Promise To Pay The Bearer

By Page Martin

A Liam Ross Novel

To my wife Sayre,

My true inspiration to keep moving forward

And to my son Liam, if not for he,

Liam Ross could not exist

Prologue -
A New Paradise

Summer 1011
Moapa River Springs

The beaded lizard lay motionless in the shadow cast by the over cropping of rock. It had been contemplating the possible meal that had come into its view. Almost eight weeks had passed since it last ate, and when it was time to eat, the lizard would eat five to ten times its own body mass. So, as the pangs in its stomach kept increasing, it awoke a sense deep inside so it knew it was now time to eat. The small bird, a mere morsel, was unaware that the venomous reptile was watching it. The bird was carelessly enjoying an early evening dinner of crane flies that lived near the springs. She would eat her fill then take some of the insects back to the Joshua tree at the springs edge that was home to her nest of hatchlings.

As the bird kept dining, the Gila, about 50 centimeters long, turned its head as the bird darted among the small pools that the springs formed. A heavy, slow moving creature, the Gila would lay in wait with his acute sense of smell, a sense so keen that it can smell small eggs buried 15 centimeters deep within the earth. When the bird was within striking distance, the monster would attack and attempt to swallow it headfirst. Its venom, a neurotoxin produced by the Gila's salivary glands, would then be injected into the bird, thus paralyzing the breathing of the helpless creature. It would then be swallowed whole, using the powerful jaws and neck muscles that allow the tenacious reptile to hold on to its prey.

The drama unfolding before Winnemucca was one he had witnessed for many of his mid-age years, a constant life and death struggle between all of the creatures of this vast desert. When standing he was almost 2 meters tall, he was the tallest in his tribe. The long ebony hair of his ancestors was almost to his waist and tied into a tail that reflected his standing within his caste. His eyes, which revealed his youth, but also proclaimed confidence and experience, were the color of the dark brown earth. His skin had the weathered texture that came with the years of exposure to the sun and the color of the darkest bark of an aged mesquite tree.

He had had been quietly resting in the shade of the outcropping, waiting for the stifling heat of the day to pass. It had been six full moons since he had left his family and friends in search of water. His trek south at times appeared pointless as day after day brought nothing but more rock, sand and oppressive heat. But now he had spent the better part of ten days exploring the vast springs that he recently been calling home, a true paradise that seemed untouched by any human. A day's walk to the south revealed a small valley with a lush river, teaming with wildlife and vast expanses of deep green wild grasses. Two days walk to the east revealed a vast body of water that Winnemucca could only believe was the edge of the earth. A body of water so large, so vast, that he could not see a shoreline in any direction. An abundance of the life giving liquid that would sustain his tribe for eons to come. He had accomplished what he had set out to do. He had found a paradise so that all of his people could now live their years in peace and prosperity.

Slowly picking up the fist-sized rock that was near to his hand, Winnemucca, now filled with a sense of joy and happiness, that six moons ago was lost and perhaps never to be found, keenly took aim at the large lizard. Throwing the rock, more gently than deadly, Winnemucca felt that today he could perhaps decide the fate of another living creature. The rock, landing harmlessly halfway between the Gila and the bird was all it took for the bird to turn and see the impending threat. Having now seen the large reptile, the bird flit off to enjoy another day of life. The Gila however, seemed to turn it's head towards Winnemucca, almost to stare deep within his soul as a warning that perhaps he would be the Gila's meal.

Dismissing the lizard, Winnemucca now had great news to share with his tribe. He would begin the long journey back to where his family await. He thought about his mate and their three children. The happiness that they would all have once they were living within this paradise, never again to experience the hardships of the desert, never again to go without food and drink. It had been five moons since the last cold and snow had fallen. Winnemucca calculated in his head that he could return to his tribe on a more direct route than the one he had taken in search of his quarry. Perhaps three, no more than four moons should pass, returning him to his loved ones. It would be brittle cold again and snow would be in the air. But he was sure that he could make the journey without incident.

The moon was half full as Winnemucca set out north. The hot arid air of the desert seemed to have an almost soft, sweet smell about it. Large dark ominous clouds were forming in the East. Low on the horizon, bright flashes could be seen building in intensity. The native knew that this was the smell of rain. It would not be long before the drops would be falling on Winnemucca's path.

Five hours had passed and the moon was behind the mountains in the west. The light that Winnemucca once had now was all but a dim cast barely lighting his path. The rain that had started out light had now become a steady stream. The flashes in the eastern sky were much closer and the deep rumble that accompanied each one was getting louder and deeper in pitch. He knew that he had to find shelter to wait the passing of the storm. A few paces on, an outcropping of rock appeared, surrounded by a small cluster of Pinion pines. Most of the trees were no taller than Winnemucca himself, but at the base of the outcropping stood one very tall, very old tree. As Winnemucca strained to see the top of the tree, he lost sight in the wet, murky dark. The tree had to be over the height of twenty men standing one on top of another. It took the wet man twelve paces to circle the base of the giant. This was an old soul, a god of the earth. Just as Winnemucca was about to arrive at the beginning of his circle a rustling in the smaller trees to his right alerted him. Perhaps a small hare was seeking shelter from the rain. If he could catch it, it would be a fine change from the roots and pinion nuts that he had been surviving on for the past week. As he slowly approached the low branches and looked down as to the direction that the beast had moved to. He noticed the print in the wet earth. It was a new print, just recently made in the wet brown earth. However this was no hare, it was the footprint of another man.

Winnemucca instantly reverted to what he had been taught so many years before by his father. He slowly and quietly let the branch he was holding lay back into place. Almost as a single motion with the branch, he lowered himself onto the wet earth and began to quietly conceal himself within the branches. Many frenzied thoughts were going through Winnemucca's mind, who was this person, had he been followed, was he still being watched? It was at that moment he sensed the movement more than seeing it. There, to the left of the small tree, just beneath the rocky over cropping, was darkness, darker than the rest of the rock that made up the over cropping. At that moment the storm intensified as a flash of lightening quickly followed by an extremely loud crash that vibrated the earth below. It was during that flash of light that Winnemucca saw the eyes. They were red eyes, almost the color of fire, peering out into the storm from the darkness that was now revealed to be an entrance to a small cave.

As Winnemucca lie quietly beneath the branches of the Pinion, water from the intensified storm was pooling in the small furrows amongst the trees. The Red Eyes were still at the entrance to the cave, reveling themselves each time that the lightening illuminated the wet dark air. What seemed as an eternity, but in fact was just a mere few minutes, even more questions and thoughts ran through

Winnemucca's mind. The foremost question, however, was "Who was this person?" However the longer that Winnemucca watched it became apparent that Red Eyes was in all actuality unaware of his presence. As he watched, it also became aware that this was this man's home. With each passing lightening flash, the area surrounding the cave entrance was revealed to hold the cast off discards of bones, rotting berries, pinion nuts and strange yellow stones the size of Winnemucca's thumb.

The flash of light and the deep ear piercing crash came simultaneously. The noise was so deafening that Winnemucca closed his eyes and covered his ears to block out the pain. The lightening had struck the top of the tree that he was hiding beneath. The earth beneath him started to tingle and Winnemucca felt a pain that he was unsure of. The water all around him became electrified. As the pain increased Winnemucca screamed and jumped from his hiding place. As he rolled to the front of the small cave he became aware of the tree collapsing all around him. Just as a large, burning limb of the Pinion tree was about to crash down upon Winnemucca, unforeseen hands pulled him safely into the cave opening. Winnemucca sat there, breathing hard, drenched from the torrent that was coming from the heavens as an unstoppable wave. As he turned to face his savior he peered into those red eyes that he had been musing about. Was this man friend or foe? This question however, would go unanswered as the Red Eyes that had rescued Winnemucca from certain death, slowly turned and went to the rear of the dry cave and lay down.

The storm continued through the night. With each passing hour Winnemucca sat near the entrance to the small cave, first peering into the darkness, alert, cautious, afraid. Then he would look at Red Eyes, who appeared to be fast asleep, curled into a ball on the hard earthen floor to the rear of the cave. Why had he saved Winnemucca? Where did he come from? Who was this man? This was the question that had Winnemucca feeling uneasy yet most curious. However speculating that he was a man was perhaps not the whole truth. His size and physical form showed that he could have been a boy of no more than sixteen years, yet when you looked into those red eyes you saw the soul of a person that had seen four times that age. How had he come to be here? Why had Winnemucca not seen any signs of this person for the last ten days?

As the rain started to taper off, the light in the eastern sky started to appear on the tops of the mountains to the east. As the rays of that early morning sun crept slowly into the cave opening, Red Eyes began to stir from his sleep. Winnemucca had decided that he had to be cautious, and take no chances with this man. Just as he made this decision, the Red Eyes sat bolt upright in the low ceilinged cave, startling Winnemucca. The Red Eyes began to sniff the air, almost as if a he were a mongrel dog. His head darted from side to side as he franticly sniffed at an odor that Winnemucca could not smell. All that he could smell was the desert after a rainstorm, the charred wood outside the cave that had once been the Pinion tree that he had taken refuge under. The sweet smell of his life that just a short time ago he had cheated by the aid of this man. In just mere seconds the Red Eyes stopped his sniffing and slowly turned his head towards Winnemucca. The eyes, that last evening showed a deep soul now displayed a feral, contemptuous look.

As Winnemucca watched the man's behavior with trepidation, the Red Eyes leapt toward where he sat. Winnemucca recoiled not so much in fear, but as a pure reflex, waiting for the blow that was sure to strike him. However, a blow did not come. The Red Eyes had thrown himself through the small opening of the cave, out into the water that had settled into the recesses beneath the now dying, aged Pinion tree. When Winnemucca looked out to the daylight he fully saw the man for the first time. He did indeed look like a feral mongrel. He was slighter of build than previous thought and Winnemucca could see the scars of many battles all over his lean frame. The Red Eyes began to sniff the air more franticly than before. A low guttural sound started to emanate from deep inside the man. A sound that seemed to belong to an evil spirit ten times the size of the man before him. As the sound built to a pitched noise that Winnemucca had never heard before, nor would he ever want to hear again, increased in volume, a breeze swept by the opening of the cave. On this breeze was the odor that had frenzied Red Eyes to his current state. An odor that Winnemucca had only once before smelled in his lifetime. A smell so powerful that it's past fragrance was forever locked into the far recesses of Winnemucca's memory. The odor of death. A death so terrible, so cruel, so unmerciful, that it had butchered his mother and father when he was just a boy. A horrid death that had decimated his entire family on that dark night so long ago, a memory that had been near forgotten as the years continued.

Red Eyes ran from the cave opening just as a pair of large, muscular legs leapt down from the roof of the cave landing just in front of the opening. Now the odor of death was stronger. The feet of the creature had a thick callous upon them from years of walking on stone and hard earth. The skin of the creature that Winnemucca could view was much darker than his, almost black. But when the legs stepped further into the sunlight it was reveled to be the color of old, dried blood. For indeed that is what it was. This was the source of the smell that had started Red Eyes frenzied sniffing and excitedness.

The pair of legs leapt off in the direction that Red Eyes had run to. Just as the legs disappeared from the opening of the cave, two more pairs came into view, even darker in color than the previous. Words, if they could be called that, were spoken loudly between the two. A shout was given and within seconds the entire cave front was obstructed with more of these creatures horrid looking legs and the vile odors that emanated from them. Winnemucca became the stone that surrounded him lest any movement from him would be his last. Slowly, one by one, the creatures left the front of the cave that was concealing Winnemucca. Once they were all gone he slowly moved even further back into the cave so that he could hide even deeper in the shadows. It was at that moment that a blood-piercing scream was heard not too far in the distance. The scream was one of shear terror. Winnemucca carefully crept to the cave opening to peer out into the daylight. Slowly he inched his head out of the cave entrance to in order to see more clearly beneath the remains of the burned Pinion tree. What he saw froze his blood.

Off just a few yards to the east a gathering of the creatures now stood. Now Winnemucca could see that they were all men. Very tall, very muscular, savage men, coated from head to toe in the dried, sticky blood that he had seen close up on their legs. Between two of the savages, suspended off the ground, being held by his arms and legs was Red Eyes. One more of the creatures had taken a knife from a scabbard and slowly plunged the blade into the chest of the trapped man. Blood started to fountain in all directions causing the men to be covered even more than they were. As the knife slowly found it's way to Red Eyes stomach, one of the bystanders plunged his hand into the steaming, open wound, pulling out and revealing a bloodied mass of tissue and organs. What happened next repulsed Winnemucca to the point that he could not hold back the bile that had been rising in his throat. The tallest of the savages, and who appeared to be the leader, placed the offal to his mouth and began to eat what was once Red Eyes beating heart.

Winnemucca vomited. When the savages heard this noise they immediately turned to see the now ashen Winnemucca on his knees with his head in the dirt. The leader of the creatures made a quick commanding movement with an out stretched arm, still holding the heart of his victim. Two of the savages quickly dispersed in opposite directions in order to circle around and come upon the cave from the direction that they had originally appeared from. It had only been seconds when Winnemucca quickly rose to his feet and turned to run in the opposite direction, however it was too late. As he started to run, he ran straight into one of the men that had been dispatched by the leader. The second savage appeared and took Winnemucca roughly by the legs. The two giants started to drag him back to where their leader awaited, all the while a rush of memories and thoughts flashed through Winnemucca's mind. He knew that he was soon to see his great ancestors, as these savages did not take prisoners. They had eaten Red Eyes heart right before his eyes, even before the man had a chance to die.

The three returned to the group of the savages and their leader. What was left of the body of Red Eyes lay in a broken heap with his arms and legs torn from his body. His head was being cut from his body by one of the bloodied men. The knife the man held was long, thin and it appeared to be very sharp as it separated Red Eye's head very cleanly from his spine. Once the savage was done with the decapitation, he cleaned the blade by licking the blood clean from knife, then he took his prize and put it in a hastily made bag from what could have been the skin of an animal, but was actually made from the skin of Red Eyes. With a grunt and an arm wave the leader pronounced that it was time to go. Some of the savages picked up the various body parts that was Red Eyes. The two that had captured Winnemucca continued to drag him as the group started out into the now heated morning of the desert.

The pain that Winnemucca felt was unbearable. Skin was being flayed from his body as he was dragged behind the group. Blood was now pouring from the massive cuts that were formed as his limbs traveled over razor sharp rocks. Where were they taking him and why was he still alive? The group started to slow as they came to a gulley near a small copse of Mesquite trees. Perhaps it was over. Once they stopped Winnemucca saw that this was a place well known to the group. A large stone stood near the center of the trees, it was covered with what Winnemucca now knew to be dried blood. All around the circle were over fifty pikes of pinion wood sharpened to a point, and on those points were human heads in many stages of decay. Some appeared to be as old as the desert while others had their eyes peering as if they were deep in thought, freshly mounted. How had Winnemucca missed this place, had he not walked in every direction from the spring?

Perhaps he was dreaming, perhaps he would awake shortly and see that this was all a bad nightmare. That realization was not to be had, no sooner than his thought came into his mind Winnemucca experienced a hot, searing pain as he felt the skin from his stomach being cut away in large pieces. As he opened his eyes he saw the once familiar flesh being handed to one of the large creatures that had abducted him. The savage took the flesh and started to craft a bag from it, the same as the bag Winnemucca had seen Red Eyes head being placed into. He knew that it would soon be his time to die. He watched as the man carefully stitched together the pieces of his stomach skin. He used what looked to be the type of reed that Winnemucca's people would make baskets and mats from, but as he peered closer he saw that it was not reeds but red strands of a ropy material. What Winnemucca did not know was these strands were pieces of muscle that had been carved and dried from the legs of a victim long past.

Winnemucca tightly closed his eyes as he waited for his time to come. Suddenly a pair of large hands grasped his head and forced his eyes open. What came next Winnemucca could not comprehend. He watched in abject horror as the leader of the savages held the bag made from his stomach flesh aloft to the sky. Words were yelled in a tongue that Winnemucca still could not comprehend. As the bag was held high another of the creatures started to place a number of the strange yellow stones that Winnemucca had seen in front of Red Eyes cave. As a stone the size of his fist was placed into the bag, the savage holding his eyes open let forth a deep guttural moan that had to have come from the bowels of hell. As this moan quickly became an ear-shattering yell, Winnemucca felt the hands around his head and eyes tighten. The leader lowered the bag and placed it upon Winnemucca's stomach and slowly started to reveal a knife from its sheath that was tied to the belt about his waist. The knife was placed to Winnemucca's throat, and without one moment of pain, his throat was sliced straight through to his spine. He felt the warm liquid as it pulsed and flowed from the fatal wound. He sensed the darkness that was slowly creeping into his vision. He faintly heard the voices of the savages as their yelling increased in volume and fervor. All of this however did not matter. The only thought that was deep upon his dying brain was not of his family that he would no longer see, but "What are those yellow rocks?"

A Means To A Way

February 23, 1868
New York, New York

Roy Stephens was a man of very few words, normally. Today however, someone was going to hear a few choice ones from him. Getting him up at seven o'clock on a Sunday morning and in a bloody snowstorm to boot! Having to wake his tired bones to come back into work when he had only just left at ten the night before. Only two hours earlier he was warm in bed with his wife Anna when he heard that dreaded knock on his front door. Why did he answer it? He should have just ignored it and pulled the covers tightly over his head. But, oh no, did he listen to his sensible brain?

"What if it is an emergency?" Anna asked as she started to rise from the warm feather bed.

"Then they can damn well go find someone else! I'm tired, I'm cold and it's my only day off before returning to that bloody salt mine tomorrow morning!" But he dragged his muscular body from the bed and started to put on his pants. "Stay in bed Anna. I'll see who it is." He looked at his Elgin pocket watch and noted that it was only four thirty!

Going down the stairs to the front entry seemed more of a chore than usual this morning. Perhaps it was the fact that he could see his breath and feel the biting cold seep into his aging joints. As he crossed to the door, the knocking increased in volume and to a fevered paced. This had damn well better be an emergency!

"Hold your bloody horses you 'dam fool! I'm moving as fast as I can!"

As he pulled open the door a gust of wind brought a small drift of snow into the entry of the house. Directly behind the snow was Kevin Crosse, Roy's Director's assistant. The boy, if you could call him that, was twenty-four years old, stood perhaps five and a half feet tall, and maybe weighed 200 pounds!

"I'm so sorry to wake you so early Mr. Stephens, but Director Wright needs you at the company, as soon as possible."

"It's four thirty on Sunday morning! What is so damn important?"

"He didn't say sir. He just asked me to come and fetch you and return with you on the double. He's been at the company all night, along with those men that came in yesterday afternoon. He's also had Mr. Durand, Mr. Pease, Mr. Nichols and Mr. Thurber with them all night. It was two hours ago that he sent me for you."

How a man of that girth could stand in front of him and be shivering as if he weighed eighty pounds confounded him. "Get inside you fool before you freeze us all to death. Go into the kitchen and put a pot on the stove while I go and get dressed."

"We haven't the time sir. The snow hasn't let up since yesterday. It's over my head in some places. It might take us the better part of two hours to get back to the company sir. Even the horse cars are not running because of the snow. We need to leave right now."

"Alright, alright, let me get dressed and we will leave."

Roy mounted the stairs to his second floor bedroom only to find Anna sitting bolt upright in bed with the covers pulled to her chin.

"Who is it Roy? What do they want?"

"It's the Director's assistant, Crosse. Wright has a major bee up his backside and he wants me back to the company right this minute." He sat his six foot six inch frame on the foot of the bed and started to pull his size fourteen boots on. "Must be he can't find his fountain pen, the old fool!" he partly said under his breath

"I'll get you both some coffee and breakfast before you go."

"No need dear, we need to leave straight away. The snow hasn't let up and it's going to be a bit of a trek downtown." Roy stood and pulled on the heavy leather coat that had once belonged to his father. "I'll be back as soon as possible. Please be sure and put enough coal in the stove as it's as cold as a crones teat downstairs this 'morn."

He bent and kissed Anna on the forehead and cursed as she slipped back beneath the warm covers of their bed.

"I love you dear."

He then pulled the covers down revealing Anna's stomach. He then bent to her stomach and kissed it twice.

"You be good to your mother my little one."

He then pulled the covers back up and kissed his wife again.

"I love you."

"I love you too. Please be careful"

"I always am" he muttered as he turned into the hallway and headed back downstairs to where Kevin Crosse await.

"Let's be off Mr. Crosse. Ready for a brisk walk downtown!"

That was two hours ago. Two hours to go what would normally take thirty minutes! But here he was, back at the job only a mere six hours since he left. The only positive reason to be back here at the company was it was warm as toast from the abundance of steam that the generating plant produced.

The company was the National Bank Note Company. Founded only seven years earlier from principals of the American Banknote Company, National was created in an act of the opposition to the growing monopoly in the engraving and printing industry. In that short seven years NBNC had managed to attract the best engravers and craftsmen that the craft had ever seen, as well as securing contracts with the United States Government to print all United States postage stamps. NBNC also produced many postal proofs, essays and postal currency for a few select foreign agencies.

Roy Stephens was one of those craftsmen that came to NBNC. He was their head Intaglio Printing Press Operator. He had printers ink in his blood. His father had been a printer, as his grandfather and as his great-grandfather had been. Roy would soon mark twenty-five years in a craft that he loved as if it were a mistress. Beginning at age twelve as a paper sander, a job generally held by a boy, to sand the edges of the reams of paper before they were feed into the printing press. Then at sixteen he was apprenticed to his father at the American Banknote Company, were he continued his education of his craft, thus becoming ABNC's head printer when his father retired after forty years in the industry.

Now Roy stood next to his presses awaiting Director Wright to explain to him why he was here. He had no sooner finished his thought as Director Wright entered the pressroom. Directly behind Wright was Joseph I. Pease, the premiere portrait engraver of National Bank Note Company.

"Stephens, I am sorry to call you in on a night like tonight. But we have an emergency order that has to be finished before Monday morning. Pease here will fill you in on all the details of the run." As Wright had no sooner made this statement, he turned on his heels and headed straight back to his front office.

"Roy, I know you must be angry, but please hear me out." Joseph I. Pease was a man of fifty. His proficiency in his craft was legendary, his artwork were masterworks. Most artists either drew or painted on a canvas or other large-scale medium, but not Pease. Joseph's full-scale works were the detailed images of presidents, statesmen and history, unmatched by no one. Joseph's medium of choice was a steel plate the size of a postage stamp.

"Joseph I am not angry with you or with Wright, I am angry at myself for answering my damn door!" The two men then shared a laugh together just as they had shared many over the years that they had worked together.

"Roy, you need to ink up Number Twelve, Fourteen and Fifteen. We need to run, what I can only assume will be proofs. They need to be run on the Crane eighty-pound white watermark stock. All strikes and jambs need to be delivered with the run sheets. Someone is mixing your inks for you now. We are adding a new formulation gold to this run."

"Thus the need for Number Twelve" Roy chimed in. "You do realize that press hasn't turned a platen in over six months. We have yet to get the ink tack right on the rollers. It always ends up drying so fast we rip the plates right out of the chases."

"I know, I know. It's a special demand from the client. They actually brought an ink formulation to the Director. It's damn odd if you ask me."

"Will I get the plates from you when I am ready?" Stephens asked of Pease.

"No, that's the other odd thing about this. Everyone but you and I have been kept apart on this job. No one, even myself, have seen the entire plate. You'll be the first."

"What are the image size and the size of the finished strike? Surely you must know that?"

"Sorry Roy, I don't even have that information for you. I was told to tell you that all pertinent information will be conveyed when "They" deliver the plates to you."

"Bloody hell. How on earth will McNeil cut the stock on the guillotine?" spat Roy. The guillotine was the large knife-press that cut both the new paper stocks as well as the finished products.

"And that brings us to the final pieces of the preverbal puzzle my old friend. No one, and I mean no one else is here. You are all on your own. Tonight you are a one man crew!"

The look on Roy's face displayed his incredulous feelings. If there had been a wall within arms length, there would be a hole in it the size of a large man's fist. How did they expect him do accomplish it all? It took at least two men to run a press, not to mention the guillotine operator, the apprentices, and the checkers of the finished products.

"Just me? Are they out of their pea-sized brains?" Roy almost hissed at Pease.

"These are all requirements of the client Roy." Pease returned.

"Just who the hell is this client? And where do they come off demanding this of us on a Sunday morning?"

"If you must know Mr. Stephens, the client is the United States of America, and that's all we are going to tell you." The voice made Roy nearly jump out of his skin. It was deep and venomous sounding. Its tone was that of finality.

Standing three feet away from Roy was a very tall man. A man so tall that even Roy had to look up to see into the man's eyes. His jet-black hair was swept off his face and plastered to his scalp with root cream oil. His facial features were that of a man that had seen hard times, battles, and a hard war. Yet even for his stature the man moved with elegance and with an eerie silence and swiftness, almost as if he were a living specter.

"Who the hell are you?" Roy almost screamed at the stranger.

"I am the person that is going to assist you with the task at hand today."

"The bloody hell you are mate. I let no one touch my presses if I don't know them, and I don't know you!"

The next action happened so fast that Roy thought this all must be a dream, a dream he would soon awake from. Placed at Roy's forehead with lighting speed was the barrel of a pistol.

"It's going to be a long day. I suggest we get started my friend." The stranger lowered the gun only when Roy nodded his head in agreement. Roy swallowed hard and tried to calm his now racing heart. He was soon to find that it was not the last time that day he was going to curse himself for answering that damn door.

Intaglio printing is the opposite of relief printing, in that the printing process is directed from ink that is below the surface of a printing plate instead of on the surface like that of letterpress. The image, that is to be printed, is etched into a metal plate often of soft steel, but sometimes of zinc or copper. Then a viscous printing ink is forced into the etched lines then the surface of the plate is wiped clean. Unlike its cousin, letterpress, intaglio printing requires considerable pressure. A standard letterpress will develop about two hundred pounds of total pressure to print a sheet of paper. In intaglio printing a pressure of over eighteen tons is needed in order for the image to be transferred to the paper.

The press is essentially composed of two bearing rollers with a movable flatbed sandwiched horizontally between them. The inked plate is laid face up on the bed, then a wetted sheet of printing stock is laid over it and a blanket plate, to ensure even pressure, is draped over both. The upper roller of the press is then turned and the bed is drawn through the rollers, thus producing the printed image. One of the unique qualities of intaglio printing is that in the finished product, the inked surfaces are slightly raised on the front and indented on the back. Depending upon the type of ink and paper used this can give intaglio prints a unique texture unlike any other printing process. Being very unique and extremely expensive printing presses, there are only 32 intaglio presses in the United States in 1868. Ten presses owned by the American Bank Note Company, sixteen of them here at NBNC and the remaining six housed at various state security printers, here in the northeast.

Roy began the startup process of the presses. A long and complicated task for a full crew, a gargantuan chore for just himself, however almost as he was one of Roy's own crew, the tall stranger with the uncanny reflexes, followed each and everyone one of Roy's steps with the next required task. When the belts coming from the gantry pulley system were ready to be attached to the flywheel of the press, Roy finally spoke.

"You have done this before."

But instead of an answer, all Roy received back was a cold icy stare. So trying to make the best of a bad situation, Roy just did as he did everyday. He put his mind into his job and continued on automatically.

"We are ready for the inks and the plates." Roy stated to the stranger. "I want the black ink first, followed by the base green and finished with the gold. I may have to run a test on the gold first in order not to have a catastrophe on our hands."

"There will be no such test. You will run the ink and not stop for any reasons. I assure you that there will be no problems."

"Look here you ass. I am not taking orders from you or taking any chances on something that could destroy my press. The test will take an hour at most. I assure you that hour spent will save us a week if we have to repair a platen."

"You are mistaken Mr. Stephens. You are taking orders from me." His words were ice as he gently opened his coat revealing the revolver in its his waistband. "I will not warn you again, there will be no test, no stalling, and no more questions. Finish your job, or you will be finished." These final words were accompanied by the stony silence and the contempt that each man held. Roy could only comply.

With the presses at the ready, inks in the hoppers, plates in the platens, all belts connected to the steam pulley system, Roy was ready for the most important asset to any printed piece, the paper stock. National Bank Note Company printed on a multitude of paper stock, from standard classic laid to woven multi-fiber, Roy had experience on all types. The most complicated of stocks however was the stock used to print banknotes. This was not so much a paper as a special rag-linen combination that allowed the banknotes its resiliency to last more than a few days.

"Well my friend, it's time you tell me the size that the stock is to be." Roy voiced, "Then you and I are going to have a 'ell of a time controlling the guillotine by just ourselves."

The tall stranger reached into his coat breast pocket and retrieved a stained folded paper. He slowly unfolded the paper and handed it to Roy.

"Your instructions."

Roy scanned the beginning of the folded sheet of paper.

"This is the size of a ten-up Greenback run. Is that what this is all about? Money? For heavens sake, we could have done this during a normal press day, not having to slink about on a freezing winters night!"

"Mr. Stephens, I suggest that you get back to the task at hand, read those instructions, and cut the sheets to the required size. I assure you that it is what is best for you."

Roy looked back at the paper and the next item jumped out at him as if it were a poisonous viper.

"One hundred sheets! That's it? Only one hundred!" Roy's voiced boomed so loud that it almost drowned out the sound of the pulley system. "That might give you only one finished piece of product! What in the hell is this all about?"

"Once again Mr. Stephens, your questions are getting very monotonous, plus you are sorely mistaken in the directions in your hand. You are to cut one hundred sheets of paper, print one hundred sheets of paper, and then deliver to me those same one hundred sheets of paper. You are to do this with no more questions. Do you understand?"

Before Roy could even acknowledge in the affirmative a loud boom enveloped the pressroom. A hole the size of a silver dollar was now in the chestnut post that was just inches from Roy's left ear. Some splinters from the fractured wood buried themselves in Roy's lobe. A small trickle of blood slowly started to seep down his cheek into his shirt collar. Roy stood frozen not wanting to move in case the man was to fire the revolver again.

"Do you understand? I shall not ask again!"

Roy nodded in agreement and slowly turned towards the pallet of paper stock to the right of the guillotine. He counted out the required sheets, rechecked his count and set the paper on the left hand table of the guillotine.

"Do you want to check my count?" he asked of the stranger.

"I already have my friend, twice as a matter of fact." He returned smugly.

Roy then went to the side of the guillotine and rotated a large wheel that moved a very large, very heavy backstop made of cast iron. He rotated the wheel until the measurement from the backstop to the knife of the guillotine measured the required width of his paper. After he set this size he returned to the front of the machine, set the paper under the knife and up against the backstop. Roy then pulled a lever, almost as tall as himself, and a top weight lowered and pressed firmly against the stack of paper. Automatically after this weight came down the 400 pound blade of the guillotine followed and cut through the stack a paper as if it were butter on a warm July evening.

After this cut was done, Roy reset the back stop for the second dimension, turned the paper ninety degrees to the right, tamped the stack of paper against the back stop and pulled the lever again. The proper size sheet had been cut. As the stranger reached towards the stack of paper a terrible, horrible, wonderful thought raced through

Roy's mind. Pull the lever as the man was removing the paper and cut off his hands! That would stop all of this ridiculous madness. It could be done. Roy had seen this happen just a few short months ago. Tom Cooper, a NBNC employee, had lost both of his hands as he reached into the guillotine to move some stock as the lever failed, sending the knife crashing down, severing his hands above his wrists. Poor Tom died as he bled to death right there on the floor next to the guillotine, his hands still holding the stack of paper that was securely held on the table of the knife.

Roy shook his head to dismiss this memory. He just wanted this night to be over and to get back home to Anna and a warm bed. The tall stranger from the government now held the stack of one hundred sheets of Crane 80 pound linen rag stock firmly in his hands.

"Come along Roy, we still have a long days work ahead of us." He called as he started to walk back towards the presses. Roy, still in a fog, followed slowly, willing this day to be over. Cursing himself that he had ever answered that knock on the door.

They started on press Number Fifteen with the black ink first. They would then go on to Number Fourteen for the green ink and finish on Number Twelve with the special gold ink. The government man adjusted the feed table to fit the size of the stock that they had just cut. Once again Roy protested, as he was about to send the first "proof sheet" through the press.

"It normally takes thirty to fifty sheets to get the first strike registered properly, what you are asking cannot be done!"

"Mr. Stephens, once again you are trying my patience. These will be the last words that you will hear on this subject. So listen closely. I wouldn't want to bring your precious wife Anna here to, how would I say it, as leverage to persuade you. It would not be pleasant for her or you. That I promise to you. Now, you have just one sheet of stock to set your register. You will then use that same sheet to set the register with the additional two colors. Understand?"

How in Gods name did they know his wife's name? Who were these people? Would they really hurt his Anna if he didn't comply? Roy decided that in order to even try this impossible foolish order, he would have to recheck every possible setting on the printing presses. Increasing the backpressure on the platens, checking the rollers, checking the register gates on the feed tables, even recounting the load of paper in the feed table. If all he had was one sheet then he had damn well better get it right the first time.

As Roy was on top of the feed table making adjustments, the large door to the outer office opened and Director Wright, Mr. Pease, and two other gentlemen, that Roy had never seen before, started to walk over to the presses. The tall stranger that had been working with Roy turned and started to walk over and meet them.

The pressroom of NBNC was set up as any pressroom of the day would have been set up. All of the presses were in a perpendicular row to each other, all oriented in the same direction. Numbered One through Fifteen. The unprinted paper stock would be fed into one end and the printed stock would be received at the opposite delivery end. However Number Sixteen was oriented in the opposite direction to the other fifteen presses. This was because Number Sixteen was NBNC's newest press. Not even six months old and its height was a bit taller than that of the other presses. Additionally, the level of the ceiling dropped where Number Sixteen was so the delivery table could not be operated properly, so they installed it reverse to the other presses. This didn't cause many problems as they very rarely ran this press because it was primarily dedicated to brilliantly colored inks, like the ones used on postage stamps and proofs.

Roy glanced over to Number Sixteen and saw what he needed just as the stranger met up with the others. Over on the feed table of Number Sixteen was what looked to be a ream of stock almost the exact size that he was setting up for on Number Fifteen. He climbed down from the feed table and pretended to make adjustments on Number Fifteen as he continued toward the delivery end. As he reached the back of the press he quickly ran over to Number Sixteen and relieved the feed table of about ten sheets. He quickly and quietly made his way back to the feed table of Number Fifteen, out of sight of the group, and inserted the sheets onto the top of the load on the press, just as the group of gentlemen started to walk towards him.

"Well Roy, are we ready to pull the first proof?" the Director asked.

"Yes Sir, we are. If you will all stand back, we will send it through right now."

The group moved back, all except Roy and his unwanted assistant. The giant flywheel of the press stated to turn slowly at first as Roy applied tension from the steam pulley system to the press. The platen stated to slowly move in and out from under the rollers. When the press finally was up to speed, only then did Roy ask his assistant to release the feed bar and let one sheet, and only one sheet into the press. Roy waited patiently on the delivery end of the press for the sheet to appear. After about fifteen seconds the formally blank, creamy white stock emerged from the platen with an intricate design now printed in deep rich black ink. Very seldom did Roy ever check the plates for mistakes, errors, cracks or other such problems. It was an impossible task to do so, trying to read etched metal, in reverse and brightly polished to match. It was much easier to await the first few printed sheets. That way each of the press operators could review them for any of the potential problems and report back to the etching department any such errors. However this time it was not an error that caught Roy's eye. It was something much larger.

A United States Note, also known as a Legal Tender Note was a form of paper money printed by the United States. The bulk of these notes issued were printed in 1862 in order to cover the costs of the new War Between the States. By the wars end the United States Government had printed almost $450,000,000 in paper dollars that had earned the nickname Greenbacks, from the backside of the note being printed solely in green ink. As true to the time, these paper notes were guaranteed by the United States Government and backed by payment in gold.

Roy had printed Greenbacks before. One Dollar, Five Dollar, Ten Dollar, Twenty Dollar, even the rare Fifty Dollar denomination notes, Roy had printed them all. What he held in his hand was unbelievable! He had just struck a proof of ten, One Million Dollar Notes! And he was going to print one hundred sheets of these! Roy did the math quickly in his head. The sum that came to him was unfathomable, One Billion Dollars in Greenbacks!

Roy's hands shook with nervousness. The assembled men moved closer to Roy to review what had just been printed. The only response was from Pease, an audible gasp. The remaining men took the sheet of paper from Roy, examined it with great scrutiny and returned it to the printer.

"Excellent Roy! Wonderful!" Director Wright exclaimed. "Proceed with the run and get these sheets set to dry before you proceed with color number two."

Color number two was the green. The sheets had to go through the press on the opposite side from the black. Normally, each sheet would have what was known as offset, ink that was carried over from the previous sheet as they stacked up in the delivery tray of the press. However tonight, Roy and his helper were removing stacks of ten sheets as they came off of the press so that they would dry quicker and not have any offset. Roy was positive that the government man would count the sheets as they were removed. He had to somehow remove the ten sheets that he had put into the pile in order to help him register the additional colors.

The pile of paper stock was moved from Press Number Fifteen and readied by the feed table of press Number Fourteen. The top ten sheets were Roy's extra sheets. Roy started up press Number Fourteen and called for the feed to begin, just as the first sheet came through to the delivery Roy called to the stranger to continue to watch the feed in order to prevent a jamb. As soon as the first ten sheets were printed, Roy removed them and stashed them under the pallet that the paper was delivered onto. Once this was done Roy walked up to the feed table and asked the man to go to the rear and watch the delivery so Roy could do his press check as it ran. By the time that the man had left another twenty or so sheets had been fed into the press. This amount in the delivery should hopefully not call any attention to the fact that it was ten sheets short.

By the time the rest of the sheets had been printed, all was well. Roy's un-nerving assistant had not discovered the extra sheets and was getting ready to prepare the notes for the final printing step, the gold ink.

All of Roy's fears in regards to the gold ink seizing the press were unfounded. Roy was amazed and proud of the fact that his years of printing had indeed allowed him to register each color to the note on just one sheet, and that sheet was perfect. Perfect color balance, perfect pressure, not a single issued had arisen. All Roy had to do was to repeat with the gold, what he had done with the green and black inks.

The gold ink was placed into the well on the press and the rollers were inked up. Roy noticed under the gas lamps that there was a sparkle to the ink. A mesmerizing sparkle that the printer had never before seen in ink.

As the drying green and black sheets were gathered up and placed on the pallet to be moved over to Fourteen, Roy very deftly recovered the hidden ten sheets from under the pallet and placed them on the top of the load. The load was moved over to the last press and loaded in by Roy's assistant. The press was started and the final image was added to the note. The gold ink produced an astounding Seal of the United States. When you turned the note in a particular direction, the sparkle made the image jump from the paper.

"This is astounding! What is the composition of this ink?" Roy asked to no one at all.

"Why gold of course." The response was droll and deadpan, almost sinister, and whispered into Roy's ear. One of the two men that Roy had not seen until they started the presses was standing directly behind him causing Roy to jump and turn with a start.

"Mate, you need to let a man know when you are standing that close. I could have fallen into the press!" Roy screamed at the stranger.

"Oh a fate that could have indeed been terrible." was the response from the thin lips.

"Well back off and let me finish my job. We only have about an hour to finish up!"

By this time almost all of Roy's ten sheets had been sent through the press and the assistant was surely waiting for Roy to come and relieve him from the feed table. Roy had to quickly remove the sheets and hide them before he could do so, but he now had company watching his every move. Roy waited for three more sheets to come through the platen. Then with the ease of a man that has plied his craft for many years, Roy deftly remove all thirteen sheets from the delivery at once and turned his back to the stranger, as if to inspect them in the light from the gas lamp. Then before the man had a chance to reposition himself to see what Roy was doing, Roy returned the sheets to the delivery, except three went into the delivery, the other ten went underneath the pallet.

Roy then went through the paces that he had done two times before that day.

The run was done. The presses had to be washed and readied for the next day. The one hundred sheets, once dried, had been trimmed on the guillotine to their exact size, they were then taken into Director Wright to be serial numbered, cataloged and packaged. As this was being done, Roy was left on his own to clean his presses. After he was done with the final ink wash, Roy cautiously removed the ten register sheets from beneath the pallet. However, something was wrong. One of the sheets slid from the pile with ease. That was something that just did not happen with intaglio printing. Roy turned the sheet and gasped as one sheet had not received any green ink from the second process and the second sheet had not received any black ink from the first step! These sheets had been stuck to each other and had gone through the presses this way. It happened, but it was not common as the tolerance that the platen pressure created on a sheet was so severe that two sheets would normally jamb a press. However, something peaked Roy's interest, he held up one of the two sheets and noticed that they were much thinner than the banknote stock. The other sheet revealed itself to be of the same thickness as the first. These pieces of paper were indeed not banknote stock, but stock being used to print some of the new issue postage stamps, the new one cent Benjamin Franklin's.

As Roy held the two pieces of paper he heard the door from the office open, and voices started to proceed toward the presses and thus to Roy. Quickly Roy folded all ten sheets of paper and shoved them deep into his pockets. He quickly picked up a pile of ink-covered rags and proceeded to the tub of turpentine used to clean the rags.

"Roy, as soon as you are cleaned up, let yourself out the back entrance and lock up." Joseph Pease yelled to him. "The director and our guests are leaving in a few minutes, so am I."

"Will do Joseph! You don't have to tell me twice to leave! Has the storm let up yet?"

"No it's still coming down. The Director has told me he is letting all staff know that we will not open until the weather is better. He has sent Crosse out to deliver the news to everyone."

"A day off! What other surprises could come on a day like today? Be safe and warm Joseph, I'll see you in a few days!"

Pease left through the office doors as Roy began to exit the pressroom through the rear doors. He turned down the gas lamps, then pulled on his heavy outer coat, tied his scarf, then opened the door to reveal that the storm indeed had not let up, but it had actually gotten worse.

"Oh well, I'll be home in a couple of hours." He mumbled as he started to close the door to the pressroom. At that moment however, Roy stopped. What was he going to do with the press sheets that were in his pocket? They weren't worth anything because they had not been serial numbered. It was actually a crime for him to remove them from the pressroom. He himself had fired apprentices for taking things of even lesser value, even scrap paper. He pulled the sheets from his pockets and walked over to the large pot bellied stove that heated the transport manager's office. The coal fire was almost out, but not quite. Roy stoked up the fire and then started to place the ten register sheets into the stove. Just as the flames from the coal lumps were about to ignite the sheets, Roy had a thought. He removed one of the misprinted sheets, the one that only had the front printed in black and gold. He placed the remaining sheets into the stove and closed the door, the sheets immediately burst into flames. Roy watched as the once white paper was reduced to carbon black. He then wrote a message to Anna on the reverse of the last banknote, removed an envelope from the manager's desk, inserted the misprinted bank note inside, addressed the envelope to Anna Stephens and then sealed the envelope with sealing wax. Roy then rummaged through the desk looking for a stamp in order to post the letter to his wife. What a surprise it would be when she opened the mail! She loved to get letters. However, Roy could not find any stamps. Well, he could just give it to her at home, then he remembered a whole pile of the one cent Franklins that had been printed and tested with the new anti-reuse process. There had to be a spare one that he could buy. All of the employees had been allowed to do this from time to time in the past.

Roy went back into the pressroom and crossed over to the anti-reuse machine. There indeed was a pile of individual stamps that had been separated from a sheet. Roy took a penny from his pocket, left it on the table and took one of the stamps. He licked the stamp and placed it in the upper right hand corner of the envelope. He then returned to the transport manager's office, placed the envelope in the out going mail sack, turned off the light then headed back out to meet the storm.

Just as Roy locked the door the storm seemed to double in intensity. Roy pulled his coat collar up tighter and started to walk to the end of the alley. Just as Roy was about to turn the corner Roy was stopped dead in his tracks by a massive blow to his head from what felt like a iron rod. He fell to his knees into the piling snow. What was happening to him? He knew he was dying, but why could he not scream? Then the second blow came, fiercer than the first. As the iron rod connected, Roy stated to fall forward into the snowdrift. Just as the darkness came and his head hit the snow, the only thing that came into his mind was "Why did I answer that damn door?"

Orders

February 24, 1868
Washington, D.C.

"The hell they will! They will never remove me from office! The bastards! Who do they think they are? I am the president of the United States and I will do what ever the damn hell I want to do!" The tone was that of pure anger from President Andrew Johnson as he stood in front of the window of the Executive Office as the winter storm lashed out against the glass panes.

The 17th President of the United States moved with angst and disdain around his office in the presidential mansion, located at 1600 Pennsylvania Avenue. It had been just two short hours since the U.S. House of Representatives voted to impeach the president, 126 to 47, for violating the Tenure of Office Act, for summarily dismissing Secretary of War Edwin M. Stanton.

"Stanton wanted to rebuild what did not need rebuilding! We have greater problems and we need to address those now." President Johnson continued his discussion with two gentlemen that were present in the office.

"But Mr. President, How do we expect to pay back the creditors? We have amassed a 500 million dollar debt that has to be resolved by August 1st or they will own the country! No more Senate, no more House of Representatives, no Presidency! Do you want to go down in the annals of history as the man who destroyed the first true democracy?" One of the two asked.

"Mr. President, we need the south to rebuild their industries so that taxes can be levied and the coffers refilled, there is no other option! We must ask for an extension to pay back the debt." The second added.

The Civil War had ended just two and half years earlier. The country was still in ruins from the four-year bitter divide between the states and then the assassination of President Lincoln. Monies had been slow in returning to the coffers of the United States Treasury, yet massive amounts of cash were needed daily to rebuild what had been destroyed. In a desperate attempt, President Johnson, by bypassing Congress, had made a covert pact with a very secretive group of gentlemen that would provide the much needed cash to start the rebuilding of the Union, thus assuring him re-election in November. However the monies borrowed were mismanaged and most diverted to other uses. It was soon to be time to repay the creditors with great interest, or else.

"Gentlemen, I am fully aware of our situation and I do believe that you are wrong about our options." Almost as if on cue there was a knock on the outer office door. The President's secretary, Colonel William Moore, opened the door and escorted three gentlemen into the Executive Office.

The gentlemen had just arrived from New York on The Baltimore and Ohio Railroad. Their travel had been slowed by the continuing snowstorm that had blanketed the eastern seaboard for the past day. Once in Washington D.C. the three went directly from the railroad station to the White House.

"Gentlemen, come in, please, sit by the fire. I trust you had a successful trip?" asked the president.

"Yes Sir, quite successful, we have the required documents and are leaving on the 5:45 to St. Louis this evening. We expect to be in the Utah Territories in about a fortnight." This reply came from the tall man that had the definite look of a military man who had seen hard battle, and was most certainly the man in charge.

"Wonderful news Mr. Black! Just wonderful! I trust that you will keep me informed of your progress trough the entire trip?"

"Yes Mr. President, we will. We will wire you from all of the prearranged locations on our way. With the best of planning and execution the items should start arriving back here in the capital no later than June 1st."

"Excellent, we need the item back here no later than June 15th as we need to meet our obligations, understood." The last was not a question from the president but an order, a direct order. The men standing before the President had sworn their allegiance to him and they were duty bound to uphold all of his orders.

The president crossed the room to his desk, a desk that had been used by President Andrew Jackson. He had had the Lincoln desk removed from the office only hours after he had taken the oath of office. He did not want an abolitionist's desk in *his* office. So he opted for the desk of, a true southern gentleman, Old Hickory. Upon reaching the desk, the President picked up an oilcloth-covered packet. Holding this out to Mr. Black, the President handed the packet to the tall man.

"Your final orders are in there. You are to open them only once you are underway. Those orders must be carried out to the letter if we are to see this once great country whole again. The transportation will be completed by the end of the month. I just received the final surveyors report that all is clear into Carson City.

We have just spent the better part of a year getting it all completed. So get to Gass and get it all settled, now. Do we have a complete understanding?"

Taking the packet and weighing its importance in his hand, Mr. Black's reply was immediate and definite.

"Yes, sir. We have complete understanding."

"Very good then. Godspeed gentlemen, Godspeed."

"Thank you Mr. President." And with that the three men departed the Executive Office. The president, now more jovial than he had been in days turned to his remaining visitors.

"Gentlemen, we are on the path to a new beginning. The beginning of a new country." The president turned from the men and looked out of the Executive Office window at the pelting storm. "A new - United States."

Nouveau Riche

March 13, 1868
Gass Los Vegas Rancho

It had been three very long years for Octavius Gass. The work that was contracted for at the end of the war was about to be finished. It had been shear luck that Octavius had found the strike of all time. He had been looking for a way to capitalize on the abundant water that flowed beneath his lands since he discovered there was an ocean of it underground. But it was that fateful day three years ago when Octavius Gass broke through an inner cavern while looking for the source of the water, that he found what fortunes and dreams were made of.

Gass's rancho occupied over 20,000 acres. The primary area of the rancho was once the U.S. Army's, Fort Baker. After the war, the War Department decommissioned the fort and sold the surrounding land to Gass for $5 an acre. The $100,000 purchase price was what some people considered $99,999 too much for the land, as it was just a barren, god-forsaken wasteland. Gass however vehemently disagreed. He had loved the desert his entire life. He was born not more than 30 miles from the place that he now called home. He intimately knew every inch of the surrounding land for over 100 miles in every direction. When Gass first found the water it created quite the sensation, he was able to pump a moderate amount to the surface and turn a once arid wasteland into lush, fertile ranch land. Those naysayers were now coming to Gass, hat in hand, begging for water.

But it was near the old burial ground that Gass encountered the first signs of what might come to be. There were hundreds of the small stones, more like thousands. All scattered about the ground of what was rumored to be an ancient sacrificial throne. When Gass started to explore the area closer, it was discovered that the alter-stone held a secret; it actually pivoted revealing an entrance into caverns below.

Gass revealed his secret to only one man on earth, his own beloved brother Samuel, a staff assistant of the former Vice President, Andrew Johnson. It was through these channels three years ago that Gass was approached to help his country. The request was unbelievable, but possible. Mine enough of what President Johnson requested, and do it as soon as possible. In return, Gass would become the richest man in the United States.

Gass had few worries in the world at this time. He was given assistance to accomplish this herculean task in the form of two hundred Chinese miners that arrived at the rancho within two months of the finalization of the deal. Another two hundred Chinese appeared about a year later to start a narrow gauge railroad that was needed to transport the mined ore to its final destination four hundred and fifty miles to the northwest. However, a man sent to oversee the operation and to push towards the set deadline, became Gass's only concern. A very tall, very large man, easily weighing in at 325 pounds and standing well over six-feet four inches, was not the sort that Gass wanted to call a friend. He had a brutal look about him, the look of a man that had seen a hard life. Not hard by circumstance, but hard by choice. This overseer pushed the workers beyond what was thought humanly possible in order to reach the set delivery date. Most workers cowered at his presence, fearing that if they even looked at him improperly that they would end up being sent out to a part of the project that no man had returned from in two years. This man was known only as Mr. Black.

It had been a beautiful day. The sun bore down but the heat was a welcome relief from the cold, near frozen days of the past few months. Gass was watching the days work through a spyglass, from the porch of his new home that he himself had built over the past three years. No other man knew more about his own home than Octavius Gass did about his. Every board, every nail, each adobe brick was set into place by his own two hands. He was afforded this opportunity once Mr. Black arrived on the scene and announced that his presence was no longer needed on a day-to-day basis in the mine. This suited Octavius just fine. He could focus on the building of his new home that would be a centerpiece for his new ranch and new lifestyle.

Years before Mr. Black and the workers had arrived, Octavius had discovered an alternate way into the mine. Once discovered he took the opportunity to widen the new entrance into the mine and disguise the old cavern entrance that he had discovered under the old alter stone. That stone was now the main focal point of Gass's fireplace in the newly whitewashed great room of his home. The former large limestone alter was cleverly disguised as part of the fireplace wood storage and cooking section of the wall. However, only Octavius Gass knew that the cooking section contained a secret. Gass had turned a portion of the cavern into a special hold and storage area that he alone would know about. A place that he could hide himself and his eagerly anticipated new wealth in case the war was to break out once again. It held an added bonus in that a section of the cavern also contained one of the larger lodes of the mine discovered three years ago. A vein that was separate and nowhere near the other ore lodes. So with meticulous detail, Octavius planned for a future that would allow him great riches from water, from fame, from cash and most of all, from gold.

So it was from the front porch that Gass had seen the smoke from the latest train heading south to the mine.

"This should be the end of the line, so to speak." Gass spoke out loud to no one there. The locomotive's whistle shrilled as the train approached into the makeshift station about a mile away.

"The last train, the last load." The words startled Gass as he turned to see Mr. Black standing just off the porch. "We should be out of here within the next sixteen hours."

"Three years, two thousand tons plus. That's quite a haul. Have all of the men been taken care of?"

"More than taken care of Gass. These men will never have to worry about money for the rest of their lives. They will all be remembered in anonymity."

Gass was not sure what to make of the remark. For the past week trains had been leaving in the middle of the night carrying workers north, as their labors were no longer needed. But being remembered in anonymity, what kind of a remark was that? However Gass quickly erased this thought as he noticed a carriage approaching down the road from the station.

"This should be your special delivery Gass." Mr. Black voiced as he stepped from the porch to meet the carriage.

Octavius followed close at hand to go and meet his fortune. He was within twenty yards when the first of two men stepped from the carriage. This man was as tall and large as Mr. Black and could have been his twin, in fact he was. When he crossed to the carriage it became evident. He blinked his eyes hard twice to make sure that he was not seeing double. With outstretched hand the new stranger spoke first.

"Mr. Gass? May I introduce myself? I am Homer Black. I trust my brother here has told you about me?" as he gestured towards his hard faced brother.

The two were identical in every aspect, the height, the weight, the hair, and the eyes, mostly the cold dark eyes. The only difference was their manner of dress.

As Gass shook his hand in return, Homer Black introduced his arriving partner.

"And this is Horace Wright, my associate." A man, almost as tall as Black, stepped from the carriage. His face was that of a specter, a large scar traversed his neck and throat. His hands the size of ham hocks gripped a dark brown, well-weathered valise.

"It's a pleasure to meet you both. Welcome to my ranch. I trust your trip was pleasant and not too long. Perhaps you would both like a place to wash up and then some supper, perhaps?"

"Thank you Mr. Gass. That would be most welcome. I have to admit, travel on a railway is arduous at best, but travel on a temporary railroad designed and constructed in less than two years for ore cars, is not proper transportation."

"Well gentlemen, please follow me. I will have my houseboy fetch your bags for you and take them to the guest quarters."

"That is most kind Mr. Gass, but we have no bags. You see we do not plan on staying long. We are close to our deadline and time is of the essence," answered Mr. Wright.

His voice startled Gass. The voice was in a register higher than most men's, almost boy-like. What Octavius Gass did not know was that Horace Wright lost most of his speaking ability when hit in the throat with a Minié Ball during the Battle of Antietam in the late summer of 1862. The deadly ammunition severed most of his throat and vocal cords. In order to save his life, what cords were left were stretched so taught that it gave Wright an almost comical speaking voice for a man of his statue.

"Well then, I will have my housekeeper set the table for a quick meal, Gentlemen, this way if you please," Gass gestured towards the great room.

In a short time Gass's servants set a marvelous table. Fresh venison, that had been caught just the evening before, had been roasted and prepared with a very peculiar sight to be found in the middle of a desert, fresh vegetables. Carrots as large as a child's arm, sugar beets as red as blood and the size of a man's fist, all sat steaming in earthenware bowls. Large pitchers of ice-cold water with fresh lemons floating in them appeared off on the sideboard of the table. Two large bottles of what appeared to be wine stood majestically in the center of the table. Both bottles hosted very peculiar labels.

"My compliments to the host. I have to admit that I am a bit astonished to see such unexpected luxuries' way out here in the middle of no where. Vegetables, lemons, ice water and wine, how do you come by them all?" Homer black quizzed his host.

"Everything that you see before you gentlemen was produced here on the ranch. The water that flows beneath the ranch allows this arid landscape to become some of the most fertile soil west of the Mighty Missi'sip!" I have converted 200 acres of desert into lush, bearing land. My orchards alone should rival those of the Tennessee Valley within five years. I have fifty pump stations planned over the next two years alone that will bring water to the surface and turn this valley into a paradise!" Gass beamed with pride as he extolled this tale on his guests.

"Well, you will soon be the richest man west of the Mississippi, if not the entire United States in just a few short hours. Should we conclude our business gentlemen?" asked Homer Black. "Horace, could you retrieve my valise my friend?"

Horace Wright, in mid-sip from a large goblet of wine, grunted an affirmation. He got up from the table and disappeared into the foyer of the grand room and disappeared outside for what seemed like an indeterminable amount of time. Of the three remaining men, Homer Black and Gass continued deep in conversation and Mr. Black remained his stoic self. Finally Wright returned with the valise.

Horace Wright opened the worn valise and extracted an oilcloth packet, and then he retrieved a rather voluminous sheaf of documents that required Gass's signature. Setting the oilcloth on the table, the sheaf of documents was handed to Homer Black. They now embarked on what would be over two hours of review and discussion on the final agreement before them. Once all of the terms had been scrutinized and finalized, Horace Wright produced a wonderfully heavy object from inside his breast coat pocket. The object was made from black onyx with what appeared to be a cap ringed in gold. The object was passed to Homer Black where with a deft twist of his hand the cap was removed to reveal a mysterious object to Octavius Gass.

"One of the newest attempts at and old task master, it is called a fountain pen. No longer we will need a quill and a pot. The days of nasty ink spills will be a thing of the past. All you have to do is make your mark on the documents the same way that you would use a quill nib." Black demonstrated by affixing his name to the documents before him. Black then passed the pen to Gass.

"It's very heavy." He remarked as he hefted the weight in his hand. He then put the nib to paper and signed his name with great flourish, and then he signed the second identical set of papers. When finished he replaced the cap and handed the pen back to Black.

"Please, keep that as a small token from the President. I am sure that he would want you to have it."

Gass looked at the man and mouthed his thanks.

"Perhaps now you would like to see your fortune?" Wright squeaked from the opposite end of the table. He then passed the oilcloth packet to Mr. Black who in turn handed it to his brother. Homer slowly unwrapped the cloth and produced one of the objects from within. He slowly handed it to Octavius.

Octavius accepted the paper and rotated it so he could look upon his new fortune.

It was a work of art! Gass had never seen anything more beautiful in his entire fifty-three years. He was holding in his shaking hands a United States Note, a Greenback, valued at one million dollars! Gass read the face of the note, he thought silently, but in reality it was out loud.

"Promise To Pay The Bearer, Cash Amount or True Returned Weight In Gold, As Of Date Specified Or At Later Date, No Sooner, Which Ever Is Greater For Payment of Interest. Note Matures in The Year Of Our Lord Eighteen Hundred and Eighty" Octavius was now very light-headed, and he felt as if he might pass out.

"Horace, a glass of wine for Mr. Gass if you would please, quickly."

"I think something a little stronger is called for." Horace replied. "I have some good old Kentucky Sipp'in Whiskey. May I pour us all a drink?" He produced a flask from somewhere unseen.

"You haven't even seen the best part Mr. Gass" Homer Black slowly retrieved the remaining papers from the oilcloth packet. "Here are the remaining nine hundred and ninety-nine notes."

He slid the neatly tied bundles of notes over to Octavius. Gass was trying to do the math calculations in his head but it was too great. Gold was currently valued at $18.93 per ounce. It had remained closely at that rate since it was discovered west, over the Sierra Nevada Range, in California in 1848. They had mined over four million tons of ore here on Gass's rancho, all mined in secret!

"If you were wondering, Octavious, it's a total sum of one billion, two hundred eleven million, five hundred and twenty, thousand, dollars."

His mind was swimming in circles. It had been three years, three years of toiling beneath his rancho. The whole thing hadn't been real to Octavius until just this very moment.

Glasses of the brown liquor were handed all around. Homer Black stood, followed by his brother then Horace Wright.

Octavius's legs would not lift him. They felt like cooked damp bread as he tried to stand. In a split moment he decided that it was best if he remained seated.

"Gentlemen, to the richest man in the United States, if not the entire world! Mr. Octavius Gass!" and with that the men all quickly drained their glasses in toast to the man seated before them.

As the trio finished they set the glasses on the table before them. Mr. Black, who had been quite quiet for the past three hours, finally asked his leave of the men so he might return to the mine in order to finish the closing. He wanted everything to be completed by nine o'clock that night, with the last train leaving at nine fifteen, and no later. The remaining three men talked of what Gass might do now that he was a wealthy man. The three continued talking until about eight o'clock when Homer and Horace asked their leave of Octavius. Octavius escorted the men to his front door, lit and handed them a Dietz Railroad lantern in order for them to find their way to the mine and the station. The air had turned to a chill, as it was still winter in the desert.

Gass returned to the great room and retrieved his new fortune. He quickly thumbed through the notes to verify that they were truly genuine and not stacked with blank pieces of paper. All proved to be true and Gass's trembling hands slowly started retuning to a somewhat semblance of normal. He had much to do tonight as they were closing the mine and sending the last workers off on the remaining three work trains. He wanted to be there when they were to dynamite the mine opening. That would put a close on one life and open the beginning of a new one for him. First he thought however, that tonight was also the ideal time for him to try his hidden secret-keep to hide his new wealth.

He crossed the expanse to the large fireplace that was the focal centerpiece of the great room. He gently pressed on the small, oval keystone that was center, just below the great pinyon mantle. The rock depressed about two inches into the surrounding stone. As the stone bottomed, an audible click was heard off to Gass's left and an unseen latch was released. He then placed a small locking stone into the recess of the keystone in order to keep the secret door from returning to its closed position while he was in his secret keep. Gass then moved over to the front of what appeared to be the firewood storage bin inset into the stonewall before him. With little effort, Gass pushed the large imposing rock, back into the wall, revealing a stone stair leading down into the secret cavern below.

Octavius tread lightly down the stone steps, as it was pitch dark. Once he was at the base of the steps he reached for a small lantern off to his right on the wall. He retrieved a wooden match from his fob pocket in his worn blue denim work pants. He struck the tip of the stick against the roughly hewn wall of the cavern. The spark from the match produced a great flash of white light until it settled into a small burning pyre of wood. He set the match to the wick and slowly adjusted the lantern's flame to reveal a warm glow of light over his secret keep.

In front of Gass, down a short tunnel from the steps, lay the starting point of his own underground railway. Octavius had laid close to three miles of mine track beneath of his wonderful home leading to the actual mine. At the end of the line was Gass' real work office and sanctuary. He climbed aboard a contraption of his own design. Instead of using a standard heavy mine handcart to speed upon the steel rails, Octavious had built a conveyance powered by a bicycle. The bicycle sat upon one rail and attached to it was a small flat car that rode the rails as well. This allowed Gass the ability to carry items back and forth from his home to his secret keep.

Octavius sat astride his Railrider and started pedaling. The track was level and well laid, so the short trip took no more than 20 minutes before he reached the end of the line. Here at the end just as at the beginning, Octavius had small turntables built into the track. These allowed him to easily turn his Railrider around with a minimum of effort, thus pointing his transportation in the proper direction.

Gass turned the well-oiled turntable with ease and set the Railrider in the correct direction for his return trip back to the house. He then walked over to a large, hand carved oak door. He withdrew a key from a peg on the wall and opened the door to his secret keep.

Over the past year, Octavius had built many shelves, cabinets and cupboards into his secret keep. In many of the drawers he had placed much of his important documents for his ranch and water operations. He chose a special place that he had crafted into the stone itself, a hiding place ingeniously hidden unless you knew just where to look for it. In this nook he placed the one thousand Greenbacks for safekeeping. In just twelve short years this new fortune would truly be his. He would have cash and riches beyond any man's dreams.

As Gass was about to return on his railway to the stairs to head back to the house, he heard an unfamiliar muffled noise from the direction of the now concealed, old entrance into the mine. He moved to the large inset rock just down the tunnel that separated his keep from the rear of the soon to be closed mine. When Gass had sealed this entrance he had decided to maintain a viewing port and hidden entrance into the mine. In the beginning it was from this spot he was able to monitor the progress of the mine once Mr. Black had assumed operational control. It had now been months since he deemed it necessary to oversee the mining progress.

He slowly removed the few stones necessary for him to peer into the mine. It was with abject horror what Octavius Gass witnessed. In the center of the large cavern that had been stripped of the precious yellow and white ore, stood what appeared to be the remaining Chinese miners, about fifty in all. However, all around them, strewn upon the floor of the cavern like discarded firewood, were the bodies of the remaining one hundred and fifty miners. The workers had not been leaving on the late night trains to the north. It was now revealed where the workers were being sent.

Off to the side of the cavern, to the side of the cowering, screaming men were Mr. Black, his brother Homer, and Mr. Wright. Before the three men, on a low-slung wagon, was a contraption that Gass had only heard about. The machine, invented by Dr. Richard Gatling in 1861, became a Northern horror of the civil war. The Gatling gun was a rapid-fire machine gun capable of firing over two hundred shells a minute. Thus allowing its user the power to tear a man's body literally in two from the shear quantity and power of the ammunition.

Mr. Black was bent over the gun feeding what appeared to be a new belt of ammunition into the gun. Once he completed this task he moved to the side as Horace Wright stepped up to the crank that was situated to the rear of the gun. As he turned the crank the shells leapt from the rotating barrels of the machine invented solely for death. The bullets ripped into the screaming men and women as appendages, arms, legs, even heads, were severed from the broken, dying bodies. Blood spewed from the bodies with such force that it appeared to be hundreds of small fountains raining down crimson water upon a crimson lake.

When the firing ceased and the smoke started to clear a little, the next horror made Gass retch his full stomach upon the floor of his keep. The three men stood in front of over two hundred murdered men, congratulating each other as they shook hands. The three men turned and left the cavern. Gas continued to hear their laughter as they made their way out of the mine.

Gass quickly returned the stones to their place and ran for the Railrider and pedaled as fast as he ever had back to the house. At the end of the line he leapt off of the seat and dashed to the steps, which he took three at a time, racing upward as the horror of what he just witnessed replayed over and over again in his head. Once he was to the top of the stairs he quickly returned the alter stone to its place and reset the keystone below the mantle. He quickly made for a room off to the side of the great room in order to retrieve his war worn Smith & Wesson Model 1 revolver. As he turned the corner he stopped dead in his tracks as he came to the window overlooking the mine entrance and train station. In the dark of the evening, a single solitary lantern light could be seen coming closer to the ranch house. He was convinced that he was next to be murdered. The entire arrangement had been a sham. It all boiled down to simple robbery. Gass called out to alert his house staff but there was no reply. It turned out that in the absence of Mr. Horace Wright during dinner, he had located Octavius's very trusted housekeeper, cook and valet and had slit their throats and had left the bodies in the kitchen.

Gass grabbed his revolver and quickly made to the front entrance. He threw open the door and as the door came to a crash against the plastered, white washed wall, he stepped out onto the porch and began to open fire at the approaching lantern. Before he could pull the trigger once more, a shot echoed from Gass's right. A sharp searing pain scorched across his right thigh as a bullet entered his thick muscular leg. The blood started to stream from his thigh as Gass fell to the floor of the porch.

He started to drag his injured body back into the house in order to take cover. Unknown to Octavius, Mr. Black had flanked the house from the right as Mr. Wright flanked to the left. The lantern that he had been firing at was a clever ruse that in the dark look to be a person slowly approaching the porch. Instead the two murderers had tied the lantern to a small wagon to the center of a long hemp rope. Each man then walked about ten yards to each the side of the wagon and slowly advanced towards the house pulling the wagon between them. This allowed them to reach the house unseen, thus allowing cover from any fire and allowing them to outflank Gass.

Gass slammed the heavy pinyon door closed as more bullets tore into the hardened wood. He slowly returned to his feet just as a thunderous crash tore through the front window of the great room. Homer Black had thrown a large flaming bucket of tie oil, otherwise known as creosote into Gass' home. The oil spread across the floor with alarming speed. Just as the pool of oil reach the table another crash to Gass's left revealed another flaming bucket of the treacle oil substance. With in seconds the entire room was ablaze.

The room soon filled with acrid, throat closing smoke as the oil seeped into the floorboards of the house. The flames increased in intensity and size as the furniture added kindling to the inferno. Gass knew that he had to get out or die. He could never make it to the rear door of the rancho and he knew deep in his soul that one of the three thugs was sure to be waiting for him there in order to put a bullet in his head. Instead, Octavius headed to the fireplace and it's hidden secret.

Trying to steady himself on his injured leg, coughing from the smoke that now made breathing more painful than the wound in his leg, Gass reached for the keystone in order to release the latch to the stairway. The smoke was now thick as pitch and began to poor out through the chimney of the fireplace. Gass was completely enveloped in the cloud, unable to breathe. He fumbled as he closed his eyes to the stinging smoke. He finally found the oval stone directly under the mantle and pushed it deftly into its socket, however he did not place the locking stone into the recess.

Through the noise of the inferno he was unable to hear the click of the latch, but he felt the low tremor beneath his feet as it released the large alter stone. Gass fell to the floor where he found he could actually see across the entire room. His house, his beautiful house that he had slaved over for the past three years was burning all around him. A lone sadness welled up in his throat as he reached the stone base and pushed with the all the strength he could muster. As he pushed the piece of limestone he lost his balance over the stairway and tumbled down into the inky blackness of his secret keep. At the bottom of the stairs Octavius

Gass lay bleeding from the bullet wound in his leg. As he lay there he continued to cough, trying to expel the smoke from his lungs. Just as the coughing started to abate a slow approaching darkness start to creep across his mind. He began to feel a sudden coldness beginning in his legs and slowly growing up his torso into his chest and then creeping down his arms. He was now shivering as if he was exposed naked to a blast of a cruel winter wind. Just as his entire body felt as if it could take the cold no longer a flash of warmth and comfort filled Gass's body then quickly left. Death had come to Octavius Gass.

Above, the alter stone returned to its concealed state and the keystone returned to its place beneath the pinyon mantle. The secret keep would continue to keep its secrets.

1

Unexpected Finds

Javits Convention Center
New York, NY
April 30, 2013

"Sold, item number 231 for $2,300 to bidder number 1631!" the auctioneer relayed as his hammer struck the top of the podium. "Up next for bid is lot number 232, Scott Catalog, United States number 117, a mint, previously hinged copy of the twelve cent, green S.S. Adriatic. We will start the bidding at $ 500.00. Five hundred, five hundred dollars, do I have five hundred..."

Liam Ross listened to the pattered drone of the auctioneer as he began his verbal eloquence. The auction, as of yet, had proven to be fruitless. Of the ten items that he came to bid on, eight had been hammered down at over one hundred and ten percent of catalog value. He had two more lots to go, but they wouldn't be on the podium until at least eight o'clock this evening. So, as he walked into the dealer bourse he thought to himself that if this artificially inflated market for mint United States Collectors Postage stamps continued to get out of hand, average collectors would just throw in the towel and start to collect McDonalds Happy Meal toys or something else. As he continued to browse from table to table of stamps encompassing virtually every country on the planet, including stamps from many countries that no longer existed, his gaze was in what had long become being on automatic search mode. His eyes quickly scanning the tabletop arrangements of the individual stamps, plate blocks, stamps on covers, and much more of the exact same items that would regularly appear in the major philatelic events. Every once and a while an item would pop out at him, thus requiring a closer, proper inspection.

"Liam, anything in particular that you are looking for?" The voice was that of an old friend of Liam's, Rex Cooper. Rex stood off to the side of his neatly ordered table consisting solely of 19th century United States individual stamps.

"Always looking for that miraculous find that will bring the philatelic word to its knees Rex. Anything new that I haven't seen yet?"

"How about a 1855 Swedish Three Skilling Banco, color error? I'll let you have it for the bargain sum of $3,000,000, I'll even let you pay in installments, say ten dollars a month for the next, say, twenty five thousand months!" laughed the silvered haired dealer.

This had been a running joke between Liam and Rex for the past twenty-five years. Liam could still remember that day shortly after he had just begun collecting stamps. He had spent hour upon hour every day after school and on weekends, searching, digging, combing through box after box of stamps in Rex's old stamp shop. One particularly rainy Saturday, Liam was convinced that he had found the Holy Grail of stamp collectors, a 1855 Swedish Three Skilling Banco, color error. He was so excited that he rushed from Rex's back stockroom into the store, tripping over a newly stacked display of stamp albums, sending them flying through the air and then sadly into a glass display case. The noise and calamity had been horrendous! The stamps flying through the air would have been comical if one of the shards of glass hadn't torn through a mint, never hinged, United States Number 2. A beautiful copy of the ten-cent black George Washington issue of 1847, worth over $2,000! Liam thought for sure that Rex was going to explode right then and there. Two customers in the store at the time, stood frozen in horror as the twelve year old slowly lifted his head to reveal his face covered with stamps that had stuck to his sweaty brow from the collision. Liam wanted to run before Rex had the opportunity to punt him through the front door of the shop. However, in total surprise to all, Rex just leaned down on the counter, the ends of his mouth curling into a Cheshire cat type smile.

"In a bit of a hurry are we Mr. Ross? I am afraid that postage for your size and shape will be a bit more than the three-centers that you have displayed. I'm afraid that postage due would be a whopper!" Rex broke out into a laugh that soon put both the customers and Liam at ease.

After a couple hours of clean up, and a very long talk with Liam and his father, who had offered to pay for the damage, the decision of all three parties was to have Liam work in the store after school and on weekends, paying back Rex ten dollars a week until the damage and the stamp were paid for.

Liam worked hard as he was determined to pay back every single penny for the damaged stamp, a stamp that he could only dream of owning one day. But after only two years, sometimes using his entire weeks pay to offset the debt; Liam had paid back almost every penny of the damage.

During that time, that wonderful time, Liam also learned. He listened to Rex dealing with his customers, he listened to the varied interests of collectors, he spent hours reading and researching every book, newspaper and article on stamps that he could get his hands on, amassing what would someday become an encyclopedic knowledge of philately.

It was a Saturday afternoon and Liam was helping Rex close down the shop for the weekend when Rex called him to the backroom.

"Liam, do you have a minute?"

"Be right there Rex. I'm just locking up the front door."

Liam finished the task at hand and went into the backroom carrying the day's trash with him.

"Yes, sir. Do you need something?" asked the now fourteen year old.

"It's payday, and according to my records, today marks the final ten dollars of your little miss-step from a couple of years ago." handing him an envelope "Both your father and I are proud at how you stayed with it and never shirked your responsibilities Liam. Good job!"

"Thanks Rex, but I feel that I owe you so much more. What you have taught me alone about stamps is priceless."

"I also wanted to talk to you my boy. I am going to do away with weekend hours here at the store and start going to some more stamp shows. I could still use your help from time to time, but I know your dad wants you to start over at his company this summer. He really needs a hard worker like you."

"I know Rex, but with my brother there, and the business being so big, I don't know what I could do."

"I'm sure that your dad has plans for you Liam. Just give it a try and see how it goes." Rex started to pull on his light jacket. "Let's get things locked up for the day, shall we?"

Just as Liam and Rex were about to turn out the lights, Rex went back into the shop, returning just a few moments later with a small package.

"Say, I almost forgot to show this to you." Handing the small, glassine envelope to Liam.

"What's this?"

"Open it up and take a look."

Liam slowly opened the glassine envelope as he had been taught to. Rex removed a pair of stamp tongs from his shirt pocket and handed them to the boy. Liam slowly set the tongs to the single stamp that was revealed in the envelope, slowly retracting the small piece of paper revealing the reverse of the stamp.

"Well, turn it over you fool." The shopkeeper laughed.

As Liam turned the tongs in his fingers, he gasped as the front of the stamp revealed itself to be a pristine ten-cent black George Washington issue of 1847.

"Rex, you found another one! That's so great! Where did you ever find it?"

"That, my clumsy friend, is the very same stamp that you so wonderfully skewered two years ago. I had an expert repair it."

"How will you ever sell it? A repaired stamp isn't worth anywhere's near its catalog value."

"Well, this one is already sold."

"Really? To who?"

"To a young man who has just spent two years paying it off in ten dollar increments."

With that news Liam's eyes grew to the size of small dinner plates.

"It's me...I mean, it's mine?"

"All yours my boy, you broke it. You bought it!"

So, it is that very moment from the past that always floods back to Liam as Rex and he banter about. Today, that very stamp holds a place of honor among Liam's vast collections.

Liam Ross was a collector. Not your average hobbyist that starts a collection as a child and then pulls it out from the attic every five or ten years as they grow older in the hope that it has magically transformed itself into a million dollar windfall. Liam was a professional collector of many rare, precious items that many sought after, but very few would ever acquire. A detective of sorts; searching not only for items to add to his own collections, but seeking out items for companies, museums and other private collectors.

Those private collectors were why he was here at the International Philatelic Expo in New York City. Three of his long time clients had been searching, for quite sometime, for some very specific variants of a rather common stamp. These variants differ only in the fact that they either have a unique number of perforations or a slightly different color. Those slight differences meant the divergence between a stamp that was worth $1.45 and a stamp that could garner as much as $45,000 at auction.

"Liam, do you have some available time this afternoon?" the old friend asked.

"I have three more items that I need to try and bid on, but that's not until later this evening. Why do you ask?"

"Well, an old friend, really my very first client, Joe Bousquet, recently passed away leaving his collection to his daughter. She really has no idea as to what her father had and I think she would like to try and get me to buy it. He probably bought most of it from me anyway, general issues and such, couple of dozen albums or so, I know I wouldn't be interested in any of it. Could you just go and give her a quick estimate? She is only here for the day. It shouldn't take you very long."

"Sure Rex, where does she live?"

"Her dad's place is in the Bronx, not to far from a subway she said. Here are the directions and her number. Take a look and see what the old coot had. It's can't be much."

"I'll take a quick look and if it just general issue items, I'll give her the name of some dealers that could really use the inventory and who will give her a fair price. How does that sound?"

"Perfect, I'll call her and let her know that you are on your way."

So Liam left the Javits Center on Manhattan's Westside, found the entrance to the Grand Central Shuttle subway entrance a few blocks away, and headed to Grand Central Station. Here Liam transferred to the number Four subway and headed uptown. When he reached the Bedford Boulevard-Lehman College stop he exited the train and headed out to the street to hail a cab.

"98-124 Webster Avenue, please." The taxi left the station and headed only a few blocks east. Liam arrived at his destination within five-minutes, most of that time they had been sitting at a traffic signal. If he had known it was so close he would have walked. Handing the cab driver a five-dollar bill for a four-dollar fare, Liam knew that it would be futile to even ask for change, so he thanked the man and left the cab.

The building was a typical Northeastern factory building, the type that was designed and constructed in the mid to late 1800's. It was a classic twin building construction surrounding an interior motor courtyard that had been converted into a parking area and garden for the tenants. Made of what was then known as city brick, the building appeared to be ten stories tall, with well kept lawns and gardens out front and a row of freshly planted pachysandra neatly along the front walk to the entrance. The front entrance was a series of two glass doors, an outer door to keep the elements at bay and the inner door leading into the main vestibule. You couldn't enter either of these two doors without a key or without being "buzzed" by one of the residents. Liam quickly located Rex's friends name on the registry off to his left and pressed the button next to it. After a series of tones a voice answered.

"Yes, may I help you?"

"Susan Bousquet? My name is Liam Ross. I think that you were expecting me?"

"Yes, please come right up. Tenth floor, apartment A." A buzzer sounded and Liam was able to open the doors into the smallish vestibule. Finding the elevator off to his right Liam pressed the single button and waited for the elevator car to come. Once the car stopped, Liam opened the door to the retrofit 1900's single door style elevator car, closed the door and then the gate behind him.

"Talk about claustrophobic! It's a bread box with a light!"

Liam remarked to himself. The car made its assent very slowly, bumping and jerking every inch of the way. After one particularly bone jawing thump, Liam actually wrapped his hands firmly around the two small wooden handrails attached to the walls and vowed to take the stairs down. The elevator finally arrived at its destination and Liam hurriedly exited the elevator. Shaking his hands to get some blood back into them, Liam found apartment A and rang the bell affixed to the middle of the doorjamb.

The door opened to reveal a woman, not much younger than Liam, dressed in blue jeans and a cropped Syracuse University sweatshirt revealing a very toned stomach. Her hair was honey blonde and cut short in a long forgotten pageboy style. She was tall, eye-to-eye as tall as Liam, however as he looked towards the floor he noticed that so wasn't wearing any shoes. As she welcomed him into the apartment he noticed box upon box stacked in just about every corner of the home.

"I'm so sorry for your loss. Rex sends his condolences as well."

Susan crossed the living room hurriedly and covered up some items that she was putting into a box.

"Thank you Mr. Ross. It's been rather difficult going though all of dad's things, but I have to get it done and back up to the university before the beginning of the week."

"Please, it's Liam. Are you a student Ms. Bousquet?"

"No, I'm a adjunct professor at the Maxwell School. I teach certain aspects of public administration and other terribly boring topics. Please call me Susan."

Liam saw something in her eyes as she described her profession. He had also noticed that she always kept her graze directly at Liam's eyes. Liam thought that it must be a certain trick of the trade for teachers in order to keep their students focused to the topic.

"Well… so I don't hold you from anything, if you could show me your fathers collection, I'll try and get out of here as soon as possible."

"Oh sure, it's in the spare room. It'll just take a few minutes. This way, down the hall" the words came across almost sarcastically.

Liam followed her down the narrow hall noticing that there were only three doors down the rather long hallway. As he neared the end of the hallway the door to his immediate left was the bathroom, and the next left was what appeared to be the master suite, if you could call it that. At quick glimpse it appeared to be a fairly standard bedroom, of about ten feet by twenty feet. Something seemed odd as Liam continued to follow Susan. All of the rooms appeared to be smallish, but the hallway went on for a good sixty feet.

They stopped at the door on the right and Susan opened it. Liam was not prepared for what lay beyond that bedroom door.

2

Recycling

Before him was what could only be described as a mirage. Nothing could be this large. Not in an apartment in the Bronx! Hell, it was impossible! Before Liam was what appeared to be a library, not a small library mind you, but a library that could easily cover over twenty thousand square feet. In this room were row upon row of shelving from the floor to the sixteen-foot ceilings, each shelf four feet wide with eight shelves per stack. Each row had perhaps ten stacks and the rows continued on forever it seemed, each shelf containing albums, boxes and file cabinets. In the center of the room was a single chestnut table that looked like an original captain's table from a 1700's merchant ship. The windows in the room had all been carefully blacked as to not let the harmful rays of the sun in, thus laying damage to the precious contents.

Liam must have stood there staring with his mouth open looking like a complete idiot. He knew he couldn't move. He didn't know what to say.

"Liam, my fathers collection." As she theatrically waved her arm across the vista of shelves. "Just a few items, shouldn't take you long I guess."

Finally Liam found enough saliva in his mouth to croak out a somewhat lucid response,

"Susan, I had no idea. Rex just said that it would take a few minutes."

"I guess Rex never really, truly knew what dad had. This was his passion for over sixty years. It's all he did, really."

"He was a stamp dealer?" he asked still not knowing where or how to even begin.

"No he was just an avid collector. Only searched out and bought the horrid little things, never sold a single one to my knowledge. Never paid attention to anything other than these damn pieces of paper."

Liam noticed her emphasis on "the horrid little things." He was about to say something when she continued on.

"Don't get me wrong Mr. Ross, I loved my father, but his hobby, his obsession really, came between us many years ago. My mother coped for many years, but in the end she couldn't take much more. They could have had a very comfortable lifestyle in their golden years, but all dad wanted to do is sit in this room twenty and sometimes twenty four hours a day, immersed in this obsession." Excusing herself, "So if you don't mind, I need to finish up in the living room before the movers show up. I'll let you get started in here."

Susan left him to himself; he still didn't know where to start. First things first, he was going to call Rex and give him hell. This was a project that would take ten people over a year to even make a dent in. Who the hell even knew what was in here. Just as Liam was about to dial Rex, Susan interrupted him.

"I can be such a ditz at times. I forgot to give this to you. My dad's attorney gave it to me to give to Rex. It should explain everything." She handed him a manila packet that had to be a good two inches thick, Rex's name squarely affixed to the center of the label on the front. "Dad was very through. Everything you will need should be in there."

Liam stood there holding the packet as Susan turned and left the room. Liam dialed Rex at the expo. The phone had just rung for the third time when the familiar voice answered.

"Rex, it's Liam. You are not going to believe this!" Liam then recounted the past fifteen minutes to Rex via the cell. "She also gave me an packet. It's addressed to you. Do you want me to bring it over to you now?"

"No, go ahead and open it. It might make some sense out of all this."

Liam carefully opened the end of the buff colored packet and withdrew the first of its contents. Liam quickly scanned the top page of the document.

"Um, Rex, you might want to get over here pretty damn quick."

"Why, what's up boy?"

"According to this, Joe has left everything to you!" There was silence from the other end of the phone, after what seemed an eternity Rex finally spoke up.

"What do you mean, left everything to me? From what you are telling me there must be a hundreds of thousands, if not millions of issues there!"

Liam returned to scanning the document.

"Wait Rex, there's more. There is a letter in here from Joe explaining that he had come across a find that might turn out to be fairly significant. He doesn't get into the specifics, only that you need to check some of his files that he has listed here. He also say's to be careful and to not take anything for granted or to trust anyone you don't know. He empathetically writes – Keep the eyes opened and check 23021868."

"That's a bit cryptic if you ask me." Rex's voice emitted from the cell that Liam had now put on speakerphone and had set on the desk so he could continue to read.

"It continues on for some ten or so pages Rex. Most of it is just rambling, but it's apparent that your friend was very paranoid. It goes on to state that some attorney had contacted him six months ago, wanting to purchase his entire collection for a client. That this client was an ardent philatelist and he would pay any amount he named." Liam continued on. "The attorney appears to have been relentless. He called Joe everyday for two weeks, always pressuring and sweetening the proposal."

"Well Liam, in today's economy people are trying to buy for far less than what things are worth and others are trying to get those things for a steal. Doesn't sound like Joe was even remotely interested. Plus it doesn't sound like Joe needed the money. "

Liam read on.

"Rex, it goes on, it seems what really concerned Joe is that there is no way that anyone could have known about his collection, that is besides his late wife, his daughter and you. So he tried to find out how this attorney's client know about it."

Still reading.

"Oh, oh, hold on Rex. Joe also states that he was starting to be concerned for his safety. That there had been at least six break in attempts in the last five months. The first about two weeks after he told this attorney to leave him alone and to go to hell, that he was not selling and to never contact him again."

"Liam, let me close things down here and I will be there as soon as I can."

"Good, I'm going to go and talk to Susan a bit more and see if I can shed any more light onto this. See you soon"

Liam closed the connection and went out into the apartment foyer to find Susan. She was busy taping up what appeared to be the last carton for the movers.

"Susan, might you have a few minutes to talk? I have a few questions."

"Only if you will help me move these cartons over to that pile. These are items that are going to Goodwill."

Liam helped the woman move the boxes, asking questions as they worked.

"Susan, first, are you aware that your father left the entire collection to Rex?"

"I am, I certainly do not want it."

"Are you also aware that your father had some break in attempts over the past few weeks?"

"Dad, called me when the first one happened. He thought it was just kids looking to get into the basement and cause trouble, that's happened quite a bit over the years. The basements a great place to party."

"Do you know if your father reported it to the super or the owner of the building?"

"Um, Mr. Ross, mom and dad owned the building, they have since dad got out of the Army. He told me he bought it at a government auction on the day the war ended. They then converted it into apartments."

"What do you mean owned the building? Who owns it now?"

"Well that would be me I guess. After mom died, dad changed his will and left everything to me, that is except the stamps. I told him I couldn't care less about those."

"If you don't mind me asking Susan, how many tenants do you have?"

"Well each floor has eight apartments, except the ground floor, and we have ten floors, however as you have just seen, the top floor here dad took over completely for his collection. The funny thing is that as tenets have left over the past few years, dad never seemed to find new ones. We're down to just three, Mrs. Meyers on the third floor, and two groups of grad students on the fourth. The rest of the building is empty. I was thinking of offering them all a buy out and sell the building. But that is going to have to wait until the summer, after finals."

That explained the long halls and the vast library as the collection room. Joe Bousquet had taken over the entire floor over the years and converted it into his library, as he needed.

"Susan, did your dad have any special security installed here in this apartment?"

"Did he! This last year or so he went over board with cameras, infrared systems, even lasers. The control center is back in the collection room."

"Do you know if he kept an archive of his security tapes?"

"Dad had everything sent to a hard drive with an array redundancy. For an older man, he was on top of computer systems and what they could offer."

Liam's mind was racing thinking that perhaps the hard drives might show or explain why Joe Bousquet had become rather paranoid in his last days. He made a mental note to check the disks when Rex got there.

"Susan, one last question if you wouldn't mind, and I am sorry if this seems not very tactful, but how did your father die?"

Susan's reply still revealed the grief of a child that had just lost a parent, a grief that takes years to finally retreat from a person.

"Dad died while he was on his way home from the bank. He used to make weekly trips to his safety deposit boxes over at New York National Bank."

"Heart attack or stroke?"

"Neither, Dad was as healthy as a horse. Dad was killed by a hit and run driver just as he left the bank. He held on at the hospital for a couple of days, but his injuries were just too severe. He died last Wednesday; I had him cremated on Friday. I am taking his ashes back up to Syracuse. When I was younger, every summer, we would go up to the Thousand Islands; dad loved it there, that's where we had our boat. So I am going to spread his ashes over the St. Lawrence River, as he requested."

"Was everything okay here at the apartment when you arrived last week? Did it look like anyone had tried to get in?" asked Liam.

"The police were here, I gave them permission to go in. That was on the day that dad was hit. I then moved in and stayed here until dad passed. I didn't see anything that looked like someone broke in. I'm sure that the police would have said something if there had been any trouble. Why, what are you getting at?"

"Oh, just the over active imagination of an individual that reads too many detective novels." Liam then remembered about Rex. "Susan, Rex is one his way over here to try and get his head around the collection. I am afraid that it will take quite a few days to get everything packed up and ready to be shipped out. How long might we be able to stay here and get on with the project?"

"Stay as long as you need." Handing Liam a spare set of keys.

"These should open just about everything, except the stamp safes and boxes. Those keys and combinations should be somewhere in his office. I don't have any plans for the apartment yet. I don't even know what I'm going to do with the building. We only have the handful of tenants left and I won't be able to get down enough to see that everything's running okay. But that's the next story, so they say."

Liam help Susan finish her packing and then escorted her to the elevator. She was on her way out to make the final arrangements for the movers in order for them to make their pick up in the morning. They said their goodbyes at the elevator door.

Liam was now going to see if he could find the security center and the remainder of the keys for the stamps. He was half way down the hallway to the library door when the there was a knock on the front door.

"Wow, Rex got here fast." Talking to himself as he went to let his old friend into the apartment. Liam pulled open the door and was about to make a smart remark about how old men can really move when it involves a pretty woman or a stamp, when Liam saw that it was not Rex. Before Liam stood a man of regular size, light brown hair cut in a popular style favored by most professionals, and dressed in what appeared to be a hand tailored Henry Poole & Co., grey herringbone cashmere two piece suit that most likely set the man back £4,500.

"May I help you sir?" Liam asked of the man before him.

"It is I who could most likely assist you Mr. Cooper." Handing Liam his business card. "My name is Trumball Nash. I represent a fellow philatelist that would very much like to purchase the late Mr. Bousquet's collection."

The accent though appearing to be English, was not. From the body language that the man absent mindedly projected, combined with what seemed to be a passing acting ability, Liam readily suspected that the man was indeed German, not from The City, London, England, as his card suggested.

"I am so sorry Mr. Nash. I am not Rex Cooper. I am Liam Ross, an associate of Mr. Cooper's. I do expect him, but not for some time."

"Well perhaps I could wait?"

"Well sir, any other time would have been fine, but you see, I am on my way out as well. Perhaps you could call Mr. Cooper later in the day and set an appointment, perhaps for tomorrow? I'm sure he would love to discuss the collection with you." Liam handed him one of Rex's cards but with his cell phone number instead of Rex's.

"A wonderful idea. Could you please inform Mr. Cooper that I will be calling soon, my client is most anxious." Did Liam perceive a small click of the heels and a slight bow? Liam led him out into the foyer, only locking one of the three locks that the door harbored, and the two men walked over to the elevator. Once to the elevator, Liam waved the man in before he stepped into the claustrophobic cage. The aged elevator returned the men to the first floor without any incident. Once outside Liam started to say goodbye to the attorney but was cut off before he had a chance to.

"Mr. Ross, could I offer you a ride to your location?" as a new Lincoln Town Car slid quietly up to the curb beside the man. The driver leaped from the left side door and quickly positioned himself at the rear door next to Mr. Nash.

"Thank you very much for your kind offer, but I have a car around the corner. But thank you again."

Liam took the offered hand and shook it before the man leaned into the back seat of the automobile. The driver quickly closed the door and returned to the drivers seat. Within two seconds the car moved noiselessly away from the curb and accelerated down the avenue. Liam watched as the car turned left at the next traffic signal, but not before committing the license plate to memory.

3

Puzzle

Liam waited at the curb for about five minutes before a cab pulled up. Rex extracted himself from the back seat, paid the cabbie and walked over to Liam.

"So, we have a bit of a project ahead of us, eh?" asked the elder stamp dealer.

"Rex, it would take a team of twenty experts perhaps six months to even make a dent in that." as he hooked his thumb towards the building.

"If it were just you and I doing all of the cataloging, and hoping that we live to the ripe old ages of 150 and 185 respectively, we might just make it through the first shelf."

With a chuckle the two men started for the front door. When they arrived back on the tenth floor, Liam let Rex into the apartment and took him straight to the library. Rex's first comment was a long, low whistle.

"Holy Shit! I don't even think that the NYC Library's collection is this large. This might even rival the United States Postal Museum's, this is gigantic!"

Liam watched his friend as he hurriedly went from shelf to shelf, trying to get a sense of what was what, acting like a boy in a candy shop.

"Liam, nothing is notated. It just bar coded and numbered."

"Well, that my friend my be our saving grace. Susan told me her dad was quite the computer expert. Let's see if we can find his computer. Perhaps it might get us started on the right path."

After casually looking for about fifteen minutes with shouts back and forth to each other about what seemed to be held on the shelves, Rex came across a locked room near the back of the massive library.

"Liam, I think I found the computer room, however, it doesn't have a lock. Did Joe's daughter mention how we might get in?"

"All she said was that everything we needed was in here."

Liam came from around one of the ceiling high shelves, waving the manila packet as he joined Rex at the door. Liam examined the door and found it to be a top of the line Master Security Products door, the type that were installed in the pentagon after the attacks of 9/11. Able to withstand small arms fire, high temperatures and even small battering rams. Liam tried the handle, but the handle stayed firm. Noting that there wasn't a single keyhole on the entire door or the doorjamb, Liam set about to find the locking mechanism.

"What we are looking for Rex is either a slot for a card key of some type of keypad that we can enter a combination into. You look on the left hand side and I will look on the right of the door."

It didn't take long; Liam found a small-concealed panel artfully hidden in the intricately carved molding around the door. Pressing at the top of the small carving the hinged door revealed a Keico KF-2000 Combination Finger Reader / Keypad electronic lock.

"Damn! It couldn't be easy, could it!" the stamp dealer expelled while looking over Liam's shoulder. "How in heaven's name are we to get into that?"

Liam thought for a minute and remembered Susan Bousquet's words, "Dad was very through. Everything you will need should be in there" meaning the manila packet.

Liam removed all of the contents of the packet and placed them on a small table that was near the door. Near the bottom of the packet was a small padded envelope about three inches wide by six inches long. Liam opened the packet and pulled out a small hand written note with some of the worse penmanship that Liam had ever seen.

"Rex, can you make heads or tails out of this?" as he handed his friend the note.

Rex removed some reading glasses from a case that was inside his coat pocket. He then perched the antique Pince-nez glasses on his nose and started to read the note.

"It's from Joe. It seems to be a bit of a puzzle. We need specific numbers for the combination, that he relates I should know by heart, and…" Rex stopped in mid sentence and seemed to turn white as a sheet.

"And what Rex?" asked Liam.

Reluctantly Rex continued on. "Um, it seems we need his right thumb! How gruesome!"

As he said these words, Rex slid down into a nearby high-backed reading chair, looking even paler than he was. He was about to excuse himself, and find a bathroom, when his former clerk spoke up.

"Now I understand, or shall I say I "dig-it"?" Standing there held between Liam's index finger and thumb, was another thumb. When Rex saw the finger, he could not contain himself and grabbed the nearest wastebasket and proceeded to vomit his lunch from today and the better part of his breakfast as well. After he finally regained a few shades of color into his cheeks, he stood up and approached Liam.

"Is that really his thumb?" pointing to the dismembered digit, covering his mouth as if he might loose the remainder of his breakfast, and possibly dinner from the night before, at any second.

"Well, yes and no. What I mean is it's not his real thumb, but a beautifully molded and crafted replica of his thumb. The detail is outstanding, you can see the ridge flow and pattern configuration in exact detail." pointing to a small occlusion on the tip, "You can even see a scar where it looks like he cut himself sometime ago. So we can scan this on the reader and get into the computer room, however we still need the numbers. Any idea what numbers by heart you know?"

"The only numbers I know by heart are my phone number, your phone number and that's about it."

"Well, let's try your phone number." Liam placed the thumb on the scanner and pressed the sequence of numbers into the keypad. The response back was a loud buzzer and a flashing screen that stated "Access Denied"

"Okay, any other idea Rex?"

"Well, like I said, your phone number."

"I can't see where that would be it, but lets give it a try."

They repeated the process garnering the same results.

"Liam, we could be here a month trying different numbers and still never get in. Any other ideas?"

"We have a bigger problem that that Rex. If I'm not mistaken this unit has a failsafe on it that shuts the system down after the third denial, so were down two strikes."

The two men stood pondering what the number could possibly be. It had to be at least five digits but no more than eight. Liam thought hard as he looked at the keypad. It appeared to be a standard keypad, a three by four grid comprising of ten numbers, a pound sign and an asterisk. It was a normal, standard telephone keypad, nothing special. When he had this thought it hit him like a ton of bricks, it was a telephone keypad, not a numerical keypad! Most locking devices only have a numerical keypad; this one had both numbers and letters, just like a telephone keypad!

"Rex, you mentioned earlier today that Mr. Bousquet was your very first client, right?"

"Yes he was, but what does that have to do with opening a door?" replied the puzzled man.

"Did you and he have a running gag, just like you and I have?"

Rex though for a minute and then he eyes revealed the answer.

"Of course! He never let me forget what the first stamp he purchased from me was. As a matter of fact it was his first stamp he bought when he returned from the war."

"Rex, what stamp was it?"

"It was nothing special, just a used copy of the 1868 reprint twelve cent Washington issue, with the F grill. Pretty bad example if I remember rightly. He made a point that he was buying it on Washington's Birthday, said it was going to be the beginning of his new discovery."

"That has to be it!" Liam excitedly proclaimed. "Well, ready to give it a try?"

"Give what a try?" the older man quizzed?

"This." Liam placed the thumb to the reader and entered the following sequence. "S-C-O-T-T-97." Scott Catalog Number 97 was the official numerical designation of the first stamp that Joe Bousquet had bought from Rex those many years ago. Simultaneously after Liam pressed the final number the electronic lock clicked and the door to the computer room opened.

4

The Proposal

Washington, D.C.
Foggy Bottom District

Untrue to popular belief, Foggy Bottom is not an acronym for a division, or even a building, connected to any of the United States Government intelligence services. In reality Foggy Bottom is one of Washington D.C.'s oldest, late 18th century neighborhoods. The true reason for this rather odd name is that the area is situated directly on the banks of the Potomac River; that lies to the southwest of the neighborhood. During the early days of the new union a large number of factories and industries were built here utilizing the abundant water supply and contributing their air clogging smoke and steam to the already naturally occurring high dew point, thus creating a fog that many visitors compared to the streets of London.

So perhaps it had not been coincidence that a group of 18th century Englishman decided to call this place home, a new home for a proposed organization that was to become one of the world's wealthiest entities. A group of individuals that could take on and solve problems no matter how great or how small. There were to be rules however, very strict rules. The first and foremost of these would be that the central core of the organization would always consist of one hundred of the nation's, if not the world's, leading contributors to all pursuits that the world itself professed. All branches of the sciences, mathematics, politics, religion and finance; especially finance.

The nondescript building, located deep in the heart of Foggy Bottom, had been designed and built by members of this organization shortly after the War for Independence. Over the years much modernization and expansion had occurred as the ages demanded, but these expansions occurred in such a discreet way that it the building never seemed to grow when one was to view it from the street. Adjoining buildings had been purchased and retrofitted over the past two centuries. Many basements and sub-basements had been added as crisis after world crisis came and went.

Although this organization still held to its core value, it employed tens of thousands of employees in offices all over the world. The headquarters in Foggy Bottom held staff upwards of two thousand. Offices held the personnel of over 200 divisions of the organization. Many of these divisions, true companies unto themselves, that had grown and flourished over the past two hundred years, carried on their day-to-day activities, furnishing the world with common everyday items such as plumbing fixtures to office machines.

Over the course of the years, one of the retrofitted buildings in this neighborhood complex had become the offices-central for the organization. This building housed the current Chairman with support staff only. Thousand upon thousands of communications came into these offices daily. Each communication, be it telephone call, email, regular mail, or even radio call, would first be screened by a team of individuals trained in specific phrases and codes, thus determining where said communication was to go and who was to receive it.

It was just such a call that had been received from the rear seat of a Lincoln Town Car some two hundred and forty miles to the northeast. After a quick series of questions with the proper corresponding answers the caller was connected to the Chairman's dedicated, private line.

"Yes." Came the voice, with no greeting, no salutation, and just curt directness.

"We have contacted the new owner and expect to have the new proposal finalized within the next twenty-four hours. Do you have any further instructions?"

"Just close the proposal and return here when you have finalized. Make sure that the other party is completely divested of everything. Understood?"

Before the party in the rear of the Town Car could even reply, the connection went dead. With nary two seconds elapsed, Mr. Nash dialed a number from memory. At the end of the first ring, a hollow emptiness opened on the other end of the line and without any tone prompting the caller to leave a message, Nash left very precise information. When he was finished leaving his directions, he entered a string of numbers into the telephones keypad closing the secure connection. Nash had done as instructed. After all, instructions received from The Centum were always crystal clear.

5

Revelations

Rex and Liam made their way into the darkened room. Rex found the light switch to the left and flipped it to on. Bank upon bank of fluorescent lights blinked on overhead, illuminating and revealing Joe Bousquet's "computer room".

"Its like mission control in here! What the hell is all of this?" Rex asked as he crossed over to one of the computer terminals on a center console.

"It appears to be a intranet system, a private internal computer system. From this system Joe could have run many multiple systems, simultaneously, doing millions upon millions of calculations. What the hell would he need a system like this for?"

Liam sat down in front of a very large LCD panel that looked to be the central system console. He looked for an on switch but failed to locate one.

"Rex, look in the packet and see if there are any specific instructions for this terminal, will you?"

Rex started to comb through the contents from the packet that they had yet to look at. After about two minutes he found a series of instructions and a card key that he thought might be the operations start up procedure. He handed these to Liam and awaited the outcome.

Liam carefully followed the instructions step by step. First tuning on power to the console, then inserting the card key that Rex had handed him. A cursor blinked to life in the upper left hand corner of the monitor, then, after step three, typing in a very long series of pass codes, the terminal in front of Liam blinked to life.

The menu that appeared on the screen was very specific. Joe had categorized it into five main categories, with each area being broken down, some into multiple sub categories. The four main categories were, Inventory, Research, Security, and Personal. Liam maneuvered the curser to the first item of the list and opened the icon. A menu of subcategories appeared revealing the multiple layers of the philatelic inventory that was in the adjoining room. Each sub menu was then arranged by decade, starting in 1770 and moving forward to the current year. Liam chose the decade 1900 - 1909 and clicked on the icon. The icon opened and revealed a massive list of what appeared to be individual United States stamps that were issued between the years 1900 -1909. Liam paused briefly, finally letting out a breath of relief.

"Oh, thank God, Joe computerized everything. Every issue has been scanned and cataloged. Well that should save you about two hundred years going through everything."

Liam selected a Scott Catalog number 298 on the screen, the eight-cent Pan-American issue. The file opened revealing that each stamp had its own barcode, associated inventory control number, high resolution scan of both the front and back of the stamp, current catalog information and a brief history of that individual stamp. Rex watched as Liam worked through the information of the screen.

"This must have taken him years! The scans alone are remarkable, the best I have ever seen." Remarked the dealer. "But why go to such trouble for a personal collection?"

Liam navigated the computer back to the main menu. He wanted to look at the security section. After a few clicks from the mouse, the screen revealed multiple windows, at least fifty, with each window related to a corresponding camera. There in the center of the screen were Liam and Rex seated at the console. There had to be at least fifteen cameras in the library room alone. There were cameras showing the front door to the apartment, each room of the apartment, including the bathroom; odd thought Liam, multiple cameras showing the outside of the building and a series of cameras that were focused on a very large darkened room.

"What's that?" asked Rex pointing to the series of darkened room icons.

Liam selected the first of the dark images and double clicked on it. The image opened to full screen and revealed the camera's location information in the lower right hand corner.

"It's say's First Floor NE. I can't make out the image, there is not enough light for the camera."

Liam went back to another one of the darkened icons and tried a different view.

"Same as the last, First Floor SE. It appears that he has a series of cameras all focused on the first floor. I wasn't really paying attention when I came in, but did you notice anything different about the first floor?" Liam asked of his friend.

"No, it was just an entry vestibule, nothing special."

"Odd." thought Liam, "Very odd. Well we had better get back to the stamp inventory and see if we can figure out what to do. What else was in the packet Rex?"

The two men retuned their focus to the packet's contents. The remainders of the items were primarily documents outlining the transfer of the collection from Joe Bousquet to Rex. Once they were finished with the papers, Liam returned to the original letter that revealed this historical cache and the rather cryptic messages to Rex about his safety.

"So, I wonder why was Joe so concerned about his safety? Was it because of the break in attempts or the incessant attorney and his offers?" Liam sat pondering his own question and was just about to take a deeper look into some of the menus on the computer when his cell phone rang.

The display on Liam's phone revealed an odd series of numbers, not a standard ten-digit telephone number. It was actually a series of fifteen numbers and two asterisks. Liam showed the phone to Rex.

"What do you make of this?"

"Don't have the slightest clue. International call perhaps?"

Liam answered the phone on the fifth ring.

"Liam Ross." The response back was at first hesitant.

"I was looking for a Rex Cooper. Might he be in? This is Trumball Nash calling." Came the return voice on the other end.

"Mr. Nash, so nice to hear from you so soon. Please hold for Mr. Cooper."

Liam passed the cell phone to Rex. Rex mouthed the words "who is it"? Liam covered the mouthpiece of the phone and quickly whispered the name of the gentleman and who he was. Rex shrugged his shoulders and took the phone.

"Rex Cooper, how may I help you?"

"Mr. Cooper, My name is Trumball Nash. I have been informed that you are the trustee of Mr. Bousquet's philatelic collection. I represent…"

Nash went on to repeat the exact same information that he had relayed to Liam earlier that day. Liam listened carefully as Rex finally had an opportunity to put a word in.

"I am terribly sorry to inconvenience you Mr. Nash, but I am going to honor Mr. Bousquet's wishes. The collection is not for sale." Then more words from Nash on the phone that Liam could not make out. After about five minutes Rex finally responded.

"That is a very generous offer Mr. Nash, but the collection is just not for sale. Again, thank you for your interest."

Rex was about to say goodbye when Liam distinctly heard the words quite clearly coming from the earpiece held to Rex's ear.

"Think it over again Mr. Cooper, don't be a fool. Particularly a dead one."

Then the line went dead. Rex held the phone and just stared at it. Rex took a deep breath, holding the air in his lungs momentarily. He exhaled as he turned slowly towards him, Liam watching as the blood drained from Rex's cheeks, leaving him looking like a walking corpse.

"Liam, I think I have just been threatened."

6

More Questions, No Answers

"Look Rex, we need to go to the police, and now. Joe was concerned about something and now he is dead. I for one would like to know more about his accident, if that is what it truly was. Plus we have all these cryptic notes left by him that make absolutely no sense. What could Joe have stumbled on that could possibly put him, and now you, in danger? I think we have just scratched the surface and it's time to start digging into this little mystery."

Rex pondered Liam's words for all of about five seconds before he replied.

"You are right. We have no idea what this could all be about, perhaps the police could shed a little light on the subject."

"Susan said her dad was hit on his way home from the bank. Let's see if I can get an Internet connection off of this system and locate anything about the accident."

Liam's fingers danced upon the keyboard, quickly opening up a pathway to the World Wide Web. Typing in the memorized web address of a popular search engine, Liam waited until the search box appeared on the screen. Liam entered the Joe's full name and the key word accident and pressed enter. Within five seconds over three hundred search responses appeared on the computer monitor before him. Quickly scanning down the list Liam was able to locate the address of where the accident took place. It was only two blocks away from the branch of the New York bank that Joe had gone to.

"The bank is about twelve blocks from here. So with the accident occurring near the bank, we should be able to located the nearest police precinct."

Liam navigated to a new screen and online program that allowed him to located various neighborhood necessities. Into this search box he input the keywords, police station and almost as an after thought the key word hospital. Within eight seconds this time, a list of just five entities appeared on the screen. Rex began to read the list as Liam wrote down the information.

"The Bronx 50th Police Precinct is here on Knightsbridge and the closet hospital is New York Presbyterian, just south of here on Broadway. That's where they must have taken Joe. Let's go and see what we can find out."

Liam started to close down the system as Rex repacked the packet with the information that Joe had left him. When they had finished, the two friends secured the computer room and walked out to the entrance door that led them into the stamp library. As they began to exit the room and close the door, Liam noticed that this door as well, was a Master Security product. He also did not remember Susan utilizing any special key or even a locking mechanism when she showed Liam into he room those few short hours ago. As he carefully looked around the casing of the door, it was revealed off to his right, that this entrance as well supported the identical finger reader and combination locks. Susan must have opened the door prior to Liam arriving, thus not drawing his attention to the security measures. He made a mental note to ask Susan about this entrance.

As the men walked back down the hallway into the living room, it was confirmed that each door in the apartment was a Master Security product, although not every door sported a keypad and thumb reader for admittance. The men left the apartment, being sure that each of the three locks were secured with the keys provided by Susan. As Liam turned the final key of the three, a very noticeable, loud click was heard deep within the doorframe. Upon closer inspection a small-concealed panel to the left of the door this time, revealed the now expected Keico keypad and thumb reader.

"Funny I didn't notice any of the security when I escorted Mr. Nash down to the street. Good thing that I only locked one lock, or we would have never gotten back in! Joe has this place secured like Fort Knox, maybe even better!" Liam laughed as he and Rex made their way to the rickety elevator.

"Rex, how about a little walk? That thing needs some serious attention, at least the stairs should be in one piece."

"Afraid of one of man's greatest marvels are we?"

"No, it's just that the last man to service that thing was Elisha Otis himself!"

The two laughed as they made their way to the stairwell.

At each level Liam and Rex checked each door onto the floors below. Most were secured with the same technology that Joe had employed in his tenth floor abode. The few that did not have any security, Liam reasoned, must be the floors that currents tenants resided. Once they reached the first floor they walked directly into the entry foyer.

"That's odd." Remarked Rex. "Didn't the security cameras all notate the first floor areas? There is obviously a first floor, but there isn't any entry from here. All of the walls look to be poured concrete."

Liam walked around the perimeter of the entry foyer carefully marking his paces as he went from wall to wall. From there Liam went outside and went to the sidewalk and turned back towards the building. Looking up at the ten stories, then down the length of the building in each direction, Liam made some quick mental calculations, noting just the one entrance door on this side. Moving, without a word and right past Rex, Liam walked to the end of the block to the south in order to see the depth of the building. Once there, he once again noted the absence of any entrances. Relocating in order to look down at the rear of the building, near a long abandoned rail spur, entrances were present but they appeared to not have been in use for some time, sealed for all eternity. Upon seeing this dead end, Liam calculated that the building was approximately three hundred feet in length, one hundred sixty feet in width and about one hundred and sixty feet tall. That put the buildings square footage at roughly three hundred and sixty thousand square feet, even taking into account the center courtyard. The building was a good-sized commercial building even in today's standards, but a considerable size venture to have been built in the late 1800's. Most buildings of this size, constructed during that time period, were either owned by one of the major railroads, a major manufacturing concern, or the United States Government. Liam's mind started to mesh the available information so that a clearer picture would appear. Lost in a fog of deep thought, Liam did not hear Rex asking him a question, just feet away from him.

Tapping Liam on the shoulder,

"Liam, son, where did you go? You are standing right here but you were a million miles away. What's up boy, something bothering you?"

"Rex, it just doesn't figure. The building is obviously a large old factory, but why would there be only one single access to the first floor, let alone the building? With that in mind that entrance into a foyer that comprises of just one percent of the entire first floor's square footage? Why not into the rest of the building? How do you access it? There are no doors that we can see from the street level. All of the loading doors on the back of the building that face the rail spur have been sealed over for what appears to be decades. There doesn't even appear to be any type of fire escape from the upper floors. In today's codes, this building is a death trap. No one would be allowed to live here. Something just isn't right."

"So, Joe Bousquet seems to have been a very protective man. Didn't Susan tell you that he had problems in the past with kids getting in the building to have parties? Maybe that is why Joe sealed everything up."

"Could be Rex. When we come back tomorrow, I think I'll take a closer look around to see if I can find some of the answers to this puzzle. Let's head over to the 50th Precinct."

As the two friends started the fifteen-block walk to the 50th Precinct on Knightsbridge Avenue, Rex spoke up.

"Liam, what exactly are we looking for? Don't get me wrong, I love a mystery as much as the next guy, but I guess I don't understand exactly what's driving you."

"I really don't have an answer for you Rex. Things just don't add up. One, a client, rather a friend from your past leaves you what could turn out to be one of the finest collections of stamps that the world has ever seen. Two, that friend dies in a hit and run accident. Three, the man had security measures installed in his home that most small governments do not even have access to and four, this man had become a tad paranoid over the past six months as someone continually pestered him to sell his collection. Add all of that to the fact, that someone just threatened your life, regarding the same stamp collection and to me that all adds up to mud. No answers, just a multitude of more questions."

With that, the two men continued their walk in silence towards the 50th precinct of the Bronx division of the New York Police Department, both of them reviewing the day's revelations in their own way.

7
Eyes and Ears

The message had been direct and explicit, as always. After committing the message to memory, a matching series of numbers was entered into the recording device, the same as the numbers entered as when the message was sent. With that series of keystrokes the information was permanently deleted.

The next project, as the message's recipient preferred to call them, was to be finalized and finalized quickly. The last project had been dealt with expediently, so perhaps a repeat performance was called for. After all, it was New York City, how many hit and run accidents occurred daily, seventy-five, maybe a hundred? How many involved a run of the mill, standard, New York City taxicab?

The taxi sat still at the curb two blocks from the building on Webster Avenue. There was nothing special about this cab, except perhaps the window tinting was a couple of shades darker than normal. The light on the roof of the 2005 Chevrolet Caprice, painted the infamous New York City Taxi yellow, noted that the cab and its driver were Off Duty. The Recipient sat behind the wheel and using a modified Nikon D700 digital SLR 12.1 megapixel camera with a Nikkor 200mm F2.0 G AF-S VR lens, was actually able to read the nametag, with exact clarity, on the uniform of the UPS driver delivering two blocks to the north. With the gentle push of the shutter release button, a rapid series of images were committed to the compact flash memory card. A quick review in the viewfinder signaled that all was in perfect working order.

In addition to the camera, placed on the seat next to the Recipient, was the latest version of the Laser-3000 listening device. This device is capable of securing audio from long distance, with extreme clarity even through glass. As the image of the UPS driver was covertly being acquired the Recipient listened to the rather risqué discussion taking place between the deliveryman and the woman who was defiantly not his wife.

The principal science of a laser microphone is that a laser beam is used to detect sound vibrations in a distant object. The beam of the laser is focused on an object either in an enclosed space or room or on an individual in the outdoors. Any type of object, a painting, a pitcher or even a pane of glass itself as long as it can vibrate, will, due to pressure waves being created by a noise or from the vocal speech of individuals, be an excellent target for the laser. Once the laser beam is bounced off of the selected object, that beam is returned the receiver unit, which converts the light beams into an audio signal. This technology has been used for decades with great success. However with the advent of events in the world today various counter measures have been developed in order to curb this form of eavesdropping. The Recipient was sure that there would be no need to worry about being detected today.

After about ten minutes of waiting, two men appeared from the building's entrance. Quickly, images of both men were taken. Full body shots, medium shots, and extreme close-ups of each man, as well as both of the men in the same frame were shot. As the photographs were being taken the conversation between the gentlemen was being committed to the memory of the listening device.

After a few minutes of conversation the two men started walking directly towards the parked taxicab. When the men were just one half a block away, the watcher deftly secured both the camera and the laser microphone in case either man were to notice the equipment. Just as the men were within twenty feet of the cab, the Recipient started the motor, moved the gearshift into drive and slowly merged into the northbound traffic on Webster Avenue, away from the pedestrians. When the cab reached the corner, the driver quickly made a left hand turn and sped down the block to the next corner in order to maneuver around the block and resume surveillance on the unsuspecting pair.

As the taxicab reached the return corner on Decatur Avenue the traffic signal turned from yellow to red, forcing the cab to stop behind a local, small grocery delivery van. The pair of men were straight ahead and in view as they crossed the street and headed towards Knightsbridge Avenue, six blocks to the southwest. The Recipient had ascertained during the recording that the two were going to the 50th police precinct to learn more about the accident of the older mans friend. Instead of following them, the decision was made to move ahead and wait for them to show up at the precinct itself. As the light turned green, the grocery van made a left hand turn, allowing the taxicab to ease through the intersection and continue on to 194th Street, moving past the identified pedestrians.

When the Recipient arrived at the 50th Precinct on Knightsbridge, plans were changed immediately. Instead of a quiet Bronx borough police station, the activity that unfolded before the cab could only be described as orchestrated mayhem. There had to be at least two hundred police officers coming and going into the large brick edifice located halfway up the street from the corner of 194th Avenue. After a quick glance at the dashboard clock it was determined that this must be a shift change at the cop house. Police cars lined both sides of the narrow avenue; with most of the cars double-parked awaiting their new occupants to start the evening shift. No way this taxicab going to be allowed to remain parked on the street anywhere near this facility.

As the taxi slowly made its way up the clogged street the Recipient noticed that directly across the street from the main entrance of the precinct, was a small park, no larger than the width of a good sized house. Inside the park were dozens of mothers and nannies watching over their charges, as they raced up and down the park's playground. Although not being able to use the Nikon or the laser microphone, it would make an ideal spot to observe the Recipient's Project.

Within minutes the Recipient located a parking spot less than three blocks away. With the gear safely stored and locked away in the trunk of the cab, but first retrieving what appeared to be a standard smart phone and ear-buds from a case in the trunk, the Recipient walked swiftly back to the park across from the police station and waited for the two men to arrive.

While seated on a bench closest to the street, ear-buds in place and while appearing to be a parent listening to music as their child played, the Recipient viewed the two men as they turned the corner from 194th Avenue onto Knightsbridge Avenue. Discreetly watching as the pair crossed the street and moved up the ten steps into the building full of police. Nothing to do now but wait until they returned from trying to find out more information on what happened to their friend.

8
Answers

Liam and Rex made the walk from Joe Bousquet's building on Webster Avenue to the 50th police precinct in a little over thirty minutes. It had been a beautiful walk in the spring air, however a silent walk as Liam was mentally trying to fit each individual piece of a puzzle together. With each piece that fit, the revealing image made even less sense, thus requiring more puzzle pieces in order to form a clear picture.

When they arrived at the police station it was a beehive of activity. Uniformed and plainclothes officers were both coming and going from the precinct house. Rex and Liam made their way up the front stairs to the entrance lobby of the building. There they were met with a cliché directly from a Dashiel Hammett novel, the uniformed officer perched high above them behind an artfully crafted 1940's style counter of dark wood. The only thing that would complete this, Liam thought amusedly to himself, was if the officer was turned out to be the stereotypical Irish cop. The amusement was dashed as the officer's nametag came into view, declaring him as Officer R. Juarez.

"Good afternoon Gentlemen, how might I help you?"

"Good afternoon, Officer Juarez, my name is Liam Ross and my associate is Mr. Rex Cooper. We would like to speak with your watch commander if that is at all possible."

"As you can see Mr. Ross, we are between shifts and extremely busy. So do you know which watch commander you would like to see, the morning or afternoon shift?"

"We are interested in some information about the accident of Mr. Joseph Bousquet, last week. Supposedly it was a hit and run. We do not know what time of day that it happened."

The desk Sergeant consulted the only item on the large counter that did not seem to fit with the 1940's décor, he entered the name of Joseph Bousquet into a high end Hewlett Packard networked terminal. Within seconds the information was displayed on the LCD panel before him.

"The accident occurred last Wednesday, the 20th at 1630, that's four thirty in the afternoon. The watch commander on that date was Lieutenant O'Brian." Quickly consulting the watch list before him, "The Lieutenant should be on in about ten minutes, would you like to wait for him?"

"Yes we would, thank you Sergeant. Where might we wait?" ask Rex.

"You can wait outside his office. Down the hall, and off to the left. I'll have an officer escort you."

With that, Sergeant Juarez call a fresh-faced uniformed patrol officer, perhaps no older than twenty, over to escort them down to Lieutenant O'Brian's office. Once they arrived at the antique style office cubicle the escorting officer showed Rex and Liam to a couple of chairs and asked if they would like some coffee.

"It's actually pretty decent stuff. One of the wives owns a coffee shop a few blocks away. She must take pity on us, sends us all we can drink!"

Rex readily accepted the offered caffeine as Liam just scanned his gaze around the large room with its noisy comings and goings.

"No thank you officer. If I may ask, is it always this hectic here?"

"No, generally it's a bit tamer, but there's a flap on as someone tried to rob one of the local bodegas this afternoon. Cop got shot in the process."

The officer left to retrieve Rex his coffee as the two men sat down and observed the chaos. Just as the fresh-faced officer returned with Rex's cup, an older man, perhaps late fifties, wearing what could be described as a good quality, off the rack suit, crossed the squad room and introduced himself to Rex and Liam.

"Gentlemen, I am Lieutenant O'Brian. How might I help you?"

The Lieutenant opened the door to his office and allowed Rex and Liam to enter first.

"Please have a seat."

The two men took the offered chairs and introduced themselves as the officer took his station behind his desk. Rex was the first to speak.

"Lieutenant O'Brian, Joe Bousquet was killed in a hit and run accident last Wednesday. I was wondering if I might get a little more information on the accident and the ensuing case?"

"If I may ask Mr. Cooper, how are you related to the deceased?"

"I am a sixty plus year friend of Mr. Bousquet's. I have had business dealings with him over these past sixty or so years."

"What type of business dealings Mr. Cooper?"

"I am a stamp dealer and Joe bought stamps from me."

Rex's response brought an almost smug response from officer seated before him.

"Stamps? As in postage stamps?"

"Yes, Sir, United States postage stamps."

"Well Mr. Cooper, as our accident investigations are kept closed to all but immediate family, I don't see how I can offer you any more information that what you have now. I am truly sorry."

The boilerplate cops speak. Liam interjected,

"Lieutenant O'Brian, what Mr. Cooper has failed to mention, is that he is also the beneficiary of Mr. Bousquet's stamp collection. A rather large and in my opinion, what will be revealed to be a very valuable collection. Also, what you may not know is that in the weeks leading up to Mr. Bousquet's tragic accident, he may have had his life threatened over said stamp collection and just to make things a bit more interesting, Mr. Cooper has had his life threatened today, over the same collection, by what we assume are the same individuals."

"Threatened? How?"

"Apparently, an unknown individual approached Mr. Bousquet sometime ago, through an attorney, wanting to purchase his collection. A collection, that we are very confident in the fact, who's existence was known by only a small handful of family and friends, three people to be exact, four after today, that forth being myself. After telling this attorney that he was not interested in selling, various break in attempts at Mr. Bousquet's home were attempted. "

"Do you know if these break-ins were reported?"

"According to his daughter, they were."

"And you now think that there may be a connection between these break-ins, the threats and with Mr. Bousquet's accident?"

"We aren't assuming anything Lieutenant O'Brian, we just wanted to get the details of the accident if at all possible."

Without a word, Lieutenant O'Brian swiveled his chairs to face the computer terminal on the credenza placed behind his desk. After a few keystrokes he scanned the information in silent before pressing the print command, then turning back towards the two men,

"Mr. Cooper, when and how where you threatened?"

"Well, it was this afternoon around one o'clock and it was over the cell phone."

"May I see your phone Mr. Cooper?" reaching his hand across the desk towards Rex.

"The call was on my cell, Lieutenant." Liam began to remove his cell from his front coat pocket. "Here is the information on the incoming number."

Liam located the recently received calls list on his cell and passed it over to Lieutenant O'Brian. Who, after a glance at the screen looked up at Liam.

"This is the incoming call? This is nothing but gibberish."

Turning the phone screen around so that Liam could see the display. There on the small LCD screen, where at one time the cryptic numbers and asterisks were displayed, when the call was received, were now nothing but a series of x's. Liam looked at Rex as Lieutenant O'Brian showed the phone's display to Rex.

"Lieutenant, when the call came through, it appeared to be some sort of international number. It was a series of fifteen numbers and two asterisks. Unlike any phone number that I have ever seen before, and I make and receive a significant number of international calls."

"Did you perhaps delete the call after it came in?"

"No I did not."

"Then how do you explain this jumble of nothing?"

"I can't sir."

"Then without some starting point I don't know how we can help with this threat, if it was a threat at all."

Right before Liam had a chance to raise his voice in response to the lieutenant's outrageous comment, the door to Lieutenant O'Brian's office opened and the fresh-faced officer that offered coffee to Rex and Liam earlier entered, bearing a small sheaf of papers.

"The accident report?" asked Rex.

The lieutenant took the papers and selected two sheets from the top and handed one to each of the two men. Rex quickly read the information and looked to Liam.

"According to two eye witnesses, it states that Mr. Bousquet was struck and killed by New York medallion cab. One of the witnesses was even able to get the license number, number A7RW." Liam continued to read as Lieutenant O'Brian interjected,

"And if you didn't know, the cab's plate and medallion number are the same. The only problem with this cab's number is that it is registered to a cab that was taken out of service three months ago and destroyed."

"Did any of the witnesses see a fare in the cab?"

"No Mr. Ross, just the driver, and that description was pretty vague. Hard to identify a person when that person is seated behind the wheel and the windows are tinted."

"Is that common in New York, tinted windows on a taxi?" asked Rex.

"No, according to New York state law, windows on medallion cabs are not allowed to be tinted, they have to remain clear. But its one of those DMV laws that rarely gets enforced."

"The report also shows that Joe was hit only two blocks from his home. He was crossing the street and the cab hit him as it was turning the corner. The car stopped next to the body for a moment then the cab sped off towards Woodlawn to the east." Liam kept reading. "Rex, one of the witnesses was one of Joe's tenants, a Ryan McIntyre. He is one of the grad students that live on the fourth floor. Perhaps we could talk to him later."

"So you see gentlemen, it was an accident, tragic as it my be, but just an accident."

"Are you continuing with the investigation?" asked Rex.

"We have BOLO's, Be On the Lookout, for the cab, but that is about all we can do at this stage." The lieutenant started to stand, signaling that the meeting was to conclude.

Rex shook the extended hand of the lieutenant in turn Liam shook the pro-offered hand.

"Thank you Lieutenant O'Brian. We appreciate your assistance, and the opportunity to look at the accident report."

"Anytime Mr. Ross, and if Mr. Cooper receives any additional calls, please do not hesitate to call." Handing a business card to both Liam and Rex. "My private line is on the reverse."

After taking the cards the two men left the lieutenant's office and headed back down the hallway towards the front entrance. In hushed tones the two men started to talk.

"Well Liam, if you ask me, that was one of the fastest bums rushes I have ever had the opportunity to experience."

"I agree Rex, I don't think that they are hiding anything, I just feel that they don't put much priority on cases like this."

The two friends started down the outside stairs, even though it was spring the air had seemed to chill a bit since they first went into the precinct. The day was coming to an end as the shadows were becoming longer. They crossed the street right in front of the playground where the few remaining mothers and nannies were gathering up their children in order to head home and start to make their dinners. Heading south, towards the train station, the men buttoned up their jackets in order to ward off the chill.

"Let's head back to the Waldorf=Astoria and call it a day Liam. I need to call my attorney and insurance agents back in Los Angeles and bring them up to speed with what Joe left me. This is going to send both of them over the deep end after I just told them last week that I wanted to start wrapping things up!"

"The old retirement talk again, eh? When are you going to listen to me Rex and just accept that you will never retire?"

"Oh, not retirement son, just a nice smooth transition into act three of my life. So, shall we cab it or take the train?"

"We'll never get a cab this time of day, they are mostly off duty, the station is just three blocks up and it's faster."

Deep in their conversation the two men did not notice the Recipient get up from the park bench as they passed by. Being just a few steps behind with some of the other parents, the Recipient was able to hear their conversation, in full detail. Instead of following the two on the train and chance losing them, the Recipient turned back towards the police station in order to retrieve the taxi. It would be much more convenient to meet up with the two friends back in Manhattan.

9

Scenes From an Italian Restaurant

Liam and Rex arrived back at the Waldorf=Astoria and each went to their separate rooms agreeing to meet in the lobby in forty-five minutes in order to have dinner and discuss the events of the day. They agreed to meet at the clock.

The clock in the lobby of the Waldorf=Astoria was created for the 1893 Chicago World's Fair by Goldsmith's of London. Standing prominently at nine feet tall, the gilded clock weighs over two tons. Sculpted around the base of the clock are likenesses of Queen Victoria, Benjamin Franklin and six United States Presidents, Grover Cleveland, Benjamin Harrison, George Washington, Ulysses S. Grant, Abraham Lincoln, and Andrew Jackson. Atop of the clock sits a majestic replica, sculpted in every detail, of the Statue of Liberty. Every quarter hour, the clock sounds the Westminster Chimes to all who are gathered in the hotel's lobby.

From here Liam and Rex decided to head down to the Little Italy section of Manhattan to a restaurant that Liam had been going to for years. They crossed through the lobby, past the famous Bull and Bear Restaurant where many of New York's tried and true financiers still held court late into the evenings. They exited the grand hotel's rear exit through the decades old revolving door out onto the sidewalk of Lexington Avenue. The mild spring day had turned into a cool, overcast spring evening with the slight threat of rain looming. Liam stepped to the curb and hailed a cab for their journey downtown. After about three minutes wait, a cab pulled to the curb, Liam and Rex took their seats in the rear and gave their destination to the driver. The driver registered his trip on the fare meter and without even looking at merging traffic, quickly pulled into the evening throng of traffic that was headed down Lexington Avenue towards the lower eastside and downtown.

Friday evening traffic in Manhattan can be some of the worst traffic in the world. However, the cabdriver knew the right short cuts thus allowing the two friends to make record time down to Little Italy. The cab deposited the men at the corner of Broome and Mulberry, just a half block walk to La Mela, a forty year old, classic family style Italian restaurant.

Liam had been coming to this little hole in the wall for close to twenty years. In that time he had never walked away dissatisfied, hungry or feeling sad. The atmosphere was one of being in a small Italian bistro somewhere in a back alley of Florence or Milan. The small two-room restaurant seated perhaps sixty people in all, with people always waiting in a line on the street, anticipating the time that they would be shown to a table. Tonight was no different. The line stretched into the next block, past at least five other Italian eateries. All the while, patrons conversing and comparing notes on their weeks that had just ended, while building appetites for the heaping plates of antipasti, buffalo mozzarella, veal piccata, and pastas.

The sight of the line discouraged Rex as the two walked closer to the establishment, it had been a long day and he was hungry.

"Wow, must be a great place! That line looks to be at least an hour long."

"More like three. When people come here to eat, they just don't seat, eat and dash within half and hour. Here you dine, the proper way. You sit, you *mangi* a little, you talk, you *mangi* a little more, you laugh, you *mangi* some more, and it goes on for hours. It's called *Alimento Lento*, in English its called *Slow Food*." Liam explained to Rex as he scanned around the crowd looking for someone. He finally seemed to focus in on the individual that he was looking for.

Antonio had been a waiter at La Mela since the early seventies. He had delivered countless plates of the luscious offerings to patrons unknown and famous, almost everyday since that opening. He had seen his share of the country's elite come and go at La Mela, each one puffing themselves up to be more important than the last, always offering their photos to be displayed on the walls of the dining rooms. But it always amused Antonio to see the look of incredulousness on the television personalities, the movie stars, and even the political heavyweights, faces when he and other waiters at La Mela respectfully declined their offerings. It just proved, that the elite were never really in touch with their surroundings. Because if any of them had taken even just thirty seconds to even look at the photos displayed all around the room, they would see that not a single one of the pictures displayed anyone that anyone really knew. These photos were the real patrons of La Mela. The butcher that supplied the meat, the baker that made the dozens upon dozens of fresh loaves, the neighborhood from blocks around. That was who were on the walls of La Mela, real people. Now to be fair, there were some older pictures from those early days, that if you looked close at, might bear a resemblance to someone of note, but that was only because they became famous only after being a member of the *family* at the dining establishment.

Every seat in the place was taken; even the window tables were fully occupied. Now if you were superstitious, when you were shown to a table in the front window, and if you were a regular that is, you would respectfully decline the offer, and wait for the next offered table. This was because once upon a time places like La Mela were favored by the New York mob, and the story went that the window seats were only there to stop the bullets as the opposition would drive by and empty their machine guns into the dining room windows. Liam tried in earnest to get Antonio's attention as the man emerged from the cramped, galley style kitchen, but he was on a mission carrying what appeared to be no less than eight giant plates of antipasti to the newly seated party in the front corner by the window.

Liam stooped to the ground and retrieved a few small salt pebbles that were left over from the winters snow removal on Mulberry Street. He gauged his timing and just as Antonio had delivered the last plate of the Italian appetizers, Liam gently threw the small stones at the window. The sound that emerged as the pebbles hit the window sounded like the hollow rat a tat tat of a cinema Tommy gun.

A man with his back to the window fell out of his chair and hid beneath the table all the while screaming "they're shooting at us!" The buxom blonde next to him let out a scream that pierced the hundred-decibel din of the dining room. Others pushed their chairs away from the tables with the intent to dive for cover

116

wherever they could find it. Antonio, used to such pranks from the local teenagers, started to grab the nearest object that he could find in order to chase after the little shits. As he grabbed an empty wine bottle and started to move to the door, Antonio looked out the window to see what direction the culprits had run off to. Instead, there was the beaming face of a long time friend.

"Pisano!" the five foot five waiter yelled as he hurried toward the open front door, tossing the wine bottle haphazardly back on the table were it's contents started to pour onto the man's head as he emerged from under the table.

When Antonio reached Liam he grabbed him in a bear hug and lifted the 225 pound, six foot one man off the street with ease, kissing both of Liam's checks as in the European custom. Meanwhile the entire restaurant looked on in stunned silence at the scene unfolding.

"My favorite lost son, you have come home!" the waiter called out, "Momma look who has returned!" all the while holding Liam aloft.

Liam started to feel the blood stop in his veins from the vise like grip that his friend possessed, with air gasping from his mouth he offered his greeting to the man.

"Antonio, it's wonderful to see you, but I can't breath!"

Rex walked over to the two men and quietly revealed that all of the restaurant guests were watching. Antonio put Liam back on the ground, slapped him so hard on the back that Liam though he might loose a filling.

"What are you all looking at? A man can't greet his lost friends? Now, go back and eat!" as the waiter admonished the crowd they all hungrily focused back on the meals before them.

Just as Antonio, Liam and Rex were about to make their way through the crowed room, they came face to face with the group that sat at the table in the front window when Liam pulled his little prank. Antonio did not look pleased.

"Where are you all a going? You have not eaten a thing!"

The man that had dove for cover under the table, now covered with red wine, squared himself off in front of the small Italian waiter. As he spoke as he started to jab a pointed finger at Antonio's chest trying to show his self-known importance.

"I have never been so humiliated in my entire life! Do you know who I am? I can make your life a complete hell!" screaming at the top of his lungs " I demand to speak to the owner about what has just occurred! I can close this place down if I wanted to!"

Antonio kept his cool as the man continued to scream at him. The restaurant had silenced once again as all watched the irate blowhard yell at Antonio.

As the man's face reddened, Antonio finally saw an opportunity to act and speak. Deftly grabbing the pointed finger and discreetly squeezing it so hard it made Rex wince, the small waiter watched as the irate customers knees slowly started to buckle from the excruciating pain in his hand.

"Sir, I am terribly sorry if you have been inconvenienced in any way. Please sit down and enjoy your meal, it's on the house for your troubles."

"And if I may sir" Liam chimed in "For causing you any harm, the wine is on me, Antonio, do you still have any of the 1985 Giuseppe Quintarelli Amarone Riserva?"

Liam watched as the man's eyes widened at the mention of one of the most noted bottles of 20th century Italian wine. Having trouble answering because of the pain in his finger that now radiated to his arm, he croaked

"Thank you. Thank you very much. That is too kind."
As Antonio helped the man to his feet and escorted him back to his window table, the buxom blond started to berate what was obviously her husband.

"Harvey, if I were you, I would call that horrid little man out and demand to see the owner. How dare they treat us this way! It's unspeakable!"

It was at that time that one of the other restaurant patrons leaned over to the woman and whispered something into her ear. Before the message had been totally delivered, the woman's eyes quadrupled in size and she loudly spoke to her now seated husband, hitting him in the chest with a quick backhand.

"You idiot, you could have gotten us all killed doing that!"

Then to Antonio,

"Mr. Mela, thank you so much for your gracious offer, but we can't accept. My husband is such an ass! There is truly no need..."

Than back to her husband,

"Harvey, apologize to Mr. Mela. Do it now! If you don't you'll be spending the next year sleeping on the couch!"

As the woman continued to dictate terms to her husband, Liam, Rex and Antonio left the main dining room through the kitchen where Liam stopped and gave Momma a huge hug and kissed her on both checks as she stirred the large pot of Bolognaise, never missing a beat. Her only response to him was that he was too skinny. The three men entered the rear dining room that Antonio reserved for only true family and the closest of friends. As they were all about to sit Antonio called over a younger version of himself.

Antonio's son, Antonio Jr., raced to his father's side and continually nodded his head as the elder rattled off an extensive list of food in Italian. The young boy raced to the kitchen to fetch his father's request. From out of nowhere, two bottles appeared at the center of the table left there by another of La Mela's waiters.

"Your wine Antonio?" asked Liam.

"The 1990 at that! We just bottled the last ten barrels last month. Donald Trump was in here last week, offered to buy every bottle. Offered me a ridiculous amount of money too! I just looked at him and said, Donald, you know that this is just simple country folk vino, just for family and friends!"

Laughing as he continued.

"His face looked like I just ran over his puppy! I took pity on him and sent him home with a case. He then looked like he had just won the damn lottery!"

Antonio poured three glasses of the ruby colored elixir, taking one, and then passing the remaining to Rex and Liam. Lifting the glass to his nose, Antonio took a deep lungful of the aroma emanating from the glass. After a second nose, a large sip was taken and after what seemed like hours the wine was proclaimed, "Wow!" by Antonio. The other two men followed suit and both exclaimed similar words of enjoyment.

"Antonio, I am so sorry, but I seemed to have lost my manors. I haven't introduced my friend to you. Antonio, Rex Cooper, Rex, Antonio."

The two men shook hands as Antonio took hold of the conversation.

120

"So, the famous Rex Cooper that Liam has spoken about for all of these years. Sir it truly is a pleasure. From what I have been told, our friend Liam here wouldn't be half the man he is, if it hadn't been for you."

"Those are very kind words, thank you and if I may, thank you for your hospitality this evening. I had no idea!"

"Ah, just a little place to get a quick bite. Been in the family for years."

"Also, out of curiosity, what happened back there?"

"Antonio, are you still shoveling that myth that you were Lucky Luciano's hit man?" Liam asked as he took another sip of the wine.

"Hey, it keeps people in line! Besides I didn't start the rumor."

"Luciano died in 1962, you were two at the time!"

"Hey, we're Sicilian, They start us young!"

All three laughed and then toasted to each other's health. Antonio excused himself, as he had to get back to the rest of his guests, it was always guests with Antonio, never customers.

Just as he left through the kitchen, Antonio Jr. returned to the table bringing the first of many platters groaning from piles upon piles of the freshest Italian food that Rex had ever seen or tasted. For the next three hours Liam and Rex ate and talked of the days activities, planning the next days projects back at Joe Bousquet's building. At the end of the feast Liam had successfully initiated Rex to *Alimento Lento*. Rex proclaimed himself a true convert, vowing to never eat in less than an hour again!

After two espresso's each, the offer of Sambuca and cigars from Antonio, the two friends decided that it was time to get back to the hotel. It was after midnight and the restaurant was still going full tilt. The party of eight in the window had left hours earlier, leaving the full price of the meal and a rather extravagant tip as well. The line outside the door had shortened significantly, but many still remained. La Mela would remain open most likely until three or four in the morning as the night owls roamed the streets looking for food to fill their stomachs after hours of drinking at the local tabernas. Liam, Rex and Antonio started to say their goodbyes in front of the restaurant.

"Thank you my friend for a wonderful evening."

Liam hugged his old friend.

"My pleasure Pisano. Don't be a stranger!"

Rex looked at his watched.

"Too late to take the train. I get an uneasy feeling this time of night, even in numbers."

"I agree Rex, let's just grab the first open cab. They have been coming by quite steadily."

Rex stepped to the curb and scanned to his right down the one-way street. Many cabs were coming towards him, but all had their roof lights off indicating that they already had a fare. Rex stepped further out into the street in order to get a better view of the oncoming traffic and any approaching cabs. He noticed a taxi sitting parked at the curb about ten cars down the street across the street from the restaurant. As he was about to suggest to Liam that they head one block up to Broome and try for a cab there, the parked cab's lights turned on and it's turn signal indicated that it was going to merge into the traffic. Rex waved with fury in order for the driver to see him. The cab flashed its headlights indicating that it saw its fare.

"Liam got one! Right down the street, come on."

It had been a long day. Liam couldn't wait to get back to the hotel and to climb between the nice cool sheets and sleep a well deserved sleep. He said good night again to Antonio and turned to walk to the cab. The cab was just about to pull even to where Rex was standing in the street, when the cab's motor raced and started to move faster. Then all hell broke loose.

The front windows of La Mela suddenly disintegrated into thousands of tiny pieces, showering the sidewalk and the guests inside the restaurant with glass. The windows of the car nearest to Liam also exploded into shards as holes appeared in the trunk lid. Off to Liam's left many people started to shout and scream. Antonio shouted for Liam to get down and Liam in turn yelled to Rex to hit the deck. As Liam was falling to the ground, a sharp searing pain entered his right outer biceps. Then the warm seeping feeling of his blood added to the increasing pain. Liam looked up to see Rex fall to his knees. He got up and using the cars for cover, ran over to help his friend. Liam got to Rex just as Rex fell into Liam's outstretched arms.

The taxicab raced to the end of Mulberry. Liam took note of the license plate number of the cab as the car turned left off of Mulberry onto Broome, running the red light. Committing the number to memory, Liam turned his attention to Rex. There, in the center of Rex's chest were five bullet holes. His eyes were open and blood was coming from his mouth as he tried to talk. Liam placed Rex on the ground, tore off his coat and used it to stem the flow of blood from his friend's chest.

"Hold on Rex, help is on the way!"

Rex's eyes fixed upon Liam's as he mouthed the words, "I love you like a son, boy." He coughed twice and more blood expelled from his lungs and mouth. After the second cough his body went rigid and then a moment later fell lax as Rex died.

Antonio rushed to Liam's side in order to help his old friend.

"Liam, is he okay?"

The look from Liam alone answered the restaurateur's question. Liam took off his jacket and placed it on Rex. It was then that Antonio noticed the blood streaming from Liam's arm.

"You've been hit. Come on, we have to take care of that." Calling out to his son who was now standing in the doorway, "Antonio, clean napkins, lots of them, quickly!

Antonio Jr. grabbed all the napkins and tablecloths that he could hold and raced to his father's side. Antonio the elder placed the napkins on Liam's wound trying to staunch the flow of blood. Antonio got Liam to sit on the curb in order to better dress his wound. Sirens now replaced the screams all around. Within seconds, armed uniformed men and women were swarming all around the street and the restaurant, shouting orders, demanding to see everyone's hands.

Paramedics arrived within minutes of the police. Triage of the wounded took place inside the restaurant in the front dining room. A few people that had been inside the restaurant, near the windows, were injured but mainly from flying glass. Luckily no one else had been shot.

Liam continued to sit on the curb of the street, almost as if in shock. However his mind had become a racing torrent. With

Antonio at his side, Liam calmly asked for him to get his jacket back from Rex. Antonio retrieved one of the tablecloths from his son and replaced Liam's jacket with it, then handing the jacket to Liam.

"Liam, what is it?"

Liam fished around the inside coat pocket of his jacket and retrieved his cell phone and the business card that he had received earlier that day. He dialed the number on the reverse of the card. The call was answered on the third ring. Antonio listened to the one sided conversation.

"Lieutenant O'Brian, Liam Ross, from this afternoon. I just wanted to let you know that we have seen the cab that hit and killed Joe Bousquet, cab number A7WR. It just went past Mr. Cooper and myself down in Little Italy. Oh, and Lieutenant O'Brian, the driver just gunned down and killed Rex Cooper. So I don't think you have to worry about that threat anymore."

Liam closed the phone before Lieutenant O'Brian even had a chance to respond.

10

Making Lists

Waldorf=Astoria Hotel
New York, New York
May 1, 2013

It was after five in the morning before Liam returned to the hotel. The Manhattan precinct had keep him at La Mela answering questions non-stop, until Liam thought he might punch out the officer in charge. To make matters worse, Lieutenant O'Brian, who had arrived on the scene, about an hour after Liam's phone call to him, refused to let him leave until all of his questions were asked and answered. After four hours of the relentless questioning and until Liam assured them all that he would not "flee the jurisdiction", was he allowed to go to his hotel.

After a quick look from the paramedics on the scene, a clean bandage, and his word that he had recently had a tetanus booster, Liam was given medical clearance to leave. He was escorted back to the Waldorf=Astoria by one of Lieutenant O'Brian's men from the Bronx. The uniformed officer insisted that he follow Liam up to his room in order to "check things out" as he put it. Liam thanked the officer but refused his offer claiming that he was a big boy and could take care of himself. He left the unmarked car with a slam of the door and entered the Park Avenue entrance of the hotel.

Liam made his way through the lobby, soliciting a few rather wide eye stares from the handful of individuals that were up at that hour. He walked straight into an open elevator, pressed the button for the 20th floor. When the elevator slowed to a stop and the doors opened, Liam waked the length of the hallway to his room without incident. He unlocked the double door to the suite, turned on the lights, threw the plastic card key on the foyer table and went into the bedroom. After kicking off his shoes he found his way into the marble bathroom, opened the door to the shower and turned on the water allowing the luxurious, but old hotel's, plumbing to heat up before he stepped inside. Standing before the mirror he noticed for the first time the amount of blood that had completely covered his shirt, affirming the reason for the looks that he had received in the lobby.

Liam's arm wound turned out to be just a graze from one of the bullets that had killed his friend. But it still hurt like hell as he took the blood soaked Brooks Brothers oxford shirt carefully off, sliding his injured arm out last. Looking down at the shirt in his hands brought the evening's events flooding back into in Liam's mind. First the laughter, the fun, the food, the excitement of Joe Bousquet's gift to Rex, then the chaos, the noise, the blood and then Rex lying dead in the street. He closed his eyes and willed that the images would go away and never return.

Liam stepped into the shower and allowed himself to stand beneath the needle fine spray of the near scalding water. After about fifteen minutes of just standing there, Liam washed his body, paying careful attention to his arm, washed his hair and then slowly rinsed him self off under an eye opening coldwater rinse. Stepping from the shower, first wrapping himself in one of the hotels thick bath sheets, Liam went back into the bedroom and called room service. When the voice on the other end answered he ordered his standard breakfast of two eggs scrambled, three links of apple sausage, rye toast with Tiptree English marmalade, orange juice freshly squeezed and a large pot of very strong black coffee. This had become Liam's favorite breakfast when traveling ever since he had read Ian Fleming's James Bond when he was a teenager. With a slight change from Mr. Bond's original breakfast, Liam was pretty much guaranteed a consistent quality breakfast from hotel to hotel with this order.

Liam sunk into the wingback chair that was at the foot of the king size bed. His entire body began to ache as the adrenaline rush from the past few hours started to subside. The same questions kept repeating over and over in his head, why was Rex dead, who would want both Rex and Joe Bousquet dead, who would want me dead? Every time the same response kept coming to Liam that the answers lay within Joe's stamp collection.

The door's soft buzzer alerted Liam that his breakfast had arrived. He slipped on a robe before he let the room service attendant into the room. After the waiter set the table in the living room of the suite and checked to see that everything was in order, he presented Liam with the check to be signed. Liam signed the chit and made sure that he put a line through the tip box and re-totaled the check amount before handing the leather folio back to the waiter. As had happened with many five star hotel room service departments, a 20 – 25% tip was now automatically being added to the bills. Plus if you didn't cross out the additional tip line many non-scrupulous attendants would add a bit more for themselves' after they left a customers room. Liam was amazed at how many normal people left their brains at home when they traveled. Where they would count every penny being returned at a supermarket checkout stand, they would never check that the charges on the bill they were presented at checkout to see if it actually displayed the correct charges. He wondered how many millions of dollars went undetected in a year from this practice?

Liam tore into the hot breakfast, clearing the plate and downing all the juice and two cups of the steaming hot coffee. It amazed him how famished he was after the dinner the night before. He reached for his briefcase and retrieved a yellow legal pad from it as well as his favorite red Paper Mate felt pen. He pushed aside the breakfast dishes and started making a to do list, a list with two columns, an immediate to do list on the left, and an Action Item list on the right of the paper. The most immediate item was to make arrangements for his friend. Rex had no family left so Liam set to the task as if Rex were his own father. Things to do from getting Rex's body flown back to California for burial, to taking care of the stamp store and even the display that was still at the Javits Center and first to call Rex's attorney as soon as it was late enough to do so in Los Angeles. He also jotted down a note to talk to the hotel about Rex's room.

Liam then moved onto the second list, the Action Item list. This list was considerably longer and had much greater detail than the first. After about forty-five minutes of composition Liam reviewed the list making sure that he had left no omission off of it. When he was assured that the list was complete he started with the first item - Call the Team.

Liam reached for the phone, but before he even had a chance to pick up the handset from the cradle the phone rang. Liam picked up the receiver.

"Liam Ross."

There was no response, just dead air, or perhaps the faint whisper of a sound of someone breathing on the other end. After two hellos, and not a response, he returned the earpiece to the cradle and then just stared at the phone.

11

Next Steps

Killing twice with the same vehicle had been risky. The death of the first man, a run of the mill hit and run, might go unnoticed for days, weeks, or it may never be solved. But a drive by shooting on a crowded downtown street, someone was sure to come forward with details.

After leaving the restaurant the taxi made straight for the Holland Tunnel and within twenty minutes the cab was securely back in the rented garage, in the run down Jersey City neighborhood, that had been secured months before. On the way to the garage the Recipient placed one phone call to the rest of the team, telling them to meet at the garage in order to dispose of the taxi. When the Recipient pulled the cab into the garage all was quiet. It would be about an hour before the other two arrived.

The Recipient utilized this time to transfer all of the gear from the cab to the Obsidian Black Mercedes CL65 AMG that quietly sat in the rear corner of the garage. When finished with the gear, every inch of the taxi was inspected making sure that not even a single scrap of paper was left behind. This was all for naught because by the days end the taxi would be completely disassembled and the parts would be spread from Jersey City to Atlantic City.

Satisfied that nothing remained, the Recipient retrieved a laptop from a case in the Mercedes and logged in to a secure website who's DNS number was known by heart. After nearly ten minutes of completing security checks was the user able to start the process of reporting in. About ten minutes into the report of the evenings activities the first of the Recipient's team members arrived from Manhattan.

"It's all over the news, mob hit in Little Italy!" reported the first team member to arrive.

"Do they say how many dead?" asked the Recipient.

"Not yet. I can log in and check."

"No, get to work on the cab. I'll check."

Deftly maneuvering the cursor on the touchpad of the laptop the recipient went to the website of a popular search engine and typed in the keywords; shooting, Little Italy, New York. After just three seconds links to various stories appeared on the screen. Selecting the first link, the computer connected to the website of the New York Post. The Breaking News section reported that at 12:30 this morning two people had been shot outside of a popular Italian restaurant in Little Italy. One person had been pronounced dead at the scene.

Only one dead, but which one, this was discomforting news. The shooter was positive that both had been killed in the drive by. A thirty round clip from the Beretta 93R had been emptied, all rounds fired in three shoot bursts. Better check another news site.

Six more sites were consulted and they all offered the same information as the first, one person dead on the scene, and nothing more. Nash and his superiors were not going to take this news lightly. The order was to take care of both of the stamp dealers, then start the collection and retrieval process on the needed item. It was critical that the item be found before the demand announcement was made. That meant that they had 128 hours to find a needle in a haystack.

The door to the garage opened and the third member of the team arrived and went straight to work on the cab without even a word to the Recipient. It would take the better part of the next five hours to strip the car, load the parts into a van and take them to various scrap yards for disposal. While the two men accomplished this task the Recipient started to look into an idea that might turn the unsettling news of only one dead, into an opportunity that would expedite the search.

Leaving the two to their work on the taxi, the recipient left the garage in order to go someplace quiet to make some phone calls. The quest was to see if the second stamp dealer was in police custody or if they had returned to the Waldorf=Astoria. The phone rang once and the voice on the receiving end answered.

"It's a beautiful day at the Waldorf=Astoria, how may I help you?"

"Mr. Rex Cooper please, I don't have the room number."

"One moment please," and the connection was made.

After ten rings the automated, in room voicemail service answered the call. Before the canned voice even had time to finish the diatribe, the Recipient pressed the "O" key on the cell in order to return to the hotel's operator.

"Waldorf=Astoria, how may I help you?"

So it was no longer a beautiful day at the Waldorf the Recipient thought.

"Mr. Liam Ross's room, please."

"One moment please and I will ring his room for you."

He answered on the first ring. "Liam Ross" came the voice on the other end. The Recipient now knew the answer. The old man had been killed, but how had Ross been missed? Deciding not to respond the Recipient listened as Ross said hello and then hello once again before hanging up the phone.

An idea was starting to bloom as to how they might be able to use Ross to their needs. It might appear to be risky, but it would save days searching time if they utilized the expert. Before the plan could be put into effect however, the Recipient had to alert Nash to the plan. Retrieving a satellite phone from the case on the seat beside, the recipient keyed in Nash's number followed by the security code. On the second ring came the familiar voice. Without so much as a hello, the Recipient launched into a detailed account of the night before and the plan that would get Liam Ross to assist them in finding the much needed, long missing item.

12

Liam Ross

Liam Ross had led a very complicated, secretive life. A life that very few people, not even his closest friends and family members, knew the complete script of. For now he sat behind the desk in his suite, absentmindedly sipping what must have been his seventh or eighth cup of coffee that morning. He was not at all certain, as he had lost count earlier. Seated in the large, high backed executive swivel chair, with his friend's murder weighing heavily on his thoughts; he began exploring his own past.

Liam Ross was born into a family that could trace it roots back to pre-revolutionary America. One of six children born to Homer and Earleen Ross of upstate New York, Liam always considered himself the neglected middle child, as there were four years of age between each sibling. This great age difference between brothers and sisters paved the future path for growing up in a family devoid of warmth and closeness.

The Ross family were owners of a 200-year-old ongoing printing concern that could trace its beginnings to the early Philadelphia company of Dunlap and Ross, printers of the original Declaration of Independence broadsides in 1776 for the Second Continental Congress. Because of this family history the Ross family was steeped in rich tradition as well as legacies. One such legacy was a signatory to the document that declared freedom from an oppressive monarch. Another lent her services to the Continental Army when an ensign was needed to rally the newly created fighting forces of liberty. More recent attributes were known to have furthered the art of offset printing, and another was an acclaimed artist and architect.

But, even with the laudable came the hushed, quiet tones of the Ross skeletons, dark sheep that brought disgrace and dishonor to the name of an ages old family. Acquisitions of witchcraft in Salem, questionable business dealings during the depression, even a sex change during the time of this country's Camelot. It was his love of history and his family's past, the good, the bad, and the ugly, that led Liam on his path to find his true calling.

Liam's siblings thought him to be a wanderer, a gadfly that could find no real grounding in any profession. Flitting from job to job, profession to profession during his impressionable twenties, never landing on anything concrete to further his life or future. However this was exactly the opposite of what Liam Ross had been doing since leaving home at age seventeen.

He had discovered the theater arts at the very early age of ten, having to appear with his fellow classmates in elementary school, in a play called The Caliph's Clock. Around that same time period Liam had acquired a passion from his older brother for the classic film monsters of the early thirties and forties and the men that made them. So when Liam Ross found out that there was an evil character in the play he was about to perform in, he wanted to create a character for himself.

The great make up artists of Hollywood's Golden Age, Lon Chaney, Jack Pierce, Bud and Perc Westmore were Liam's inspiration. It fascinated him how they could turn an actor into a creature that would come alive on the screen in order to terrorize the countryside sending the unknowing villagers into the hills in abject fear. Liam would spend all of his time after school each day trying to find out how these wizards would apply putty, spirit gum and hair to the faces, hands and bodies of actors, turning those ordinary men into the vile denizens that survived even today, in the imaginations and under the beds of every child in the world.

So Liam Ross's first foray into the magical world of stagecraft began with the desire to not look like the other fifth graders that were dressed alike in various table clothes and old used curtains. With the simple application of rubber cement and cotton wool to his upper and lower lip the shy adolescent transformed himself into the crafty, evil Grand Vizer. That simple process allowed him the ability to become someone else, a way to escape. From that day forward his life would be different.

Liam would find every book he could get his hands on in order to learn about stage makeup, special effects and animation. He begged his artist father to show him the concepts of light and shadow, as well as drawing and painting. He would spend every Saturday afternoon glued to the television watching Monster Movie Matinee, then to race off with his friends pretending to be the evil scientists, creatures and demons that had come to life before them on the small television screen. As he got older he filmed movies on his grandfathers borrowed 8mm Kodak movie camera, with friends and neighbors bringing his creations to life with special effects, stop motion animation and make up.

At age twelve his family moved from the city to a small village about thirty minutes away. It was here at the junior and senior high school that Liam really discovered acting. This small school allowed him to devour all aspects of the fine arts, theater, music and science. Trying out for and acting in just about every play that the school would stage, his talents grew performance by performance. Now older, and being able to explore and connect various arts and crafts with the more disciplined sciences, Liam was able to take his makeup and special effects abilities to new heights.

As school continued on and Liam became a sophomore, some of Liam's teachers thought he was not as grounded as he should be, for he had yet to think about a serious profession. It was nonsense to think that anyone from this small town could do what Liam wanted to do. Most thought Liam's future was ready made for him at his family's printing business. He had been working there after school since he stopped working at Rex's, and his time at the printing company brought him the opportunity to learn even more about art and a place to learn about the workings of machines and tools that he could apply to his love of the stage. But he continued to butt heads with his older brother who ran the company, since his father died. Liam had lost any desire to join the family business.

So printing was a profession that was not to be. Luckily there were a few individuals that would push Liam to find his own direction. One of these people would be the father of Liam's best friend Michael Roberts, the chief of the local volunteer fire department and chief of the region's international airport fire department.

For years fire departments both professional and volunteer, would stage mock emergency drills in order to better train their members. These drills, though productive, never really carried the atmosphere or danger of a real emergency. It was soon after Michael's father had seen, what he considered professional effects and makeup work that Liam had created for a local Halloween fundraiser, that he approached Liam with an idea, could Liam incorporate realistic special effects and makeup, creating the sense of urgency and danger of an actual emergency, into one of the staged mock fire drills?

Liam jumped at the chance of a challenge. He was given a small budget, ten volunteers and an old school bus in order to create the drill. Working everyday for a week, conscripting Michael as well as friends from the drama club and stage crews, the deadline of the following weekend was met. The idea was to create a realistic as possible drill in order to train and then critique the volunteer fire department's team members to their skills and performance under pressure. Blood, broken bones, trapped people, smoke and even fire effects would be incorporated into the exercise.

Liam felt that the only way to accomplish this was to stage the drill as secretively as possible, not allowing any of the volunteers to know that it was just a drill and that the accident scene was just that, a staged scene. After laying out the entire plan to Michael's father and the rest of the fire department's line officers, and with much coaxing that the more realistic the better, did the officials okay the mock drill.

It was staged on a Tuesday evening that the department regularly held training classes. Most of the volunteers were at the station going through the required in-station drills and activities. It had been arranged with the county fire authority to send an alarm to the station as if it were an actual emergency. The call came in as a school bus involved in a single vehicle accident and injuries were reported. The chief ordered the ambulance, Engine One, and both heavy and light rescue trucks to roll. The accident scene was two miles outside of town on the Old Valley Road. When all of the crews arrived on the scene, chaos greeted them.

The twenty-passenger school bus was on its side, in a drainage ditch on the side of the little used road. Flames and smoke choked the immediate area with acrid, foul odor and heat. Bodies were strewn on the ground, some up to twenty feet away from the bus. A pair of legs was visible under the overturned bus, streaming blood from a compound fracture of the victim's femur. Cries of help and ear piercing screams emanated from the smoke filled cabin of the bus.

The first teams on the scene immediately started what they were trained to do. The engine company produced a Mattydale lay of hose from the truck to the nearest hydrant about one hundred yards away. Within two minutes the hose was attached to the pumper by way of the hydrant, two hand teams pulled 1-½ inch hoses and began a coordinated attack on the flames from the bus as well as the flames that had spread to the surrounding field.

The ambulance personnel began a triage of the scene, identifying all of the victims and setting up a staging area for treatment before transport to the local hospitals. Light rescue teams began the task of extricating each of the victims from the bus and handing them off to the paramedics and then to the ambulance team for treatment. The heavy rescue team had begun the rescue of the person that was trapped beneath the bus. Victim by victim, rescuers applied dressings and bandages in order to stop the more serious bleeding. Splints were applied to broken limbs and extraction boards were artfully placed and applied, beginning a well-choreographed movement to extricate the injured from the interior of the bus.

It had been about five minutes into the drill that one of the volunteers on the hose lines made it to the source of one of the spot fires in the field. After fighting a particularly smoky battle, the nozzle-man finally thought that they had an upper hand on the fire. When the hose leader approached the source in order to put the final water on the blaze, did he notice that something was not quite right. The fire was not burning the grass in the field but was coming from a well dug pit that had been lined with open five gallon buckets of fuel oil. The nozzle-man looked back at his rear hose man ready to exclaim "What the hell?" and was greeted by one of the assistant chiefs with his finger to his mouth, motioning for him to be quiet.

One by one, various volunteer team members started to discover that things with this accident were rather odd. It was when the last victim had been pulled from the bus that a shout from one of firemen finally revealed the canard. By that time the chiefs had been afforded the best opportunity ever to evaluate the team under duress. Once this point had been reached the chief called for everyone to stand down. It was at that minute that some of the rescuers that had not quite put one and one together had the living daylights scared out of them as most of the very seriously wounded victims just stood up and started to applaud their hero's. Two of the heavy rescue team fainted when the assistant chief working with them, pulled one of the trapped legs out from under the raised bus, placed it on his shoulder and then swung it as if it were a baseball bat, then saying "Home Run!" Team leaders reported that all had performed wonderfully, there had been some mistakes, but that was why they were here, to learn.

After about two hours of critique and clean up everyone left to return to the station. Liam finally made it back to the station to meet with the chiefs about an hour later after he was sure that all effects and props had been secured. He was greeted with cheers and shouts of well done from the fifty or so that had gathered in the station bays. Everyone remarking at how realistic the exercise had been.

After an hour of congratulations and accolades, Michael's father pulled Liam into the chiefs office and after expressing his sincere gratitude, did he ask Liam if he wanted to try it again, but on a much larger scale.

So after three months of planning and a larger budget, Liam had an opportunity to stage a much larger mock disaster drill for Chief Roberts at the airport. They had been given an out of service Boeing 707 for training use. The fuselage of the beaten up beast had been securely delivered to an unused potato field belonging to an old friend of the chief. It was here, about three miles from the end of the airport runway, that Liam staged and choreographed a flawless mock disaster.

This had been a much harder drill to conceal. Word got out to the media quickly when it was over heard on the emergency band radio that multiple fire departments were all rushing to the scene of a downed aircraft. Panic really ramped up in the media when it was discovered that the plane was a 707.

It was never revealed to the media until the very end of the exercise that this had been a drill. Chief Roberts and the airport team had taken some heat from the local constabulary for not disclosing any of the drill details to anyone, other than the participating departments chiefs. Some locals were irate at the pure media speculation of what was happening and how the fire chiefs would not allow any media anywhere near the rescue site. But in the end, one by one, the media outlets, the locals and officials saw the brilliance and the need for just such an exercise. Liam had even garnered local celebrity as the boy who brought down a plane with his special effects and realistic makeup.

Liam continued to hone his craft after the mock aircraft drill. It was during the summer that the Ross family held their non-yearly ongoing tradition, a family reunion picnic. It was at this gathering, that his Uncle Robert, whom no one had seen for over a decade and who he had not seen since he was eight or so, approached him during a family softball game.

Rumors about Uncle Robert had been swirling for years in the Ross clan. Most thought that after a promising education, graduating Summa Cum Laude from Princeton, that Robert would enter the world of politics. First a local race, then after a year or two on to the state level, and eventually onto the national scene perhaps in the senate. At least that is the life that his father had mapped out for him. Instead, about two weeks after graduating Princeton and at that year's reunion picnic, Robert announced to the entire family that he was joining a commune in California.

Robert was heard from very sparsely over the next seven or so years. Un-frequent cards at Christmas and at birthdays became the norm. So after a decade the family just dismissed his actions as just one of those Ross's that were no longer spoken of, another black sheep.

So it was quite the shock and surprise of all that on that beautiful summer afternoon, Robert Ross strolled onto the softball field. At first no one recognized the man, as he wore his hair beyond his shoulders and a beard that looked like it hadn't been trimmed in decades. He had taken up a place on the first base line and started cheering on the players, heckling some, calling each by their first name. After a few minutes of the playful caterwauling, Liam's Aunt Dawn walked up to the man to ask him to be quiet or leave, as this was a private family gathering. But only when she got to within three feet of the bearded onlooker did she realize that this was her brother.

So after many hours of questions, and even many more whispered comments amongst the elder family statesmen as to his appearance, did Uncle Robert have an opportunity to talk to his favorite nephew. After the customary chitchat about school, music, clothes and girls, did Robert ask Liam about his plans for the future. Liam told his uncle about his love of the theater and the movies. That perhaps he might go and try his hand either on Broadway or out in Hollywood, in order to learn even more.

Robert listened with rapt attention as Liam explained the various ideas that he had wanted to explore in theatrical make up. How he wanted to perfect his techniques and abilities so that they were so realistic that even a person sitting right next to one of his creations would not even know it was a person in disguise. Also how with his new techniques that he might even be able to offer new ideas into the world of prosthetics for people that had lost limbs either in accidents or in war.

After about an hour of listening, Uncle Robert finally stopped his overly exuberant nephew in mid sentence on how the use of silicon was better suited to the making of human flesh than that of liquid latex, to tell Liam the real reason as to why he was there. He asked Liam if he could keep a secret, and he meant a secret so important, that he could not even breath a single word of it to his own mother. After Liam assured his uncle that he was indeed capable did Robert reveal to Liam a very deep, closely held confidence. A secret so unbelievable, that at first Liam thought his uncle might have had one beer too many and a bit too much sun.

Robert's harbored secret was that he was not as appeared. He was not a wandering hippie living for the past ten years in a commune in California, living off the land, protesting the overbearing, far reaching government that most of his kind proselytize to any individual within earshot. He had in fact been working for that very same government since he had left Princeton. He went on to tell his nephew how he had been approached during his junior year at the famed university, as to how he had certain talents and how those talents could be used to help others. But it was not until his uncle asked him to go for a ride, did Liam truly believe his dear uncle.

Once on the highway, about ten minutes away from the picnic, did Liam ask his uncle where they were going?

"Uncle Bob, are you sure that this is not some sort of joke?"

"Don't believe me, eh?"

The evidence of disbelief was right before Liam, Robert's 1975 Ford LTD.

"Bob, we're riding in what could only be described as a death trap on four wheels. You know F-O-R-D, found on road dead. Has this car even seen an oil change in the past 200,000 miles? Ten years with the government, I would think that you could afford something just a bit nicer."

"Sarcasm, that's it, isn't it?"

The discussion went back and forth, with each of them trading barbs until Liam noticed that they were leaving the highway.

"So, the airport huh? Have to get out of town before the family comes after you with a razor and comb?"

"Wait and you shall be delivered unto the light oh smart ass!"

Instead of staying straight on the main road to the international terminal, Robert veered right down a road with a posted sign that stated "No Trespassing, Property of the United States Government."

"Man, the lengths that you will go to egg on a story! What, are we going to end up at some dead end deserted road with a bunch of pretend feds standing around?"

No sooner had Liam even spoke these words than Robert coasted the car to a stop just feet from a locked gate that appeared to guard an entrance onto one of the airport runways. As he sat there with his jaw slack, ready to concede to his uncle that this was a great gag, the gate opened and two black vans appeared from nowhere. From the rear doors of the two vehicles, six men appeared, each holding what appeared to be compact sub machine pistols. Each of the six wore the standard issue dark grey suit, dark sunglasses and custom molded radio ear piece in the their right ears.

Robert's car was flanked on all sides by the six imposing figures. Liam could only watch as his uncle rolled down his window and flashed a wallet that he had produced as if by some magicians slight of hand. After what could be determined as the lead machine pistol's careful scrutiny of the wallet and some hushed dialog between the two, did Robert roll up his window and the six men left the perimeter of the car, heading back into the vans before them. The vans started to pull away and Robert followed them onto the tarmac.

As soon as Robert's car cleared the closing gate, another van appeared and fell in behind Liam and Robert. The four vehicles traveled across the southern tip of the runway to an area of the airport that Liam knew to exist, but had never seen due to it's high security access for an USAF tactical fighter group. As the trio of vans and one rather decrepit Ford LTD cleared into the USAF secured area, Liam felt his heart jump into his throat. There before him, in very familiar livery of white, blue and gold sat a Boeing VC-137, more widely known as a Boeing 707. The livery of the plane identified it to be one of the planes consigned to the office of the President of the United States.

"That's...that's Air Force One!" Liam hoarsely croaked as he pointed a finger to the jet, now just yards away.

"It's only Air Force One when the president is on board. When it is consigned to other duties it is known as SAM 26000" was Robert's response.

"What's it doing here? And what the hell do you have to do with the President of the United States?" Liam sat rigid on the bench seat, almost as if in a state of shock. The Ford LTD rolled to a stop just to the rear of the cargo-loading ramp of the jet. Robert started to get out of the car when he noticed that his nephew had not moved an inch, his eyes were as wide as saucers.

"Come on, I'll give you a tour!" he shouted as he slammed the door to the car and started to walk towards the inclined ramp leading up into the bowels of the plane. Sheepishly Liam followed his Uncle's lead, reluctantly closing the car door and almost falling flat on his face after tripping on the ramp and from being in a complete daze.

Liam made it to the top of the ramp where he saw his Uncle, holding a clipboard and in conversation with some of the men that had surrounded the car earlier.

"Liam, I'd like to introduce you to my team leader Special Agent Terry Krom. Special Agent, my nephew Liam Ross."

"The one that caused all of the commotion?" asked Special Agent Krom.

"One in the same. Thought I give him a quick tour before we head back out."

"Yes sir, take your time. Our estimated time of departure isn't for at least another ninety minutes. Don't forget to show him the chariot!" quipped the agent.

"Chariot, what chariot?" asked the now inquisitive teen.

"All in due time. Let's start in the cockpit and work our way back. What do you say to that?"

"I say that I never would have believed it if I wasn't seeing it with my own eyes! My Uncle, a G-Man!" exclaimed the now eager Liam.

For the next hour the two poured over the aircraft, Liam's questions were non-stop. Whenever Robert didn't have the answer he found the person that did. From how the plane refueled in mid-air, to how the Secret Service and the Air Forced maintained the plane nick-named Angel, and it's crew Angel Maintenance. When they finally returned back to the rear cargo area they were in time to see the presidential limousine being loaded into the bay.

"Want to see the Chariot?" asked the elder Ross.

The president's limo rolled to the base of the ramp.

"Are you kidding? The President's car?"

"Sure, why not! Hop in!"

Liam ducked his head as an agent held the door open for him. As he crouched to the rear seat and turned to sit, he noticed the array of electronics in the bulkhead before him. Telephones, radios, a television, and a piece of equipment that his Uncle told him was called a facsimile machine, a way to send printed documents over phone lines, were all on and making an array of beeps and tones.

"Pretty neat, huh? Asked Robert. "What to see something really cool?"

Robert picked up the phone in front of him and within two seconds quickly rattled off a string of numbers and alpha characters to the unseen person on the other end of the handset. In ten seconds the facsimile machine came to life, spewing out a printed sheet. Robert removed the sheet from the machine and handed it to Liam. He now held in his hands, what appeared to be an FBI file on the seventeen year-old son of an artist from Syracuse.

"I have an FBI file? What the hell is this?"

"Liam" came his name from his uncle "I have more than just my secret to talk to you about. I need to talk to you about the real reason why I am here."

"Real reason, what real reason? I don't follow you Uncle Bob."

"Believe it or not Liam, I work for a division of the government that you have probably never even heard of, it's called the Central Security Services or CSS. It's a part of the National Security Agency. Our core mission is to protect the United States security systems and to aid and produce any foreign signals of intelligence information. Information technology is going to explode in the next twenty years. Computers, big and small, will become a part of everyday life; information will become one of the most valuable assets a country can ever control. So, to put it a bit more bluntly, we are spies."

"I...I..." was all Liam could muster.

"Here's why I am here today. No one else in the family knows any of this, and you can't tell them. Do you understand?"

Liam nodded his head in the affirmative.

"I am here today because of you, believe it or not. You came to our attention a couple of months ago when you did that mock jet rescue. A couple of the Air Force Crash Response team members filed a report, and gave you glowing remarks as to how it appeared to be a real disaster, and as to how professionally it was pulled off. Those remarks made it up all he way to my desk at CSS. It seems that without even knowing it, you did some remarkable feats out there that impressed the hell out of some of the intelligence chiefs in D.C. So, after the connection was made that you were my nephew, we did some checking and, voila, I'm here to talk to you about becoming a consultant for the CSS."

"What does that mean, consultant?'

"Well, like me, you might disappear for a couple of years while you get some specialized training by the CSS down at Quantico. Then the agency will help set you up in the make up and effects business. From time to time you will be called on to provide some services for us."

"Is this all legal? What kind of services?"

"Well, we might have the need to get some high official out of the country undetected. Or we might want to fool someone into thinking that a federal witness has been assassinated or something in that effect, in order to insure that they remain alive for trial. Thing's like that, so that's where you come in with your make up and effects"

"Wow, sounds pretty cool Uncle Bob, but do I really have to disappear for that long?"

"Liam, this needs to be kept super secret. No one, and I mean no one can know about this. But I can understand where this has been a shit bucket full of information to digest in just one night. I want you to take a few days and think about it, really think about it, then, we will talk again. How does that sound?"

"I think that I can do that Bob. How do I get a hold of you if I have any questions?"

Robert gave Liam a card with a special phone number on it.

"This phone number can reached me twenty four hours a day, seven days a week. I have the phone here in my pocket at all times."

Robert pulled out a device that looked more like it had come off of a Star Trek movie set.

"Is that really a phone? It works anywhere?" asked Liam.

"Any place and anytime. All you have to do is call that number" referring to the card in Liam's hands.

"Look Liam, We have to head out in a few minutes. I am going to have one of the local agents take you back to the picnic, so, are we cool?"

Once again Liam just nodded his head in the affirmative.

Liam watched as the Boeing VC-137 made it's taxi to the runway and then off to runway 21R. Within three minutes the plane was off into the evening sky. The local Special Agent motioned Liam over to a car that was waiting with its engine running. Within a half an hour, Liam was back at the picnic with the rest of the family, unable to concentrate on the evening's BBQ offerings, just staring off into space. Liam's young life had just taken a turn to what was to be the first of many, wonderfully, terrible adventures.

The next three months were agonizing for Liam. He had secretly met with his Uncle a number of times, getting ready for the time that he would disappear and head off to training. The day seemed to never get there fast enough, but it finally did. The story that was told to family was that Liam was off to an internship program at a major theme park in Orlando, Florida. There he would work and study new techniques in animation, special effects and make up, with hopes to secure a job with that company after the program was complete.

Instead Liam spent the next two years at various training facilities in and around the Washington, D.C. area. From basic law enforcement instruction to very intense training in firearms, microelectronics, forensics and his beloved theatrical make up. For those classes Liam was astonished to see that the instructor was none other than the make up artist that won the first Academy Award just a few years before.

Liam buried himself into everything that they taught him. Days would fly by and nights would be full of studying and preparing for the next day's grueling schedule. On the rare occasion that there was a night off, Liam and three other trainees, would head out to either the local movie theater or off to the beach for a picnic or barbeque. These four were all close in age, in their early twenties. At first none of them even spoke to another soul for fear of reprisal from one of the instructors, plus they all noticed that the older recruits never socialized with each other. But it was soon revealed that the reason the older recruits never spoke was that they were actually intimidated by the younger team members. So once this was deciphered, the "Fearsome Four" as they had been nicknamed by the instruction staff, opened up to each other and became close friends.

During the training Liam was sent out on some live training exercises. His first was what he felt was a simple make up job for a federal witness that the U.S. Marshalls had to relocate without the man's former gang knowing where he was. The project turned out to be a simple two-day "gig". One day to prep the subject and one day to execute. The job went flawlessly, primarily due to the fact that the subject turned out to be a small boned, rather slight male in his early forties. Liam was able to transform the former gang leader, amusedly with much objection from him, into a rather attractive female in her late twenties. The effect was so realistic that when Liam, the two agents in charge and the witness left the federal courthouse, they passed within two feet of the former gang leader's first lieutenant. The gangbanger hooted and whistled some rather descriptive catcalls at his former leader without even having a clue as to who it was. Everyone was suddenly in panic mode when fed up with the whistles and hoots, the former gang leader turned on his six inch high heels with ease and flashed the international symbol of discontent at his former lieutenant. Everyone froze, sure of the fact that they had been blown before they even got to the car. But sanity was restored when the bald slob of a gangbanger spouted off some expletives in Spanish about her being a tease and a whore, turned on his heel and stormed off with his low rider pants seeming to dust the ground while six inches of his white boxer shorts were exposed at his waist.

There were more and more of these gigs as the days turned to months then into years. After the two years of training were up, it was decided by the higher ups at CSS that Liam would indeed be sent to Florida in order to open up a special effects business in order to support an emerging film industry in Central Florida.

Everything went smooth as silk over the next five years. Liam hired his three friends from the CSS academy to work with him in Orlando. The handlers at CSS had no objections to this as the Fearsome Foursome were often used as a freelance team, and having them together in one place afforded the organization some efficiencies. As the years went by, the team was asked to do fewer and fewer assignments.

Soon it had been over eighteen months and not one phone call from either his uncle Robert or his handlers at CSS. This proved beneficial as Liam and his team's work became more and more in demand from the top Hollywood producers. Before they knew it the team had work scheduled for the next three years, and it would be a demanding three years. The work became so intense that Liam found himself not involved in the actual production end of the business, but more and more wrapped up in the day-to-day aspects that it takes to run a successful organization. Liam and some of his team members began to grow disenfranchised with the work that they had once loved. Producers became more demanding as budgets became leaner. So when a larger effects house approached Liam about a merger, Liam instead suggested a straight sale of his company to the latter. So within two months, Liam's company was fully acquired by the Hollywood effects company and he now looked to new adventures.

It was during this time that Liam grew, not just physically, but emotionally and spiritually as well. Not yet even twenty-seven, he discovered that he had many distractions to occupy his long time thirst for learning. He had discovered wine and fine dining one evening while in France on a film shoot years ago. His gastronomic passion soon turned to into obsession, an obsession that added a few pounds to his six foot two muscular frame, and a weight condition that Liam would continually battle for years to come.

It was also during this time that he became a collector. No one knows exactly why, not even himself. But with the financial means, the ability and love of travel, plus always having had an inquisitive demeanor about him, Liam would embark on this new passion as more than just a hobby or an investment. Coins were soon added to his stamp collection from his youth. He then pounced on small rare artworks and artifacts before moving into fine vintage wines, which transpired into early 20th century collectable toys, film memorabilia and even classic film monsters. Liam Ross certainly and truly was a renaissance bon vivant.

Liam's attention was brought back to the present when the phone on the desk rang. Liam reached over and lifted the handset from the cradle and answered.

"Liam Ross."

"Mr. Ross, it's Lieutenant O'Brian, I hope that I am not disturbing you."

"No, Lieutenant, I was just finishing some breakfast. Is there any news?"

"No, nothing yet. I wanted to see if you had the time to go to Mr. Cooper's room with me. I will be at the hotel within the next forty-five minutes."

"I appreciate the offer Lieutenant, shall I meet you in the lobby?"

"I first have to see the manager about getting hotel security to open the room."

"That won't be necessary, I have a key to his room. Whenever Rex travels, rather traveled, he always would give someone else a spare key. He was always loosing them. How about I meet you in his room?"

"No, I would rather that you not go into his room without me Mr. Ross, how about I meet you in your room?"

"That's fine, I am in room 20R. Use the Park Avenue elevators, I will see you in forty five minutes then."

Liam hung up the phone and just continued to sit staring out the widow that faced north up Park Avenue. He needed some help.

13

The Team

Belmont Heights
Long Beach, California
May 1, 2013, 5:30 AM PDT

It wasn't even light out yet and the phone was ringing. Looking up at her bedside alarm clock through bleary eyes, Liz Gallagher cursed herself for not setting the answering machine to no rings. Who in the name of god calls someone at this hour! Don't they realize that I just got to bed an hour ago! "That new game was addicting and I had to break it!"

Even with this one-sided dissertation in her head the phone continued to ring. After the sixth ring she finally gave in and called out "Answer Phone". With that phrase the automated, whole home phone system, that Liz had been perfecting for the last three months, opened a connection with the caller on the other end.

"Who ever the hell this is, it had better be damn important. It's 5:30 in the morning! And if it's not urgent I am going to hunt you down and rearrange your credit history!" was her greeting seemingly shouted at the ceiling as she lay in her bed.

"Liz, it's Liam. Rex is dead. He was murdered." Came the voice from hidden speakers in the room.

When Liz heard her former boss's voice she sat bolt upright, unable to respond as his words just starting to register in her now awake consciousness.

"Boss, is that you? What did you say?"

"Rex is dead Liz. He died in my arms last night. He was murdered."

"Why, how, where?" was all she could respond with.

"We were in New York at the International Philatelic Expo. We went to dinner… It's a long story, but I need some help. Do you have some free time?"

"Sure, whatever you need. I'll jump on the next flight out. I think I can be there by dinner your time. Do I need to bring anything?"

"Just you and that pretty little brain of yours. Oh, and don't call me Boss, you know what it spelled backwards is, right?"

"Yeah, Double S-O-B" she laughed "How could I forget."

"And Liz, I'm calling the guys in too. I could be in real trouble here. Do you know if they are around?"

"Kyle is in Florida at the old shop. They brought him in to upgrade one of the animatronics from the space center exhibit. He was the only one that could remember the old programming system. John hooked up with a local theater group in Denver. I think he's still there as the artistic director. Last I heard from him, he was into round three with soon to be ex-wife number two. Cell numbers and emails are still the same."

"Thanks Liz, you're the best" and almost as an after thought "and Liz, be careful. What's going on here really stinks. Go back to the old protocols."

"Got it Boss, see you tonight."

They both hung up at the same time. Something was wrong, very wrong in order for Liam to mention the old protocols, Liz thought to herself. They hadn't done a job for the CSS in over four years. What had Liam spooked?

158

"Call Consolidated Airlines" were her next words as the automated phone system dialed the airline so she could make a reservation to New York. As she waited for the airlines antiquated answering queue to connect her with a live human being, Liz made her way to the bathroom in order to start her day.

Liam's next phone call was to his former top electronics and mechanical whiz, Kyle Gale. When Liam first left the CSS and was setting up shop in Orlando, Kyle was the first to join him full time. After graduating MIT at the top of his class, Kyle had been approached by the NSA, in a rather unique, backwards way, regarding the SST or Super Satellite Technology, otherwise coined by the conspiracy theorists as SuperSatTrap. This supposed technology, could literally pull electronic conversation signals from the air and from all types of cables. Allowing the government to eavesdrop on every single piece of electronic communication that was being sent, from all over the world, provided that certain identified code words were spoken within a sentence structure, as Kyle was soon to find out.

So, around two o'clock one morning, outfitted with a modified time delayed tape recorder/dialer of his own design, Kyle was attaching the device to a payphone just outside the White House in Lafayette Park. The recorder was timed to call the President's private bedroom phone number.

The phone number, he had "borrowed" from a girl that he had had a brief love affair with a year ago, who just happened to work in the White House Telecommunications department. Kyle broke it off with her shortly after he discovered that for "fun" and sexual arousal, she liked to verbally spar at an outrageous volume almost every night. These arguments were always about nothing of any importance and just for her demented pleasure. So one night after one of the marathon shout fests, Kyle found himself in her living-room with a glass of single malt in one hand and her personal address book, that had just happened to conveniently fall out of her purse, in his other hand, opened to a page that was titled "Super Secret" phone numbers. Kyle had forgotten about the handful of the so called "Super Secret" phone numbers, until he was out with a woman whom he had been trying to get a date with for over six months.

When she finally said yes, Kyle spent the better part of ten days, outlining and planning the perfect evening. When the night finally arrived Kyle and his date were seated at a table in one of Washington D.C.'s most romantic and famous powerbroker restaurants. As the two were having a pre-dinner glass of champagne and having a normal decibel conversation, the oral Mike Tyson approached from nowhere and began to launch into one of her famous verbal fist-de-cuffs as if she had just caught him cheating on her! As his date for the evening ran from the table and mouthed the word "asshole" silently at him, it was at that precise moment Kyle remembered the phone numbers from a year ago. After almost fifteen minutes of her voluminous logomachies, and with three waiters plus the Maitre de dragging her out of the establishment, Kyle decided that a lesson needed to be taught.

Kyle never stopped laughing from the minute he had tapped into the payphone's number in order to hear the conversation that he had placed on the tape recorder. It was 3:30 am and Kyle's programmed tape was reading back a rather lengthy confirmation order for pizzas, to a rather groggy President of the

United States, pizzas that needed to be delivered to his former lover's home within thirty minutes. Holy shit, he thought, the damn phone number really works! Kyle was still laughing when three members of the NSA security team, plus ten agents from the Secret Service, politely broke down his front door, about 30 minutes later.

Liam indeed found Kyle at the old Orlando shop, and within five minutes had brought Kyle up to speed on what was happening. Liam gave Kyle a shopping list of things that they might need in New York. Kyle would pull the gear together and drive up from Orlando. He would be in Manhattan first thing the next morning.

Liam's final call was to John Andrews, who was the actor of the group. John had been approached when Liam had seen him in a performance of Frankenstein at a local theater. The performance was outstanding. The dialogue and the acting, was superb. The make-up of the Creature, the role in witch John was portraying, held Liam's attention through the entire three-act performance. At the end of the play Liam made his way back stage in order to meet and congratulate the actor.

Liam stopped at the stage manager's desk and asked where he might find John Andrew's room. The stage manager directed him to the dressing rooms that were located under the stage, two stories down. As Liam located Andrew's door and knocked, he was greeted with an eloquent "Entre vous" in an English accent. Liam opened the door, half expecting to see the actor seated at the makeup table removing the grotesque appliances that turned the actor into the creature. Instead, Liam was welcomed into the room by what appeared to be a boy, a boy of perhaps fifteen at best, without a speck of makeup in sight, either on his face or on the table in front of him.

"I would like to see John Andrews if I may" was Liam's request.

"At your service, Sir" came the response, still in the over acted, English accent. Seated in a reclined make up chair, reading what appeared to be the latest issue of *Famous Monsters of Filmland*, while scarfing down what appeared to be a slice of pepperoni pizza the size of the actors head.

"I must be mistaken. Are you John Andrews? The actor that just played the role of the Creature?"

"I am he sir, and just who might you be?"

"I'm Liam Ross. I am a make up artist."

The boy seated before Liam jumped up so quickly that Liam thought that he was perhaps being electrocuted.

"The Liam Ross? The Liam Ross? You did the make up in "Gormet". That is one of my most favorite horror films. Are you really, him?" The English accent now appeared to be from one of the plains states, probably Iowa.

"That was one of my first and worst films. You actually saw it?"

"Eleven times, it was amazing! The story was dog shit mind you, but the effects were the best!" the boy crossed over to where Liam was now standing and energetically shook his hand until his arm almost came out of it's socket.

"Well thank you for the praise Mr. Andrews, I greatly appreciate it. However, it is I that want to thank you for a wonderful performance tonight. It was one of the best adaptations of Shelley's Frankenstein that I have ever seen. I am though a little perplexed."

"How so Mr. Ross?"

"Please call me Liam."

"No shit? That is so cool! Thanks Liam. So way are you perplexed?"

"Well I half expected to find you in the throws of removing your appliances of the Creature, yet here you are, only 10 minutes after the curtain came down, and you look as if you have just had a three hour facial. How could that be possible?"

What came next both surprised and shocked Liam at the same time. The boy standing before him suddenly appeared to grow almost six inches right before his eyes. The actor then bowed his head and placed it into his hands that were open before him. Unnoticed to Liam, the lights dimmed and an eerie glow emitted from around the soffits of the dressing room. A low sound that Liam recognized as the voice of the Creature, emanated from within the hands that were covering the thespian's face. The sound built until the entire room was filled with the hair-raising tone. Slowly, John Andrews lowered his hands to reveal the hideous face of Mary Shelley's tormented creature.

"What the hell?" was all Liam could muster. "That is amazing? How did you do that? I didn't see a mask or appliance anywhere? Where were they hidden?"

Then, as if by magic, right in front of the makeup artist, the actor's face returned to normal. All Liam could do was stand there with his mouth opened, unable to speak.

"What? How? It's not possible…"

"I have been experimenting for the past two years with different techniques in order to create characters for the stage." John picked up a small remote and returned the room lighting to normal.

"As you know Mr. Ross, I mean Liam, 99 percent of all theatrical effects are created with various light sources or the lack-there of. What I have been doing is working with new make up bases that when applied in normal light, have absolutely no visual effect. But when seen under the correct, and corresponding wavelength of light, the effect is revealed."

Stepping to within inches of the actor, and carefully reviewing every inch of flesh, Liam was unable to detect any signs of the makeup.

"Unbelievable... just unbelievable. That is just amazing. Not unlike how John Barrymore did it in Dr. Jekyll and Mr. Hyde in 1920 for Paramount."

"It's really a very old technique that I am trying to bring new, updated technology to."

"Would you be willing to show me the effect again?"

With that John Andrews showed Liam the effect and then the entire system for staging the effect. First the smaller system installed in the dressing room, then the larger system on the stage. When they were done reviewing all of the minute details that went into the process, three hours had passed. It was well past midnight, yet the two continued to talk well into the morning about make up and effects of the great Hollywood masters, from Lon Chaney to Willis O'Brien and then to the more modern creators such as Rick Baker. John was even able to get Liam to reveal some of the tricks that Liam had perfected in his short career. From that evening on the two became good friends.

Liam dialed the phone number that he had stored in his iPhone for John. After three rings the connection was made and Liam heard the snooty English accent from so many years ago.

"Rat Race, head Rat speaking."

"I heard that the rats were winning."

"Pure rumor and innuendo spread by my competitors to sully my sterling reputation!" came the reply.

"How are you my old friend?"

"As well as can be expected I guess. Having some ups and downs in life lately Liam."

"Marriage number two turned sour?"

"No, more like number two turned to number two!"

"Sorry to hear that John. I wish that I could help, but truth be told I need your help right now."

"Anything for you LR, just name it."

John Andrews had taken to calling Liam in the same manor that actors of old called Cecil B. DeMille, just by his initials. At first this drove Liam up a wall. But after the fourth or fifth thousandth time, it was the norm between the two friends.

"John, a very good friend of mine from way back was just murdered here in New York. Something's not right and I need help getting to the bottom of this before something else happens. I need you here as soon as possible."

"I will be packed and on my way within the hour."

"Great John. Come straight to the Waldorf when you land. Also John…"

"Yeah LR?"

"Protocols."

"Understood."

14

Suspicions

Liam's last call was to Rex's attorney, Ken Whitelaw. As it was still early, there was no one in his office yet so Liam left a message for Mr. Whitelaw to call him as soon as possible. Liam hung up his call and noticed the time. He was expecting Lieutenant O'Brian within twenty minutes. He quickly put on a one of his favorite Brooks Brothers Pinpoint Oxford shirts. The sales agent told him the color was called Light Salmon. Light Salmon my ass, thought Liam, it's pink, pure and simple. Thank God he was one of a handful of men that could pull off a pink shirt, other wise it could be an issue!

Liam left his suite and headed straight for the bank of elevators, right down the hall. It always amused him whenever he thought of the purely trivial. Like that in most large hotels the elevators would take forever to arrive. However here at the Waldorf it always seemed that they arrived at your floor just seconds after pressing the call switch, just one of the many things that he loved about this old, classic New York City hotel. The doors opened and Liam stepped into an empty car. He pressed the G button and stepped to the rear of the car as the doors slid to a close. He turned to face the front of the car and looked up at the intricate molding detail in the elevator car. He had been in any one of a dozen elevator cars in this hotel and each and every one of them still had all of the original details from the opening day of the hotel in 1931.

The interiors were all hand crafted from solid mahogany. The hand carved dental molding circled the base of the crown moldings that secretly concealed the lighting fixtures for the car. The brass railing that circled three of the cars walls were reportedly one of the few items that had survived from the original Waldorf=Astoria hotel, built in 1893 by William Waldorf Astor, that was located at the site that The Empire State Building now occupies.

Liam was lost in these details as the car came to a halt at the ground floor. He exited the car and went left into the massive lobby of the hotel. In the southeast corner of the lobby, next to the Bell Captain's desk is a small, unobtrusive room, located behind a set of glass paneled French doors. This room at one time was the day check room for the Bell Captain, but in recent years had been turned into a VIP check in. Not that Liam considered himself a VIP of any sorts, it just happened to be a perk of this hotels frequent nights program, that anyone who stayed in any of the chain's hotels over forty nights a year had use of these VIP services. Forty nights – Liam wished that he had stayed only forty nights in hotels last year. The last he checked his travel-calendar he had stayed in various hotels, inns and bed & breakfasts over 185 times last year alone. This year was on track to beat that tally, easily.

Liam opened the door to the VIP Services and peered in. No one was at either of the two desks. He checked his watch and realized he had but ten minutes to get back to his room and meet with Lieutenant O'Brian, but he needed to alert the hotel that he was going to need three more rooms for a few days. After waiting for three minutes Liam left the VIP room and crossed the short distance to the Front Desk. Liam waited in line for about one minute before he was called to the next available desk agent.

"Yes sir, how may I help you?"

"Hi, I'm Liam Ross in suite 20R. I stopped in at VIP Services, but no one was there. I was hoping to speak with Jane if possible about setting up three more rooms for me. Is she in this morning?"

The desk agent, perfectly dressed in the hotel's livery of a dark, charcoal gray double breasted suit with the faintest pin strip in cream, checked the daily log on the computer terminal in front of him.

"I can't seem to locate her schedule Mr. Ross. If you would excuse me for a minute or two, I will check with the manager."

The twenty something year old, excused himself and left through a perfectly concealed hidden door located within the mural that adorned the wall behind the front desk. Liam knew his wait would not be long. As he waited for his agent to return he stood to his side and leaned against the stomach high counter looking out into the ornate lobby of the hotel. People were always coming and going at the Waldorf=Astoria. Most hotels had a check in policy of mid afternoon. However if you stayed frequently at the Waldorf, you were allowed to check in whenever you needed to, another one of the perks. Liam was about to check his watch again when he noticed another of New York's greatest attributes standing in line.

She had perfectly styled red hair almost to her shoulders. Liam estimated that she must be late twenties or early thirties, over six feet in height, then he noticed the four-inch, red soled, Christian

Louboutin shoes. A quick mental calculation made her to be a true height of about five feet-ten inches. On her perfect figure she wore what had to be a French designer business suit of a tailored jacket and pencil skirt in black silk crepe that came to length just below her knees. Beneath the buttoned jacket was what appeared to be an ivory silk blouse with French cuffs that extended just over her delicate hands. She trailed behind her a standard issue rolling overnight case with the Y & L pattern of the famous Paris designer. She was absolutely stunning, breathtakingly gorgeous; she had to be a model. Liam didn't fully realize that he was standing there staring, with his mouth slightly agape until she started to walk right toward him. Like a kid caught red handed looking at a copy of Playboy, Liam tried to regain his composure and turned back towards the desk to cover up his soon to be red face. Why she was walking towards him? He was about to turn and apologize for staring when she turned to her right and stepped to the agent behind the desk, in the line right next to Liam.

At that time Liam's agent returned with the answer to his query.

"Mr. Ross, Miss Reese is in a meeting and unavailable. She will be more than happy to set up your additional rooms for you, when she is free. If you would leave me the names and check in dates of your guests, I will see that she gets the information."

"Thank you. That will be fine." Liam wrote down Kyle, John's and Liz's info and handed it to the agent. As he turned to walk back to the elevators, he walked behind the redheaded woman that was now deep in conversation with her desk agent. When he passed his senses were aware of the most amazing scent that he had ever smelled. He was unable to recognize the woman's perfume, but it was intoxicating. A scent that seemed to clear his mind of all of his troubles of the past twenty-four hours and mysteriously place him on a beach sitting next to this enthralling beauty.

Just as Liam left the deeply carpeted reception lobby and his shoes touched the marble of the elevator hallway he felt a touch on his shoulder. Liam turned to see who had just tapped him.

"Mr. Ross, I thought we were going to meet in your room?"

Standing before Liam was Lieutenant O'Brian and one of his detectives looking as if they had just been dragged in from the rain.

"Oh, Lieutenant O'Brian, You startled me. Yes we are going to meet in my room. I just had to change my hotel arrangements."

"Not leaving New York already, are you?" asked the Lieutenant's associate.

"No, as a matter of fact I am lengthening my stay a bit. Just in case you need me for anything." Liam lied through his teeth to the detective.

"Mr. Liam Ross, meet Detective John Conner."

Liam proffered his right hand.

"Detective."

The officer returned the handshake.

"Mr. Ross."

"Why don't we go up to Rex's suite? I have the key with me" offered Liam.

Liam pressed the elevator call button, one of the doors to the left side of the hallway opened. Being polite, Liam motioned for the two policemen to enter before him. After they entered the elevator car Liam stepped inside and pressed the floor button marked 18. Just as the doors started to slide shut a voice from outside called.

"Please hold the elevator!"

Liam quickly pressed the door open button to return the sliding door to its fullest open position. Standing before the three men in the elevator was the redhead that Liam had been absent-mindedly starring at in the lobby.

"Thank you gentlemen. I appreciate the help."

"Our pleasure Miss." The response was from Detective Conner.

The aroma of the woman's perfume suddenly filled the small elevator car with its heady scent. Liam was barely able to ask the woman what floor she was going to, as his mind raced back to the moment he first saw her.

"Floor please?"

"Oh, it looks to be the same as yours, the eighteenth. Thank you."

Liam pressed the button once again then stepped to the side of the car. None of the occupants spoke a word as the eighty-one year old elevator car sped upward. After only about a minute, because there were no stops, the elevator arrived at the eighteenth floor. The car silently slowed and then the door opened. Liam held the open door button until all had exited the car. The three men watched as the redhead walked silently down the thickly carpeted center hallway.

"That is one hot piece of ass if you ask me" came the crass comment from Detective Conner.

"We didn't ask you." Came the somewhat stern reply from Lieutenant O'Brian.

"That gentlemen, was a lady." Liam remarked as his gaze followed the retreating beauty down the hallway.

After an awkward moment, the two policemen looked to Liam for direction.

"Which room Mr. Ross?" asked Lieutenant O'Brian.

"Rex was in Suite 18N, down the center hallway to the end, then left to the end of the hall, the room is on the right."

The three men fell into step down the hallway watching as the redhead disappeared down the hallway that they were about to turn to. As they turned they saw the woman stop, turn, unlock and then disappear into a hotel room door. The men continued down the hall until they came to suite 18N. Liam stepped forward to open the door. Once the door was open, he once again gestured for the officers to proceed first. After all three were in the foyer of the suite Lieutenant O'Brian turned to Liam.

"Mr. Ross, could you please wait here in the foyer on the marble flooring until we have had a chance to look around?"

"Not a problem Lieutenant."

Liam turned to his left and sat in the overstuffed chair that was placed in the foyer, crossed his legs and waited. After only about two minutes, Lieutenant O'Brian returned and asked Liam into the living room of the suite.

"Mr. Ross, when was the last time that you were in Mr. Coopers room?"

"Oh, I don't really remember the exact time, but if I had to venture a guess I would have to say about 7:00pm two days ago.

We had a drink before going to dinner. Why do you ask Lieutenant?"

"We are just trying to map out Mr. Cooper's activities for the past two days."

"Well, I can tell you pretty much everything, except for the times that I was elsewhere at the Philatelic Expo. But I assure you Lieutenant; Rex would not have left his table in the bourse. Just how can any of this be related to what happened to Rex?"

"Because we are trying to see who really wanted Mr. Cooper dead, Mr. Ross."

The response was quick and crass but not from Lieutenant O'Brian. Detective Conner had spate out Liam's name as if he had a mouthful of acid.

"And you are thinking that I had something to do with his murder? Are you both insane? I was almost killed myself you jackass!" Liam's temper was starting to build as what the Detective said started to sink in.

"What about the report we gave to you just yesterday afternoon." Turning to Lieutenant O'Brian, "If I had something to do with his murder would I have been with Rex to file the report with you then? If I remember correctly you gave the whole incident the big heave ho."

"That could have just been you starting to build a good..."

Stop it now John and that's an order!"

Lieutenant O'Brian cut of Detective Conner mid sentence.

"Mr. Ross, we are just looking at all of the pieces. We are as much in the dark about this accident as you are."

"Accident? Accident? Are you out of your fucking mind! Rex was shot with a Beretta 93R firing what I assume was 9mm Black Talon ammo from a 30 round clip!"

"How are you aware of just what model, type and form of ammunition was used Mr. Ross." The two detectives peered at Liam with sharp cold hard eyes.

"Because I'm not an idiot and I've been in the film effects business for years. I have handled all types of machine pistols, handguns, shotguns and rifles. As for the ammo, I had a piece of the shrapnel hit me in the upper arm. It was easy to put one and one together from there you clowns!"

Liam was not going to tell them the real reason why he knew what model gun was used and he was sure as hell not going to take these accusations.

"Please Mr. Ross. Stay calm. We didn't mean to upset you. It's just that there are way too many unanswered questions. Like the next one for instance, do you happen to know if Mr. Cooper was married and if not, do you know who might be his beneficiary?" asked Lieutenant O'Brian.

"Mr. Cooper was not married. I mean he was once, a long time ago, but she passed away over 20 years ago. As for who his beneficiary is I have no idea."

Detective Conner appeared from the bedroom.

"There is nothing in there but his clothes, no computer, no files nothing."

"Mr. Cooper's files and computer would be at the Philatelic Expo in his bourse space. You will find his booth on Level Three, Section A, Booth 1046. I have a set of keys for the locked cabinets. Just to let you know I have alerted show security as to what has happened. There will be three security guards at Mr. Cooper's booth until I find out from his attorney what I need to do with his belongings."

This too was a lie, but Liam was going to call the show management office the second these two had left.

"Here are the keys to the locked cabinets." Liam handed the keys to Lieutenant O'Brian. "I would appreciate it if you would return them to the head of show security when you are finished. I, as well as his attorney, have a complete inventory list as to the contents in the cabinets. If you need to remove anything, I will have security note the inventory control number and photograph the item. Do you have a problem with this Lieutenant O'Brian?"

Detective Conner spoke up first as he crossed over to Liam.

"You little shit! You don't tell us what to do or how to do it!" Now pointing his index finger at Liam's chest, "Get it! We are the fucking NYPD, we do as we want!" The last poke was hard and it connected solidly with Liam's sternum.

He didn't even see Liam's arm move, it was that fast. Liam was so fast that he had grabbed the Detective's finger, spun him around and now held Conner's finger and arm behind his back. Before Conner even had a chance to respond, Liam let go of the Detective and pushed him toward Lieutenant O'Brian.

"That Detective was assault. I have the right under New York City statutes to defend myself in any way or means in order to protect myself. I will not allow you to treat me this way. I will be filing an official complaint with the Commissioner's Office within the hour." Liam stood still waiting for the hotheaded Detective to retaliate. Just as he predicted, Conner started to lunge at Liam but was stopped with a meat hook for a hand from Lieutenant O'Brian.

"Mr. Ross I apologize for the detective's actions. He was out of line."

"What the fuck? Boss, how can you..." Conner was stopped cold.

"There is no need to bring this to the Commissioner's attention. I will personally see that Detective Conner is reprimanded. Now Detective, apologize to Mr. Ross."

"The fuck I will..." was loudly conveyed by Conner.

"Detective! Now!" was even louder.

Sheepishly Conner bowed his head, swallowed hard then looked up at Liam.

"Mr. Ross I am sorry for my actions. In no way was my intention to cause you any harm. For this I am truly sorry."

It was Liam that held his hand out first after hearing what Conner had to say.

"I accept your apology Detective. I too am sorry for the way I reacted. I had a little stunt training with martial arts for film work. I guess my instinct just took over." This too was a lie.

"Lieutenant O'Brian, is it okay to pack up Rex's personal items here at the hotel and get them shipped back home?"

"I don't see why not. There is nothing here that we need for the investigation. I will let you know after we have checked his items at the Expo as to their disposition. As for your schedule Mr. Ross, you are staying to the end of the Philatelic Expo?"

"I am actually staying a bit longer now. As you know, Rex was the beneficiary of Joe Bousquet's stamp collection. I need to catalog the contents and make arrangements to get it shipped back to Rex's warehouse. It's going to take some time."

"Do you have Mr. Coopers' attorneys information? I would like to contact him about Mr. Cooper."

Just as Liam was about to give Lieutenant O'Brian the information his cell phone rang.

"Well, there's a coincidence for you. It's Ken Whitelaw, Rex's attorney. If you will excuse me for a minute."

Liam turned and walked out to the foyer in order to have a little privacy.

"Coincidence my ass." Conner mumbled under his breath but loud enough for Lieutenant O'Brian to hear.

"And as you know Detective, I don't believe in coincidences" was O'Brian's response.

"Ken, it's Liam. I've got some pretty bad news. Rex is dead. He was murdered last night here in New York."

"Liam, please tell me that this is some kind of a sick joke."

"Sorry Ken, it's true. Go to the New York Post website. It should be front page."

There was a moment of silence as the attorney typed in the URL information.

"Got it. Oh shit, it says that there were two people involved. Who was the other?"

"I was the other person Ken. I got hit in the arm, but I'm okay."

"How can I help Liam?"

"As soon as they release Rex's body I will get it ready for transport back home. Do you know if he had any specific funeral plans Ken?"

"Let me go and pull a copy of his will, hang on a minute will you?"

"First Ken, can I give the local detectives your contact information?"

"Yeah, sure. No problem. Give them my cell as well."

"Thanks, I'll hang on."

Liam cupped his hand over the mouthpiece of his cell and he relayed Ken Whitelaw's contact information to Lieutenant O'Brian. Just as he finished Ken came back on the line.

"Liam, I'm back. Okay, here is Rex's most recent Last Will & Testament." Ken paused briefly as if he was reading.

"Liam, didn't Rex ever talk to you about this?"

"He tried to Ken, I just didn't want to listen. I kept telling him he had decades left."

"Well, I can tell you that he named me as the executor of his will. So we can dispense with a lot of the formalities. He also had a living trust in effect so we don't have to worry about probate on his estate."

"What about funeral services Ken?"

"This states that he wanted to be cremated and have his ashes spread over the lake in the Adirondacks where his family vacationed when he was a boy."

"Can I take care of that here in New York?"

"Shouldn't be a problem Liam. I'll fax whatever releases are needed to the coroner there. Just where are you?"

"His body will be here in Manhattan. I don't have any of the numbers yet."

"Don't worry about that. I'll have Denise my assistant handle all of that. I'll also send you a power of attorney that will allow you to close out Rex's account there at the Waldorf. I'll send a fax right to your room."

"Thanks Ken. I would also like to set up a small memorial here at the Philatelic Expo. These people were really his family."

"That would be great Liam. Let me know when it is set and I'll fly down for it."

"Also Ken, I need to let you know about something else."

"Sure Liam, what's up?"

"It could be the reason why Rex was murdered."

"Really, what is it?"

"Yesterday, Rex found out that he was the beneficiary of a rather large and important stamp collection from one of his long time clients."

"Could it be worth anything?"

"It could run into the millions Ken, maybe tens of millions. We never really had a chance to review any of it. I do know that the former owner may have been killed over it as well."

"Are the police aware of this?"

"Yes, Rex and I went to them yesterday when Rex was threatened."

"You really think that this is all connected?"

"I'm certain of it. So what should I do with this collection?"

"Well I guess anything that you want."

"Anything I want? What the hell are you talking about?"

"I guess now is as good a time as any to tell you. You are Rex's sole beneficiary."

Dead silence.

"Liam, did you hear me? You own everything. Don't you have anything to say?"

"Oh shit! That's all I need."

Looking a bit pale, Liam closed the phone connection and went back into the living room where the two detectives were still waiting.

"Sorry to keep you waiting gentlemen. That was Ken Whitelaw, Rex's attorney. He is going to file the necessary paperwork with your coroner so that when Rex's body is released it can be cremated. He also informed me that he is the executor of the will and has given me permission to settle Rex's affairs here in New York. So if you don't mind, I need to get back to my room and start making some arrangements."

The three men started to walk towards the front door of the hotel suite. As Liam opened the door the door on the opposite side of the hallway opened at the exact same time. Due to the form being backlit from the light within the room, Liam did not immediately recognize the woman coming out of the room. When he smelled her perfume, he snapped back to the present, it was the redhead from the lobby, once again.

"So, we are neighbors, how nice," she remarked as she closed and locked her door. "Have a nice day" was all she said as she turned and walked down the hallway presumably heading to the elevator.

Lieutenant O'Brian and Detective Conner made their way into the hall. Liam pulled the door to Rex's suite closed as he watched the redhead turn the corner to the central hallway. Lieutenant O'Brian broke the silence.

"So, did Mr. Whitelaw have anything else to say Mr. Ross?" The three started their walk toward the elevators. When they reached the central hallway and turned, Liam expected to see the redhead waiting for the elevation, however she was nowhere to be seen. Liam then returned his attention back to Lieutenant O'Brian's question.

"That Rex wanted to be cremated and his ashes scattered around a lake up in the Adirondacks. We also spoke about having a small memorial service at the Philatelic Expo, most likely in two days. The stamp dealers were really Rex's family since his wife died."

The men reached the elevator bank, Liam pushed the down button for the officers and he pushed the up button for himself.

"That's all Mr. Ross? Nothing else?" Conner chimed in.

"Also that he was the executor and that Rex had a living trust in place so there will be no probate issues."

The familiar two dings of the elevator signaling that the car was going down chimed. The door opened and the two policemen stepped inside and turned to face Liam in the hallway.

"He did mention one other little thing" Liam spoke as the door to the elevator started to close.

"And what was that Mr. Ross?" asked O'Brian. The door was now three- quarters of the way closed.

"Nothing much, just that I am Rex's sole beneficiary. I get everything."

The door shut tight and started its journey down to the lobby. The elevator to the right of the one the officers boarded, chimed once and the doors opened. Liam jumped on quickly and hit the button for the twentieth floor and then quickly hit the close door button. Liam knew that it was an adolescent move but he didn't want to get into that discussion with the police at this time.

The elevator car arrived at the twentieth floor in three seconds. Liam quickly exited the elevator and almost broke into a sprint to his suite. Once there he retrieved the fax that Ken had sent, grabbed his wallet with his ID and headed straight back out to the elevators. Liam hit the down button and once again waited no more than sixty seconds for the car to arrive. When it did arrive it was empty. He had half expected to see Lieutenant O'Brian and Detective Conner standing there with handcuffs out, waiting to haul his ass off to the precinct for that bonehead move. Well he would most likely run into them waiting in the lobby.

The car arrived at the lobby and Liam was surprised again, no cops. Instead of searching for a pre-seeable trip to One Police Plaza, Liam headed right to the VIP Services office. When he got there he was relieved to see Jane Reese sitting behind her desk. As Liam entered, Miss Reese stood up to greet him.

"Mr. Ross, so nice to see you this morning. I have the information that you left with the front desk earlier. I was just in the process of setting the additional rooms up for you."

Jane Reese had become a fixture for Liam here at the Waldorf, almost a personal assistant. But in the ten years that they had known each other, Liam could yet get her to call him by his given name, not that Liam hadn't tried everything to get her to call him by his first name. She was a professional, and would stay a professional to the end. Liam had to admire that. She was however a bit of an enigma. Whenever Liam saw Miss Reese she was always dressed in the hotel corporate attire, same charcoal grey suit with light cream pin strip, but with a skirt instead of pants. Also instead of a tie, Jane always wore a silk scarf in the hotels colors.

Jane did however have one personal fancy, one private indulgence that not many people knew about. She always wore the most up to style eyewear. Every time that Liam saw her she had to have been wearing a different pair, he couldn't remember seeing her wear the same pair twice, she must have hundreds. This morning she was wearing what appeared to be a genuine pair of Prada oval glasses in muted red. The famed six squares and Prada logo prominently displayed on the temples. They made her eyes look mysterious and quite lovely.

"Good Morning Jane, how are you today?"

"Fine, thank you Mr. Ross."

"Jane I need some help with another matter. Would it be possible to speak with George?"

"Mr. Boldt? I am sure he would love to see you Mr. Ross. Let me go and get him for you." Jane Reese left her office through the rear office exit and returned in less than three minutes.

"Mr. Boldt is on his way. He will be here momentarily."

"Thank you Jane, I greatly appreciate it."

"I have the other three rooms all set up for you. Do I need to make any pick up arrangements at the airport?" she asked.

"That won't be necessary Jane. Two of them are flying in, but I don't know their flight information. Mr. Gale will be driving up straight from Florida and he should be here first thing tomorrow morning. Could you see that his room will be ready when he arrives? He will also need parking for a small truck, perhaps a twenty-four foot bobtail."

"I will let the garage know. Everything will be taken car of."

The rear exit doors that Jane had left through earlier opened and a well-dressed man in his late fifties entered into the office. George Boldt had been with the Waldorf forever - literally. It was actually a running joke in most major hotel circles. George Boldt was the great-great-great grandson of the first George Boldt, a self-made millionaire, who influenced the development of the urban hotel as a civic social center and luxurious destination. He was the first General Manager of the original Waldorf=Astoria and the sole owner of the acclaimed Bellevue-Strafford Hotel in Philadelphia. His most remembered achievement was perhaps one that went unfinished.

In 1900, on Heart Island, a privately owned island in the middle of the St. Lawrence River, George Boldt started construction on what was at the time the largest construction project in upstate New York, Boldt Castle. Boldt started building the tribute to his wife Louise, and both expected the castle to become a major international landmark in the region. **Equally distinctive is a huge yacht house built on a neighboring island where the Boldt's had another summer home and a vast estate, incorporating farms, canals, a golf course, tennis courts, stables, and a polo field, where they stayed during construction. However all work ceased on the castle in 1904 when Louise died abruptly.** Today the castle is open as a tourist attraction and is located just outside Alexandria Bay, New York.

"Liam, so great to see you!" The hotelier gave Liam a firm handshake and a quick man hug "I am sorry that I haven't had a chance before now. Is everything okay?"

"Actually it's pretty crappy George. Do you remember my friend Rex Cooper?"

"Of course I do. He set me on some wonderful stamps as investments a few years ago. I understand that he is with us now. Correct?" he quickly looked at Jane and she nodded her response.

"Well actually George, Rex is dead. He was murdered last night down in Little Italy."

There was an audible gasp from Jane as her hand shot to cover her mouth in shock. George Boldt's complexion turned ashen, he steadied himself until he could sit in the nearby client chair.

"Liam, I am so sorry. What can I do to help?"

Liam held out the fax that he had received from Ken Whitelaw.

"Here is a copy of the Power of Attorney". I am going to close up his room and accounts here at the hotel. I will move everything over to my room. If you have any questions, please contact Mr. Whitelaw. His number is there on the fax."

"No hurry Liam. I will have all charges stopped as of last night. Take your time packing up his room. Weren't you and he here for the Stamp Expo? What about his display and inventory?"

"That's a great question George. Jane, is there anyway that I could rent one of the meeting rooms and hire some round the clock security?"

"It will be taken care of within the hour Mr. Ross." Jane moved back to the rear of her desk and started right in on her computer.

"Liam, I know that Mr. Cooper also had a safety deposit box here at the hotel."

"He always did George. He would transport the rarities back and forth everyday. He didn't fully trust event security. Can you continue to hold the box until I am ready to check out? I am the only person allowed into that box."

"Consider it done." The man stood having regained his balance. "Just let me know if there is anything else Liam. Call me anytime, day or night."

"Thank you George." The two men shook and Liam started out the door but stopped just before exiting and turn back.

"Jane?"

"Yes sir?"

"I love the new glasses." He turned and left the office not seeing her face turn the identical shade of red as her glasses.

15

Bruised Egos

Lieutenant O'Brian and Detective Conner arrived in the lobby of the hotel and debated whether to return upstairs and confront Liam Ross.

"I still think that you should have let me arrest that son of a bitch for attacking a police officer."

"John you know damn well that you lost your temper back there. It would have only ended up bad for you and the investigation would go no where" O'Brian assured the younger officer.

"He's dirty, I know he is."

"He may be that indeed, but we need to get more information before we make a move."

"What about the asshole's news about being the sole benefactor? That has to bring us somewhere."

"I want to get down the Tombs and see if CSI has dug anything up on the shooting. You need to go back to the office and start digging into Mr. Liam Ross's background."

16

Tea For Two

Liam was about to enter the elevator lobby when he realized that he was hungry, very hungry. The events of the day may have jumbled his mind with partial facts and information but he always worked on his stomach and his stomach was telling him it was time to eat something. He decided not to head out as he had left his wallet and cash back in the room. He had three choices in the hotel this time of day, Oscar's, the Bull & Bear and Peacock Alley. Oscar's was great for breakfast; the Bull & Bear was a bit stuffy for a mid afternoon bite, so he decided on Peacock Alley.

As with the rest of the hotel, Peacock Alley has a rich and treasured history. On opening night of the original Waldorf=Astoria in 1893, Oscar Tschiry, the maître d'hôtel, stood in the background as New York's society flocked to the hotel to see all its finery. As the matrons of society paraded with their lavish gowns and millenary Oscar was to have overheard Mr. Robert Baker, the society editor of the New York Herald,

"Look at them strutting and preening along that corridor, they look just like peacocks. If I may say so that's not a bad name for that corridor. Mind if I call it that in the paper tomorrow?"

"Sounds like a good name to me." Oscar told the reporter. The hotel manager George Boldt came by just then and Oscar repeated it to him. He apparently mouthed the words over and over again while stroking his beard, and then uttered, "It fits!" And so Peacock Alley got its name. From that night it became known throughout the country as the Main Street of Fashion. Some thought it an actual street, and mail has often been addressed to it even today.

Years later when Oscar Tschiry was interviewed in an article for the opening of the new Waldorf=Astoria, where the rebuilt Peacock Alley was to be a main feature, he was quoted as saying, "The Peacock Alley was no part of the original hotels plan. Mr. Hardenbergh, the hotel's architect, did not design it with any such idea in mind. To us," "states Oscar, "it was just a corridor in the hotel. Why ladies decided to congregate there that night, nobody knows. But they couldn't have selected a more fitting background, a more elegant rendezvous."

Liam walked to the hostess stand at the front of Peacock Alley where an older woman, whom Liam had noticed on many of his previous visits and who had been with the hotel since the sixties, greeted him.

"Good Afternoon Sir, welcome to Peacock Alley. May I help you?" Her greeting was very upbeat and cheerful.

"Yes, table for one please?"

"Yes sir" as she picked up the small daily menu "please follow me."

She wound her way through the densely placed tables, with Liam close behind, weaving their way through the nearly full establishment with its scores of matrons from New York society. Even today, this was where you were meant to see and be seen. High tea at the Alley had become a coveted invitation and only available to those in the "Know" or so it seemed. Just as they were about to reach the rear most table of the restaurant Liam heard a voice from his left.

"Why hello neighbor. Fancy seeing you at tea."

Liam turned and there was the ravishing redhead from earlier. He tried to return with a pithy comeback but all that came was "I beg your pardon?"

"I find it quite unusual for a man, especially one that is so young and alone, to be at High Tea."

This time Liam was prepared.

"Well I find some of the old customs most relaxing, Mrs...?"

"Hodge, Miss..., Rebecca Hodge, Mr.?"

"Liam Ross." Ever the gentlemen Liam offered his right hand in greeting. Miss Hodge shook it not as a businessperson would shake hands, but with a delicate placing of her hand into his.

"It's a pleasure to meet for the first time, again. Would you like to join me instead of sitting alone?"

"It would be a pleasure. Are you sure I won't be an intrusion?"

"No, not at all. It will be nice to have a conversation with someone my own age for a change."

Liam called the hostess over and explained that he would be sitting with Miss Hodge. Within seconds a busboy came to the table bringing with him a utensil setup, a water goblet and a teacup.

"So Miss Hodge, what brings you to New York?" asked Liam as he settled into the table.

"I am here visiting my aunt. We meet at least once a year here in Manhattan for some shopping, and we always come to the Waldorf for tea. Unfortunately, she became ill and was not able to join me this year. So I decided not to waste the trip and came by myself. How about you Mr. Ross, what brings you to New York?"

Liam always liked to introduce himself with the true term for stamp collecting. Nine out of ten times it received raised eyebrows, particularly if the individual was not listening intently.

"I'm a philatelist. I am in the city for an expo at the Javits Center."

"A stamp collector? Really?"

Impressive thought Liam, smart as well as beautiful.

"More of a stamp finder. I locate stamps for a handful of clients. I find elusive issues for their collections."

"Fascinating. Can that be a lucrative business?"

Normally, Liam's radar would have started screaming loud and clear when a person asked this type of question. A seemingly innocuous question could be the beginning of an attempted robbery. However, call it the strain of the past evenings events, or more than likely the beauty of the woman seated before him, Liam answered her question with no concern.

"It can be if one is cautious. Believe it or not there is more forgery in the stamp business than in all other collectable markets combined. That even includes fine art works from all the great artists."

Before Rebecca had a chance to respond a waitress approached the table and asked for their order. They ordered the high tea opting for more savory items than sweet. As for their tea choice, it was a bit more complex. Tea was grown and cultivated in over one hundred countries. There are at least six main varieties of tea, white, green, black, yellow, oolong and pu-erh. Each one of these had a multitude of subsets that numbered into the hundreds.

Liam held the rather extensive list before him and tried to make a decision. It could be a more daunting process than that of choosing the right wine for a dinner party.

"What type of tea are you in the mood for Mr. Ross."

"Please, call me Liam. I am having a rather difficult time in choosing it would seem, Miss Hodge."

"Please Liam, call me Rebecca. It seems that I am having the same indecision. Shall we leave it up to the Tea Steward?"

"Excellent idea. Miss could you please have the Tea Steward make the choice for us?"

"Yes sir." Was all the waitress offered as she left the table.

"So Miss, er… Rebecca, what is it that you do? That is when you are not having tea at the Waldorf=Astoria?"

"Oh, I have one of those, boring, common, garden variety type jobs. I am just a claims adjustor for Eastern Mutual Insurance."

Liam heard the response but he was still mesmerized by her beauty. He was having a very hard time focusing. His body was starting to tell him that he needed some sleep.

"Oh I am sure that you lead a very exciting life in the claims adjustment world."

"Have you ever watched paint dry before Liam?"

"No, I can't say that I have."

"That's how glamorous my job is. If it wasn't for New York being a short train ride away, I just might go crazy."

"Do I take that that you are based in Connecticut?"

"Hartford to be exact, you know your insurance sir, I'm impressed."

Their conversation continued with the small, getting to know you conversation until their tea arrived, where they were from, how many siblings they each had, all the information that two people share when there appears to me a mutual attraction.

While deep into this banter their tea arrived with a grand flourish. The selections that they had ordered were a beautiful sight to behold. Small cucumber sandwiches, chicken salad with almonds, rosemary scones and of course clotted cream. They did order one sweet as a finish, the classic delicate cookie Madeleine's. The two ate and talked for the next hour with each person revealing small tidbits of their pasts and present, favorite movies, classic restaurants, vacations they have had and vacations that they dream about. They were about to order another pot of tea when Liam stifled a yawn.

"I am so sorry. I had a rather late night last evening and I haven't really caught up on my sleep. Would you mind terribly if I called it an afternoon?"

"Oh Liam, I am so sorry for monopolizing your time. If I had

known we could have done this another time."

Liam waved to the waitress for the check.

"I've had a lovely time Liam."

"And I as well Rebecca. Might I hope to see you again while you

are here?"

The check came and Liam signed it to his suite.

"I do have quite a bit free time this trip seeing where as my aunt will not be making it. Would it be to forward of me to invite you to dinner this evening?"

"Not at all. It would have to be a bit later if that is not a problem."

The two got up from the table and started to walk to the exit of Peacock Alley.

"I love to dine continental style!" she exclaimed.

"How late would you like to make it?"

"How about nine? Is that too late for you?"

"Not at all. How should I dress?"

"You could wear a cardboard box and still be the best dressed

woman in the room."

Liam remarked as the pair reached the elevator lobby.

"I think that I can do better than a box."

Rebecca remarked with a sultry wink. Liam saw this as he pressed the up call button.

"How about cocktail dressy, but not formal?"

The elevator announced its arrival with the customary one bell. They entered the elevator after letting a couple of businessmen exit the car.

"Sounds perfect Liam."

Liam reached forward and pressed the buttons for both the eighteenth and twentieth floors.

"The twentieth floor, I thought we were neighbors?"

Did Liam detect a bit of disappointment in Rebecca's voice?

"No, I am on twenty. My friend is, or rather was, across the hall from you. Should I call for you at your room, or should we meet in the lobby later?"

"Let's meet in the lobby, if you don't mind."

The car arrived at Rebecca's floor. Liam held the door open for her as she exited the elevator. Liam stepped into the open door as to say goodbye to her, as well as to hold the door open. He was not going to walk her to her room. He felt that it might be a bit strange after having just met her.

"Well then Rebecca, till tonight?"

Liam extended his hand and as before Rebecca placed her hand softly in Liam's. She then placed her left hand over his. Covering his hand from both sides.

"Till tonight."

She leaned forward and gave Liam a quick small kiss, first on his right cheek, then on his left, very European. When she was finished she let go of his hand, winked once again, turned, and walked down the central corridor towards her room. Liam realized that he had been holding his breath since she kissed his cheeks. He exhaled loudly and spoke to nobody there.

"Unbelievable."

Liam stepped back out of the elevator door; let the doors close and continued up to his room in order to get some much-needed sleep.

Back in the hotel lobby, a watcher had viewed the entire meal with the redhead and the stamp dealer, while expertly not reading a copy of today's Financial Times. One beauty of Peacock Alley was that it was open to the rest of lobby; its bounds marked with small potted Fichus trees, making it an ideal surveillance location. The viewer watched as the two finished their meal and made their way to the elevators. Where they waited until the elevator door opened, and after allowing two men dressed in business suits exit, entered the car to go up to the private rooms of the hotel. When the door closed the watcher noted the time by way of a wrist watch, folded the pink sheets of the cover newspaper, got up out of the one of many large high backed chairs that dotted the hotel's lobby, and walked towards the Lexington Avenue exit of the hotel, where once outside, hailed a cab.

17

Reunion

The pounding of the drums was unbearable. The darkness that surrounded Liam was inky black and near suffocating. Where was he and why did it feel as if he were floating? The drums increased in volume and intensity then in an instant, stopped. Where the hell was he? It wasn't until a crash, the decibel like that of a car careening into a brick wall, that Liam sat bolt upright. He was in a pitch-black room and sitting in what he only assumed was a bed. The drumming, that Liam still could not explain, started again, but this time closer as if someone was pounding on a door. As Liam rubbed his eyes trying to clear the cobwebs in his mind, he realized that he had been deep in REM sleep. Before he even had a chance to call out to the unseen cacophony, the pounding stopped and with another tremendous crash the bedroom door burst open flooding the dark space with the brilliant light emanating from the living room of the hotel suite.

"Stay right where you are!" came the shouted words.
Liam instinctively rolled off of the bed furthest away from the intruder and into a crouch. He had still not completely focused his eyes and was not going to take any chances with any sudden movements before he was able to identify the intruder. All Liam was able to focus on was the silhouetted shape of a very large person standing in the doorway to his bedroom. An unseen hand reached to the light switch that was just inside of the doorframe.

Seconds later the room was filled with harsh light from a dozen wall sconces inside the suite.

Standing before Liam was a large man, a very large man. He was dressed in a navy blue blazer, tan pants, and sporting a very short military haircut. In the classic two handed shooters grip, dwarfed between two hands the size of small boulders, was what appeared to be a Sig Sauer P229 Equinox, a .40 caliber automatic, favored by most of the United States' governmental agencies. Liam's mind automatically registered the threat and silently cursed at him self for not having a weapon close at hand. Assessing the situation, Liam felt that the only option that lay before him was one of playing at being incredulous.

"Who the hell are you and what right do you have just barging in here? Identify yourself this instant!"

"Mr. Ross, We were asked to check on your safety."

"Credentials, now!" barked Liam.

Holstering his weapon the large man went to remove his identification from his left hip pocket. All the while Liam was scanning the room for some sort of weapon. The big hand slowly held up what appeared to be an ID card and a badge. Liam slowly rose from the crouched position beside the king-size four-poster bed.

"Okay, toss them to me."

The security guard tossed the shield wallet towards Liam. Liam caught the small leather case and opened revealing both a printed identification card and a badge of a known covert security firm. The ID stated that the big man was one Reginald Dwight of 214-85 East 39th Ave., Long Island City, New York. Liam looked at the man with skepticism.

"Reginald Dwight? Really? Reg Dwight, as in, Elton John? You must be kidding." Liam tossed the wallet back to the big man, whose face was still stone set, expressing no facial expression.

"Yeah" shrugged the guard as he holstered his weapon. " Both my parents were big fans. Funny thing is I can play a pretty decent piano." He held up his fingers and moved them as if there were a phantom keyboard in front of him.

"Well Reg, who the hell told you that I was in trouble and to come bursting in here like it was Fallugah?"

"That would be me." Came the small voice from somewhere behind the big man that was still standing in the doorway. Slowly, making her way around the behemoth and into the room was the lithe figure of Liz Gallagher.

"What? Not happy to see me?"

Indicating with the tilt of her head towards Liam's groin. It was at that point that Liam realized that he had taken his nap naked. Now aware that both Liz and the security guard were staring at his rather flaccid manhood, Liam quickly grabbed a pillow that was hanging half off the bed and shielded his exposed body.

"What the hell Liz! You could have just knocked!"

"I did Boss, for over fifteen minutes. It was at that point I became just a tad concerned and talked to the office."

"But telling them to storm the damn beach? What the hell for?

"Liam, correct me if I am wrong but didn't you tell me…"

Liam cut her off in mid sentence as he moved towards the closet in order to secure a robe.

"Mr. Dwight, as you can see, I am all right. I don't think that we will be needing your assistance anymore today."

Liam stepped into the large walk in closet and retrieved one of the hotels luxuriously thick robes. Stepping back out of the closet he crossed to where the security man was still firmly planted after entering the room. Shaking the man's hand, Liam once again assured him that everything was indeed all right.

"You do understand Mr. Ross that I will still have to file a report?"

"Understood Reg. I will inform the office of the incident and the hotel that I will take care of the damage to the doors." Ushering the man to the front door of the suite where Liam noticed that there was no damage. Opening the door and looking towards the big man, Liam must have had an odd look on his face, almost as if saying, what the…?

Grinning and holding up a small plastic card was another man dressed identically as Reginald Dwight but perhaps he had four more inches of height on the first behemoth and six more inches across his chest, the guard responded in tune.

"Master key. No need to break down a door anymore." The two smirking men left the suite and headed down the hallway where they walked side-by-side filling the entire width of the corridor. Liam closed the door after the guards had exited and turned to find Liz standing there with her arms folded across her chest, tapping her foot on the marble floor of the foyer. She looked amazing, pissed as hell, but amazing just the same.

Liam hadn't seen Liz, whom he affectionately called his right hand, for almost two years. Liz had always been athletic and never let her body turn to mush. But it was sometimes difficult at best to gauge what lay beneath her sophomoric clothes when she ran the effects shop for Liam. Liz was prone to wearing sweatshirts of various educational institutions that were always three sizes to big for her and Levi 501 blue jeans that most people swore she slept in. But standing before him was a different Liz Gallagher. Her once long brunette hair was now a stunning blonde with highlights and tones, cut in a very stylish, trendy short style. She was wearing a smartly cut charcoal gray business suit and medium high black pumps. Around her neck was an elegant choker of perfect Mikimoto Minuette pearls that highlighted her absolutely flawless complexion. Liz Gallagher could very easily be mistaken for Charlize Theron.

"Liz, what the hell were you thinking?" still staring at the sight before him, "Wow, you look amazing."

"First things first, you said follow protocols, so I did. After pounding on your door for 15 minutes, and knowing full well that you were in your room, and getting absolutely no answer, I felt it was time to call in the marines."

Pausing to take a quick gulp of a breath,

"Secondly, thank you." Then, while turning slowly so that Liam could see her, "So you like?"

"Woof! What has happened to my quiet, shy little girl?"

Liam's response would have been taken out of context by any other person perhaps eliciting a slap across the face, but not by Liz. She knew that because they were both professionals, there would never be anything other than banter between them. God knows when Liz first met Liam she had tried to jump him, but in the end the two felt that it was best that they remain objective and because of that decision, the two became the best of friends. At times throwing banters and barbs at each other; like brother and sister.

202

"Okay, so you alerted the marines. How much time to I have before I need to contact Uncle Robert?"

Looking at her watch "Oh, about thirty seconds." But before her words even trailed off, Liam's cell phone started to ring out in the living room. Liam crossed the plush carpet and picked up the ringing iPhone.

Long before Apple computer introduced their person-to-person videophone capabilities, the CSS tech geeks developed their own, 8.2 gigabyte encrypted video conferencing for smart phones. The technology could only be used in approved device to approved device, thus matching the software protocols with internal encrypted smart chips that would change encryption codes every half-second. Liam pressed the answer key on the touch screen. Immediately Uncle Bob's face filled the 4.5-inch diagonal LCD screen.

"Nephew, so nice to se you in one piece."

"Morning Robert, sorry about jumping the gun."

"Not a problem here. Just a bit strange to have someone call the OUD line with rather outdated codes, four and a half year old codes to be exact."

OUD – Operative Under Duress was a special coded communications line that any operative of the CSS called in order to receive backup in case of an unexplained emergency, in this case, Liam not answering the knock on his hotel room door quickly enough.

"Sorry about that Uncle Bob" came Liz's voice as she walked closer to Liam in order for Robert to see her in the frame of the smart device.

"The boss here specifically said to use the old protocols if anything felt wrong or off, so I did." Liz was the only person that Liam knew that could call his uncle, Uncle Bob, who was now the Director of Operations-CSS.

"Good God Liz! Is that you?" Uncle Robert's eyes widened as he was seeing Liz for the first time since almost five years earlier. "I don't even recognize you! You look ravishing Lizzy."

"Thanks Uncle Bob, it was time for a change."

Liam interrupted the two.

"Rob, have you heard what's going on up here?"

"Nothing more than the morning intel report on suspected suspicious activities. You have time to read me in?"

Liam and Liz spent the next fifteen minutes bringing Liam's mentor up to speed. If it had taken anymore time Uncle Robert would have cut them off and expressed his displeasure with them not getting to the point quick enough.

"Do you need any help from me Liam?" asked Uncle Robert.

"I don't think so, not at this time. I really don't know what we are up against yet. Kyle and John will both be here by morning and we will be able to get our toes a bit wetter. I will keep you apprised if we find anything out of the ordinary."

"Okay nephew. In the mean time I am going to have tech services send up some updated phones for Liz, Kyle and John. I assume that yours is still up to date with the latest software?"

Even after leaving the CSS, Liam had been expected to maintain contact by checking in every two weeks at first, but then monthly as time went on. In order to do this he had to have the latest communications equipment, most times equipment that was generations ahead of what most consumers knew existed, even though they looked identical to the current models. A decades old agreement with one of Apple's founders, allowed the CSS specially modified equipment for their sole use. However once equipment arrived from Apple's CEO, modifications that even the tech guru would foam at the mouth about, were installed.

"Thanks Robert. I'll see that Kyle logs them in when he gets here."

"Also nephew, I think that you should place paper with the NYPD, quietly of course, for the four of you to have carry permits. I don't think that we should be taking the events too lightly."

"I'll jump right on that Uncle Bob. I have my gear coming in from the airport now. Cost a bloody fortune to check it from LAX. Gate agent gave me a rash of shit saying that it was over way over the accepted weight limit" then sarcastically " don't really know what they mean, it was only 1500 pounds of computer and imaging equipment!"

Robert let out a rare laugh as he saw the pixie expression on Liz's face.

"Just make that three sets of permits Liz. I already have a CCP (Concealed Carry Permit) for New York City, part of being an upstanding philatelic dealer. I am however, going to start to carry, instead of keeping it in the safe."

"As I think you all should." Chimed in the mentor from the small LCD screen. "Check in with me by the end of the day tomorrow to let me know if this needs to become official."

"Will do, talk later." And with that Liam closed the connection.

"Do you want the Glock, Boss? I can call Kyle and if he hasn't left yet, he can bring it from the shop with him." Liz asked.

"I'm going stay light for the time being, I'll use my Storm." Quipped Liam, "It's down stairs in the safety deposit box."

He crossed the living room dropping the iPhone on the desk as he went by.

"I'm going to get dressed. Be out in a few" He disappeared into the bedroom in order to make himself more presentable.

Liam's primary choice of weapon had always been his intellect, however sometimes situations called for him to be a bit fuller prepared. When these few rare instances occurred Liam preferred to carry the PX4 Storm sub compact automatic from Fabbrica d'Armi Pietro Beretta, the centuries old Italian firearms manufacturer founded in 1526 in Bresica, Italy. This small weapon allowed for Liam to discreetly conceal it either by a shoulder holster, or in a holster, specially made to fit in the small of his back. Although small, this pistol used universally found, full load, 9MM rounds, allowing seventeen rounds in the magazine and one in the chamber. This gun had saved Liam on a number of occasions and he knew that if he needed to use it would serve him well.

As Liam was changing, Liz followed him into the master suite and sat in one of the over stuffed armchairs next to the un-made king sized bed and called to him through the open door to the dressing room.

"Liam, just what is going on? I haven't been able to find any new information, except a few small news item in the local papers."

"Well Liz, from the outside it doesn't appear to be anything more than an attempted robbery. Joe Bousquet's death was ruled a hit an run so that is not going to go anywhere else."

"So why are we here?' was her response

Liam's response was anything than definitive.

"Good question Liz. I just can't put my finger on it, I just have one of those feelings."

"Ouch! When you get those feelings insurance companies get nervous!"

Liam emerged from the dressing room. He had changed into a pair of charcoal grey, almost black, worsted wool summer weight slacks. His dress shirt was a Brooks Brothers button down, pinpoint oxford in a muted grey. His tie was one of his favorites, a multi-colored Jerry Garcia. Liam went to the other armchair across form Liz and sat down, pulling on his shoes.

"I've set up room reservations for you and the guys. Go downstairs to the VIP Check In and ask for Jane Reese, she will take care of you. I also asked her to set up a conference room so we could bring Rex's show exhibit back from the Expo. Can you check on that status?"

"How about dinner reservations for tonight? John should be here in plenty of time. We won't see Kyle until tomorrow, late morning at best. I guess you don't feel like Italian, so how about Thai? Greek? Or just some good old comfort food at the Palm?"

Liam stood up and went to the dresser and retrieved his wallet, money clip and watch. He was never one to be flashy when it came to men's jewelry, more of a laid back realist, but he did however splurge on one item. When he was a boy Liam discovered the novels of Clive Cussler. Cussler's main hero was Dirk Pitt, a modern, devil may care adventurer working for NUMA, the National Underwater Marine Agency. Pitt favored a dive watch from his years in the navy, a time worn Doxa dive watch. Liam spent hours reading these novels, escaping into the world of NUMA, and it wasn't long before he became hooked. As soon as he was able to afford one, he bought a Doxa Sub 1000Ti Professional sporting the classic orange watch face. Instead of the stainless steel band, Liam opted for a divers band of neoprene and Velcro. It was this watch that he fastened onto his left wrist.

"The Palm sounds good. Make a reservation for two…"

Before Liam had a chance to finish his sentence there was a light knock on the door of the suite. Liam continued on to Liz as he went to answer the door.

"We should see Kyle by four AM. I just received a text from him stating that he was able to get out of Orlando about six hours early and you know how he drives like a maniac. He will be dead tired and cranky when he gets here so make sure that his room is waiting for him." Liam reached for the knob of the front door without looking into the peephole to see who it might be.

"As for John, he has, …" Liam jerked opened the door to reveal John Andrews standing in the hallway. "… been here since this afternoon." Slapping the actor on the back. "He was in lobby when I had tea this afternoon."

John just stood there with a blank stare on his face, positive that his former boss had not seen him earlier, clenched fist held up, as he was about to knock on the door once more.

"Then I'll make the reservation for three!" Liz spouted as he saw John and ran to hug him. Liam however pulled on a medium weight raw silk sport jacket that complemented his ensemble.

"No just two." Proclaiming. "I … have a date."

Liam then left the suite with John still standing on the doorstep, and Liz sporting a blank stare with her jaw agape. Liam was easily twenty yards down the richly decorated hallway when John was able to finally speak.

"How does he do that?"

18

Drinks, Dinner & Dessert

Liam was waiting in the hotel's grand lobby, perusing his emails that he had received earlier that day, when he looked up and saw her walking towards him. Liam stood up from the chair and watched in rapt fascination as she moved closer from the elevators. Liam knew that she was beautiful, but his brain could never have had prepared his eyes for what was walking towards him at that moment in time.

Her models' figure was now sheathed in lustrous black silk satin. The dress had the finest of spaghetti straps that traversed from her sweetheart bodice, over her bare shoulders, and ended in an intricate lace-up back. The length of the dress fell to just above her knees and scalloped about six inches lower in the rear. When she walked a slit was revealed that showed even more of her sculpted legs, which appeared to be encased in the finest silk stockings. Her shoes were another pair of Christian Louboutins'. However instead of her delicate pumps from earlier she wore the famous designers Lady Bow, open toe sling backs with an almost five inch stiletto heel.

Her red silken hair was now coiffed in a 1940's style that revealed a long, slender delicate neck. A distinct impression rose from her perfect delicotage and ended at the base of her throat, which was perfectly accentuated by the slightest protuberance of her clavicles. Between these salience's she wore a necklace of what could only be described as liquid silver. A rope of silver strands so fine that when her pulse beat, each thread shimmered as if were thousands of diamonds woven together as a precious thread. Her green eyes were now smoky gray and showcased expertly applied shadows and liners. On her lips was a shade of red that Liam could only compare to a fine pinot noir.

As she glided across the lobby many a head turned, both men and women alike. People not only stopped to envelop themselves in her aura as she passed, gazing upon her shear beauty, but also to see whom this Venus, this modern day goddess, was going to meet.

As she neared Liam, he sensed that all eyes were fixed upon him. She floated to a stop, leaned in and kissed him once on his left check, then once on his right. As she was leaning back she stopped and saw a shimmer in the eyes of the man standing before her. She saw him swallow as if his entire mouth and throat had closed tight from being trapped for months in a desert. She leaned forward once again, only this time she kissed Liam full on the lips. The warmth of her lips pierced through Liam as if it were twenty below zero in the lobby. They broke their kiss and looked at each other.

"Well, good evening, Miss."

"And a good evening to you Sir. I hope that I am dressed properly for the occasion?" She held both of Liam's hands up as she stepped back to show off her dress.

"Rebecca, words alone cannot even begin to describe the beauty that radiates from you. You look stunning!"

"Well thank you sir. Might I say that you are dressed impeccably as well?"

Liam watched as she literally eyed him from head to toe and when finished returned her eyes to his.

"So what do you have in store for this simple insurance girl from Hartford this evening?"

She was anything but simple, Liam thought to himself.

"A mini adventure, but only if you feel up to it. I thought we would start with a glass of bubbles, then move onto to dinner."

"Ready, willing, and starving, if I may say so."

The pair crossed through the main lobby, past the elevators and into the hotel's Park Avenue lobby. Here they crossed over the intricate detail of Louis Rigal's "Wheel of Life" mosaic and down the stairs to the front entrance of the hotel. The doorman hailed a cab, and within minutes the two were headed to their first destination of the evening.

"Where to?" asked the cabbie.

"15 Vanderbilt Avenue, south end of the block if you could." Responded Liam.

"I've never heard of Vanderbilt Avenue. Where is it located?"

"It's not too far, we should be there in a few minutes."

With the finish of his response the cabbie pulled to the corner of Vanderbilt Avenue and East 42nd Street.

"Grand Central Station? Are we going somewhere?"

Liam did not answer as he helped her from the rear of the cab and then paid the driver.

"This way my lady." Liam extended his arm in order for Rebecca to take a hold of it. They passed down Vanderbilt Avenue about ten yards and went into the old cabstand entrance for the grand old terminal. They entered a nondescript door and found themselves in a well-appointed foyer with a rather steep set of marble stairs leading to a second floor.

The pair climbed the stairs with ease and stopped at a hostess stand just outside a large brass and mahogany door. The dower-faced hostess was attired in the typical Manhattan uniform of all black. Black skirt, black shirt, black stockings and black shoes. Liam wondered what would happen to any of these fashion plates if one day black were finally decreed passé. Perhaps if they had to wear a color they might actually have to smile for a change. Liam snickered to himself.

"Do you have a reservation?" asked the twenty something.

"I was under the impression that the Campbell Apartment did not accept reservations. Has this changed?" asked Liam.

"As you can see sir we are terribly full, it will be at least a two hour wait." the uninterested hostess said not to Liam or Rebecca, but into the air as she was moving to great someone that appeared to be more important.

Liam scanned the room and noticed at least a dozen unoccupied tables.

"Not off to a good start am I?" Liam remarked to Rebecca. "Give me a minute, please?"

Liam left Rebecca standing near the hostess stand. He walked toward the hostess that was allowing some rap music star of minor importance that Liam did not recognize, into the club.

"Miss, I hate to bother you, ..." Liam was cut off by the curtness of the hostess.

"I told you sir, it is going to be at least two hours before I can seat you. I suggest you try the Marriot Hotel Bar down the street."

No it was Liam's turn to stop the impolite little gen-xer in her tracks. Gently he placed his hand on her shoulder and whispered.

"Miss, stop right where you are." Liam said firmly. "My name is Liam Ross, and if you check with your manager Mr. Rogers, you will see that I do not need a reservation nor do I need to go and find the hotel bar down the street. If you want to continue your employment here, I suggest that you call him immediately.

The hostess's face lost all color.

"Do you know Mr. Rogers?" was all she could croak.

"Dearly." Was all that Liam responded.

Reluctantly, she picked up the intercom and pushed a button that would soon ring at the desk of Mr. Philip Rogers. When the other end answered, she cupped the mouthpiece of the handset and turned her back away from Liam and Rebecca so that she might converse in somewhat private.

After what was about a minute, all Liam could hear was a continual string of

"Yes, sir. Yes sir. It would be my pleasure sir. I am so sorry sir."

The girl turned back toward the pair, gently returned the phone to its cradle, picked up two drink menus and spoke to Liam.

"If you would follow me please, this way to our best table."

She led them through the three quarters empty lounge and brought them to a table that was placed directly in front of the largest fireplace that Rebecca had ever seen. The hostess placed the two menus on the table and muttered that someone would be there shortly to take their drink order.

"What did you say to her Liam?" asked Rebecca as she lowered herself into one of the most luxurious chairs that she had ever sat in.

Liam waited until Rebecca was seated and then he took the chair directly across from her.

"Oh, I just reminded her that, you could catch more flies with honey than you can with vinegar." Rebecca shot Liam a rather quizzical look.

"I may have also told her that I happen to know her boss and if she really enjoyed working here that she might want to check in with him. That's all."

"So, a man with connections. This night sounds like it could be a night to remember."

A waiter, attired in a perfectly cut staff suit of the New York Central Railroad of the 1930's, approached and asked if they knew what they might like to drink. Liam noticed that the man's nametag declared the waiter as George and responded with his given name.

"George, my name is Liam, Liam Ross and this is Miss Hodge."

"A pleasure to met you both."

"George, what we would like this evening is not on the menu, but if you check with Mr. Rogers, he will confirm that I have a locker here. That would be locker B-1. In that locker you will find a case of 1998 Veuve Clicquot Ponsardin Rose Reserve. Please bring us a bottle and two flutes, would you?"

"Yes sir! My pleasure!" and the waiter hurried away as if on a mission of national importance.

"So, happen to know her boss, eh?" Rebecca crossed her legs it the way that only a woman can do. Liam caught himself staring at her gorgeous limbs.

"Just a bit" Liam answered sheepishly as he held his thumb and forefinger together indicating a small measurement. "In all actuality, Philip Rogers is one of my clients. One of my oldest actually."

"So he is a stamp collector as well?"

"Oh, I am sorry if I gave you the impression that I was just a stamp dealer. I happen to deal in other collectables as well on a case-by-case basis. I handle acquisitions for private individuals as well as museums, businesses and the odd auction house. Philip has a rather unique hobby. However I would be transgressing a confidence by mentioning what the hobby is with out his permission. I hope you understand?"

"By all means, I can see that you are a man of integrity as well as taste, a rare asset in today's society. So tell me about this place." She asked as she looked around the room.

"I've been coming to Manhattan for years and I had no idea that this even existed! It's lovely!"

"The Campbell Apartment, as it is known, was actually an office for a man by the name of John Campbell. He leased this space from William K. Vanderbilt II, the grandson of Cornelius Vanderbilt, the founder of the New York Central Railroad. It was not as the name would assume, living quarters, but an office. Campbell was one of America's old time financiers. He also was on the board of directors of the railroad."

The bottle of champagne arrived and Liam took a break regaling his tale of the apartment. George made quite the flourish of opening the bottle, the tearing of the lead capsule, the wiping of the cork, the gentle removal of the cork from the bottle without the cork flying into inner-space. After all, nine out of ten times that just allows the wine in the bottle to build up pressure and send it raining all over the unexpected, plus it is a terrible waste of good champagne.

George poured a small amount in the flute closest to Liam. Liam tasted the wine and proclaimed it perfect. George then poured Rebecca a glass.

"I hope you like this. It's one of my favorites. It has a wonderful, delicate taste on the palette, perfect tiny bubbles, and best of all no headaches in the morning. You can drink bottles of this all night long and run a marathon the next morning."

"It's wonderful! I could get used to this very easily!"

"Mr. Ross?"

"Yes George."

A second waiter appeared at the table and set out a small silver tray with toast points and a covered terrine in the shape of a duck.

"Compliments of Mr. Rogers, Paté de fois gras."

The second waiter revealed the coveted delicacy by whisking away the upper half of the duck terrine. Inside was the delicate, velvety smooth liver pate that was once shunned in some circles. It was however making a come back into gastronomic circles after a process was developed without the need to force feed ducks in order to engorge their livers. This was just that type of paté, from a farm on the banks of the Hudson River, some 45 minutes north of Manhattan. Liam spread some of the liver on a toast point and held it so that Rebecca could try it. She gently, almost seductively, took the toast and sampled the fois gras. The look on her face was all the confirmation that Liam needed.

"So, how does that taste?"

Quickly shooting her hand to half cover her mouth as she chewed,

"Would I be too forward if I said that that is truly orgasmic?" She took a sip of the chilled rosé champagne, "Oh my God! It just went to multiple orgasmic! The flavor of the wine and the fois gras together is amazing!"

"Welcome to the world of gastronomy, Miss Hodge."

Liam offered a toast with the champagne. As the two touched glasses and they sipped their wine a large, very well tailored man in his mid-sixties, graying haircut with precession styling and wearing tortoise shell glasses, approached their table. Liam got up to receive the visitor.

"Liam! How nice to see you again!"

The large man embraced Liam with a bear hug of a greeting. It took almost a minute before Liam felt the circulation return to his extremities.

"Philip it's wonderful to see you. May I introduce to you Rebecca Hodge. Rebecca, Philip Rogers, Manager of The Campbell Apartment.

Rebecca held out her hand in order to greet Philip. Philip took her hand in a very continental way and kissed the back of her hand.

"Enchanté Mademoiselle. It is a pleasure to meet you."

"Philip, do you have time to sit?" asked Liam "Join us please."

"I have a few moments, besides how can I refuse one of my oldest friends."

"Mr. Rogers, thank you so much for the lovely fois gras. It is one of the most wonderful things that I have ever tasted!"

"My pleasure Miss Hodge, and please call me Philip."

"So Philip, Liam tells me that you are also a client of his."

"That I am. I to am one of those individuals that can lose all self control when it comes to one of my collections."

"What is it that you collect, if I may ask?"

"Ah, direct to the point, but first, has your companion told you of the history of The Campbell Apartment and the real reason that we met?"

"He started to, but he has been unable to finish."

"Well with Liam's permission, I will complete the tale."

A waiter appeared with another flute and filled the glass for Philip and then added to the others.

"So where did you stop your tome my friend?" asked the manager.

"We were very close to the beginning. I had just told Rebecca about Mr. Campbell and his being on the Board of Directors of the New York Central."

"Oh he started with the boring stuff, did he? Liam was always one to be a stickler for the obtuse. Let's get into the juice, shall we. After Mr. Campbell, John, arranged this lease, he became a very powerful person in the world of New York finances. Some would even say that he had his fingers into the power politics of the nation at that time. This room was his office, not a living quarters as some believe. Mr. Campbell used the word apartment in the same sense as the British do."

"Philip took a sip of the champagne.

"This magnificent room was once considered to be the largest floor space in all of Manhattan. Campbell commissioned a well-known architect, Augustus Allen, to turn this space into an opulent office, a space worthy of his wealth. Mr. Allen turned the room into what you see here, a recreation of a 13th century Florentine palace.

Philip Rogers directed their attention towards the ceiling some twenty-five feet overhead.

All of the details that you see are original, however most have been restored."

He then directed their gaze towards the oversized fireplace that they were seated by.

"The fireplace was never a working fireplace. Some say that John Campbell had a secret entrance, or more importantly secret exit, hidden amid its woodwork. To this day, no one has found any evidence to that fact. The safe however is original and Campbell had it installed so that anyone that came to this room would realize that they were in the presence of a very wealthy man. And people did come to this room, quite frequently. Campbell was quite the ladies man, and he always held lavish parties here in this office. He had a pipe organ installed, that we are in the process of restoring now. "

Rogers pointed towards the bar.

"Our bar is the original bar that he had hand crafted out of quatre-foil and mahogany. It matches the balcony just outside."

"It is beautiful, it is all just amazing." Remarked Rebecca.

"Campbell used this office until his death in the late 1950's. He had become just a former shell of his well off self, but a lease is a lease. Campbell's lease for The Apartment was in effect until his death at the grand sum of $100.00 per year."

"You must be joking!" exclaimed the redhead.

"When it comes to this place Rebecca, Philip never jokes." Interjected Liam.

"We have not a copy, but the original lease, framed and hanging in my office."

"What would a space like this lease for in today's market Philip."

"We have had offers of $3,000,000 for The Apartment."

"$3,000,000 a year is a nice bit of rent."

Liam now chimed back in.

"A month, Rebecca. $3,000,000 a month!"

Rebecca looked as if she were a deer caught in the headlights of an oncoming car.

"My god, that's twelve million dollars a year for just 3,500 square feet. That would make it some of the most expensive real estate in the country."

"More like in the world." Philip drained his champagne glass and Liam refilled them all.

"So after Mr. Campbell died, the property reverted over to the current owners, who to this day remain very secretive. All I know is that on my paycheck is a company called Central Eastern Transportation Underwriters Management, some sort of an insurance company."

Philip paused to take a drink from the freshly filled champagne flute.

"So, how did the two of you meet?" asked Rebecca.

"As part of a collection phobia, my dear" was the mangers response.

The look on Rebecca's face was registered as interest and a touch of confusion.

"May I finish the tale Philip?" as Liam asked, Philip nodded his head in assent.

"Our friend Philip here is known all through New York, if not the Eastern Seaboard, as being quite the historically accurate restorer. Every project the he touches has to be one hundred percent historically perfect. No reproductions, only the originals."

"I could see that in some instances that that could present a few challenges."

"Oh, if you only knew! The sleepless nights, the tracking things down blind alleys, and the hundreds if not thousands of individuals that are just out to rob or cheat you!"

The club manager's passion, as well as a small amount of anger from the past was visible in the eyes that were behind the tortoise shell glasses.

"One day I received a phone call from a friend of a friend. They told me that Philip here was in need of a special kind of detective, one that finds things instead of people. My friend knew that this was sort of an avocation of mine; so, I took Peter's information and contacted him."

Rebecca was hooked. She was leaning forward in her chair, rapt of the tale from the two men.

"What was it that you wanted Liam to find? Historical documents, gold, jewelry, what?"

"Oh nothing as exciting as those, but something terribly more valuable!" Philip too, seemed to be getting into the telling of the tale even though he had heard it countless times in the past.

"What Peter needed me to find was a rug."

"A rug? As in carpet or hairpiece?" she asked.

"A Persian carpet that in 1925 cost $3,000,000 dollars. This carpet was a wall-to-wall, hand crafted masterpiece. A true one of a kind!"

Rebecca let out a low whistle.

"$3,000,000 in 1925, how big was this carpet?"

"What do you say Philip, about thirty feet wide by sixty feet in length? Would you say that that is about right?" Liam queried.

"Measurements are spot on my dear friend."

"That's a large rug, I will give you that, but I have seen Persian carpets even bigger, so what makes it so special?"

Liam continued.

"What made this rug so unique, and warranted the cost of $3,000,000 in 1925, mind you that would be worth over $37,000,000 in today's money, was its colors. The reds were the deepest of crimson, the blacks the darkest of midnight, and the gold, well let's just say the gold' rivaled the purest of the pure."

"That's because it was pure gold!" Philip had leaned into Rebecca and almost whispered this revelation to her so no other patrons could over hear him.

"Pure gold, woven into a rug! That must have been the most beautiful carpet on the planet. Tell me Liam, did you ever find it?"

Liam and Philip just leaned back in their respective chairs. They both had grins as wide as their faces, looking as if they had both just devoured the preverbal bird. Liam ever so slightly just nodded down towards the floor. At first Rebecca did not quite understand his facial tic, but it soon registered. Once she realized Liam's motion she almost went almost as white as a January snow storm.

"You mean to tell me that I have been sitting here drinking champagne on a $37,000,000 dollar carpet, spun with real gold? You must be pulling my leg."

"Trust me dear, your leg has not been pulled. This is the genuine article. I found it in all places in a second hand, Baptist church consignment shop in Albany. They thought it was just a lobby size rug from an old hotel that was torn down in the fifties. It was so big, they could never sell it."

Excitedly Rebecca had to ask.

"Well, how much did you pay for it? I simply must know!"

Philip jumped back into the conversation.

"That's the best part of the story! We didn't pay a one thin dime for it! It was so large, and took up so much space that they offered to pay Liam to cart it away!"

"So, someone just gave you a $37,000,000 rug? Just like that?"

Liam sensed a bit of disgusted in her comment.

"If you are thinking that we stole this rug from a disadvantaged church, just wait on more minute. Once I got the rug here and we all say that it was in absolutely perfect condition, just needed a little cleaning, Philip here sent that church an anonymous donation in the amount of $500,000. I even relinquished my finders-fee of $250,000 to the same church.

"It's like something right out of a movie. Hasn't anyone ever tried to steal pieces of it? A square foot must be worth something like two grand. That's pretty tempting for a girl!"

You could see figures being mentally converted to shoes in her mind.

"That is why that the entire world thinks that this is just a faithful reproduction and nothing more. I trust my secret is still safe with you my dear?" asked Philip.

"To my grave, that will go to my grave with me."

"Thank you my dear." Peter rose "And with that, I must make my apologies. I have some staff issues to deal with."

"Not on my behalf, because of the hostess Philip?"

"Liam, your incident was just the cream that finally formed on the top of the bottle. I feel that she hasn't done this institution proud with her service. At times only letting in her friends while other, more prominent, New Yorkers are left to wait in the lobby as they stare at empty tables. No, the time has come for her to find other employment."

"Well please, make it known that it wasn't just my doing. She looks like she could do some damage if she was in her right mind."

"Will do Liam. I am off!" with that Philip bent low and kissed Rebecca on the check and took her hand.

"Till we meet again Cherié!" and with that he was off, weaving between his guests, stopping every so often to as to welcome someone, or to even say hello to an old friend. Within minutes he had disappeared.

"Well, that's some start to the evening if I say! Drinking champagne on a $37,000,000 Persian carpet. How will you ever top that?"

Liam stood and held his hand out to Rebecca.

"On to round two."

The couple left the The Apartment and hailed a cab right outside of the entrance. Liam gave the cabbie the address and within ten minutes Liam and Rebecca were being escorted to their table at Le Cirque on East 58th.

They had a table with a wonderful view of the entire restaurant. The maître d saw that the two of them were attended to and went off on his way to great a well know morning television talk show host. As it was getting late they both decided to not eat too heavy. Rebecca asked for Liam to order for her. The choices at Le Cirque have always been limited, but that still never makes for easy decisions.

The waiter arrived and Liam started his order.

"I think that we will both have an order of the Lobster Risotto to start."

"Excellent choice, sir. And if I may suggest, the chef has some wonderful truffles blanche. If he has any left would you like some on the risotto?

"That would be heaven," remarked Rebecca.

"For the main course, let see… How are you on fish Rebecca?"

"I love it. I try to eat it at least three times week."

"The Poisson it is. We will both have the Daurade en Croute de Sel, and we'll make our dessert choice a bit later, if that is alright."

"Excellent choice sir! Shall I send the wine steward over sir?"

"Yes, please, thank you."

Within less than thirty seconds the sommelier arrived tableside.

"Good evening sir, good evening madam. I am Michael. How might I be of assistance this evening?"

Sommeliers and wine stewards served a vital importance in upscale restaurants such as the one they were now dining at. However, Liam had been studying and collecting wines for years now and had developed a very astute palette. As with his love of food, Liam made it a life's mission to always try and pair the right wine with the dish being served. This allowed him great chances of experimentation but he also was not one to fall into the restaurant claptraps of wine lists. As most bottles were priced over five times their retail equivalent.

"Michael, we are staying light this evening. We are both starting with the Lobster Risotto and then moving on to the breem in salt crust."

"Wonderful decisions sir. Then might I suggest a light red this evening?'

"Well, I was going to be a little more traditional and go the with the white. How about a nice mid-age Corton Charlemagne?"

"Wonderful choice sir! I may have a few bottles of the Latour 2002 left in the cellar."

"That would be a wonderful choice Michael. Let's start with a bottle of that."

With the choices made, Michael hurried off to an unseen cellar cavern, as the restaurants literature read, but in reality a large temperature controlled room in the basement, in order to locate Liam's wine of choice.

"So, a gentlemen, a philatelist, a detective of sorts, and now a wine connoisseur. What other surprises do you harbor Mr. Liam Ross?"

Before Liam had a chance to answer, wine glasses arrived and within seconds Michael returned. The sommelier opened the bottle and handed the cork to Liam. Most people have the urge to smell the cork, as it has been portrayed countless times in the movies. Liam did not. He checked the hardness of the cork to see if it had become spongy. If it had, it would have allowed various bacteria to enter the wine and cause many off flavors and aromas. The cork yielded very little when Liam pressed it between his thumb and index finger, a very good sign especially for an older white wine. Michael had now poured a tasting sample into the fine Riedel white burgundy glass that had been placed in front of Liam. The golden straw color of the wine danced under the light from hidden ceiling sources. Many have classified the fine white Burgundies' as the wines of the gods, and this vintage was no exception. Liam's draught caused his taste buds to awaken and his palette react with a veritable cornucopia of flavors. Liam's reaction was anything but snobbish.

"That is amazing! Wonderful!"

"The 2002's have become some of the finest vintages ever produced."

The sommelier poured Rebecca a full serving and then returned to fill Liam's glass. Rebecca lifted her wine glass in a toast.

"To you sir, a truly remarkable individual."

Liam countered.

"And to you Miss, a true beauty. Thank you for a wonderful evening."

Rebecca's next comment took him a bit by surprise.

"And it's just beginning."

The two touched glasses and sipped their wine just as the Lobster Risotto arrived.

The waiter was true to his word.

There on top of the risotto were five or six of the largest shaved slices of white truffles that Liam had ever seen. They both attacked the risotto with abandoned flourish. The flavor of the lobster, gently mixed with earthiness of the truffles, was brought to new heights when followed with a taste of one of Côte de Beaune's finest.

"I have just experienced a piece of heaven." Was all Rebecca could manage after her sixth forkful of the risotto.

"Wait until the fish arrives. I promise you another taste that will have your taste buds exploding."

The rest of the meal was an exceptional experience. The two talked and compared dining experiences of their pasts. When the table had been cleared and dessert, coffees and liqueurs offered. They both decided to pass as they had early mornings the next day.

As it was a short walk back to the hotel, they both agreed that the night was pleasant enough to try and bare a walk. As they passed 55th street Liam noticed that Rebecca was perhaps a bit chilled. Ever the gentleman, he took off his sport jacket and placed it over her shoulders as they continued to walk and talk. Arriving back at the hotel within twenty minutes.

They walked right onto an empty elevator. Liam pressed the button for Rebecca's floor.

"Would you mind if I escorted you to your room?"

"I would have it no other way, thank you."

The elevator let them out on the eighteenth floor. As they walked down the hallway Rebecca leaned into Liam and very carefully, never missing a stride, removed her shoes.

"The true devil's bane of beauty, high heels. I love them, I hate them!"

"Ah, the perfect dichotomy!"

They reached her door and Rebecca retrieved her key from her evening bag. After two ill attempts of inserting the key, the lock finally yielded. Rebecca stepped into the room as Liam waited at the door.

"Liam, would you like to come in?"

Liam was torn. Here was perhaps the most beautiful woman that he had ever spent time with and he would be lying if he said the thought of making love to her had never entered into his mind. As his mind was still scrambled from the events of just twenty-four hours ago and he was still standing on just a few hours of sleep, he felt it best if he decline.

"Rebecca, as much as every fiber in by body is screaming at me to come in, I feel that I should decline. Please believe me, it's not that I'm not attracted to you, just the opposite. I hope you understand."

Rebecca leaned forward and kissed Liam full of the lips. He felt her lips part lightly and a slight darting of the tip of her tongue slid into Liam's lips. Liam responded as he placed his left hand on the small of her back. The soft touch of the fabric against her, coupled with the erotic touch of her kiss, caused a stir in Liam as he felt himself becoming erect. If Liam did not stop right this second, a situation was going to arise.

She wrapped her arms around his neck and kissed him deeper, her tongue slowly moving across Liam's lips. After a full two minutes of passion their lips parted and Rebecca leaned close to Liam's left ear and whispered.

"Oh, I can tell that you are attracted. If you could only feel how attracted I am to you."

They broke their embrace and Rebecca stepped back inside her room and took off Liam's jacket.

"I am here for a few more days, but I have a business meeting all day in the Bronx, perhaps dinner the next night?" Liam hoped that he was not pushing.

"I have to wait a whole forty eight hours?" Her moist lips formed into an irresistible pout.

"If I could only make time move faster, trust me I would!"

"Then it's a date." She leaned into Liam once again and kissed him warmly and wetly once again.

"Good night. Thank you once again for a marvelous evening." She then closed the door.

Liam was standing there in the hotel's hallway, in front of a closed door, letting the tingle of her last kiss linger. As he started to walk away towards the elevators he realized that her kiss was not the only thing lingering.

19

Updates

"Ross and the woman, they were both followed?" Trumball Nash asked.

"Yes" came the disembodied voice of the Recipient from the cell phone.

"The woman is in her room at the Waldorf, as Ross is in his. From what we heard, it appears that Ross is planning on returning to the Bousquet building in the morning."

"Do you feel that Ross has the article in his possession?" asked Nash.

"I don't think so, not yet. He hasn't been out of our site the entire day and night. He hasn't had a chance to locate it yet."

"Then why isn't your team pulling that building apart to find it?"

"Sometimes it is best to approach a difficult situation from an opposite direction. Mr. Ross is the expert, why not let him do the heavy work and locate the object for us? If I were to send in a recovery team now, their after presence would only make acquisition even more difficult. Plus there is no telling where Joe Bousquet hid the item. It could take months to search everything in that building. Months, as you are aware, that we do not have."

"Then you are sure that Ross is aware of it?"

"Why else would the old man have contacted him?"

"I never assume anything anymore and neither should you." shot back Nash. "I'm giving you seventy two hours to get this resolved, I suggest that you step things up or you can convey your excuses to the Chairman in person."

"Mr. Nash, it does not bode well to make empty threats. You had months to find what was lost. In just twenty-four hours I have taken the necessary steps to assure complete and total success. There will be no excuses, at least, none that I have to worry about. I wonder if you could say such a thing as to your part Nash."

Nash swallowed hard as he heard the mono-toned, cold words. His response stuck in his throat.

"You have all of the necessary assets in place?"

"In place and ready to proceed on my command. We will have the article within seventy two hours."

Nash listened as then line went dead. He looked at the phone and heard the cold words still echoing in his brain. He had to report to the Chairman. He looked at his watched and noted the time, three o'clock in the morning. He weighed the question whether he should report now or wait until later that morning.

He wrestled for a full three minutes before he dialed the contact number from memory. He realized that he was starting to sweat in the cool morning air. Dreading the fact that he did not have the object as he had promised the Chairman. After the familiar hollow tones of the encryption devices, a voice that sounded as it had been up for hours, responded.

"Do you have the item?"

"Not yet Chairman. We have had to approach this from a different direction."

Nash retold the entire days events to the Chairman, detailing the next steps to come.

"I assure you that we will have it within the next seventy two hours."

"An excuse Nash? Your last assurance was twenty-four hours. Perhaps I have sent the wrong man to accomplish this relatively simple task."

"I have no excuses Chairman. It is just taking a bit more time because this Ross is now standing center in the picture. His presence is just a slight inconvenience but one that is easily surmounted. The acquisition will be finalized."

"See that it is Nash, because if it is not I will relieve you of your position."

Nash knew all to well what that meant.

20

Protocols

Waldorf=Astoria Hotel
New York, New York
May 2, 2013

The morning came too early for Liam's taste, but it was his own damn fault. He had only been asleep for four hours when the ringing of the telephone announced the wake up call from the hotel switchboard. He dragged his dead tired body from the warm bed and headed into the cold marble bathroom. As he went through the dressing room he picked up his jacket that he had tossed on the couch the evening before. When he went to hang the jacket in the closet he caught the scent of Rebecca's perfume from the night before. He closed his eyes and remembered her kiss on his lips and the feel of her breasts against him as he held her. He hung the jacket up in the closet and continued into the bathroom, turned on the shower and then headed over to the sink. He had just started splashing water on his face when the ring of the suite's phone pierced the noise of the running shower water. Years ago the hotel had installed telephones in just about every room of the hotel, that included all of the bathrooms as well. Liam reached for the handset and answered.

"Liam Ross."

"Morning Boss, how ya doing?" came the voice of Kyle Gale.

"Kyle, glad you made it, any problems?"

"Nope, made it in record time. Didn't have to stop for any scales, even in Virginia."

"Have you had any sleep?"

"Had a few hours and about three gallons of coffee, so I'm raring to go. I loaded everything on the list that you faxed down to me. Can't say that the shop's new owner's were very happy to see me loading up the gear that you had in storage there. I think in the back of their minds they might think that you are setting up a new company. You know, ready to take work out of their mouths so to speak. You might want to call them and reassure them. They didn't want to believe me."

"Will do, I'll put in on the list."

"So where do you want all the gear? Not here at the hotel I would venture to guess."

"Assumption is correct. Drive it up to the Bronx. We are going to set up out there for the next few days. I'll text you the address."

"You want me to wait for Lizzy, John and you?"

"No, why don't you head out now, we'll jump on the subway in about thirty minutes. So we will most likely beat you out there this time of the morning. Also, Kyle, I haven't had a chance to completely scope out the building, so as of right now the only elevator that I know of is a small passenger car in the main lobby. We need to get everything up to the top floor so it's going to take a few trips."

"No problem Boss. I'll scope things out when I get there."

Liam hung up the phone and sent Kyle the address of Joe Bousquet's building in the Bronx. He then made a quick call to Liz, who in turn called John, laying out the plans for the morning. He told them that he would meet them in the lobby in half an hour. He then jumped into the shower and rushed through his morning rituals.

Liz and John found Liam waiting in the Grand Lobby of the hotel. When they walked up to him he was deep in a telephone conversation with a person or persons unknown. Most people might not have called it a conversation as Liam only had a chance to weigh in occasionally with a "but", "no really" or an "I assure you". When it was all said and done Liam looked as if he had just gone five rounds with a ranked welterweight.

"Who was that?" asked Liz as Liam shoved the phone back into his pocket with just a bit of disdain.

"The new owners of the old shop. Kyle gave me a heads up that they seemed a bit perturbed that I might be setting up a new shop, thus violating the sales agreement. I tried to tell them that I wasn't, but they didn't seem to want to believe me. Threatened a law suit for fraud, breach of contract, you name it, they threatened. So, I'll deal with that problem later. Right now we need to get up to the Bronx. Let's go."

The three associates left the hotel through the Lexington Avenue exit and headed two blocks north in order to get on the uptown bound, number four train.

After an uneventful thirty-minutes, the trio arrived in the northern most recesses of the Bronx. As Liam had learned just two days before, it was quicker to walk to the building than to try and catch a cab, so the brisk walk took just fifteen minutes. When the three had left Manhattan the day was shaping up to be a typical dreary spring morning. However now the day's outlook appeared more favorable as the sun was starting to break through the gray overcast skies.

Liam escorted Liz and John into the building and up to the top floor that had been Joe Bousquet's library. When Liam opened the door to the stamp collection he saw the looks on his associates faces. Their eyes went wide; both of their jaws dropped and hung open for a count of ten until both silently mouthed the words "holy shit". Liam thought to himself that that is what he must have looked like when he first viewed the collection. John was the first to respond.

"Unbelievable! Just unbelievable!" was all he could respond.

"Boss" Liz finally chimed in, " this is gigantic. I've never seen a space so large in an apartment building, not just here in New York, but anywhere. It has to be over twenty thousand square feet."

"Closer to thirty." The voice that came from behind and made them all three of them turn in surprise. Susan Bousquet was standing behind them holding a steaming cup of coffee between her hands.

"Sorry to startle you. I was in the kitchen when you came in."

"Liz, John, this is Susan Bousquet, the owner's daughter."

"Former owner's daughter, Mr. Cooper is now the owner of this postal nightmare!" Liam quickly made the introductions before either Liz or John mentioned Rex's fate.

"It's a pleasure to meet you." Susan shook both Liz's and John's hands. "Can I offer anyone a cup of coffee?"

"That would be wonderful, why don't I help you. Liz, why don't you get started on setting up your computer and John, could you wait downstairs for Kyle?" With that Liam and Susan left the stamp room and went down the hall to the kitchen.

Yesterday when Liam was at the Bousquet home, he had not seen the kitchen. It was Liam's turn to have his jaw hang open, again.

The room that he had just walked into could only be described as pure heaven for a professional chef. The entire open format kitchen encompassed about six hundred square feet. Another carefully laid out deception of the apartment's floor plan revealed. The ceiling was at least sixteen feet in height, thus heightening the illusion. The gleaming stainless steel appliances were all professional models, from the walk in refrigerator to the ice maker installed at the wet bar. Hanging above the soapstone topped center island was a chef's hanging rack containing a vast collection of pots and pans, Liam recognized most, but some were unfamiliar to him. Off to the right of the island was a small dining area and with it was another door.

"In to the dining room?" Liam asked Susan as he motioned towards the door.

Susan pulled three coffee mugs from a cabinet to the left of the stainless steel sink that could double as an Olympic wading pool.

"No, Dad's wine cellar. Take a look, it's unlocked."

Liam walked over to the door, turned the antique knob, and pulled heftily on the insulated door. Another marvel awaited on the other side.

It wasn't a large cellar by any means, perhaps twenty feet wide by twenty feet long and was a good twelve feet from floor to ceiling. The redwood racking ran floor to ceiling and wall-to-wall with what Liam estimated to be a capacity for over four thousand bottles. There also appeared to be very few empty spaces for new acquisitions. Towards the rear of the cellar were both wooden crates and corrugated cases, again stacked almost floor to ceiling, each container holding either six or twelve bottles of mostly newer vintages. The temperature in the room was a perfect fifty-five degrees.

The appellations ranged from Napa Valley and Santa Barbara in California to just about every known growing region in France, Spain, South America, and from some countries that Liam had no idea produced wine. All of the well-known wine makers were represented; Chateau Mouton Rothschild, Chateau Lynch-Bage, Olivier LaFlaive, Rochioli, Au Bon Climate, Grace Family, Mulderbosch. Other, more obscure wineries were equally represented as well. It appeared that Joe Bousquet was a true wine connoisseur.

"Simply outstanding, a wonderful collection." Liam remarked to Susan who was now standing in the doorway, holding a tray with coffee, cream and sugar.

"And a shame if you ask me as I don't drink!"

The look that Liam returned must have been one that required a response as Susan continued on.

"Sorry, no sorted stories or the such, it's just I never developed a taste for alcohol. God knows dad tried for years to teach me all about wine and food, the food took, not so much the wine."

Liam walked to the doorway and relieved Susan of the tray and placed it on the soapstone island.

"Susan, I need to talk to you for a moment."

"Of course. Is there something wrong?"

"Well, actually there is. Why don't you sit down?"

The two took seats at the small antique dining table in the alcove. Liam didn't know where to begin so he quickly decided to start with the events of two nights ago.

"Susan, two nights ago, Rex Cooper was killed while in Little Italy."

Susan face really did not display any emotion. This was not because she was devoid of them, she just didn't know how to react.

"How, what happened?"

"He was killed in a drive by shooting as we were leaving a restaurant."

This time look on her face was of concern, fear and perhaps confusion. After a few seconds she was able to speak again, but her voice wavered as she continued.

"Oh my God are you alright?"

"I'm fine, the police are looking into the situation. But I must tell you that there seems to be a possible connection to your father's death."

"But my father was in an accident."

"It's not looking that way Susan. Rex and I went to see the police the afternoon that we were here. We explained to them about the odd happenings here and how your father may have been threatened over his collection."

"How do you know all of this?"

"Rex was threatened that very same afternoon. The police will be looking into any possible connections between his murder and your fathers so called accident." Liam changed his course of thought for a moment.

"Susan, if I remember correctly, did you say that you were heading back up to Syracuse?"

"Yes, I'm leaving on Friday, why do you ask?"

"Might you have a friend that you could stay with until then?"

"Why, am I in danger?"

"I don't think so, I just think that until the police can put the pieces of the puzzle together, it would better to be safe than sorry. Particularly if whoever is involved in all of this, knows that you are here alone with your father's stamp collection."

"Yes, I can stay with my friend Beth she... The stamp collection! What do I do about that damn collection now?"

Liam had only known the girl two short days and he felt that it might sound just a bit unbelievable if he told her the contents of Rex's will.

"Do you trust your father's attorney?"

"John? I trust him with my life. He wasn't just dad's attorney, he also happens to be my Godfather. Why do you ask?"

Liam handed her a slip of paper with Ken Whitelaw's name address and phone number on it.

"Here is the name of Rex's attorney. You should have your father's attorney call him as soon as possible."

Susan took the information from Liam and excused herself from the kitchen in order to call her Godfather. Liam picked up the tray of coffees and returned to the collection room.

Liam entered the collection room to find Liz unpacking and setting up her computer. He brought the tray of coffee over to the table that she was working on.

"How did she take the news?" asked Liz.

"I think it shook her up a bit. She's calling her attorney now." Just as Liam responded a chime to the rear of the voluminous space sounded. He looked to Liz.

"We found a freight elevator behind the end shelving. John took it down as Kyle pulled up about ten minutes ago with the truck."

"Well, I might as well make myself useful and help them unload."

Liam went to the rear of the space and found John and Kyle deeply involved in a discussion as the two moved boxes off of the freight elevator. Over the years the two friends had embarked on many of these, somewhat theoretical and philosophical discussions. The only problem is that most pertained to conspiracy theories that the majority of people would dismiss as pure supermarket tabloid fodder. Today was no exception. Today's discussion consisted of whether or not a church in lower Manhattan hid the remains of a fourteenth century European Templar Knight. The two friends had almost convinced each other that when given the time, they should head out and reveal the true secret.

"And then you can find the massive treasure, write a movie about it and become rich beyond your wildest dreams." Liam laughed, as the two were ready to drop everything and head out at that very moment for their urban spelunking adventure.

"Hey Boss, where do you want all the gear?" asked Kyle

"Let's just quickly stack it up here and then I can give you all the sit-rep."

For the next twenty minutes they emptied the truck and stored all of the items on the upper floor of Joe Bousquet's building. When they were finished they rejoined Liz who had her computers up and running. Just as they were all about to sit down Susan Bousquet returned from her conversation with her father's attorney.

"Liam, may I have a moment?"

"Certainly Susan." The pair left the stamp room and went out into the hallway.

"Well, my Godfather and I have just finished a conversation with Mr. Whitelaw and I can't tell you how it was a major load off of my mind Liam. He explained all of Mr. Cooper's wishes and he is sending all of the requisite paperwork to John. He wanted to wait until all of the legal I's were dotted and T's crossed in order to turn over everything to you, but I told him that I trusted you."

She reached into her pocket of her jeans and extracted a ring of master keys and a folded piece of paper.

"Mr. Ross, I am going to take your advice and go back up to Syracuse today. You last mentioned that it would take a few days to catalog dad's collection..." she handed Liam the keys and the paper. "If you would like, please make yourself at home here and take as long as you need. I have no plans for the building yet, and as of right now I really have no intention of even returning to New York anytime soon."

"Susan, that is a very generous offer, thank you."

"Liam, I loved my father dearly, but right now I just need to get on with my life. This talk of dad possibly being murdered is very disturbing and I just want to have good memories of him."

"Susan I understand completely, as you no doubt know now, Rex was more than just an associate of mine, he was really my second father. He was my grounding when my dad died. God knows I was a handful for my mother. I would have turned out very different if it hadn't been for Rex."

"I have everything that I need packed up, so I'm going to head out. My contact information is on the paper. Please, make yourselves at home. Actually you could stay here instead of in the city. There are more than enough bedrooms and if you haven't seen it yet, dad had a small efficiency room back in the stamp room, really nothing more than a bed and a bathroom. That should save you a small fortune in hotel bills."

"Susan we just might take you up on that offer, thank you."

Susan turned to leave but she turned back and leaned into Liam and kissed him on the cheek.

"Thank you Liam. Please let me know what happened to my father."

"I will Susan. I will."

Susan turned again and walked down the hallway towards the front door. When she reached the door she turned once again and called out to Liam.

"One other thing Liam, I have instructed John, my godfather, to send over to you the appropriate papers. I am giving you dad's wine collection as a thank you."

Liam was almost speechless.

"Susan, you can't! That collection is worth ten's of thousands of dollars. If not more!"

"I can and I did, thank you again Liam Ross. Enjoy!" and with that Susan Bousquet closed the door behind her. Liam just stood there looking at the door. After what seemed to be ten minutes but was really only two, Liam returned to the stamp collection. He explained that they were free to use the apartment for as long as they needed. It was decided that by Saturday they would all move out of the Waldorf=Astoria and work out of the Bronx. It was now time to get to work.

Liam brought his old team fully up to date with all of the information that he had. It was now time to start to dig to see why Rex and Joe Bousquet had been murdered.

"Are we going to bring the police in on what we find?" asked Liz.

"Not yet" replied Liam "I need to find out all of the details and if we involve the police they are only going to tell us to stay out of the way. No, let's keep this in house for now. I can however guarantee you that we will be hearing from Lieutenant O'Brian and Detective Conner. They don't appear to me to be the types to leave me off of their radar. I think that Detective Conner thanks that I may have had something to do with Rex's death because of my inheritance."

"So Boss, where do we start?" Kyle was next to chime in.

"Let's start with Joe Bousquet's files."

Liam walked over to the large captains table in the middle of the room where Liz has set up her computers and extracted a manila envelope from his case.

"This is what was left for Rex from Joe. We thought that it was just ramblings of someone that may have gone off of the paranoid deep end, but now I think it was Joe's way of leaving Rex a clue."

"Any idea as to what kind of clue?" Liz asked as she started to read the paper that Liam handed to her.

"No, not right now I don't, but I think that Joe's computer may give us an idea."

Liam retrieved the small, white box that held Joe Bousquet's replicated thumb and went over to the computer room. Liam opened the room and turned on the lights. As he unlocked the security device with the thumb no one even questioned him on the detached digit. They had all made similar prosthetic devices for special effects in film work for years and all could spot a fake appendage from a mile away.

The loudest gasp came from Liz Gallagher when she entered the room and saw the computer arrangement.

"Holy shit! Liam this is some of the most advanced, state of the art gear. What the hell is it doing here?"

"Well, I think that Mr. Bousquet may have harbored a little secret from his family. He must have been company connected."

"You mean at the CSS or the CIA, FBI, NSA or Secret Service?" John Andrews asked in one of his many stage voices.

"Yes." Was Liam's response "I believe that Mr. Joseph Bousquet of 98-124 Webster Avenue, New York, New York, was not as he appeared to his family, I also believe that he was a freelance consultant to some of, if not all, of the agencies that you named John."

"That would definitely explain all of this gear. Please tell me that you have start up instructions, please?" Liz was as excited as a small girl on Christmas Eve. Liam reached into the packet and removed the instructions and gave them to Liz. She sat right down at the center of the console and went through the detailed system startup.

It took all of five minutes before Liz had everything up and operating. As the three men looked over her shoulder, she then spent a few more minutes familiarizing herself with the system desktop.

"Okay gents, I got it." Her fingers flew as she entered data into the touch-screen keyboard. "This is set up very efficiently." Her right hand maneuvered the cursor across the screen. "These files here are the stamp collection and from what it is showing Liam, you've got about one hundred and ninety years of licking and sticking ahead of you Boss."

"Very funny, ha, ha, ha." Drop the comedy and get back to the files.

"No sense of humor I tell ya." Liz screwed up her nose and went back to the keyboard. "Okay, again," pointing to the computer monitor "these folders here are just stamps, at first cursory glance, nothing more than inventories and current price evaluations. These files here seem to be his personal papers" continuing on "these files here are building related, tenants, contractors, security system, etc, etc, etc." moving the cursor again only to stop in the lower right hand corner of the screen where no files were located. "However these aren't the only files." Liz looked to Liam only to recognize a look that she had first experienced years ago.

"Liz, there is nothing there."

"Oh, sure there is. You just have to look real hard."

"My eyes are wide open missy computer geek. What the hell are you talking about?"

"This…"

The screen background appeared to be just a repeated geometrical graphic design. Liz used a keyboard command to zoom in on a section of the screen, revealing what was actually a series of very small designs making up the background pattern. The pattern was consistent throughout the entire screen with the exception of the lower right hand section where Liz now placed the cursor. She clicked the mouse again and the design enlarged, revealing a series of heavily clustered lines and dots, running from left to right in a sentence order, different from the rest of the pattern. Kyle was the first to offer up a solution.

"Morse code dots and dashes?"

"It looks more like flea footprints if you ask me." Came John's high pitched, comedic voice of a popular animated movie flea.

"No… open your eyes!" Liam sounded excited as he grabbed for Rex's envelope once again and pulled out the paranoid instruction letter that Joe had left. Quickly scanning the document Liam found the sectioned that he remembered.

"Keep the eyes opened and check 23021868. Keep the "I's" opened. Each set of a line and a dot is a letter "I". They're Shadows!"

"Lost you on that one LR, Shadows, what the hell are Shadows?" John now appeared to be more interested in the topic at hand. Liz explained.

"Shadows are a form of visual cryptography, a hidden image within another image."

""Like an Easter Egg?" asked Kyle who was almost as adept as computers as Liz but more from the hardware side of things, not programming.

"Similar, but a bit trickier. With an Easter egg nine out of ten times the image is just hidden. It is revealed only when your cursor rolls over the invisible item. Then the image becomes a standard clickable link into a program. With Shadows, the images are always there, not invisible. They are akin to micro printing on currency and stamps. Images so small that they cannot be seen by the naked eye alone. But with Shadows the real secret is that each image is just a piece of another image. You may have a couple of images that make up your final image or you could have millions. The real trick is to open each item in the correct order, then the packet will reveal itself and you can enter."

Liam now looked a bit worried.

"What if you open a item in the wrong order?"

"There's a catch."

"There's always a catch!" grumbled John.

"What's the catch Liz?"

"The catch is that once an item is opened in the wrong order, you have to start over again at the beginning."

"Well that doesn't seem like such a big deal. You can copy and paste your previous work into the field if that happens" responded Kyle.

"Sorry boys, not that easy. Every Shadow program that I have ever seen also incorporates some type of redundancy. If you miss a sequence and have to start over again, the starting point moves as well. In other words you have an entirely new beginning image!"

"Damn, this could take years" was all Liam could offer.

"Only if we don't have the proper algorithm Boss. Joe Bousquet must have left some kind of a clue or key, just give me some time to get into this."

"Alright then Liz, you start on the hacking, Kyle, could you start in on the reprogramming of the access locks in the building. Susan gave me the master access key so that we can change what ever we see fit to change." Liam reached into his pocket and handed the keys over to Kyle. "I suggest the building's main entrance, the entrance to this library and this control room should all be reprogrammed. Make them compatible with all of our biometrics. Also did you get a package from Uncle Bob this morning?"

"Yes sir. Brand new iPhones complete with expanded bag of dirty tricks. I activated and logged them in with the service this morning then assigned them to the team." Liam looked to the three as they all held up their new cell devices. "I do need to update yours later, should only take a few minutes. Something new that Uncle Robert sent down."

"Good job Kyle, thanks" and with that Kyle was off to accomplish his task.

"What do you want me to do LR?"

"John, why don't you to do a complete recon of the building. See if we can map out the entire building. I would love to know what access points there are and what we need to be aware of. Liz, can John use the other terminal to access the security section of the system?"

Liz rolled over to the other terminal and with a series of lightening fast keystrokes and had the monitor up and running for John. He jumped into the nearest chair and attacked the files that were on the display monitor.

"Call me on the cell if anything comes up, any of you. I'm going to browse through the other room and see what is really there."

Liam walked out of the control room and into the massive stamp library. He stood and surveyed the roughly thirty thousand square foot room. He had never seen so vast a collection and his mind was swimming just trying to calculate the shear number of stamps in this room.

He knew that an average United States singles stamp collection could be contained in about six high quality albums and have over five thousand issues amongst the volumes, so that averaged out to over eight hundred stamps per volume. Just looking around there appeared to be well over his initial estimate from just two days ago. Liam now calculated in his mind that there could be close to three hundred thousand albums here. Quickly doing the math he estimated that there could be over one hundred and fifty million stamps in this room, and if some of these albums were stock books, multiples of the same issues in a series of pockets bound on each page, that figure could easily double. He walked over to the southeast corner of the room and slowly walked northward down the first row of shelving. As he passed row upon row, stack upon stack, album upon album, he stretched both of his arms outwards, covering the five-foot span from shelf to shelf. His fingertips swept over the bindings of each of the albums within his reach, with each album denoting the standardized Scott Catalog numerical system and a more up to date barcode identifier. It appeared that each album contained one United States issue, and just one issue alone.

Liam stopped about ten feet down the first row and extracted a volume from his left that was bar coded and noted as Scott Number 5A. Liam knew this to be the 1851 issue of a one cent blue issue depicting an image of Benjamin Franklin. He carefully opened the album and what appeared on its pages was pure astonishment.

Liam was holding in his hands an album that perhaps contained over one thousand of this particular issue. These were in all grade stages of mint, with most in Post Office fresh condition, meaning that they looked as if they had just come off of the printing press. Liam scanned the shelves again and noticed that there were over twenty albums, all with this stamp's Scott number. He set the first album down and slid out another album and opened it. Here were the same issue, not in the same condition, but in a condition that serious collectors would pay over $10,000 USD a stamp. Liam extracted yet another album from the shelving, once again with the same Scott number of 5A. This album revealed used copies of this issue, and these copies were considered to be in XF-Superb Condition. This meant that the stamp was very well centered with at least nominal margins surrounding the image, one margin may be perhaps a bit more unequal than the others on either the top, bottom, left or right. Stamps in this condition could sell for over $5,500 USD.

Liam quickly scanned the album and calculated that this album of used issues alone had a catalog value of over $4,000,000 or a wholesale value of roughly $800,000. Then the real nightmare hit Liam. He realized that this one album, which he held in his hands, could create a problem, a very real problem in the philatelic world. If word were to get out about this collection, the values of stamp collections around the world would plummet over night. Never in the history of stamp collecting had this many copies of one issue of a fairly rare stamp, in these fine of conditions, ever been assembled, or even know to exist! That is with the exception of when the stamps were first printed in 1851!

Liam placed the albums back into the rack and continued to walk down the aisle. He was about half way down the first aisle when he had an idea and quickly returned back to the control room.

"Liz, John, have either of you seen a barcode scanner in here? You know, one of the handheld type used in grocery stores?" John started opening drawers in the rack behind the control console. Both Liz and John joined in the search.

"Found one LR, correct that, found ten!" John called out to Liam. "They all seem to be charged and ready to go."

"Let me have one, would you John." John handed Liam the scanner and Liam left the control room.

"What was that all about?" asked Liz

"I guess when you gotta shop, you gotta shop!" smirked John.

Back in the main library, Liam returned to the aisle that he had just left. He turned on the hand held scanner and pointed the laser reader at a barcode symbol on the spin of an album and pulled the trigger. Within ten seconds the onboard screen filled with multiple lines of information and images. The information contained the Scott Catalog stamp identifier, Joe Bousquet's inventory control numbers, photo scan numbers of the issues, where they could be located on the main computer, and the total amount of issues in that particular album. At the top of the screen, right before all of the information, was a high-resolution scan of the issue devoted to the album. It appeared to be a perfect specimen of that issue, which at one time Liam thought could have only come from either the American Philatelic Society's reference library or from the only known complete private collection of United States stamps, the collection of Benjamin K. Miller. This collection was donated to the New York Public Library in 1925 and remained on display at the central library until 1977 when a theft occurred at the museum. The collection was then taken out of public exhibition and placed in storage, not to be seen by the public for the next thirty years. In 2006, an agreement was struck between the library and the United States Postal Museum in Washington, D.C., where the collection remains on display today.

But Liam now knew differently. The scanned image of the stamp that appeared on the scanner, most likely was contained within that album. Liam looked at the information and just shook his head in disbelief. He continued down the aisles of the library, spot-checking albums barcodes has he walked. Each time the same type of information was displayed on the hand held device and each time Liam just shook his head in disbelief.

Liz and John had both been deeply focused with their tasks at hand at the terminals. John had been able to locate an online blueprint of the building with all of its security devices outlined. He had also been able to find a complete list of all of the tenants of the building, current, past and present, since Joe Bousquet bought the building in the late 1940's. He also located a locked folder that was labeled as the history of the building. John tried every possible way in order to gain access to the information in that folder. After a fourteenth failed attempt he decided to leave that task to Liz for later and he launched the security camera program.

Just as when Liam and Rex launched the program days ago, the screen in front of John came to life with over eight different images from that same number of cameras. John scrolled through the various menus and spent the next thirty minutes correlating the cameras to their locations on the blueprint. When he came to the first and second floor cameras he ran into the same issue as Liam and Rex, it was just too dark to make out any features on those floors.

Liz was still hunched over her monitor when both Liam and Kyle came back into the control room.

"Boss, I might have something for you in a hour or so. I think I've got a way into this Shadow."

"Did you find Joe's algorithm?"

"No, I did a scan on all of the drives and didn't find a thing that was even remotely close, so I started writing my own."

"Just like that, you started writing an algorithm to break a one hundred and twenty-eight layer encrypted Shadow?" Kyle asked as he sat in a chair next to her.

"Writing one is the easy part, having it work is the challenge," quipped Liz.

"What did you find out about the security system John?"

"I've been able to isolate all of the systems, both visual and auditory, everywhere in the building with the exceptions of floors one and two. The lighting for the cameras is non-existent down there. What's on those floors?"

"Don't have a clue. Rex and I didn't get the chance to have a look around."

"Well, no time the present Boss" Kyle chimed in.

"I agree. John, could you stay up here with Liz? For he time being no one should go off on their own." Then Turning to Kyle, "What comm link did you bring?"

"I brought the next gen IFB's." Kyle continued as he passed out the tiny in ear communication devices. "Range is three times that of the older models and the ear buds are smaller and fit snugger in your ear."

"Any con's to this model?" asked Liz.

"None that I have found, but as we all know, that doesn't mean that there isn't any." Kyle was referring to an operation a few years earlier when the first IFB system was introduced into the surveillance world.

The IFB or Interrupted Feedback (sometimes called an interruptible fold-back) systems are used in broadcasting and motion picture production for crew communication, audio monitoring and cueing. The IFB is a special intercom circuit that consists of a program feed sent to an earpiece worn by talent via a wire, telephone, or radio receiver (audio that is being "fed back" to the talent) that can be interrupted and replaced by a television producer's or director's intercom microphone. On a television news program for example, a producer can talk to the news anchors, to tell them when they are live on the air and when to begin reading off the script on the teleprompter or cue cards. These in ear devices fast became the ideal surveillance tools, as they were small and often undetectable when worn. Combined with a highly directional miniature body microphone, communications by an operations team can be conducted in complete stealth.

However, legend has it, when these relatively newly miniaturized systems were first tested on a mission, an accidental crossed signal sent an FBI team's communications through a wireless baby monitor, waking both the individual under surveillance and the baby, causing a rather precarious hostage standoff situation.

"Okay, can I have a sound check everyone?" asked the technical expert.

"Test one, two, three…" Liam responded first.

"Five by Five Boss…" as Kyle monitored the audio via his laptop.

"Ten, nine, eight, seven…" responded Liz.

"Loud and clear Bright Eyes."

"Mary had a little lamb, its fleece was no longer white as snow due to all the pollution from the coal fired electric plant." wisecracked John.

Kyle just looked upped from his laptop and gave his friend an icy cold stare.

"What? Too politically correct for you?"

"Alright Abbott and Costello, knock it off." Liam retrieved a pack back just like Kyle's. "Let's start on the second floor Kyle.

John, talk us through what you see on the cameras. Liz give a shout when you have something." With that Liam and Kyle headed out of the apartment to the main passenger elevator lobby.

The elevator was still waiting on their floor. Liam and Kyle boarded and closed the door then the wire cage. Liam pressed the "2" on the floor indicator and the small cage started its descent. When the elevator came to a stop, Liam opened the cage and then the outer door. When they stepped out of the small cage they were in the lobby on the first floor of the building.

"That's funny, I could have sworn I hit two. Oh well, no harm, no foul."

The pair got back into the car and repeated their actions. This time the elevator started its ascent. When the car came to a stop again, Liam and Kyle once again exited, however, this time they were totally perplexed. They now stood on the landing of the elevator on the third floor!

"Impossible! I know that I pressed two." A bit miffed, the two got back on the elevator, however this time Liam, slowly and very deliberately, pressed the indicator with the numeral "2" centered on its face. Just as before, the elevator started its downward travel. Once again when the car stopped, Liam and Kyle opened the doors and stepped out. Right out into the first floor lobby.

"Alright, now I'm just pissed off! What kind of joke device is this?" barked Kyle. At that moment their IFB's came to life and John was talking in their ears.

"What are you two doing? I have visual on you both in the lobby. What happened to the second floor?"

"Well, that was the plan, however I think we hurt the elevators feelings when we forgot to include it in our plans" joked Kyle as Liam once again stepped into the elevator.

Instead of pressing a floor indicator, Liam ran his fingertips over the brass panel that held the buttons.

"What's up Boss?"

"Well, it appears that the second floor is locked off, however there does not seem to be any lock for that floor, no mechanical key, switch or cardkey."

Liam continued his inspection of the brass panel. Just below the orderly rows of buttons was a speaker inset into the operations panel. A common device in older elevators but a device that was always accompanied by some sort of call button, some way of signaling an operator or maintenance staff member in case of emergency. This elevator however did not have one.

Liam bent down on one knee in order to look at the speaker closer. Just as he was at eye level he detected a very faint red glow coming from within the speaker enclosure. Very carefully Liam ran his fingers over the die cut speaker grill. When he came to the upper right hand corner of the grill he felt the slightest inward give when his finger passed over one of the slotted screws that held the grill in place. He pressed harder on the screw head until he heard a faint audible click. When he removed his hand, the grill pivoted downward like the loading gate on a truck. Here behind the speaker grill was another finger reader identical to the one on the library door upstairs. Liam opened his backpack and retrieved the copy of Joe Bousquet's finger. Liam pressed the replica to the scanner then entered in the numerical code. Once completed Liam closed the elevator doors and pressed the number two button on the elevator panel. The elevator started its upward movement once again.

"Careful man, wasn't he?" remarked Kyle.

"Very careful man, he definitely had secrets," responded Liam.

This time the elevator stopped and Liam and Kyle exited into a darkness that was blacker than black. The faint glow from the elevator car barely cast a glow three feet onto the floor before them. Both men removed flashlights from their backpacks and trained their beams into the inky blackness.

"John, we're in. Kyle you go ten paces to the left and see if you can locate a light switch. I'll do the same to the right."

Each of them went their separate way all the while scanning the wall for a switch. Liam was about near to the end of ten paces when Kyle's voice came over the IFB.

"Got one here Boss, but it doesn't look real."

"I'll be right there."

Liam double-timed it over to where he saw the glow from Kyle's flashlight. Two steps away from where Kyle had focused his beam, Liam swung his light onto the wall. There on the earthen red brick was the switch. A switch that looked like it had just came from the set of a Frankenstein movie.

Liam stepped in to look closer at the evil looking device. The switch was a double knife style, which had not been in use for over a hundred years. Upon closer examination Kyle saw an inscription on the cast metal base plate read it out loud.

"Edison Electric Light Company, N.Y., N.Y. 1878. Well, it definitely looks like something from Edison's time."

"Kyle, this switch was most likely installed by the man himself. New York was Edison's first commercial venture into electric companies." Liam then gave John and Liz the heads up over the IFB that they were going to try the switch.

Kyle grasped the twenty-four inch long handle in both of his hands and firmly planted his feet in order to heft the switch into the on position. This was un-necessary as the switch moved with such ease that the initial movement nearly caused Kyle to lose his footing and stumble into the wall. Liam caught his friend and steadied him as Kyle closed the circuit on the switch.

There wasn't a flash or sparks as so commonly depicted in the movies when a giant switch is thrown. Slowly the blackness in the room was replaced with a warm glow from expertly focused, hidden lighting fixtures. What was revealed to Liam and Kyle was simultaneously echoed in their ears from Liz and John upstairs as they watched from the computer monitor.

"Oh My God."

21

Time Capsule

"Is it for real?" Kyle whispered to Liam standing at his side.

"It's either real or we just entered a time vortex."

The two were now standing at the edge of a well-lit room that encompassed the entire floor of the building. The room length Liam estimated to be five hundred feet and 100 feet at its width, 50,000 square feet. The ceiling was higher than the apartment upstairs. It was at least twenty feet in height. The interior construction appeared to be that of a modified post and beam construction.

Standing guard down the center of the massive room were massive thirty-six inch square wooden posts, spaced equally every twenty feet. Emanating from the tops of the wooden columns were equally impressive beams, two feet square, spanning from post to post. The whole structure was reminiscent of a child's building toy, but one on steroids. Liam reached out to he nearest post and felt the warmth of the dark brown wood.

"Most likely Chestnut." he commented. "Trees had to be over 100 years old when they were felled. John, Liz, are you both seeing this?"

"Unbelievable, you could fit an NFL field in there if it wasn't for the posts." came the response back in their ears.

"The trees had to have been the size of redwoods!" exclaimed Kyle.

"Not as tall as redwoods but they could grow to over one hundred-fifty feet in height and could go over ten feet in diameter, hard as a rock as well. The tree is all but extinct now in North America. Most mill and factory buildings here in the northeast, from the 18th and 19th centuries, were built from them."

"Why the beefy construction up here on the second floor? Also, I thought this building was from the early 20th century?" said Kyle.

"What ever was stored here was very heavy. Come on, we have to see what's on the first floor."

Kyle and Liam returned to the elevator.

"I don't remember seeing another entrance on the first floor from the lobby. Maybe something from outside?" he asked Liam.

"John, anything on the monitors for the first floor?"

"Still dark LR."

"Okay, let's go and see if we can find a way in."

Kyle closed the outer door and then the inner wire cage of the elevator. Liam was about to press the button for the first floor when he had an idea. He retrieved the false thumb once more and pressed it to the scanner's surface. Once the scanner completed it's process, Liam pressed the number one button on the elevator. The elevator started its slow descent. When it came to a halt instead of being able to open the front wire cage and door opening, the rear of the elevator opened automatically, revealing the same inky blackness that greeted the pair on the second floor.

"I'm impressed. I couldn't even tell that there was an exit there," said Kyle.

"He had a lot of secrets." was all that Liam responded with.

Without splitting up as before, the two men both went to the left, shinning their flashlights upon the brick wall. Just as expected, they came upon an identical knife switch set upon the wall. This time Liam threw the switch and the hidden lights started to come on one by one as the electricity completed the circuit. Just as on the second floor, the lights illuminated a monstrous space and it's post and beam construction, but this time there was more to the room. Laid out in perfect order before Liam and Kyle was a silenced ancient factory.

"Unbelievable." whispered Liam.

"You can say that again." came John's voice through the IFB.

"Do any of you know what you are looking at?"

Kyle walked over to the closest of the machines.

"Some kind of museum with old machines I venture to guess."

Liam joined Kyle at the first machine.

"I can't believe it, I just can't."

"Believe what Boss?" Liz asked over the IFB.

"This place seems to be an exact mockup of an 19th century print house."

"Complete with replica machinery." added John in Liam's ear.

"No, that's the amazing thing, all of these machines are in fact genuine. Each and every one of them original."

266

Liam walked over to what he recognized as an Intaglio printing press. With admiration Liam walked around the press and ever so gently touched the dials, levers and knobs as he circumnavigated the machine.

"This really is absolutely amazing." He stopped at the delivery end of the press. "This is an actual 130 year old Intaglio printing press. Only governments are supposed to have these. If one of these were to get into the wrong hands, someone could literally print money for free. How in hell did it get here?"

"Um Liam" Kyle interrupted from about thirty feet away, "There are two more over here."

Liam looked slowly around the room and started to recognize the various other pieces of equipment, from the printing presses, to a Boston Machine Works slitter, to a spotless Shniedewend & Lee guillotine used to cut paper.

"Every thing is spotless." Kyle remarked. "It looks like these were all just oiled yesterday." He ran a finger over the cool metal. "I wonder if they would still work?"

"Let's find out."

Liam walked over to where he and Kyle had turned on the power for the lights. There next to the knife switch was a series of levers connected to a machine that ran a good fifteen feet long and looked like a large hog lying down with it's four legs underneath it. This was what Liam was looking for. Liam closed another knife switch on the wall and the machine leaped to life, first with a low pitched hum but shortly the factory was filled with a syncopated rhythm of the large motor.

Suspended up in the rafters of the facility, were a series of shafts and belts that ran the length of the room and dropped to each piece of equipment. This was the motive power for all of the machinery.

Liam moved to the first in a series of levers and slowly engaged a clutch pedal with his right foot and then pulled the lever towards him. The ten inch wide leather belt that was connected to the large wheel started to flap as the wheel came up to speed. Liam slowly released the clutch as the cam moved into high speed. The shafts overhead came to life as the main shaft slowly wound its way up to speed. When the noise of the machinery evened out Liam shouted to Kyle to engage the operations lever next to the guillotine. Kyle pulled the lever and the flywheel on the side of the cutter came to life. Liam joined Kyle at the knife.

"Watch this."

Next to the guillotine on a wooden pallet was a stack of paper about 36" long by 24" wide. Liam removed a good four inches from the top of the pile and placed it onto the polished cast iron table. He then spun a wheel beneath the table until an indicator dial just above the top framework of the machine indicated 18. Liam then slid the paper into the mouth of the machine until it came to rest up against a solid metal stop. Liam then stepped to the right side of the guillotine and pulled on a lever with both hands.

As the lever was released, a deafening crash as well as a silvery flash bellowed from within the machine. First a half-ton metal clamp fixed the stack of paper into place rendering it unmovable. Then, less than a second later, a blade sixty inches long and twelve inches wide, weighing 400 pounds, came crashing down into the stack of paper cleaning slicing through the telephone book thick stack of paper as easily as a baker slices through a loaf of fresh bread.

"Damn! Could you imagine that on an arm or leg?" Liz asked over the IFB

"I get chills even thinking about it" said John.

"This thing is over a hundred years old. No safe guards then, but I bet there were a lot of men called lefty." Quipped Kyle. "How in hell did you even know how this thing worked?"

"I grew up in a print-house. I was using one of these things when I was ten. Cut a model car in half. Put a chip in a $3000 blade, couldn't sit down for a week. But I digress; the operation of the modern version is not much different than this one. However now they are designed with all kinds of safety's and stops. The only way to get hurt on one today is to just be plain stupid."

They continued on with their search of the first floor factory. As they went past the various machines, Liam and Kyle confirmed that each and every apparatus was in working condition. The last area that they checked were the small row of offices that sat near the walled up loading dock doors. The first three offices revealed little, nothing more than some antique furniture and empty wood boxes.

In the office nearest to the large overhead door they found a clerks high desk, a row of mailbags on the wall, and a wooden bookshelves stacked full with old ledgers.

"I'm going to check out the loading dock area." Kyle said and left the clerk's office. Liam crossed to the bookcase and scanned the titles on the spines of the ledgers. Most were labeled with just a date with each book containing an individual month. The dates represented were from 1859 through 1872. Liam extracted the first book in the shelf and opened it. The end-sheet of the book was void of any markings. Liam then turned the flyleaf to reveal the title page of the ledger.

As with most printed documents of the day, craftsmanship was paramount and this daily ledger was no exception. An intricately designed typeface proclaimed the company's name who's ledger Liam held. Liam felt a lump in his throat when he saw the badge and name of the company, National Bank Note Company.

Liam gently turned the pages of the ledger. Each page held daily production information for the venerable printing company that once printed corporate stock certificates, negotiable documents, and all of the currency and postage stamps for the United States, as well as other countries. Just as Liam finished with the first ledger and was about to return it to the shelf, Kyle came back into the office.

"Nothing out there Boss. It looks like the three loading dock doors are still working, they open into the building, but the doorways have been blocked up on the outside. They were sealed up with cement block so that means they were blocked up within the last forty years. What did you find?"

"An archivist's dream. It appears that our Mr. Bousquet has assembled many major pieces and key documentation of the National Bank Note Company. These ledgers show us exactly what the firm printed from 1859 through 1872 when they were forced to merge with the American Bank Note Company."

"What do you mean forced?" asked John.

"Well a national scandal almost bankrupted the company in 1869. The scandal was known as Black Friday. A group of influential investors, including President Ulysses S. Grant's brother-in-law, tried to corner the market in gold." started Liam, "It was only four years after the civil war, the country was massively in debt and the currency of the day, the Greenback, became unredeemable. Because of the perceived worthlessness of the Greenbacks, gold coins were forced out of circulation, thus rendering the country's credit very precarious."

Liz chimed in. "But I thought right after the war the government launched a gigantic search for precious metals in the new territories."

"That they did, but to no avail, whatever gold mines that were discovered during that time period were all privately owned. The government bought up what ore it could to shore up the treasury, and that was all accomplished very shadily during Andrew Johnson's administration. Some senators from the northeastern states at the time even suspected President Johnson of diverting the gold out of the treasury by sealed presidential order only to route it to a secret southern society, but nothing was ever proven."

"So how did National almost go bankrupt?"

Liam replaced the ledger that he was looking at and removed the bound edition that was dated October 1869. After a few minutes of reading he was able to answer Liz's question.

"According to the production ledger, the largest order ever placed with the National Bank Note Company occurred at that time. It was for a the printing of over $1,000,000,000 of newly designed United States Greenbacks."

"So how could what should have been a very lucrative contract, almost bankrupt a company?"

"It shows here that over 25,000 pallets of the newly designed and printed currency were to be delivered to the United

States Treasury. Only that it was rejected and that National Bank Note Company was never compensated."

John let lose a low whistle over the IFB.

"Damn, 25,000 pallets of cash never paid for? The manufacturing costs alone had to have been a small fortune back then. Why was the cash rejected?"

Liam continued to read further in the ledger.

"The ledger doesn't make any reference to why. It does show that 30 days later the inventory was handed over to the American Bank Note Company, with once again no compensation to the National Bank Note Company."

"So how did National stay in business for another three years?"

Liam retracted another ledger from the bookshelf.

"January of 1870 shows that the only U.S. Government contracts that National had from that point on were for postage stamps. The rest of their income appears to be from private contracts, that's it."

Liam returned the ledger to the shelf and removed the final ledger of 1871.

"Well this shows the completed transfer of all inventory, equipment and other assets to the American Bank Note Company, and the end of the National Bank Note Company."

Liam closed the book and returned it to the shelf with the others.

"Liam" over the IFB.

"Yeah Liz?"

"I'm in. I found the password.

"Great job! How'd you do it?"

"Well, I ran a simple number generator first to see if that could get us in. Got lucky when I started with numerical date configuration. Password that came up was 08091951. Mean anything to you?"

Liam typed the numbers into his iPhone's notepad in calendar order, 08/09/1951.

"No, doesn't ring a bell. Anyone else have an idea?"

"Let me run the date through an Internet search," said John.

"While John is working on that, what's in the Shadow Liz?"

Liz started scrolling through the list of folders and files.

"Okay, I got a folder here that is labeled *Building History 1861-1872.*"

"Sounds as good as any place to start."

"Boss, I'm going to send this down to you so you can read it yourself. Be there in a few seconds."

With a few keystrokes Liz sent the file's information to Liam via a wireless Internet connection. Within one minute Liam's iPhone alerted him that the file was available. He opened the file and scrolled through the folders list of files stopping on the file title *Building History 1861-1872.*

"Okay" Liam highlighted the file name and opened the folder. He then opened the first file listed in the subfolder. He read the first five lines before he remarked.

"According to Joe's files on the building, construction was started on June 1, 1858 and completed on April 12, 1861."

"That's the date that the Civil War broke with the firing on Fort Sumter." Kyle replied.

"You'll never guess who the first owners were."

"Who Boss?" asked Liz.

"The building was financed and built for a firm by the name of Danforth & Perkins &Co., the predecessor of National Bank Note Company." Liam continued "It turns out that this was their warehouse, the main factory was located at 1 Wall Street in Manhattan, right across the street from Trinity Church."

"Ha! Told you so!"

The volume of the comment from John echoed in everyone's IFB's.

"Not so loud! You almost blew out my eardrum you stage hack!" said Kyle.

"Trinity Church! See! The church that we were just talking about earlier, you see it's tied to everything!"

Liz tried to bring the conversation back to the topic at hand.

"Down boys, it is purely a coincidence. Everything was located around that church in 1859. It was the center of the city at that time. So Liam, why would National have their main shop in Manhattan and a warehouse all the way out here? Wouldn't it take the better part of a day to get from there to here?"

"I'll answer that when I get back upstairs Liz. Be right up."

Liam and Kyle retraced their steps, shut the power down to the equipment and lights and took the elevator back up to the stamp library. Liam walked back to the security center and took a chair by Liz.

"Turns out that August, 9 1951 was the true recorded date of the end of WWII," reported John.

"Joe was a real stickler for details. Susan said her father told her he bought the building the day the war ended. Liz, please bring up the building file. I noticed a file in there I want to take a closer look at."

Liz expanded the folders directory and opened the directory for Liam. He scanned down the list until he came to a file labeled NY&H.

"Open this one."

Liam pointed to the file on the screen. The file expanded and displayed on the computers desktop was scanned image of an old survey map of the City of New York. On the map were a series of roads, canals, and avenues. He also noted a small blinking icon on the lower right hand corner of the map.

"What's this?"

Liz maneuvered the cursor to the icon and doubled clicked it. A transparent overlay of the map appeared.

"Looks like Joe scanned a second map and overlaid it on the original survey map. Look at the legend." Liam pointed to the faint legend on the overlay.

"What does it say right here?"

"Hang on Boss, let me dial down the transparency."

Liz made the overlay appear less transparent. When she did the legend became legible.

"Another surprise, Joe was full of them."

On the screen before them was a key to current and proposed railway lines for the New York & Harlem Railroad in 1859. One of the lines ran directly from the Wall Street area directly to the building that they were sitting in, in the Bronx.

"Liz, what you have before you are the beginnings of the New York Elevated System, circa 1859. National Bank Note Company had the NY&H run a line from the main building to the warehouse here in the Bronx. Only makes sense as Cornelius Vanderbilt owned the majority of the NY&H and would have tried to secure major shipping contracts both locally and nationally to support his steamships and fledgling railroads. Can you pull up a current NYC Subway System map?"

With a momentary search on the Internet, Liz found a .jpg version of a system map. She made a few graphics corrections and overlaid the new map on the scanned image from 1859.

"See the current MetroNorth line is an almost perfect match. Before the city moved most trains below ground, the city was teaming with private elevated railways. This line was owned by Vanderbilt's New York & Harlem branch line. There must have been either a spur to this building or they moved the line in the early 20th century."

"So after the war Joe bought this building. Do you think he knew what it was?" asked John.

"Well the more and more we learn about Joe Bousquet I think we'll find that he was defiantly a company brother. He must have stumbled onto this building during the war and waited until the end of the war to buy it. I think some of the other files here will layout the timeline for us."

"I'll jump on it first thing in the morning, okay Boss?" said Liz "Right now I seem to have stumbled onto another little secret here in Shadow."

Liam looked at the screen at what Liz had found."

"Could take hours." He looked at his watch and noticed that the day had slipped away. "Tell you what, all of you must be beat, why don't you take the day tomorrow and wrap things up at the hotel. We'll move operations out here on Saturday morning."

"Sure thing Boss. Do you need any help tomorrow?"

"No thank

Liz. I'm going to clean up some of Rex's arrangements, spend some time in the library and then have dinner with a friend."

Liz, John and Kyle packed up their gear and walked over to the subway and caught the next train back into Manhattan. Liam spent the next forty-five minutes exploring Joe Bousquet's apartment. He located three well appointed bedrooms, each with it's own full bathroom, a small area that had been converted into a gym complete with a circuit trainer, and a office complete with business equipment and wall to wall book shelves. The last room he went into was the master suite. He opened the door and was astonished to find a room almost five times the size of an entire New York City apartment. Everything in the room was custom. The oversized king bed sat on an elevated area of the suite. Next to the bed was a sitting area with two full-size couches, two recliners and an oversized coffee table. A door on the far wall revealed a custom built, walk in closet that could easily be used as small warehouse. Custom racks for shoes, suits, socks even dirty laundry lined all four walls. Recessed lighting illuminated all the shelves and drawers with what appeared to be carefully balanced light. A center island contained a touch screen terminal that could be used as a wardrobe inventory system. Liam just shook his head and smiled as he closed the door.

The bedroom had an exit out onto an outdoor terrace that faced south towards the Manhattan skyline. Liam walked outside and over to the parapet that surrounded the terrace. He retrieved his cell phone, located the Waldorf=Astoria's number and pressed connect. The operator answered on the second ring and Liam asked for Rebecca Hodge and waited for the operator to connect him.

When she answered she was a bit out of breath.

"Hello."

"Rebecca, it's Liam Ross. Am I interrupting you?"

"No Liam not at all. I just walked in and rushed to answer the phone."

"I wanted to call and see if we are still on for dinner tomorrow evening?"

"I am if you are."

"Wonderful. I was wondering if we might try something a little different. You game?"

"Just tell me when, where and what to wear."

"How about seven o'clock, I'll have a town car meet you outside at the Park Avenue entrance and as far as what to wear, I wouldn't even venture to begin to even have a clue as to what the most beautiful woman in New York should wear!"

Rebecca laughed.

"Well tell me at least if it's formal, business or casual?"

"Intimate dining with a casual flair. Does that help?"

"Yes, I think it does."

"Well then, till tomorrow evening?"

"Till tomorrow evening."

Liam disconnected and watched the last of the sun's orange, red and purple light slip beneath the western skyline.

22

Cote de Beouf

Bousquet Loft
Bronx, New York
May 3, 2013

Liam awoke early the next morning in his room at the Waldorf=Astoria. By six he had showered, shaved, packed and eaten breakfast. He left a message on Jane Reese's voicemail that he would be checking out and that someone from his team would be contacting her to pickup all of his and Rex's belongings.

Liam then spent thirty minutes making some arrangements for that evening and returning phone calls from the day before. Including one from the New York Coroner alerting him that Rex's body had been released and sent to Gang's Funeral Home as directed by Rex's attorney. It was too early to call Ken's cell and alert him that everything was being taken care of so Liam called his office and left the message there. At eight o'clock Liam called Gang's Funeral Home and confirmed the cremation arrangements for the next day at 3:00 PM.

Liam had a full day of errands ahead of him and his first stop was back at the Philatelic Expo. He met with a handful of fellow dealers and told them about the arrangements for Rex. They assured Liam that they all would be in attendance for their colleague and old friend. Liam left the exhibition hall, walked out to the traffic lanes then hailed a cab. Liam gave the cab driver the address in Little Italy. Being after rush hour the cab made the journey in a little over twenty minutes. Liam had the cabbie drop him at the corner of Broome and Mulberry. He paid the driver and then walked the half a block to where the nightmare had begun forty-eight hours earlier.

The scene at the restaurant was quite different than two nights before. There were no police cars, no crime scene tape, no broken glass from the bullet-shattered windows and no bloodstains on the sidewalk where Rex had died in Liam's arms. Everything looked normal, as if nothing had even occurred here. Just another day in Manhattan.

Liam climbed the three short steps into the restaurant and was met by a busboy that was mopping the floor from last nights patrons. In broken English-Italian he tried to explain that the restaurant was closed. Liam just walked right by the teen, past the counter and right into the kitchen. Antonio was right where Liam knew he would be. Sitting at the small kitchen table, that his mother use as her prep table each day, nursing a coffee cup. When Antonio saw Liam he shot up and called to the busboy in Italian.

"Marco, un cappuccino per favore, due colpi del espresso. Pronto!"

"Cappuccino made with two shots of espresso, you have a mind like a steel trap my friend, never forgetting."

The two friends embraced each other and then sat down. The coffee arrived within seconds.

"Liam, I am ever so sorry about your friend. If there is ever anything that I can do to help, just let me know."

"Thank you Tony, I greatly appreciate that. But it is I that needs to offer an apology to you my old friend. I am afraid that Rex and I brought this tragedy upon your restaurant."

Dismissing Liam's comment with a wave of his hand,

"Think nothing of it. The real tragedy is that it has brought the ghouls out of the woodwork. We no sooner cleaned up from the other night when the city's sad underbelly descended upon us. That is the true crime, the sickness of the vultures. I've closed the doors until next week. By then it will be yesterday's news."

"Tony, but what about all the business that you will loose?"

"Not another word, the staff is grateful for a few paid days off, God knows I could use a couple off as well. Besides, when you tell customers down here that you are closed due to a death in the family, there are no questions asked. They will all be back."

Liam took the death in the family comment and closing of the restaurant to heart. This meant that Antonio was honoring his friend. Liam was too choked upped to even respond. When he got up to leave once again his friend of fifteen years gave him a bone-crushing bear hug.

"Be safe Pisano. You need anything, you call me."

"Grazie Antonio, Grazie."

Liam walked the few short blocks over to the number Four train in order to head up to the Bronx. Liam walked down the subway entrance stairs and walked right onto a train heading uptown. Liam sat in a corner all to himself, reflecting on the events of the past days and starting to feel a bit melancholy. At the Lexington stop a family got on the train and sat directly across from Liam. Mom and dad had their hands full trying to contain three toddlers. The three were so excited that they were going to the zoo to see the monkeys. One of the children would start to mimic a monkey with chattering and scratching his head, dancing about, when his siblings would both join into the fracas. After watching the children for a few minutes, Liam forgot about his dark skies and began to laugh at the trio dancing around the subway car. By the time the conductor's tinny voice on the intercom called out his stop, Liam felt like a new person.

Instead of a cab, Liam opted to walk the mile over to one of the greatest treasures in all of New York, a gastronome's Camelot, Mecca for serious devotees of all things culinary, Arthur Avenue in the Bronx. Ask any New Yorker about Arthur Avenue and you will either receive quizzical looks or non-stop admiration about the best place in New York for meats, cheeses, pasta, just about anything Italian. The real conundrum is most New Yorkers have never even heard of this place, while those in the know, know it as a not a so well kept secret.

Liam had his shopping list committed to memory. First he started at The Retail Market, a collection of small vendors that had it's start in early 1940 when New York's mayor, Fiorello LaGaurdia, wanted to relocate the food cart vendors that lined the street of New York. Little has changed since then and when you set foot on the avenue you almost feel like you are stepping back in time.

He started at Vincent's Meat Market where he asked for a freshly trimmed 32-ounce, dry aged, prime, bone in rib eye. The butcher behind the counter asked Liam how long he wanted the bone. Liam asked if it was possible to cut it to around six inches. The butcher responded that that would not be a problem and also asked if he should French-trim the bone. Liam was prepared to do this back at the loft but was more than happy to have the butcher complete, what could be an arduous task. Liam paid for his purchase and headed back into the market in order to find the rest of his shopping list. After an hour of going from store to store, and stall to stall, Liam had assembled all of the ingredients necessary for his dinner with Rebecca.

Liam hailed a cab at the corner of Author Avenue and 187 Street. He was back at Joe's building with twenty minutes. He paid the cabbie and hauled his purchases up to the apartment. He then spent the better part of an hour familiarizing himself with Joe Bousquet's kitchen. He found all of the equipment that he would need, including a whole house stereo system. As part of that system, Joe had installed a computer hard drive as his music source. After a few minutes navigating the system's menu Liam set it to automatically select various instrumental compositions. With the evenings music decided he set to work prepping that evening's dinner.

Liam had decided to go very old school New York with his menu. He would start the evening with his take on the classic Oysters Rockefeller, followed with a classic steak house salad. For the entrée he was going to prepare a Coté de Beouf with a deglazed pan sauce, accompanied by Gratin Dauphinoise, delicately sliced potatoes, baked with herbs, cream, garlic and Gruyere cheese. To finish the evening's gastronomy, dessert would be the venerable classic, Mousse Au Chocolat.

He started with prepping the beef. The rib eye that the butcher trimmed for Liam was perfect. It had the perfect amount of marbling and the steak measured at a good two inches thick. He sprinkled a generous amount of kosher salt, garlic powder and a small amount of freshly cracked black pepper on both sides. He then wrapped the steak tightly in plastic wrap and deposited the meat in Joe's commercial walk-in refrigerator.

Next he found a mandolin among Joe's collection of kitchen utensils. Unlike the musical instrument this instrument would make fast work of slicing the Yukon Gold potatoes. Liam set the slicer to a little over 1/16" in thickness and then went to work cutting the tubers. After slicing the potatoes, Liam let the slices soak in a 50/50 mixture of water and milk until he needed them. He then changed blades and quickly shredded the needed cheese.

Liam located Joe's collection of Le Creuset enameled coated cast iron cookware. He found the perfect size low dish for the potatoes and started the assembly. Working quickly, he started in one corner of the greased baking dish, placing each individual slice of potato, overlapping the previous slice by half. He continued until he had covered the entire bottom of the dish with two layers.

Liam then sprinkled a liberal layer of the shredded cheese on top of the potatoes. A light salt and peppering and it was time to repeat the layers of potatoes. He continued the same process until the pan was filled to just below the rim. He then covered the top of the potatoes with the remaining cheese. Covered the dish with plastic wrap and pressed down, compacting the multiple layers of the potatoes. He removed the plastic and set the dish aside.

Now it was time to prepare the wet mixture of the potato dish. Liam minced three cloves of fresh garlic, cut some butter into small pieces then added the two ingredients to a pan along with cream and about six fresh sprigs of thyme. This was brought to a gentle boil and then poured over the potatoes.

Liam had brought the convection oven to temperature and placed the pan of potatoes in to bake for about ninety minutes. When finished baking, Liam would let these set out of the oven until the potatoes had cooled, then sliced them into small squares right before serving.

Liam quickly made the chocolate mousse following a recipe that his mother had taught him when he was just a boy. The rich dessert consisted of just six ingredients, 12 ounces of chocolate, ¼ cup of black freshly brewed coffee, four separated eggs, 2/3 of a cup of sugar, 2 tablespoons of dark rum and a ½ teaspoon of vanilla extract. Liam went through the preparation almost without thinking as he had made this favorite many times. When finished he spooned the thickened mixture into two martini glasses and set them in the refrigerator in order to chill. As he closed the door he wished that he had thought to make this yesterday as this dessert only got richer the longer that it set. Oh well, if hindsight was 20-20.

The salad was a simple prep and he would leave that until it was time to serve it. Besides he had learned long ago, after stressing too many times when making dinners for guests, that there was nothing wrong with giving them a little show while they sipped a glass of wine and sampled a hors d'oeuvre. But he did need to prep the oysters.

Most people might turn down the opportunity to sample one of the world's best gifts, oysters. It was very true of the old adage that it must have been a very brave man to eat the first raw oyster, but oh what he had discovered! Although Oysters Rockefeller were not served raw, you did need the freshest oysters possible and no place in the United States could offer up a better selection of these fresh bivalves than New York City. Liam's love of oysters stemmed from trying them in just about every place he traveled in the world, but his all time favorites were the famed Blue Points.

After having almost been harvested to extinction, the Blue Point was making a tremendous comeback in the waters of the southern shores of the Long Island Sound. Liam had found a wonderful fishmonger in the Author Avenue market and had secured six of the most perfect specimens that the man had. Liam had been assured that these oysters had been harvested from their beds just that morning, and the classification tag that the monger showed Liam proved just that.

Oyster Rockefeller can trace its roots to Antoine's in New Orleans, one of the oldest family restaurants in the United States. It was created in 1899 and named after the richest man in the world, at that time, John D. Rockefeller.

The oysters are served on the half-shell, lightly broiled and served hot. Over the years, various chefs have taken this classic and adapted it to their own means, and Liam was no different. After the oysters were shucked into a bowl with their liqueur, the juice from the fresh oyster, Liam steamed some fresh baby spinach then plunged it into ice cold water in order to stop the cooking process and to preserve the rich, dark green color. He then made a light stuffing of fresh seasoned breadcrumbs, minced garlic and onion, olive oil, herbs and melted butter. Once combined, he placed a spoonful of the mixture on the drained, cooled spinach leaves that he had lined in the bottom halves of the empty oyster shells with. On top of this stuffing, one of the shucked oysters was placed, later on top of each oyster, a dollop of freshly made hollandaise sauce and crumbled bacon would be added right before cooking.

Liam found a low rimmed baking sheet and covered the bottom with rock salt that he had bought at the hardware store. On top of the salt he placed the six oysters, wrapped and refrigerated until 30 minutes before he was going to serve. The rock salt was an old New England Yankee way to gently cook the oysters without the fear of the shells exploding in the broiling process.

He had arranged for a car service to pick Rebecca up at seven so that meant the earliest she would arrive would be seven forty-five, so he had a little over an hour and a half. Liam convinced himself that he had plenty of time for a shower, shave and a change of clothes.

The shock of Susan's gift of the wine cellar was not real to him yet. He stood just inside the doorway and a surveyed the thousands of bottles that had been collected. After a few minutes Liam was able to understand how Joe had organized his collection, white wines on the left, reds on the right, and sparkling and dessert wines in the center rack.

Liam searched for the perfect white wine to serve with the oysters. He was looking for a full-bodied, not too heavy on the oak, chardonnay. He found the perfect bottle, a 2008 Olivier Laflaive Puligny Montrachet. For the main course he wanted an older wine to showcase with the beef. Rack by rack he removed amazing after amazing bottle, vintages going back to the 1940's. A whole section devoted to the amazing 1961 vintage from Bordeaux. Liam finally made up his mind on a rather unique choice. Tucked far below on one of the bottom racks Liam discovered three bottles of a little gem of a 1989 Santa Barbara California Pinot Noir. He removed two of the bottles from the shelf and took them into the kitchen.

He set the first bottle on the counter next to the seating area. What Liam did not see was the piece of old hardened wax that had stuck to the bottom of second bottle. When he set the bottle down, it pitched forward onto the stone counter, smashing the bottle and spilling its ruby contents all over the soapstone. Liam quickly grabbed a towel and cleaned up the pooled wine, cursing to himself over the loss of an excellent bottle of wine.

He went back into the cellar to retrieve the third bottle from the rack. When he pulled the bottle out of its space he was surprised to notice that the bottle was conspicuously lighter than it should be. He looked at the bottle's shoulder level but was unable to determine how much wine was in the container because the glass appeared to be discolored black.

Liam went to turn the bottle so he could see the label, however the bottom of the bottle came off in his hand as he rotated the bottle. He peered into the bottom of the bottle, but was unable to see into it because of the dim light of the wine cellar.

In the brighter kitchen light, Liam was able to see a paper inside the darkened cylinder. Liam slowly retracted the paper to reveal a glassine packet a little larger than a standard household envelope. Carefully he opened the flap of the packet to reveal an aged, yellow envelope inside. Rather risk damage to the paper, Liam retrieved a pair of stamp tongs from his case. Gently he removed the paper from inside the glassine packet and set it on the counter.

The paper was an envelope, an old one. The recipient's address was written in a flowing script, the purplish-black hue of the ink was most likely iron gall ink from the mid 19th century. The postmark in the upper right hand corner announced that it was mailed in New York on February 25, 1868. The recipient was Anna Stephens, 46 Essex Street, Manhattan, New York. The reverse of the envelope held a faded red wax seal that had been broken open. Liam delicately opened the envelope and extracted its contents.

The paper from the envelope was different than standard paper of the day. It seemed heavier than most and had very pronounced threads within its compound. The paper had been folded over as a tri-fold then folded in half once again. Liam unfolded the first fold and revealed a message in the same flowing hand that had addressed the envelope, it read; *Anna my dearest, I told you some day we would be rich beyond our wildest hopes and dreams, Your loving Roy.* Liam slowly unfolded the remaining two folds. When fully opened, what Liam held in his hands was truly unbelievable, a sheet of ten, one million dollar U.S. Notes. Missing was the printing on the reverse, or Greenback, side.

This couldn't be real it had to be a fake. The largest known Greenback was a one thousand dollar denomination Demand Note, and the only known example that still existed was on display at the Smithsonian Institution. Liam was about to take the paper into the stamp library in order to better examine it under one of the scanners that Kyle had brought up from Florida, when his cell phone vibrated in his pocket.

"Liam Ross."

"Is this the wonderful man that had a limousine, complete with champagne, whisk me off to a far away land called the Bronx?"

"Guilty as charged, I'm afraid" was his response.

"We should be there in five minutes, Sweetheart."

Liam looked at his watch and saw that she was going to arrive a good twenty minutes early.

"Well, call when you arrive and I will come down and greet you."

"Be there soon."

Liam returned the letter and envelope back into the glassine packet, and then carefully inserted the packet back into the wine bottle. He set the bottle on the kitchen counter out of harms way. He was about to check the white wine to see if it had sufficiently chilled when he was startled by the door buzzer. Liam pressed the button to unlock the downstairs door. Liam made it to the front door and opened it just as Rebecca was stepping off the elevator with a champagne flute in one hand and a bottle in the other. She crossed the short distance to where Liam was standing, stopped and gave him a very hot, very wet, lingering kiss.

"Hi honey, I'm home!" She breathed into his ear. She slid past Liam and handed him the three quarters empty bottle.

Liam stepped aside to let her in. He welcomed her when he was finally was able to breath again.

"What a lovely place! Is it yours?"

"No I'm sort of house sitting for a few days. Please make yourself at home.

Liam showed Rebecca into the living room.

"May I take your coat?"

""Yes, thank you." Rebecca removed her coat only to reveal what a beautiful woman would consider dressing casually. She was wearing a beautiful multi-colored silk peasant blouse, whose colors shifted as she moved, and deep rich blue designer jeans that accentuated her lithe, well sculpted legs. She was also wearing yet another pair of the famed red soled Christian Louboutins', which Liam now assumed was her favorite shoe designer. She struck a pose with her hand on one hip in order to show off her ensemble.

"Too casual?" she asked.

"Stunning! Perfect! Gorgeous! No compare... and the clothes are nice too."

Liam received a warm, heart-felt laugh and a hug from Rebecca with that comment.

"Another glass of wine, then perhaps a quick tour?" Liam asked his guest.

"That would be lovely."

Liam led her into the kitchen and before they were even three feet into the room Rebecca let out a muffled response to seeing the culinary heaven.

"Oh my! What an amazing kitchen! It smells amazing in here, are we eating in?"

"If you don't mind. I don't get to cook all that often and I truly love to."

"Have a wonderful man make me dinner? You won't hear any complaints out of me."

Liam then poured the last from the bottle of Laurent Perrier Rosé champagne into two clean flutes and handed one to Rebecca.

"This is perhaps the most delicious champagne that I have ever tasted" she remarked.

The two toasted to friendship and life, clinked the glasses, and drank some of the rose colored wine. Liam then turned to the steak that had been warming to room temperature on the counter.

Taking a heavy cast iron skillet, He placed a tablespoon of vegetable oil in it then heated the pan on the stove until the oil just started to smoke. Then he placed the steak into the pan and started to sear the sides of the beef. Once the first side had cooked for four minutes, Liam turned over the steak and cooked the opposite side for another four minutes. Completed, Liam removed the steak from the pan and let it rest on a plate for twenty minutes.

"Okay, I am very impressed. You do look as if you know your way around the kitchen."

"I struggle through."

"So what's on the menu for this evening, that is if you don't mind me asking?"

Liam ran through the menu and looked for any tell in Rebecca's face if she did not care for something, he saw no such response. Liam then went to work on prepping the salad.

In most classic American steak houses you will always find a common salad on the menu. If for some reason it is not there, all one needs to do is ask for it and ninety-nine out of a hundred times, the guest will be accommodated. The salad? A simple wedge of cool, crisp, iceberg lettuce, with chunky blue cheese dressing, tomatoes optional.

Liam prepared the dish by slicing half a head of lettuce in half, then placing the lettuce on ice-cold plates that Liam had removed from the freezer. Next he liberally drizzled a mixture of freshly crumbled Maytag Blue Cheese and extra virgin olive oil over the wedges. Liam would then season these with a small amount of freshly cracked black pepper right before serving, but until then, the plates were returned to the refrigerator. Liam then turned the salamander broiler on low and placed his Oysters Rockefeller on the bottom rack and set the timer for fifteen minutes.

"Now for the nickel tour."

Liam showed Rebecca around the apartment. She remarked on the décor and was very complimentary to the owner as she went from room to room. They lingered on the terrace outside of the master bedroom, sipping their champagne, while the lights of the city started to appear one by one.

"Liam it is so beautiful here. I am having a wonderful evening."

Liam set his wine glass down and moved closer to her. He circled his arm around her waist and brought her close to him, they kissed. Liam tasted the combination of the wine and her lipstick while inhaling her intoxicating scent. Still holding her he slowly released her lips from his, and watched as her closed eyes slowly opened.

"Me too." He said in a whisper and kissed her again.

The pair left the terrace and went back inside as a chill started to settle into the spring night air. On their way back to the kitchen he guided her right past the stamp library. He didn't consciously omit the room more than he heard the steady chirp that was the timer for his oysters.

Back in the kitchen Rebecca took her same place at the counter and Liam took his place on the opposite side. He tied on a half chefs apron in order to assure that his shirt and pants did not fall victim to some errant splash or spill. He then removed the tray of oysters from the broiler and plated three for each of them. He then placed the steak into the oven.

"Oh, that looks wonderful!" remarked Rebecca.

"My version of Oysters Rockefeller." Responded the chef. "I hope that you like oysters, I was taking a gamble."

Liam then uncorked the bottle of Puligny Montrachet that had been resting in a silver ice bucket. He poured a small amount into one glass, sampled the wine, and then poured each of them a glass of the golden wine.

Rebecca took one forkful of the savory mollusk and her eyes and mouth conveyed it all.

"Oh my God. These should be illegal! This is pure heaven on earth."

"I thank you Madame, one of my specialties.

She lifted her glass and delicately sipped her wine.

"Oh, I could get very used to this."

The two just chatted about their day until the thermometer buzzer sounded. Liam removed the steak from the oven, removed it from the skillet and wrapped it tightly with a piece of foil. Then returning the skillet to the stove Liam added his ingredients one by one, butter, kosher salt, freshly grated black pepper, heavy cream and finally one half cup of cognac that he flambéed. Once this was done he poured the contents of the pan into a small sauce ramekin. All that was left to prepare was the small side dish of haricot verts, small, French style green beans that he quickly sautéed in olive oil and garlic.

With the meal all prepared, Liam sliced the streak and plated the feast.

"Are you comfortable here at the counter or would you like to move to the dining room?" Liam asked of Rebecca.

"Oh, it's just lovely right here" she proclaimed.

Liam retrieved the bottle of red wine that he had opened earlier in order to breathe, poured each of them a glass, then he sat down next to his guest.

Their discussion spanned many topics interspersed with compliments to the chef each time Rebecca tasted something new. About forty-five minutes into the dinner Liam poured the last of the Pinot Noir.

"Ah, another dead solider" he remarked. Liam watched as Rebecca drained the last bit from her glass.

"It's still early, how about another bottle?" she asked coyly holding out her wine glass.

"Your wish is shall be granted."

Liam got up from the counter and started towards the wine cellar. Just as he was about to open the door Rebecca called to him.

"Here's a bottle!"

Liam turned and saw that she had found the fake bottle that he had left on the counter. As she picked up the bottle the bottom fell onto the soapstone counter breaking into multiple pieces. Quickly following the bottle's bottom the glassine packet fell onto the counters surface. She was startled and dropped the bottle onto the counter. As it hit the stone it shattered into a hundred shards. Rebecca now appeared to be quite distraught.

"Oh Liam, I am so sorry, I didn't mean to…"

"Don't worry about it" as he reached the counter and retrieved the glassine packet from the pile of glass in front of him. He then set it off to the side as he went over to the kitchen sink cupboard.

"I'm so sorry, I didn't know that it wasn't a bottle of wine. I mean it has the same label as the one we were drinking. I am so sorry" she continued.

"Rebecca, please don't worry about it. It's just one of those trick containers that you can hide things in. It's really nothing." Liam found a small dustpan and broom under the kitchen sink.

"Are you sure, I feel so awful for dropping it like that."

"Really, it is quite alright. No sense crying over spilt milk, or in this case broken glass."

"So what was hidden in the bottle?" she picked up the packet and had removed its contents before Liam had a chance to react.

"Oh, nothing really. Just an old envelope and letter."

"Oh what fun! Who is it from?" Rebecca started to remove the letter from the envelope and Liam stopped her and gently took the envelope away from her.

"Sorry, it's a very old letter and it needs to be handled with gloves, plus it's not mine and I feel a little funny having stumbled across it myself. I hope you understand." He set the packet and it's contents off to the side.

"Oh, certainly Liam. I didn't mean to pry."

"So how about that other glass of wine?"

Rebecca walked over to where Liam was standing and stopped just mere inches from him. She reached both of her arms up and wrapped them around the back of his neck. As she leaned in close to him she whispered.

"How about some dessert instead?"

She closed her eyes as her mouth found Liam's lips. She began exploring Liam's tongue with a lingering French kiss as Liam reached behind her and pulled her closer to him. Their tongues locked into a dance as they explored each other's mouths. The warmth of her mouth set waves of electricity throughout his body and Liam felt himself become extremely aroused. After a full two minutes, of perhaps the most amazing kiss Liam had experienced, Rebecca gently closed her mouth and broke their kiss.

"What room are you staying in?" she asked him in a low raspy voice.

"In the master" was all Liam replied.

As she turned around she grasped Liam's right hand and led him out of the kitchen and down the hallway to the master bedroom.

23

Walk of Shame

Liam awoke from a deep sleep. He had just had one of the most intense dreams that he could ever remember having. A dream so realistic it would be difficult to believe that it had not been real. He moved his left arm in order to retrieve his watch from the nightstand. When he fully extended his arm he hit another pillow instead of the nightstand. Beneath the grogginess of the dream he realized that he was sleeping on the wrong side of the bed. He sat up onto one arm and tried to clear the cobwebs. After two minutes he remembered that he was not in his hotel room, but in Joe Bousquet's loft. The evening before came flooding back into his memory. It had not been a dream just the most intense love making that he had ever experienced.

Liam looked to the empty bed next to him, unaware as to where Rebecca was. The digital clock on the nightstand reveled that it was just 2:55 AM. He sat up on the edge of the bed and noticed the sliver of light pouring from under the master suite bathroom. He was about to get up when the light under the door turned off and the door to the master suite bathroom opened slowly and quietly. A dark shadow slowly started to walk over to the bedroom door.

"Time for the walk of shame?" he asked Rebecca.

"Oh lover, I didn't want to wake you" she walked over to where Liam sat on the edge of the bed.

"I was out like a light, the wine must have gotten to me. I'm so sorry that I fell asleep."

She leaned over and kissed him.

"Don't worry about that one bit. You told me yourself told me that this has been one hell of a week. To tell the truth, if I didn't have to be on a train back to Hartford tomorrow, I mean later this morning, I would still be lying beside you."

She kissed him again, and as she did she slid her hand between Liam's legs and felt him as his hardness returned.

"Perhaps even enjoying Act Two."

Liam grabbed her and pulled her down onto the bed next to him.

"Act two? I thought we would be up to at least Act Four or Five!" Liam kissed her passionately.

"When can I see you again?"

"How quick can you get to Hartford?"

"I suppose I could re-arrange my schedule and be up there next weekend. Is that son enough?"

"Then I shall re-arrange my schedule as well."

Liam held Rebecca close and tight he did not want to let her go. He kissed her once again and they both got up off the bed.

"Oh Liam, please don't get out of bed, I'm fine."

"Nonsense, I will take you back to the hotel."

"Really, that's not necessary. I called the same car service that brought me over here, when I was in the bathroom. They should be downstairs waiting."

"Well at least I can walk you to the car."

Liam walked Rebecca out of the apartment, into the elevator and then down to the lobby. He held open the front door and let Rebecca out first. The air smelled fresh with rain. Small puddles had accumulated on the sidewalk in front of the building and the streetlights reflected on the wet streets. The town car was waiting at the curb. It's engine ticking softly as it idled. Liam went around Rebecca in order to reach the car first. He opened the rear door to allow her to get in. She stopped in front of him and kissed him goodbye.

"I had a wonderful evening Mr. Liam Ross."

"I as well Miss Rebecca Hodge."

"I'll call you when I get back to Hartford. I'm going to miss you."

"If you only knew how much I was going to miss you."

They kissed one last time. Rebecca slid into the warmed leather seats of the town car. Liam closed the rear door and knocked on the front passenger window in order to tell the driver to make sure that his account was billed. The window slid down silently, releasing the water that had settled on the outside of the glass. Liam leaned down to offer his instructions and was startled to see that the driver was a woman.

"Yes sir. How may I help you?"

Feeling a little relieved that Rebecca would be safer with another woman as a driver, he asked the driver to make sure that he was charged and that she should put on his bill a thirty dollar tip for herself.

"Thank you sir. That is very generous. Good night."

With that the window returned closed and the black car slid away from the curb. Liam stood for a few minutes as he watched the car off in the distance. He then returned to the loft and the warmth of the king size bed. Liam stripped off his clothes and climbed between the sateen sheets of Egyptian cotton and beneath the thick goose down comforter. Liam relived the entire evening in his mind over and over again, seeming to focus on the dessert course. After twenty minutes Liam fell back to sleep, with a boyish grin on his face.

24

Third Rail

The crash woke Liam from a dead sleep. It was the type of crash that you perceive in your dream but when you awake it has really happened. Liam sat bolt upright in bed and listened to see if he heard anything else. He got out of bed and put his jeans on. He then quietly pulled on his shirt and slipped his feet into his Jack Purcell sneakers without even untying the laces. He then quietly moved out the bedroom door and stopped in the darkened hallway. He flatted himself up against the stamp library door and listened, no noises. He was about to walk down to the kitchen when he saw the small beam of light move on the floor outside of the kitchen entrance. The light was coming from a small penlight that was held by a figure dressed entirely in black. Liam ducked back towards the wall and cursed himself for not having his Glock. The gun was still securely in his room safe back at the hotel.

As soon as the shadowy figure went into the kitchen, Liam slowly crept down the hallway and stopped at the entrance. He ducked down low and quickly shot his head around the corner of the doorjamb in order to surveil the room. He did this three times, each time focusing on a different part of the kitchen. On the third try he saw the figure over near the sink shining the LED pen light over the surface of the counters.

Liam hastily put together a plan. The evening's dinner dishes were still on the counter about ten feet inside the door and to the right. He would crawl over to the counter and hide on the opposite side as the intruder. He might be able to reach one of the steak knives that he and Rebecca had used during dinner. He would then figure out step two, once he got that far.

Liam checked the position of the figure once more and watched as he started to walk over to the sideboard near the wine cellar. Liam took his chance. He quickly and quietly crab-walked over to the counter stools and stopped to listen. He sensed that the intruder was still over near the wine cellar from the sound of glasses being moved about. Liam checked from the end of the counter to see what direction the figure was looking, it was a good sign he was still bent over the books and papers that were on the wine cellar sideboard. Liam noiselessly stood up and grabbed one of the unused steak knives. And shot back down for cover. He now had at least some form of a weapon.

Liam peered around the edge of the counter once again. The figure has finished the search of the sideboard and was walking toward the dining counter and Liam's hiding place. Liam squatted on his feet and steadied himself by the cabinets that supported the counter. Liam now heard the intruder very close, as he was just four feet away on the other side of the counters. Liam knew that what he was doing was reckless. He did not have a plan, or even a proper weapon. At that time he also remembered something that his Uncle Bob had told him years ago. That in most home robberies, the average homeowner is the one that most likely ends up being injured and even killed with his own weapon, be that a gun, knife or even baseball bat. Well, Liam felt that he had a couple of things going for him. He didn't own this house and he was a bit above average when it came to confrontations.

Liam listened intently tracking the visitor via a floor plan of the kitchen in his mind. The noises stopped suddenly and then Liam noticed the telltale rustle of a glassine envelope. It sounded as if the packet with the Greenback was being opened. About fifteen seconds elapsed when Liam heard the figure quietly emit just on word – Bingo.

Liam waited, as he had counted on the thief to return the way that he had come. He was right. Within seconds Liam heard the padded footfalls approach his hiding area. It sounded as if the thief was double-timing his pace on the exit. Liam had hoped for this as he had the element of surprise on his side. Liam melted even closer to the cabinets and waited. Just then the black clothed legs of the intruder appeared to Liam's left. Liam silently quick counted two and then lashed out with a side sweep of his left leg.

Liam's leg connected with the hard surface of the intruder's tibia. As Liam finished his leg sweep the figure crashed to the ground, falling forward, face down. Liam quickly jumped from his hiding place and onto the thief's back. He jammed his right knee into the small of the intruder's back with all his strength behind it. He then grabbed for the masked covered head with his left hand as his right held the steak knife. Instead of a hand full of hair, Liam's hand came away with a black sailors watch cap. Liam paused just a second to comprehend what was in his hand. That two beat pause proved to be costly to Liam.

In just those two counted beats, the prone figure underneath Liam, kicked out with such force that it through Liam off balance and back into the counter cabinets, dropping the steak knife. His head struck the hardened surface of a hinge as he fell backwards. The figure started to get up and was now in a three-point runners stance. Liam leapt for the intruder's 0legs but was just a fraction of second late and connected with nothing but air, as the bandit tore out the kitchen door and into the loft's living room. Liam got up and took off in pursuit. The figure was about twelve feet in front of Liam as they crossed the dark massive space. He was heading for the drapes in the corner of the room.

The intruder made it to the drapes and ducked behind the floor length fabric. Liam skidded to a brief stop about six feet from the curtains. He was not about to wildly jump into a potential ambush. Liam reached for a large coffee table book off to his right, and flung it with all of his might at the curtains. The book connected with a thud and what Liam thought would be the expelling of air as if one was just hit in the solar plexus. Liam then reached for another book to throw but stopped as he heard the sound of a metallic thump. Liam then ran to the drapes and tore them down from the rod above his head. As he did, he saw what was most likely the source of the crash that had awakened him. There on the floor was a small pile of window glass that the intruder had broken in order to reach into the loft and opening the latch to the window.

Liam stared out the open window at the loft's fire escape. There, just one floor below, was the shadowy figure racing down the aged metal stairway. Liam jumped out of the window out onto the platform outside. He then made his way down the winding stairs as fast as he dared on the slippery wet metal treads.

Liam was just one floor above the ground when he heard the sound of the ground ladder being extended. Liam made it to the final platform of the fire escape and peered into the access hole that was the exit onto the ground ladder. The ladder was empty. Liam looked over the railing to see the figure running at a full clip south down Webster Avenue. Liam grabbed both sides of the ladder and slid the final sixteen feet to the ground. The side rails were slippery than he thought. He hit the wet ground with a bone-jarring thud that sent a shockwave from his legs into his teeth. Dampening the pain he turned and took off into the dark after his quarry.

Liam was not in the best of shape, nor had he become a couch potato, but he was starting to fall way behind. He was struggling with his breathing, almost feeling if he were choking from lack of oxygen, until he remembered that he had to breathe in through his nose and out through his mouth. Once he employed this oft used runners technique, his rhythm and paced picked up and Liam started to regain a faster pace.

After about two minutes Liam had a hunch as to where the thief was running. This hunch was got even stronger when the thief turned right onto Bedford Park Boulevard. Liam calculated that they were now just three blocks away from their destination.

With one block to go Liam was gaining on the shadowy figure. They were about to reach Jerome Avenue when the thief left the sidewalk and sprinted across a vacant lot. The vacant lot abutted up to the ground level subway yard for the Number 4 line.

Liam was now just yards behind the thief when they reached a ten foot high chain link fence that surrounded the rail yard and protected the uninformed from walking out onto a train track. The black clad figure scaled the fence in what appeared to be just one leap. Liam jumped as high as he could, reaching out for the top of the fence, grabbing onto the chain link as he landed. Still a good four feet from the top, Liam climbed to the crest of the wire then dropped the ten feet to the wet earth. Upon hitting the ground, Liam tucked and rolled to avoid breaking an ankle or a leg. Once up from the ground Liam took off in the direction of the thief.

Liam ran full out to the edge limestone ballast of the roadbed and the first set of train tracks. He quickly pulled up and skidded to a halt just as the thief was crossing over the steel rails of the third set of tracks. Liam carefully ventured out onto the first set of tracks deliberately placing his feet on the cold concrete ties that held the rails in place. Liam stepped over the first rail and reached the opposite side and the lethal *Third Rail.*

Third rail systems are a means of providing electric traction power to subway trains, and they use an additional rail, called a conductor rail, for that purpose. On most systems, the conductor rail is placed on the sleeper ends outside the running rails, but in some cases a central conductor rail is used. The conductor rail is supported on ceramic insulators or insulated brackets. A metal shoe on the outside of the subway car makes contact with the third rail and transfers 660 volts of direct current, to the electric motors that power the cars. If a human were to touch both a third rail and the ground at the same time, the end result would most certainly be a horrible death by electrocution.

This is what Liam was trying to avoid, any contact with the third rail. Many times a person may make contact and not realize it until it was too late. An errant piece of metal lying on the ground but also touching the conductor rail was all it took, thus electrocuting the unsuspecting pedestrian.

Just as Liam had carefully picked his way over the first set of tracks and was about to cross the second set, a familiar sound emanated from his left, the unmistakable tone of a subway horn. Just then from around a gentle bend came the tell tale glow from the lead car's headlight, now illuminating Liam.

He jumped back just as the train sped by at over 40 miles per hour. Holding his breath, Liam stood fast just three feet from the speeding train. Urging all of his muscles to remain still and planted in that one spot, as the wind generated from the passing train urged to pull him into it's slip stream. After eight hundred feet of train passed, Liam finally began to breathe again. After his breathing returned to normal, Liam continued the chase after his quarry.

The thief had made it to the other side of the yard and was scrambling up onto the passenger platform. Liam quickly found his way through the remaining tracks and made it to the platform. The early morning riders had started to appear and the platform was starting to clog up with people on their way to work or school. Liam started running down the platform just as a downtown train pulled into the station and it's riders started streaming out of the ten cars. Liam kept his eyes fixed on the back of his target as he made his way through the throng of mixing passengers, now just two cars away from catching up to the figure in black. Just as Liam thought that his thief was about to go to the far end platform to exit, the announcement over the loudspeaker on the train announced that the doors were closing and to please stay back. Liam watched the thief dash to his left and run onto the departing train.

Liam was about ten feet away from the subway car entrance in the car behind the car where the thief had entered. Watching the pneumatic doors closing, Liam sprinted for the closing doors and like a baseball player sliding into a base, dove headfirst into the narrowing gap. Only to land with a skid and a crash into the far side of the railway car, narrowly missing an older gentleman with a collapsible grocery cart.

Liam picked himself up and started down the half full train car. He knew that the next stop was about five minutes away and he wanted to get into the next car before they pulled into the station. Using the ceiling mounted had rails to steady him on the speeding train; Liam made it to the end of the car and the motorman's quarters. As this was not the lead car, there was no one in the cab for Liam to ask to alert the police. Liam peered out the leading window into the next car. The car was fuller than his and he had difficulty locating the thief. After thirty seconds Liam spotted the black costumed felon, near the forward car exit.

Crossing between subway cars can be extremely dangerous and is frowned upon by the transit authority, as demonstrated by the emblazed graphic on the lower half of the stainless steel door. Liam didn't have any other option. He tried the door handle and breathed a sigh of relief when the handle gave way and he was able to open the door. He had just stepped out onto the small open vestibule. Just as he was reaching for the handle to open the forward car, the train eased around a sharp bend to the right; making Liam loss his balance and crash into the safety chain. He shot his hand out quickly and grabbed the safety chain on the opposite side of the small platform. He pulled himself back to his feet just as the track straightened for the next station.

The train was just one hundred feet from the station's elevated platform as it started to slow in order to stop at its designated location. Liam tried the door leading into the forward car only to have the door be jammed. He slammed into the door with his left shoulder trying to force open the entry. He tried three times, each time with more and more force, until finally the door opened on it's corroded hinges.

Liam burst into the car and was met by a wall of bodies standing in front of the exit; waiting for the train to stop. He nudged his way through the crowded car and was within arms length of the thief when the train stopped suddenly and the crowd surged back towards Liam, knocking him off balance. He regained his balance and was about to once again grab the figure by the back of the neck when the glass and stainless steel doors opened and the throng of people waiting to exit moved as one mass.

Liam was carried out the door with the mass as he watched the thief break just feet to his left and run for the station exit. Liam yelled.

"Stop that thief!"

Liam pushed his way out of the mass of passengers and was about to take off after the filcher when he had a better idea.

On the platform was a small newsstand sporting various newspapers, magazines and snacks for sale. Off to the side of the small stand was a metal trashcan that stood about three feet high. Liam grabbed this can, quickly emptied its contents onto the platform floor and lifted the thirty-pound receptacle above his head with both hands. He took aim at the fleeting figure five yards away and threw the can with all of his strength.

The metal can flew through the air and was about to find its mark when some of the awaiting passengers started screaming with calls to "watch out". Liam watched as the can hit the black clothed thief in the legs tripping them and sending the intruder flying off the platform onto the tracks below. Liam started to run to the edge of the platform. He was ten feet away when an ear-piercing scream erupted and cries of "No!" emanated from all around.

Liam muscled his way through the gathered crowd at the edge of the platform. Just as he got to the edge he observed his quarry lying on their stomach on the track below, trying to right them-selves from the fall. Just as the figure was about to stand up they reached out in order to grab something in order to regain their balance. Sadly the object grabbed was the top of an unprotected section of the third rail. As the fallen person's left hand touched the top of the hard steel a blinding flash shot from the contact. Then the pungent smell of ozone and burnt flesh wafted to the platform causing many of the gathered passengers to retch onto the platform. Oddly enough not a single scream or cry for help left the pour souls lips as the 660 volts of electricity surged through the body. The now burning figure continued to burn and spark until the motorman from the stopped train had the foresight to call and have the power shut down.

It took over three hours for activity to return to normal. The local transit police detained Liam until the detectives from the local precinct arrived. Much to Liam's displeasure one of the first detectives to arrive was Detective Conner.

"So, Ross. You really seemed to have stepped in it this time."

"Detective, as I told the other officers, I was chasing a thief and unfortunately they fell onto the track when I tried to stop them."

"Someone tried to rob you on the train?"

Liam once again regaled his movements from earlier that morning, leaving nothing out, including what item that the thief had taken. Detective Connor just stood there stone faced as Liam finished his story.

"What a crock of shit Ross! You most likely snapped and just killed an innocent person in cold blood!"

Connor spun Liam around by the shoulder.

"Liam Ross, you are under arrest for murder."

"Murder! Are you out of your fucking mind Connor?!!" Liam yelled so loudly that the CSI unit near the body took notice. Connor just smirked at Liam as he placed handcuffs on him.

"You are! You are out of your fucking mind Connor! I don't think you want to do this!"

"Is that a threat Ross? Is it? 'Cause if it is I'll make sure they loose you for a day or two down at Rikers. The gang bangers there are just going to love you."

"Look, you asshole. You have no proof of anything, this is bullshit and you know it. You're still pissed off because of the other day!"

"Oh, I just knew that we'd be getting another chance at you Ross. You smelled dirty then, and you just proved it! Maybe we will now look into that hit and run a bit closer. Maybe it was just that, a hit. After all it looks like you stand to make out pretty well with your friend dead."

Liam moved to within inches of the cops face.

"So help me Connor, you malign Rex Cooper just one fraction of an inch and I will see to it, that you never see the light of day on duty ever again. Get it?"

"Back up asshole!" Detective Connor pushed Liam in the chest. Liam stumbled backwards. From off in the distance a booming voice echoed down the platform.

"Connor!" came the exclamation.

Just then Lieutenant O'Brian walked over to where Liam and the detective stood.

"Connor, explain yourself, now!"

Detective Connor retold the events leading up to the death of the thief. Leaving out just a couple of the salient details that Liam had relayed to Detective Connor.

"Is this true Mr. Ross?"

"Not quite Lieutenant. What your colleague failed to tell you is that the item that the thief took should still be on them. Also I should think that the security system back at the loft should clear things up fairly quickly."

"Well, let us see if this certificate is on the body, shall we?"

The three walked over to the side of the platform where the coroner was just about to take the body away. Lieutenant O'Brian called over to the medical examiner, a man that looked to be about twenty years past retirement.

"Doctor Jamison. Did you find anything on the body?"

The doctor brought over a box that Liam assumed was evidence. When the Doctor reached the group he stopped and set down the box on a waiting bench. He removed the cover ands extracted four plastic bags with the telltale red tape marking them as evidence.

"Just these Sean." He held out the bags to the detective. Lieutenant O'Brian looked at them and then held them so Liam could see the contents. There in the four evidence bags were four small piles of ash. Charred remains from when the thief had grabbed onto the third rail. Liam's heart sank. Just then the medical examiner looked directly at Liam and chastised him.

"You, young man should be ashamed of yourself, hitting a poor defenseless girl like that. Only going to be able to identify her by dental records. Not one ounce of flesh that hasn't been burned."

Liam just heard the word "girl" and heard nothing else.

25

All The News

Bousquet Loft
Bronx, New York
May 4, 2013

It took the better part of four hours, plus the video surveillance footage from the loft to convince Lieutenant O'Brian, that in fact Liam really was chasing an intruder and thief. The police however didn't believe the story of the sheet of million dollar greenbacks. The only proof of their existence was an envelope full of ash sitting at the crime lab. Given enough time, modern forensics will deduce the facts from the evidence. Liam was just seeing Lieutenant O'Brian, the crime scene unit and a swarm of other officials out the front door of the loft when Liz, Kyle and John arrived.

"Selling tickets to the policeman's ball?" shot John as he hooked a thumb towards the retreating policemen.

"No, I had a bit of an incident here last night, break in and robbery." Liam replied.

"Any damage Boss?" asked Kyle.

"No, not really, just my pride. I've got a gold shield who has a hard-on for me and for the life of me I can't figure out why."

"What did they get Liam?" asked Liz.

"Well, that's part of the story that I need to tell you all, and believe me when I tell you, you aren't going to believe it!"

Liam spent the next hour recapping the events from the night before as well as the details about the chase and the female intruders death.

"Ten Million bucks?!! Were they for real LR?" asked John.

"The printing looked authentic and the age of it appeared correct. The only thing that felt off about it beside the reverse not being complete was the weight of the paper. It seemed a bit thin and light for a Greenback. So if I had to venture an educated guess, I'd say that they were genuine but perhaps a sample or a proof."

"But according to everything that you know the United States never printed any denomination that large," stated Liz.

"That's what is so puzzling. This must be the secret that got Rex and Joe killed."

"So with out the certificate I guess were dead in the water?" asked Kyle.

"Not necessarily" Liz piped in, as she was now turning on the computers.

"What's on your mind Liz?" ask Liam.

"Okay tell me everything that you remember about the certificate."

Liam started at the beginning, remembering every detail from when he found the secret bottle in the wine cellar up unto when the thief stole the certificate. The exact details as he remembered them, the size of the sheet, the size of the individual bills, the colors on the bill, and the engraving style. He even remembered the date printed on the bills, February 23, 1868.

"The date! That has to be it! How could I be so blind?" Liz shouted as her fingers flew over the keyboard typing instructions into the computer.

After just a few short minutes Liz called up the file directory that was in the locked file they had accessed two days before.

"There was one strange sub-file that wasn't even visible when we unlocked the main set. It is shadow file within a shadow file."

"A puzzle wrapped in an enigma in other words." Liam stated.

"Exactly" Liz focused on the screen in front of her. "If my hunch is correct, this should do it."

Liz maneuvered the cursor over the area within the file directory. As she moved the cursor down the list of file names she reached the end of the list.

"Where's this secret file?" quipped John.

"Patience is a virtue" she replied while being in total concentration.

Just then the cursor found the shadow file and the background beneath the cursor changed to a darker color than the rest of the desktop.

"It's right here! Now all we have to do is double click on the shadow."

Liz clicked on the seemingly empty space and slowly a dialogue box appeared asking for a password.

"This is where the date comes in. It appears that Joe was a numerologist. In other words he loved numbers. So far all of his passwords have been some type of number or sequence. So all I have to do is enter the date that Liam remembers on the certificate proof and that should be our key in."

Liz entered the date as a string of numbers first she tried 2231868, nothing happened. Then she added the zero to the beginning of the string. Yet again there was no response from the file. She continued on entering the same set of numbers, forward, backwards, with hyphens, even variations of spelling the date out and using simple cipher codes, all the while John and Kyle kept track of her efforts on a nearby whiteboard. After forty-five minutes, and three hundred and fifty six combinations she threw her hands up in defeat.

"I don't get it, I was positive that Joe was leaving us a clue" she retorted as she was frustrated at her failure. "How could I be so wrong?"

"Well, your track record with dating of late is well known!" ribbed John.

Liz was about to throw the nearest item at John when Liam interrupted the potential bloodshed.

"Liz I don't think you got it wrong at all." He smiled at the trio as they looked at him as if he had magically grown a third eye in the middle of his forehead. "You are right, the date is the password."

"Um Boss, in all due respect..." started Kyle.

"Liz, what did I tell you when you first got into the locked file? Because of the real date for the end of WWII?"

"That Joe Bousquet was a real stickler for details. How does that fit Boss?" asked Liz

"A little item that few, but history buffs and scuba divers, have in common." He replied.

Just then Liz slapped herself on the forehead with the heel of her right hand.

"I'm such an idiot, international dating!"

"International dating?" both Kyle and John asked. Liam explained.

"In 1898 during the Cuban revolt against Spain, the United States Navy sent the second of the it's pre-dreadnaught ships, The Maine, into Havana Harbor in order to protect the U.S.'s interests in Cuba. In order to try and pull the U.S. into the war, it is assumed that the ship either struck an underwater mine or it was sabotaged, we still don't know how. The only way to send word back to Washington about the tragedy was via an underwater telegraph cable that the navy had deployed from Cuba to Florida. In order to authenticate that the wire in deed came from our side it had been decided that the Navy would change the order in which the date was written. Instead of the date being written as 15 February 1898 a slight simple switch was made to February 15, 1898, thus confirming it was real. So since the late 1800's the United States adopted the new order of writing dates."

"But why SCUBA divers?" asked John.

"Because modern SCUBA was perfected by Jacque Cousteau and being French that was how he made his notations in his log books. So it just stuck in that community," responded Liz as she entered the older international date sequence of *23021868*. Once she hit the enter key the computer monitor came to life.

The encrypted file contained over one thousand individual documents and scans. In order to make faster sense out of what they had just discovered, Liz printed three copies of the file directory and gave one to Liam, Kyle and John. She continued her search on the monitor. Each of them took a different page of files so that they wouldn't be looking over the same information. After about ten minutes Liam found the first item.

"Liz, open up file number *23021868.Scan001.jpg.*"

Liz opened the file. The image that flooded the HD monitor looked as if it were the real thing tape to the screen. There in high definition clarity was a scan of the 10-up sheet of one million dollar greenbacks. John let out a long low whistle. Kyle added to the reaction.

"Holy shit, its for real."

"You mean was. This is now just a pile of ash" came Liam's forlorn comment.

"So you really think that this is what got Joe and Rex killed?" asked Liz.

"This seems to be the most probable of answers, however it looks like it could be more." Liam pointed to a single line on the list of files in his hand. "Liz can you open up this one please?"

She highlighted the document listed as 23021868.History.doc. The program opened and then the document filled the secondary screen. Liam started to scan the text.

"These are Joe's notes. It looks like he found the letter in a pile of old family papers, right before he went into the service in 1943. He didn't really start to do any research until he mustered out in 1947. It also appears that his interest in this building and the National Banknote Company began at the same time." Liam continued reading. "In between work assignments he would spend his time tracking down everything that he could find on NBNC." Liam fell silent while he read further. "He goes on to note that the big find was when he was able to purchase the former company's operation and production ledgers."

"The ones downstairs in the production offices?" asked Kyle.

Liam grabbed a pen and pad and wrote down a series of items. He tore off the sheet and handed it to Kyle.

"Kyle could you and John head down to the first floor and bring back these ledgers?"

Kyle took the list and he and John headed down to the museum.

"Okay Liz, let's look at some of these others folders, shall we?"

Liz and Liam had sifted through three folders each before Kyle and John returned. Kyle set down the four journals that Liam had requested. He then set down a small, leather bound book. No larger than a modern day pocket book.

"What's this?" asked Liam. "Picking up the smaller book.

"It was wedged behind the ledgers in a loose panel of the book shelf. When we took the ledgers out the panel fell open."

Liam opened the clay red leather book. On the flyleaf of the tome was the inscription *Diary of Anna Stephens*.

"Who's Anna Stephans?" asked John.

Liam set the book aside and took up the first ledger.
"She was the person that the envelope in the wine bottle was addressed to."

Liam opened the first ledger, the bound edition that was labeled, *Director's Journal*, and located the entry that he was looking for. He handed a second ledger to Liz, the one marked *National Bank Note Company Employees*.

"Okay, February 23, 1868." Liam scanned the page. "It states here that the Director of NCNB"

Liz consulted her ledger, "that would be a Percy Wright," Liam continued.

" I summoned my lead pressman, Roy Stephens, on Sunday the 23rd at 2:30 in the morning." Looking up from the ledger. "So Roy Stephens must be Anna Stephens husband." Liam turned back to the ledger. "He also writes that he sent Crosse."

"Hang on a second," Liz turned the pages of her ledger until she found the correct entry. "Okay, it shows that a Kevin Crosse was the personal assistant to the Director."

Liam read down in his ledger, his eyes straining to read the faded brown ink on the yellowing pages.

"It appears that on that night there was one hell of a snow storm. It apparently crippled the city with over three feet of snow. It took Crosse and Roy Stephens over two hours to return to the plant." He read some more. "Wright's next notation is a couple of hours later. He writes that the A.J.'s Washington men are giving the orders and not being too kind about it."

"A.J.'s Washington men?" asked Kyle.

"That's all it says, A.J.'s Washington men." Liam read on to himself until he came across another piece of the puzzle. "Okay, here's something. Wright goes over what the plans for that morning were. He entered the project into the *Order Ledger* just as he would have any other order." Looking up from the book he pointed to one of the two unopened books on the table. "Look in that ledger and try to find the order placed on February 23rd."

John opened the leather bound book and started his inquiry. After two minutes of searching he spoke up.

"There is nothing in here with that date. It jumps from February 21st, to February 26th."

"No ordered entered at all?" asked Liam.

"No, absolutely nothing." responded John.

"That's odd. Wright specifically wrote that he entered the job in the *Order Ledger* as he would have any other."

Liam continued reading the Director's Journal.

"There is nothing else in here for that date as well. What is strange is that the next entry is not until three days later, on February 26th. Plus the entry is not by Percy Wright. It's by a member of the NCNB board of directors."

"What is the entry?" asked Liz.

"It is with heavy heart, that our Director Mr. Percy Wright, has succumbed to a tragic and senseless accident. A search for a new Operations Director shall begin forthwith with the entire weight of the NCNB Board of Directors."

"Hey Boss, something that you should see here."

"What is it John?"

"I was wrong when I said that there wasn't any additional entries for February 23rd. It appears that a page from this ledger is missing."

John handed Liam the ledger. Liam looked at the edge of a page and noticed that it appeared to have been cut from the book. Liam flipped through a few pages of the journal and noted that each printing job was posted the same way, in a left hand column was the customer, date, delivery date, item to be printed, sheet size, inks colors, etc. Then in a column on the right of the page the identifying quantities of paper, ink, etc. He paged back to where the entry should have been. Perplexed, Liam just sat, staring at the ledger.

Liz and Kyle had not been idle. Liz had started an Internet search for any additional information that may help with the puzzle and Kyle had picked up the *Diary of Anna Stephens* and had begun to read it.

Liz first ran a search to find out what were the major New York City newspapers in 1868. Not unlike today with various websites on the Internet, newspapers were the record keepers of the day. Every little nuance or happening on a street, in a neighborhood, or in a city, most likely would have been noticed. From the birth of a baby to the breaking news of the day, that was sometimes over a week old! Major cities had at least two but in some cases ten different publications.

One newspaper kept returning search results on the Internet – The New York World. Founded by Jay Gould in 1860, the respected New York City publication was in continuous printing until Joseph Pulitzer bought the journal in 1883. Pulitzer's form of yellow journalism and his promise to use the paper to "expose all fraud and sham, fight all public evils and abuses, and to battle for the people with earnest sincerity" connected with the lowest common denominator, turning the paper into the largest circulated rag in New York after just two years. After the circulation began to dwindle the paper ending up merging with the Evening Telegram in 1931.

Liz tried to gain access into the archives of the now lost newspaper only to keep being rebuffed on her efforts. Finally after gaining access to the files through the New York Public Library, was she able to begin a hard search. She found accounts of the Blizzard of 1868; over six feet of snow fell upon the greater New York metropolitan area bringing the city and it's boroughs to their knees. She checked the paper on the day of the event that they were searching, as well as three days either side. It was two days after the event, located on the fifth page of the paper that she found the little thirty-seven-word notice.

Prominent Businessman Drowns in Tragic Accident

Tuesday, 25th, February, 1868

Tragedy struck last night when the body of

respected businessman, Mr. Percy Wright,

was pulled from the waters of Fresh Pond. It

appears that Mr. Wright was ice skating when

he fell through the ice. No services will be held.

"Died from ice skating? I don't know about you but doesn't that sound a tad strange?" asked John.

"Liz, how old was Wright? Is there anything in the ledger?" Liam countered.

"According to this he was born in 1811. That would have made him fifty-seven at the time of his death."

"Does anyone here believe that a fifty-seven year old man went ice skating during a blizzard?" Liam looked at the blank faces of his colleagues. "Didn't think so."

It was now Kyle's turn to join into the fray. For the past twenty minutes he had been reading *The Diary of Anna Stephens*.

"No shit!" he cried out. " Listen to this. This will make Wright's death sound even more circumspect. Anna Stephens writes that her husband Roy never returned home from going into the shop, as she called it, on the morning of the 23rd of February. There are similar entries everyday for the next month until this one.

"31st March, 1868. Today I have learned that my dearest husband Roy's body was found frozen in a half melted drift of snow in the alley behind the shop. It appears that he had fallen and struck his head and perished this earth during the blizzard of last month. It wasn't until the thaw that they found his body. My poor, poor, dear Roy, what ever shall I do? The baby inside of me is soon for this world but how shall we survive with no husband and no father?"

"They found Roy Stephens dead as well, a month later? Seems like a tidy coincidence does it not?" asked John. Everyone looked to Liam.

"Well you all know how I feel about coincidences." He remarked. In unison the trio voiced their response "There is no such thing as a coincidence!"

"Okay, we have four dead men, two in 1868 and two more in 2012, a mysterious printing of one million dollar greenbacks, and some cryptic clues as to what was printed by the second largest money, bond, and stamp printers in the world. Sound about right?" asked Liam.

"That's about the best of it LR. Where do we go from here?" asked John.

"Liz, the access to the New York World archives, can you call up the papers for the next two months?" asked Liam.

"Sure, what are you looking for?"

"National events of the day. What was happening outside of New York, Washington DC in particular?"

Liz had the fastest fingers in the business. With lightening speed she accessed the New York Public Library archives. Within minutes she had the next two months of newspapers accessed.

"Where do you want to start?" she asked.

"Can you do a word search?"

"These seem to be searchable PDF's. What do you want me to search for?"

"First, Let's try the NCNB Directors name."

Liz input Percy Wright and linked the search to all of the documents. The search took just seconds.

"Plenty of Percy's and plenty of Wright's, but no hits with the combined tags."

"Okay, lets try Roy Stephens."

Again the search took mere seconds. Liz started paging through the results.

"Once again, lots of Roy's, even more Stephen's, But wait, here's one with both tags in the result." Liz read the article out loud.

"Anna Stephens, wife of the late Roy Stephens, died on Thursday morning last, in childbirth. Mrs. Stephens gave birth to a healthy baby girl."

A quiet came over the friends. After a moment Liz spoke.

"The family was certainly saddled with their share of tragedy."

"Okay, one more let's try AJ Washington." Liam pressed on.

The third time was the charm for Liz.

"Bingo! Dam, there has to be over ten thousand responses." She started to groan until she saw the tags. "A good 98% of these are all for one person."

"Let's take a look." Liam moved over to view the monitor. The results were there in the paper, plain as day. Kyle and John squeezed in order to view the results.

"Why do I feel a really big headache coming on?" asked Kyle.

"Oh, could it be that we are about to stir up a very old hornets nest?" replied Liam. "This could be fun!"

"Can't we just let that sleeping dog lie? Huh, pretty please?" added John

"Oh I don't know. It might be kind of fun to go down to Washington and see if we can pin four murders on the former President of the United States – Andrew Johnson."

26

Greed Is Good

Foggy Bottom
Washington D.C.
May 4, 2013

Nash had only been in this room once before. Many years ago when he was first brought to the attention of The Centum. On that day, long ago, he stood at the rear of the room while his mentor championed his abilities to The Chairman.

Nash was now seated in one of a pair 240-year-old hand carved Windsor chairs. The chairs were arranged in front of a very large, yet elegant desk that was fabled to have been made from The Alter of Pope Leo III. It was at that Alter that the Pontiff crowned Charlemagne as Roman Emperor on Christmas Day, 800 AD. The desk was on a large elevated dais twelve inches higher than the rest of the room. This was a very old, intentional technique, to make those present feel respectful and subservient to the person on the dais.

The Chairman was off to the left side of the dais pouring three fingers of a 150-year old single malt scotch from a distillery The Centum once claimed in the Highlands of Scotland. The dark amber liquid sparkled in the light as The Chairman walked over the desk. Never in a thousand years would Nash expect The Chairman to share, yet alone offer him a drink. He was here for one purpose and one purpose alone.

"So Nash, by your presence, I trust that the acquisition has been completed?"

"Yes Chairman, we have acquired the article."

With outstretched hand the Chairman asked for the certificate,

"May I have it please?"

"There was an accident when we finally acquired the certificate."

The Chairman took the news in stride, and responded with almost with a bit of comic tone.

"Accident? Oh please, do tell."

"Our person was able to successfully infiltrate the Bousquet loft. As you know, Mr. Ross has taken up residency in the last two days. Well, he awoke when our expert was in the apartment. Liam Ross confronted her then chased our expert from the loft, out onto the streets, finally ending up at the nearby subway station."

The Chairman lifted the cut glass tumbler and took a sip from the malt whiskey, while signaling with the wave of an arm for Nash to complete the story.

"Please continue."

Nash shifted in the hardwood chair and repositioned himself. Even though the thermostat in the room was set at a comfortable seventy-five degrees, Nash felt like he was sitting fully clothed in a sauna. He removed his pocket square from his jacket front pocket and wiped the tiny beads of liquid that had formed on his forehead. When he was finished wiping the sweat from his pate he returned the cloth to its pocket. All he wanted to do now was get through his report while holding his composure, then to get the hell out of here and have a good long drink of his own.

"Well, Ross chased her onto the platform of the station where there were a few morning commuters. So with the platform being a bit crowed, our expert was able to place a bit more distance between herself and Ross."

The Chairman now held the heavy glass with both hands and stared at the man seated below. Nash looked into the cold staring dark eyes that were fixed upon him and swallowed hard before continuing.

"Well, just as our girl…"

The Chairman cut Nash off in mid-sentence and reprimanded the man.

"That is a sexist comment. She is not our girl, your girl or even my girl. So please Mr. Nash, treat Ms. Kelly with the respect that she has earned."

Nash now could not even swallow. His mouth and throat felt as if he had been drinking sand. He was barely able to respond to the Chairman.

"I am so sorry. I did not mean to be disrespectful. I apologize, it will never happen again."

Nash did not perceive any indication either positive or negative from the Chairman, so he continued.

"Just as Ms. Kelly was about to exit the station, this upstart Ross picked up a garbage can and threw it at her from behind. The garbage can then hit Ms. Kelly in the legs, knocking her off balance where she fell off of the platform onto the tracks."

Nash continued.

"She must have hit her head when she fell, because she appeared to be groggy when she started to get up. She made it to her knees but she then made the misfortunate move and grabbed the third rail of the track, the rail that carries the power."

"And what became of Ms. Kelly?" asked the Chairman.

Nash looked down at his shoes and dropped the volume of his voice before he continued.

"When she grabbed the rail she was electrocuted. It took over five minutes before the MTA could cut the power. All that was left of her was a charred corpse."

"What became of the certificate?"

Nash now felt as if his world were about to close in all around him, after all, it was he that was meeting Ms. Kelly at the station in order to retrieve the certificate.

"I tried to get down to the tracks in order to retrieve it, but there were too many people. The police arrived within minutes and the medical examiner after that. After a while I saw the ME give the lead detective a plastic evidence bag filled with ashes, it was the certificate."

"Of this you are certain?" The Chairman asked sternly.

"I am positive, because Ross asked the same question. I can only assume that he wanted to retrieve what was stolen from him."

For the first time since he arrived Nash felt a bit more at ease as he completed his report. He shifted in the chair once again, looked down at his crossed legs, and absentmindedly remove a small piece of lint from the fabric, as he awaited a response from the Chairman. The Chairman sat unmoving in the high-backed leather executive chair and peered into the glass of single malt.

After a few minutes the Chairman lifted the glass and swallowed the remaining liquor in one draught. When finished, the Chairman stood up and walked back over to the bar, removed a glass from the display on the zinc topped bar, reached for the bottle of single malt and poured three fingers of the liquid into the glass. The Chairman then stepped down from the dais and walked over to Nash and pro-offered him the glass.

Nash looked pensively at the Chairman, almost uncertain as to what to do next. He slowly reached for the glass and looked to the Chairman once again. This time Nash received a response in the form of a nod. He took the glass then a small swallow at first, but he finished the drink with his second quaff.

"Careful Nash, that's a one hundred and fifty year old single malt, the last bottle on earth. It should be sipped, savored." The Chairman remarked returning to the dais then to the imposing desk, finally taking a seat.

Nash was grateful for the drink. He now felt as if his bad news had been received without judgment on him.

"What would you like me to do next?" he asked.

"Return to New York, take a few days off. We will be starting the next phase of the operation by weeks end. I need you well rested for your part. Understand?"

"Yes, thank you." Nash stood and then set his empty glass on the small table that was placed between the two chairs. "Thank you also for the drink."

Not waiting for a response, Nash turned and quickly departed the Chairman's office, quietly closing the door behind him.

No sooner had Nash left than a door situated to the rear of the Chairman's office opened, in walked the Recipient. Without a word the Recipient walked to the very same chair were Nash had sat, looked at the chair with disdain and chose instead to sit in its twin. The Chairman looked at the Recipient and then looked towards the office door. With just that mere glancing gaze, the Recipient removed a cell phone, punched in a series of numbers as a text command, and then pressed send.

The response came within one and a half minutes. The phone vibrated and the Recipient held up the phone to view. The Recipient smiled at the response displayed on the small LCD screen then looked up to the Chairman and nodded. What had transpired in that mere ninety seconds was nothing but housekeeping for the Centum.

Nash had exited the Centum offices a quickly as he could. He just wanted to get back to New York and take the Chairman's advice – to relax for a few days. After all, the next phase was going to be crucial and everyone had to be at his or her best.

Nash walked from the revolving door of the building and saw his driver that had picked him up at the airport. Earlier he had asked the driver to wait, knowing that he would be returning to New York as soon as the meeting was over.

The driver had just replaced his cell phone in his pocket. Nash walked to the rear of the car and waited for the driver to open the door. Nash bent low getting into the car in order to avoid hitting his head on the lower than normal sedan door opening. He sat in the rear passenger seat of the car, but before Trumball Nash even had a chance take a deep breath and relax in the plush rear seat of the Mercedes S600 the driver placed a silenced Beretta

Model 21 pistol to his forehead and pulled the trigger twice. The .25 caliber ammunition found its way deep into the brain of Trumball Nash without exiting his skull and therefore not making a mess in the rear of the luxury car.

Nash had been relieved of his position due to incompetence. The Chairman expected perfection from everyone and Nash's lack there of had almost jeopardized the operation. The Recipient filled the Chairman in on the rest of the details regarding the loss of their agent and the destruction of the certificate.

"With the certificate destroyed we should be able to continue on with the operation. Will this Liam Ross continue to be a thorn in our sides?" asked the Chairman.

"He's just a stamp dealer, a nobody if you ask me. So I have pulled all of our assets out of New York and have started the next phase of the operation. What is the opening bid expected to be in the morning?"

"It closed on Friday at $1,432.00 an ounce. We expect the opening bid to be a bit higher at first, once we release our surprise the price should plummet. Once it retreats to $100.00 or less an ounce we will start buying everything that we can get our hands on. This will be done in small amounts spread over thousands of accounts. That way nothing will alert the Commodities Futures Trading Commission. Although, by the close of business each day it will appear that all available quantities are still available for purchase, even thought there is nothing left to buy. Within two days the United States will have no option than to sell its stockpiles further weakening the dollar. Within four days the rest of the world's economic strongholds will follow suit. A day later the rest of the stock markets will crash as banks declare insolvency because you won't be able to give it away. The world will be in full panic mode throughout the weekend."

"If history repeats itself, hundreds of thousands of people will be bankrupted over night. Thousands more will kill themselves," added the Recipient.

"A minor inconvenience, nothing more. Come Monday morning our computers kick in and launch our attack. The price should skyrocket for the remaining quantities, even as high as $5,000 an ounce. By then we will control over eighty-three percent of the world's gold."

"Then the stage will be set for Act Three," added the Recipient.

27

LOC

Library of Congress
Washington, D.C.
May 6, 2013

Liam and John left Manhattan the evening before on Amtrak's Acela Express, after spending a few hours on the computers with Liz and Kyle. The high-speed train left New York's Pennsylvania Station and delivered them to Washington's Union Station in just three hours. However it was too late to go to the library when they arrived so they checked into The Willard to get a few hours rest.

The pair found themselves at the main entrance to the Library of Congress at eight o'clock the following morning. Liz had contacted a former classmate of hers that was a curator at the library and whom was able to get Liam and John into the Special Collections area of the library. Liam greeted Anna Byrnes with a warm smile and a handshake.

"Once again Anna, I would like to thank you for taking this time to help us out. I can't tell you how grateful we are."

"Anytime Mr. Ross. Liz is an old friend and she has spoken of you often. She clued me in on to what you were working on. However I can be of help, just ask," replied Anna. "Let's walk over this way."

"Please, it's Liam. We are looking for any information regarding President Andrew Johnson in 1868."

"Pre or post impeachment?" asked Anna.

"The time frame that we have narrowed down to is late January to mid-February of that year."

"So that would be just prior to President Johnson learning of the charges. Are you looking for the Congressional Record or public accounts of the President?"

"Well, what we are most interested in would be his private writings, diaries, calendars, his daily schedules, if at all possible," asked John.

"Well, you are very fortunate that we do have most of President Johnson's private papers. Presidential libraries didn't exist until President Theodore Roosevelt suggested that the files of a presidency be saved for future generations. It wasn't until his fifth cousin, President Franklin Roosevelt, became the first president to form a library. Up until then presidential papers were the property of the families and most were either destroyed or just given away. A handful of papers have made it to the LOC over the years, President Johnson's being some. But I must warn you, it's not a very comprehensive collection."

They continued to walk until they arrived at the entrance to the Special Collections department. Here Liam and John had to present ID and sign forms agreeing to the rules and regulations. With that behind them, Anna escorted them through the retina-scan security system and into the collection's main reading room. Anna escorted them to a private reading room. John asked where he could set up a laptop computer.

"You can set up here." Referring to the worktable in the middle of the room. Anna then handed Liam a slip of paper. "Here are the Library's WiFi codes. Liz asked me to give them to you. Now where do you want to start?"

"Is there a directory of what is available to view?" asked Liam.

"You can access that as well on your laptop. Here let me show you."

John turned the computer around so that Anna could access the database. After a few keystrokes Anna returned the computer to John. Liam moved to where he could look over John's shoulder at the screen. John started scrolling through the rather short list of books, documents and papers, perhaps four hundred documents in all. Liam read the list to himself as it appeared on the screen. At first pass nothing jumped out at either one. So they started over once again. With this pass they identified five documents.

They opened one file at a time. The first file was nothing but a draft of a letter from the President to the newly elected British Prime Minister, Benjamin Disraeli. The second document was nothing more than a proposed menu for a state dinner that was to happen in June of 1868. The third document was follow up information on the Alaska Purchase that the administration had brokered a year earlier. The fourth and fifth documents were dead ends as well, both relating to the suspension of then Secretary Of War Edwin M. Stanton, the act that most historians consider the basis for President Johnson's impeachment trial.

"Let's go back to the beginning. There has to be something here." Liam watched as John performed a reverse scroll. About half way back up the list Liam pointed to the screen.

"Hold on. What's this file here?" he asked.

John once again spun the computer around so that Anna could view the monitor.

"Which file?" she asked.

"This one here." Liam pointed to the file name on the screen.

"That appears to be a document that hasn't been scanned into our system yet." she replied.

"Why would almost an entire collection on one subject be available digitally but just one file would not?" pondered John out loud.

"Good question, let's find out." Anna removed a copy of a request form from the stack on the table. She wrote the files identifier number and library division down. She walked over to the telephone on a desk in the corner. Anna called the department that was listed as the department that held the document. After only a few short minutes conversation she hung up the phone and returned to the two men.

"It appears that the file in question is a book, perhaps a diary. It seems that most of the Johnson collection came from one source just five years ago. Most of the items were in excellent condition, but apparently this book was in a damaged state. It hasn't been restored yet so that is why the public scans have not been made available yet. It's not slated to be restored for another six months. I've asked for the book to be brought up from the Restoration Archives"

Before Liam could ask Anna a question there was a gentle knock on the door. Anna opened the door and let a Library docent into the reading room. After Anna signed a few forms, a special library storage case was presented to her. She was then was given three pairs of white gloves by the docent, who then left the room.

Anna opened the box and revealed a desk diary that was bound in calfskin. Anna put on the white gloves and gently lifted the book from its case and set it on an acid free paper desk blotter that was on the worktable. She then delicately opened the cover of the book. The first page of the diary was blank so she turned to the next page. There in a bold hand, was the sweeping penned script, *Personal Diary of A. Johnson.* Beneath the title were the dates *January 1868 – June 1868.*

"Jackpot!" remarked John.

"It appears to be the timeframe that we were looking for but let's not count our chickens yet, Mr. Andrews. Let's see what's inside first" was Liam's response.

Anna started to read the first page and noted that it was written in the first person.

"It appears to have been written by the President himself, not his secretary. The first entry is on New Years Day 1868. His notation is " *I can only hope that the New Year presents me with better options than the past.*"" She continued reading. " He goes on to write that the Bastards in Congress don't have him down yet. That "*there will be a new dawn coming.*""

Anna turned the fragile page.

"Here's another, "*January 21 - Wonderful news! More than 50 miles laid in one day!*" Fifty miles laid in one day? What does it mean?" asked the librarian.

"He must be referring to railroad track. But I thought the record of ten miles in one day wasn't set until almost a year later in 1869 during the building of the Transcontinental Railroad? John commented to no one in particular.

"Let's move forward to the first of February, can we?" asked Liam.

Anna carefully turned three pages until she finally found the first entry for February 1868.

"Here's the first entry for February." Anna moved the book closer to Liam

Liam put on a pair of the white gloves and took the diary from Anna. He slowly read the first few entries to himself. He finally stopped reading when he came to a rather cryptic entry, and read it out loud.

"*February 2 - Have received updated information on Gas. Need to be ready to finalize the transfer by early next month. Must have collateral processed. Send Black to wrap things up.*"

"Gas? What gas? Asked John.

"What does he mean by must have collateral processed?" asked Anna.

"The entries for the next week or so are pretty normal day to day things. Here's another entry that seems out of place. "*February 24 – Storm has closed most of Capital City. Black has returned with collateral and wonderful news. Leaving this evening and will be in the CC in a fortnight .The South may rise again!*"

The three just looked at the diary in stunned silence. Wondering if it might burst into flames any second.

"Did I just hear you correctly, Boss? That President Andrew Johnson was a southern symphonizer?" ask John.

"It's a well documented fact the Johnson was not totally behind Lincoln's policies and the reconstruction. That issue alone may have been why he fired Stanton." added Anna.

Liam continued.

"That's not all. There is another entry two weeks later. *"Wire from Utah Territory confirms project complete. Collateral unnecessary. Gas no longer a problem."*

"That sounds rather ominous" John said to Liam.

"I think it's time to get Liz on the phone."

"Will do LR." John started to call Liz via the voice over Internet protocol program on the laptop. With in four rings Liz's voice came through the computers speakers.

"Hey Boss, how's D.C.?"

"Real Cheery. Liz we are here with Anna. Can you go to video please?"

Within seconds Liz's image was placed center screen on the monitor.

"Hi Anna! How's tricks?" asked Liz.

Anna stepped closer to the computer in order to be center of the camera.

"Tricky if you ask me Lizzy" was all that Anna could say.

"What's up guys?" Liz replied.

"Lizzy, can your fire up Joe's computer and see if he has any reference to a *Gas* anywhere?"

"Sure thing. Give me a sec." Liz turned her back to the camera in order to log onto Joe's system. She came back within a minute.

"I've got three hits Boss."

"Go for it Liz."

"Okay, the first one is fairly self explanatory, it's the gas bill for the building. The second hit is for an alarm company's service call on a Radon gas detector in the basement and the third is for the replacement of a gas stove in one of the units in the building."

"Well that's three strikes," quipped John. "There must be a clue in the President's diary."

Liam, lost deep in thought, turned the book around and started to review the pages. John and Anna brought Liz up to speed about their progress and the discovery of President Johnson's diary. After ten minutes Liam focused on the February 24 entry.

"Liz, the date on the certificate is February 23rd correct?"

Liz brought the image of the stolen certificate up on the screen.

"Correct, February 23rd, 1868."

"So we have a document dated the 23rd and a entry in the diary made the next day." Liam read the entry that caused them all to pause earlier. "*February 24 – Storm has closed most of Capital City. Black has returned with collateral and wonderful news. Leaving this evening and will be in CC in a fortnight .The South may rise again!*"

"CC in a fortnight." Liam kept repeating the same phrase. "Liz, can you pull up a map of the United States from 1868?" Once again within seconds a map filled the screen. "Now can you run data search with the combination C and C.?"

Hundreds of dots appeared on the screen all over the map from the Atlantic to the Pacific.

"Okay, now for the tricky one. Can we interpolate travel times in 1868 based upon a two week journey starting in Washington D.C. on the evening of February 24th?" requested Liam.

"Give me a few minutes. Let me run a data mine program." Liz called up multiple databases and then let the computers run a simulation. Four interlocking shaded circles spanned across the United States and Canada. Anna was the first to spot it.

"Here!" she pointed to the screen. "In Nevada! Carson City, it fits!"

There on the edge, of the western-most circle, was Carson City, Nevada.

"Liz, how did you come by this data?" asked Liam.

Liz consulted the output of her data mine program.

"Most of the information is quarried from The National Railway Historical Society archives, with more data contributed by the Southern Pacific Railroad Archives. Followed up with historical weather data from NOAA."

"That has to be it Boss" added John.

"Okay, so someone named Black leaves Washington D.C. on a snowy evening on February 24th 1868, to end up in Carson City, Nevada two weeks later." reviewed Liam.

"Don't forget with the full knowledge and power of President Johnson" added Anna.

"Okay Liz, next search. Let's try the name Gas in a search of 1868 Carson City."

"Coming right up. I'll start with the 1860 Census roles."

"Liz you might also want to add both army muster roles for the Civil War, Confederate States of America and Grand Army of the Republic."

"Will do." Liz continued on with her input. Liam began to pace and think out loud once again.

"So, we have an unheard of document being printed in secret on a Sunday night in February 1868 on the direction of A.J.'s Washington men." He was referring to the information in the NBNC ledgers. "We also have information in President Johnson's diary the next day that some collateral has arrived and a Mr. Black will be leaving that evening, to what we now surmise is Carson City. I thank that it is safe to say that the collateral that is referenced in the diary is the one million dollar greenbacks printed at NBNC."

"But why Carson City?" asked Anna.

"Besides being Nevada's capitol, Carson City was also home to one of the country's largest mints, specializing in gold coinage. There has to be a connection there," continued Liam.

Liz chimed in from New York.

"Boss, no hits on Gas in Nevada during that time frame. There are however a number of hits for a Gass."

"Two S's not one, that makes sense. The telegraph operator that sent the message to the White House most likely sent the telegram by dictation and just spelled Gass with one S when taking the message." Liam turned to the video screen and Liz. "What are the main references Liz?"

"Most of them are mentions of a Octavious Gass and his commendations for service during the Civil War at a Fort Baker. It then goes on to show that Gass purchased the land that was Fort Baker after the war. Turns out he was a then modern visionary. Found a way to pump water from underground aquifers and turn the desert lush. He was ready to lunch a series of pumping stations when his ranch burned to the ground one night and he was never seen again."

"When did this happen Liz?"

"The newspaper archives are dated May of 1868 but the articles printed mention that the fire happened somewhere around March 13th or 14th, 1868."

"Two weeks later, a fortnight, coincidence Boss?" asked john.

"More likely another murder."

"There's one more piece of data that came up in the search Liam, although it's probably not related seeing where as most of the Gass references are in Southern Nevada. This is from the northern part of the state."

"Where's the data from?"

Liz read a bit further down the entry.

"This is from a Station Masters log entry. It notes that the final *Gass* train arrived from the south at 1:06 PM on March 14th, 1868."

"What city?"

"Carson City."

"So there's the connection. There must be more in the diary," Liam said.

Liam looked at the Johnson Diary and then he gently picked the book up from the table blotter. When he held the book in his hand he started to flip the pages of the diary one by one, looking for any additional entries. When he shifted the weight of the tome from his left hand to his right, his right thumb acted as a stop against the fore edge of the book. As his thumb moved up the paper he noticed and irregularity among the thickness of the pages. He closed the cover of the diary and turned the book over in his hand so that the collected bare pages were in full view. He noticed that the end of the diary pages did not meet the rear cover of the book. As if something has been pressed in the pages of the book. He opened the book to the last page.

"Anna, has this book been cataloged other than for restoration?" he asked.

"I can find out. Let me call back down to the Restoration Archive."

Anna called down to the same person that she spoke to before. It was a quick conversation.

"I have asked that the head of the Restoration Department come up for a few minutes. They should be right along shortly."

Liam remained focused on the book. Gently running his gloved fingers over the endpaper of the book. Did he notice a slight give in the paper? He traced his fingers over the entire page checking to be sure that the slight give wasn't just padding in the book. Liam stopped and looked up when there was a knock on the door.

"Come in." called Anna.

The door opened and a woman, perhaps in her late forties entered the room carrying a black executive folder and wearing a white lab coat, the type that you would expect to see on a doctor in a hospital. Anna greeted the woman and made the introductions.

"Dr. Eileen Leonard, This is Liam Ross and his associate John Andrews."

Dr. Leonard shook each of the men's hands.

"How can I be of service Dr. Byrnes?'

"If I may Anna?" Anna nodded her head towards Liam. "Dr. Leonard we are doing some research into the presidency of Andrew Johnson trying to authenticate some papers that we acquired in an auction." Liam lied, as he didn't want too many people to know what they had just found out. "We have just spent sometime with his diary of early 1868 and we were wondering what the providence of the book might be?"

Dr. Leonard opened her folder and consulted her file.

"It appears that we received this book, as well as a sheaf of documents, from a distant ancestor of the late President. It notes that the documents had been passed down through his family since there were given to his great-great grandfather in 1880 by President Johnson's widow, Eliza Johnson."

"Doctor, do you know if any restoration worked has been preformed on this diary?" Liam pointed to the book open on the table.

"Other than just placing it in a controlled environment so that any deterioration would cease, no. Nothing has happened to this book since we received it. Is there a problem with the book Mr. Ross?" asked Dr. Leonard.

"No, there is nothing wrong, it's just that I have noted an anomaly with the diary" responded Liam.

"Anomaly? How?"

Liam directed everyone's attention to the rear of the book.

"Here at the rear of the diary on the end leaf. It appears that a blank page has either stuck to or has been sealed to the rear cover of the diary. You can detect a void around the edges, and a slight give in the center. Almost as if something is underneath the paper."

Dr. Leonard removed a pair of gloves from her coat pocket and placed them on her hands. She then turned the book to face her. She then ran her fingers across the rear endpaper of the book. She repeated the same steps a half a dozen times.

"It appears that you might be correct Mr. Ross. There does appear to be a void underneath the paper."

She removed a pair of document tongs just like the ones that Liam used in his stamp collecting profession. She then removed a set of magnifying glasses from her coat pocket and put them on. She carefully checked all the edges of the adhered paper to see if there were any voids that she might be able to loosen. She found a small void in the adhesive on the bottom of the page.

"Let's see if we can loosen this page here. If not we can take it down to the lab and try some non-evasive solvents."

She very gently slid the end of her tongs under the lip of the opening. She then very slowly moved the tong tip to her right to see if there was any give top the paper. Luckily and surprisingly, due to the age of the adhesive, the edge separated from the rear cover with very little pressure and without any damage to either the page or the rear board. She continued at a painstakingly slow pace until the entire paper was free. Dr. Leonard then gently lifted the page with her tongs and open it so all could see.

There under the paper, in the void that Liam had detected, was another piece of paper. Only this one had been folded in half in order to fit within the diary. It appeared that the President had deliberately hid the paper. The room had become so quiet; you could feel a gentle swoosh as air came through the air conditioning vent in the ceiling, twelve feet overhead. Dr. Leonard was the first to speak.

"I'll need to go and get another pair of tongs in order to open the paper. I wouldn't want to damage it."

Liam spoke up.

"If I may doctor." He handed her a duplicate pair of the documents tongs identical to hers. She looked to Liam as if to say how. He responded to her before she even had a chance to ask.

"I'm a stamp dealer. I never travel without a set" was his response.

Dr. Leonard took the pro-offered tongs and gently placed both pairs between the folded edges of the paper. She took a deep breath, over filling her lungs, then, holding her breath, she slowly parted the folded paper. All the while praying silently that the paper was not too brittle. She had done this exact same maneuver thousands of times before in the course of her career. After want seemed like hours, Dr. Leonard finally opened the folded sheet. There on the table in front of everyone was the missing page from the National Bank Note Company *Order Ledger*.

"Holy shit! It's the missing ledger page" sparked Liz over the computer monitor.

"Missing ledger page, what ledger?" asked Anna.

Liam had no choice but to tell as much of the story that he felt comfortable sharing. He still did not reveal the information about the certificate.

"A ledger from the National Bank Note Company of New York, Dr. Leonard. They printed currency, stocks, bonds and postage stamps for the United States government in the late 1800's." Liam continued on. "I represent the individual that owns most of the historical artifacts of the company. We stumbled upon these ledgers and with them a small mystery. We are trying to track down what became of some documents that may be related to a robbery and two murders."

"Murders in 1868?" asked Anna.

"No the murder of my friend and mentor, Rex Cooper and a colleague of his, Joe Bousquet. They were both killed in New York over a stamp collection and something that was hidden within that collection."

"I'll have to alert the director immediately" responded Dr. Leonard. "I don't know we have gotten into here. Mr. Ross are you sure that this is your missing ledger page?"

Liam turned to the computer screen.

"Liz, can you set the ledger under a camera so that we can compare this page with our ledger?"

Liz quickly connected a camera to a document stand and connected the camera to the computer. She then placed the ledger on the table and opened the book to where the page had been cut out.

"See Dr. Leonard. First the page is the proper size, and if you look closely at the top of the page you will see three little skips in the cut where someone first started to remove the page. Liz, zoom in on the top of the page please."

The page became larger on the monitor screen.

"These skips in the cut." Liam pointed out the jagged cuts on the page. "Are identical to the cuts in the ledger Dr. Leonard. This is our missing page without a doubt."

"Remarkable" Anna said in a hushed tone.

"And you came here hoping to find this Mr. Ross?" asked Dr. Leonard.

"I can assure you that we had no idea that we would come across this when we came here this morning. We were just trying to get a better understanding as to why two people in New York have died over a one hundred and forty-five year old piece of paper."

"Well Dr. Byrnes, I need to contact the director and I suggest that you come with me." Dr. Leonard started to fold up the ledger page.

"Dr. Leonard, would it be at all possible to take a scan of the ledger page with us? It may help us with our search. I'll also see that my colleague in New York scans the ledger and that they get it to you as soon as possible."

"I will have to ask the director. I need to make sure that the library is not in some sort of legal hot water here."

"Can we call you later to find out about the director's decision?"

"I'll call you later Liam," answered Anna "As soon as we go over everything with the director. How can I reach you?"

"We'll be here until the morning. We are at the Willard. After that your best bet is to get in touch with Liz in New York. You hear all of that Liz?"

"Got it Boss!" was her response through the computer monitor.

Dr. Leonard had completed packing up the ledger page and the diary and was about to leave the reading room.

"Dr. Byrnes, are you coming?" she asked shortly.

"Liam, can you see yourselves out?"

"No problem Anna. I look forward to hearing from you" he answered.

The two women left the room. Anna closed the door as she trailed Dr, Leonard. Liam and John stood at the edge of the worktable in the center of the room.

"So LR, where to now?" asked John

"First to the hotel to shower and change, then let's call Uncle Bob and see if he would like to join us for dinner."

"Then what?" asked John.

"Fancy a little trip?" replied Liam.

28

Fly In The Ointment

Calls had been made and received, a great number of times in just the past six months alone. In the eight years prior to the first call there had been no communication at all. She had been warned that she would be called someday, and that someday finally came.

The meeting with the Director of the Library of Congress had gone well. He had found the whole situation, at first, quite unbelievable but once the facts had been laid out he realized that this could bring some much needed publicity to the library. When you had publicity you were able to squeeze more funding out of Congress and more funding is what they needed at this time.

The Director had instructed Dr.'s Byrnes and Leonard to continue on with the trail that had just been uncovered. He also allowed a scan of the ledger page to be sent to Liam Ross, as long as the library received the promised scan of the ledger.

So it was about three hours after meeting with the Director, that she found herself making a phone call to the number that she had committed to memory so many years ago. She had been in a position to help The Centum by locating and gathering many documents and books that the organization required in order to see their plan carried out. The phone line went through the familiar hollow clicks, tones and beeps that occurred every time that she called. As usual, on the sixth ring, the voice came on the line.

"Yes?"

"Liam Ross has discovered a rather interesting piece to the puzzle. He is continuing on with his search."

She then updated the listener with the information that she had learned in the past few hours, information that had left the listener silent. She asked what they needed from her next. At first she thought that the line had gone dead, but after a few seconds she received a response.

"We will have more for you. Be prepared."

After hearing the response, Dr. Anna Byrnes hung up her phone.

29

Go West

Liam and John sat at the Oyster Bar in Old Ebitt Grill, waiting for Uncle Bob to join them. Since leaving the Library of Congress earlier, Liam had been deep in thought, and as John told Liz what the Boss was up to. They both agreed, "This is when things get expensive!"

Liam was nursing a stein of Yuengling Lager, a crisp, full beer from the oldest brewery and purveyor in the United States. Meanwhile, John had ordered six-dozen oysters with his beer. He was systematically making his way through the five types of succulent bivalve mollusks, stacking the spent shells up in a tower as he downed each raw morsel.

"LR, if you don't attack some of these now, I'll be forced to get more!" John called out as he slurped the chilled delicate flesh.

Before the first oyster had even left the shell he was adding a small amount of lemon juice to his next victim, preparing it for his gastronomic feast. His system was down to perfection, he would follow each forth oyster with a long quaff of the wonderful golden, ice cold, lager. He was about to consider the fresh Chesapeake Bay Blue Crabs for dinner when Uncle Bob walked over to them.

"Gentlemen, I trust that you have enjoyed your short stay in our fair city?"

Uncle Bob shook John's hand then gave his nephew a long bear hug. When they broke their embrace Uncle Bob saw in Liam's eyes that he was a million miles away.

"Hey Kid, where are you?"

Liam focused and returned his attention to his uncle and his friend.

"Sorry Uncle Bob, just trying to fit all the pieces of the puzzle together. No matter how many times I do, it always comes down to the same thing. I end up forcing a few pieces into place with a sledge hammer."

"Okay, first we order, then we eat, after that you can run read me in"

The three ordered a bucket of jumbo, fresh steamed crabs. Once the food arrived at the table they all attacked the container of the crustaceans. Liam didn't even realize that he was so hungry and it wasn't until John pointed it out that they hadn't eaten since they left New York.

When they had finished, the table was cleared of the pulverized crab shells and a pot of coffee was ordered. Liam spent the next hour running the entire scenario for his uncle. Every detail, every step, every facet, nothing was omitted from the past six days. Through the entire hour Uncle Bob did not utter a single sound. He just sat opposite of Liam at the table in the far corner of the restaurant and drank cup after cup of the strong black coffee. When Liam had finished he waited for his Uncle's response. When he did not get one he spoke up.

"Too many holes?" he asked his Uncle.

His Uncle had always been able to listen to a project run down, then find the weak points and omissions to any plan, however well thought out. After a few moments of reflection, he responded.

"There are precious few that have the resources large enough, or quite frankly smart enough, to handle something like this and keep it quiet." He continued, "Ten years ago I would have bet you a months take home that a rogue nation was behind this, but even today despots crave publicity." Uncle Bob picked up his refilled coffee mug and stared into the steaming dark brown liquid. "No, this has avarice written all over it. So you have to ask the question, who is the greediest?"

"That is one of the puzzle pieces that I hammer the hardest on." Liam responded.

"Bob, any suggestions as to what our next step should be?" asked John.

"If you want my advice, I suggest that you continue to follow the trail that you are on."

John looked confused, so Uncle Bob added as he picked up the black leather food check folio.

"In those immortal words – Go west young men."

Uncle Bob paid the check and the three walked out into the mild capitol evening.

"I parked over at your hotel, so I'll walk you back."

It was a short two-block walk to the Willard. The three men crossed F Street by the Hotel Washington and continued down the block towards the Willard. In front of the Willard Office building a small crowd of sightseers were posing for photographs with the landmark hotel in the background. A man in his early fifties came up to the trio and asked if one of them might take a photo of his wife and himself.

"My pleasure sir." John replied as he took the proffered camera from the man.

Liam and Uncle Bob stood off to the side as John helped pose the couple. John then raised the camera, ready to take the photo when an ear-piercing scream shattered the night atmosphere, and all hell broke loose.

A woman and her companion were seated in a street café, off to the left of Liam, John and Uncle Bob. The woman was on her feet shaking a man, that had been seated across from her, all the while screaming at the top of her lungs.

"Oh my god, please somebody help him. I think he having a heart attack! Somebody call a doctor!" she called out while people just stopped and stared.

Liam and Bob reacted first. The two ran over towards the man and woman, Liam called out to John.

"Call 9-1-1!"

John quickly handed the camera back to the posed couple and pulled out his cell phone as he ran towards Liam and Uncle Bob. He dialed 9-1-1 and was connected directly with a 9-1-1 operator instead of an out of the way highway patrol station. (The new District Emergency Response System allowed for this new pinpointing technology). After the second ring an operator answered.

"9-1-1, what's your emergency?"

A bit winded, John was just ten feet from Liam and Uncle Bob as he gave the operator his information.

"I need paramedics in front of the Willard Office Building on N.W. 15th Street. A man is having a ..." John was unable to finish his sentence.

In the commotion, from out of the shadows of the large concrete columns of the office building's esplanade, a figure clad in black rushed towards Liam, Bob and John.

Just as John was three feet from Liam, the figure pulled out a hardened steel collapsible security baton, extended it to its full length, and with full force struck John on the side of his right knee. John let out a cry of pain. As he was falling to the ground, the attacker followed with a second blow to the left side of John's head.

Liam heard John cry out and looked over in time to see the figure raise the baton directly behind Uncle Bob, ready to bring it down on his skull.

"Uncle Bob! On your six!" shouted Liam.

Uncle Bob pivoted to his right on his left foot turning one hundred and eighty degrees. In the flash that it took him to turn, he saw the steel baton out of the corner of his eye, as it came swiftly down towards his head.

As Liam called out to his uncle, he took evasive action towards the attacker. Liam lunged towards the man's arm, trying to stop the baton from hitting his uncle. He connected with the dark figure's forearm just as Uncle Bob crouched into a leg sweep, trying to take the attackers legs out from underneath him. He only connected with the attackers right leg, only causing him to loose his balance. The actions of Uncle Bob and Liam caused the attacker to waiver and drop the baton, but he quickly regained his balance as Liam tried desperately to hold onto his right arm. The attacker freed his arm away from Liam's grasp and then spun away to his left, untangling his leg from Uncle Bob's hold. He took off running towards the street.

"Uncle Bob! Are you alright?" shouted Liam.

I'm fine, John's down though!" replied Uncle Bob. "I'll see to him! Go! Go get the bastard! Are you carrying?"

"I never carry in D.C.!" Liam shouted as he got up off the ground.

Uncle Bob removed his back up Smith and Wesson Police Special .38 from an ankle holster and tossed it to his nephew.

"Go!" cried Uncle Bob.

Liam caught the revolver on the run and took off after the assailant. Liam made it to the curb and saw the figure in black as he crossed the street running into Pershing Park. Liam had one foot off the curb when the telltale claxon horn of one of D.C.'s many tourist buses sounded. He pulled back to the curb, feeling the wind of the Routemaster Double Deck bus pass inches from him. After the bus passed Liam took off at a full sprint across N.W. 15th Street into Pershing Park. He was a good one hundred yards behind, but he slowly started to gain on his target as he noticed that the attacker had a slight limp, most likely caused by Uncle Bob.

Liam followed the figure in black as they ran past the Pershing Park Pond with its stylized waterfall, then past the Bex Eagle statue, having closed the gap to a little more than fifty yards. People walking in the park stopped and stared as the two men ran past, with Liam calling out for the assailant to stop. He didn't want to attempt a shot, as there were too many people around. It amazed Liam that no one even bothered to even try and stop the evading figure.

They exited the park at the southwest corner and the attacker shot across the intersection on the diagonal, causing traffic to slam on their brakes to avoid hitting the runner. When Liam made it to the street, horns were blaring and a few people had gotten out of their cars to inspect the damage from the chain reaction crashes.

Liam was winded from his continued pursuit but he willed himself on, as he was now just twenty yards from John's attacker. The fleeing figure had now cut down the visitor's path that led to the White House Ellipse Visitor Pavilion. From there, there would be little cover in the wide-open expanse.

They broke from the tree-lined pathway and were now on the roadway that encircled the Ellipse. Liam was so close that he could now hear the man talking to himself as he ran on. He also saw the flashing lights and heard the sirens coming from the northern end of the Ellipse. Liam was now ten yards behind, when he sensed, more than he heard the car come up from behind him. The car swerved and Liam dodged to avoid being hit. As he fell to the soft grass adjacent to The Boy Scouts Memorial he performed the classic tuck and roll and returned to his feet.

The car braked to a hard stop and the front passenger door flew open. Simultaneously the dark figure jumped into the awaiting black Chrysler 300 as the door closed and the car accelerated away towards the south exit of the Ellipse, leaving a trail of smoke and black tire tread behind.

Liam looked for the license plate in order to commit it to memory, but the plate had been covered over with a dark material. Liam stood there in the roadway looking at the fleeing vehicle when he realized that the oncoming sirens were now right behind him.

He also realized that he was standing in the middle of the road, just three blocks away from the White House, with a gun in his hand. He carefully laid the gun at his feet and waited for the arriving Park Police cars to come to a stop.

The Park Police had been alerted to the pursuit from one of the alphabet agencies. After a brief hold at the Ellipse, Liam convinced Sergeant Green, the officer in charge, that he was the individual that was indeed chasing the assailant. This was doubly confirmed when Sergeant Green escorted Liam back to the Willard and the original crime scene. Uncle Bob flashed his credentials to the officer so Liam was not held.

Liam was a bit confused when he returned to the Willard. The paramedics were loading John, who was awake but not totally alert, onto a gurney getting ready to transport him to George Washington University Hospital. But the gentleman that was having a heart attack was nowhere to be seen.

"What the hell? Where is everyone?"

"It was a set up nephew. We, more like you, were targeted. The heart attack was a staged diversion."

"How's John?" Liam asked as he walked over to the rear of the ambulance.

"The hit to his head was just a glancing blow, going to have a small headache for day or so. However he took a really good hit to the knee. The baton shattered his patella, he's going to be down for a while."

"How you feeling John?"

"Right now I'm feeling no pain. This morphine is amazing shit! Give me more of this and I'm good to go!"

"Look, they're going to take you to GW and patch you up. You just need to take it easy for a bit."

The medics finished loading John into the rear of the ambulance. John tried to get up off of the gurney.

"No way Boss. I'm in this fight to the end." he collapsed back onto the gurney.

"Sorry Buddy, you need to get better. Now take a nap!" Liam called out as he closed the second door. "I'll see you at the hospital."

He signaled to the driver that he was good to go. The ambulance pulled into traffic with its lights flashing and its siren cutting a pathway down the street. Liam pulled out his cell phone and hit speed dial number one, set the phone to speaker then he turned to Uncle Bob. Liz answered the phone at the loft in New York.

"Liz, there has been an accident, John's been hurt."

"Oh my God! Is he alright?" Liz then called to Kyle who was sitting at the other end of the computer console. "It's Liam, John's been hurt."

Liam relayed the evening's events for Liz and Kyle. He then ran down the options for the next steps and the gear he needed for a trip to Carson, Nevada.

"Also Kyle, could you bring my big blue make up kit?"

"Sure thing Boss. How about your special case?"

"Wouldn't hurt to bring it along."

Uncle Bob joined into the conversation.

"Kyle, I'll call and have a G5 waiting at LaGuardia. Fly down here to Andrews and pick up Liam. You should be here in three hours if you hit the ground running. Then you can both head out to Carson City."

"Uncle Bob, with all that has happened I'm worried about Liz being alone."

"I'm fine Boss, don't worry" Liz replied to Liam.

"As soon as we are done at the office here, I'll take you out to Andrews and head up to New York myself."

"But Liam, Uncle Bob, I'll be fine." Liz protested.

"No Liz, this has moved into the playing for keeps category. I rather be safe, than sorry. I'll be there in a few hours," announced Uncle Bob.

30

Cutting Edge

Uncle Bob and Liam finished with their reports and headed out to Andrews AFB where the agency housed their small fleet of aircraft. Within 20 minutes of arriving, the plane that Robert sent to New York to collect Kyle, was taxiing in front of the small terminal. A general aviation fuel truck pulled to the side of the Gulfstream jet and waited to start the refueling process. After the jet turned its engines off, the entryway towards the front of the plane opened and the stairway lowered, softly touching the tarmac. Liam and Uncle Bob waited for the all clear, and then boarded the jet.

Kyle was seated at the worktable area of the roomy jet. On the polished wood surface in front of him were a series of enlarged aerial photographs.

"Latest Keyhole images?" asked Uncle Bob, referring to the now not so secret Keyhole Spy Satellite technology.

"No, Google Earth." Kyle responded rather blankly.

Surprised, Uncle Bob picked up one of the enlarged shots.

"Damn, I had no idea, Google had this high resolution capabilities."

"New GeoSat 10 technology. What most people don't know is that Google bought a small company called Keyhole Inc., which really refined the technology. Believe it or not Keyhole was actually a CIA owned company. So this new stuff is not too far behind the NSA's current stuff if you ask me" replied Kyle.

"Are these of Carson City?" Uncle Bob asked.

"Areas in and around Carson City, Nevada" replied Liam as he picked through the stack of images on the table.

Uncle Bob put the aerial image back down and retrieved a different image. Liam stopped thumbing through the 9 x 12 photos as his eye caught something in the photograph. . He picked up t a magnifying glass and trained it on a small area, just south of Carson City.

"What do you hope to glean from these?" Uncle Bob queried.

"Looking for some clues to a railroad that was in operation in 1868." Liam answered without looking up.

"How the hell do you do that?" he asked.

"Looks like we might have our first clue." Liam announced " Here about twenty miles south of Carson City. What looks like an old culvert trestle. This also appears to be overgrown roadbed." Liam pointed the area out to Uncle Bob and Kyle.

"Looks like a good a place as any to start looking." Kyle replied.

At that moment a rather attractive female flight attendant boarded the airplane and cleared her throat. All three turned to look at the visitor.

"Mr. Clooney, your plane to New York is ready."

Both Liam and Kyle looked at uncle Bob and silently mouthed *Mr. Clooney*? Uncle Bob smiled and headed off towards the front of the airplane to follow the ground attendant off. . Just as he was about to exit the plane he turned to Liam and Kyle,

"What fun is it being in this business if I can't be someone else?"

He laughed as he started down the stairs with a wave. A male flight attendant appeared from nowhere and instructed Liam and Kyle to take their seats, fasten their seat belts and turn off all electronics as they were ready for departure as well.

The two men each selected their own butter soft leather seats on opposite sides of the plane. Liam had just settled into his seat when the plane started its journey to the taxiway. Liam looked over at Kyle and noticed that his friend appeared to be fast asleep. A skill that he had been able to accomplish whenever he called upon it.

Liam picked up the stack of aerial images and began to look at each one in turn again making notes as he went along. As the plane was rocketing down the runway for take off, Liam found himself whistling *I've Been Working On The Railroad.*

Liz looked up at the antique register clock on the wall of the stamp workroom. It had been only four hours since Kyle had left the loft in the Bronx and flew to Washington to join Liam. She looked out of the workroom window and marveled at the first light of morning rising over the eastern skyline.

She was beginning to feel the toll of the long hours of sitting in front of a computer monitor. At least she had been able to track down a few more leads regarding Octavious Gass in the early spring of 1868 and the mystery of his disappearance. She had learned of Gass's history with the army and his purchase of the former army fort site. She had gone through server after server to finding various western territory newspaper archives from the summer of 1864. After what had amounted to almost the entire night and early morning hours, Liz compiled a rather lengthy compendium for Liam. These notes comprised of a newly adjusted timeline with the recently obtained information on former President Johnson from the LOC, early territorial maps that encompassed the State of Nevada. Lastly, high resolution scans of every square inch of the front and reverse of the unfinished greenback, which everyone was now referring to as the *Gassback*.

She had also found some obscure lists for materials used to construct a railroad spur, which had been ordered by an H. Black from the United States War Department in 1866. The bill of ladings attached to the lists revealed that these supplies were to be delivered to the *Gas Rancho, Las Vegas Springs, State of Nevada* by rail and overland wagon. Liz just assumed that some overworked clerk in war torn Washington in 1866 had miss-spelled Gass's name. Liz included these in the briefing to Liam as well.

She had just completed composing the email to her boss and was about to press the send button when she noticed a movement on one of the security monitors, with her peripheral vision. She stared at the monitor for a full two minutes and seeing nothing, she pressed the send button and finally spoke to herself.

" Now I'm jumping at shadows!"

Liz put a fresh pair of white cotton gloves on, and then picked up the diary from the camera stand that had been set up on the worktable. She placed the diary into a protective plastic container and returned it to a safe that they had discovered behind a sliding panel in the control room. A large old safe with a finger scan locking mechanism. Kyle had reprogrammed the scanner, so they could store the archive items

When they first opened the safe, Liz discovered a series of stamp albums that had the title *Rare* and a number inscribed on each spine and cover. She didn't dare open any of the albums for the fear of ruining some stamps. She made a mental note to tell her boss of this discovery, as she had forgotten to in her last email.

She closed the door of the massive safe, emblazoned with a 19th century style graphic that boasted *Cary Safe Company, Buffalo, New York, The Safe and Secure Safe.* She then pulled up on the latch that would activate the locking mechanism. Returning to the workroom she collected the NBNC ledger. As she was walking to the control room she stopped at the window and noticed a storm was coming in from the south. Off in the distance a flash of lightening illuminated the pre-morning, murky sky. Liz silently counted the seconds to herself, like she had been doing since she was a little girl, to estimate how far off the storm was. When she reached a count of ten the low rumble of thunder vibrated the panes of glass in the window.

"Ten miles." She remarked to no one.

Liz stood and watched the storm, clutching the ledger to her breast. She was lost in her thoughts of childhood when the sound of her cell phone ringing almost made her jump out of her skin. She answered the iPhone as if she had had a full nights sleep.

"Hi, Uncle Bob, are you here yet?"

"Yes, I'm in New York and standing downstairs. Could you come and let me in please? It's starting to rain."

"Be right down." she answered hurriedly, ran to the control room to check the monitor then seeing Uncle Bob she left the stamp workroom walking briskly to the upstairs lobby.

Once in the lobby she stepped through the open door of the elevator cage. She closed the door then the metal grating then pressed the call button marked one. Slowly the elevator transcended down. Liz stood and listened to the noises of the lift's hydraulic system. Standing in silence, facing forward, staring at the elevator door, unconsciously clutching the ledger as if it were a small infant not wanting to be put down.

The elevator came to a stop at the first floor. She opened the door and cage to the small car and exited into the well-it lobby. She walked quickly to the front door only to find Uncle Bob standing on the stoop, his suit being ruined from the deluge that had suddenly erupted from the skies.

Liz gave Liam's uncle a quick hug and welcomed him to New York.

"Sorry you got caught in that downpour. It was a really beautiful day here. Not a cloud in the sky."

"Just my luck. I knew I should have brought an umbrella!"

"Let's go upstairs and get you a towel so you can dry off."

The pair walked over to the open elevator door.

"Bob, I need to stop on the way up and put this back." Nodding to the cradled book. "I don't feel like it's safe out in the open upstairs."

"Is that the ledger?" Uncle Bob pointed to the clutched tome in Liz's arms.

"Yes, the beginning to a century's' old mystery." Liz located the screw near the speaker grill and pressed, opening the concealed finger scanner. Liz placed her right thumb on the device and waited for the scanning process to be completed. Once that was finished she entered her new numerical code on the keypad, then pressed the first floor button on the elevator.

The concealed rear elevator doors opened and the two stepped into an inky blackness. The only light that could be discerned was the occasional lighting flash that illuminated the high, frosted, wire mesh reinforced windows.

Liz worked from memory when she watched and listened to Liam and John just days earlier, when they had first discovered the secret to the first floor.

"Uncle Bob, follow me."

"Follow you? I can't even see you! It's so damn dark in here!"

"Hug the wall and walk to your left. I'm about ten feet ahead of you."

Liz felt the wall as she made her way to the antique switch boxes. Once there she found the correct lever for the lights and switched it on. The hidden lighting instruments blinked on one by one, until the monstrous space was bathed in a warm glow.

"Holy shit!" was all that Uncle Bob could muster.

"That was our reaction as well." Liz gestured to the factory before her "Welcome to the reconstructed press room of the National Banknote Company, circa 1868!"

"I didn't believe Liam when he told me. Nothing has been constructed with such detail. Not even at the Smithsonian!" Uncle Bob's head slowly turned right to left as he scanned the room, taking in image after image, machine after machine.

"Now for the really cool part." Liz said.

She walked over to the series of belts, pulleys and levers and engaged the drive system. The room sprang to life. Uncle Bob's eyes opened even wider.

"Okay, even I have to admit that that's pretty amazing! It all works?"

Liz just nodded her head as she started to walk over to the clerk's office that contained the journals.

"I just want to put this back with the others. I just have a feeling that it would be more secure there than just one book being left out upstairs."

"Sound thinking. Which way to the clerks office?" asked Uncle Bob.

"Over near the rear of the pressroom, that seemed to be the shipping area."

The two walked over towards the small row of offices that were set against the buildings outside wall. They were about twenty feet from the office when Uncle Bob sensed a chill breeze passing him in the pressroom.

"Is there an open window or door some where?" he asked quietly.

"I don't think so. Liam had Kyle and John surveyed the entire floor before shutting it down."

Then Liz tasted an acrid metal taste in the back of her throat. Then Uncle Bob caught the telltale smell of cordite as a stronger breeze wafted past them. Uncle Bob removed his Glock from his shoulder holster and pressed himself up against the wall outside of the clerk's office, Liz was right beside him.

" Lizzy, are you armed?" Bob asked Liz.

"Unh-unh left it up in the workroom." She whispered.

"I'm going to go over to where the odor is coming from to check it out. You stay here." he directed.

"No way. Where you go I follow," she countered.

In the classic two-handed pistol grip, Uncle Bob slowly made his way to the source of the odor and breeze. Liz fell in behind him still holding the ledger. When they came to the clerk's office door they peered in the opened doorway. The small room was in shambles. Furniture upended, the drawers in the desk had all been opened, their contents dumped into a pile on the floor. The bookcase of ledgers was completely empty; the individual books were strewn about the floor. Most of them open, many having pages torn from their bindings. . Liz stepped into the small cramped office and knelt by the pile of books. She picked up a book just like the ledger she held. She then dropped it back onto the pile.

"They are all ruined!"

"Someone or ones were obviously looking for that book of yours." Uncle Bob whispered as he nodded towards the ledger that Liz now held even tighter.

"The breeze seems stronger and colder now, it feels like it is coming from up ahead." Uncle Bob said.

Very cautiously the pair slowly made their way out of the clerk's office and into the shipping area, constantly looking forward and back, making sure that no one was following them. They then saw the dim light coming from a hole, about twenty-four inches in diameter, in the outer brick wall. Small bits of brick and motor fanned out across the warehouse door. Two pairs of footprints appeared in the dust.

Without speaking a word, Uncle Bob turned to Liz and held up two fingers. Liz silently acknowledged with a nod. They then slowly moved towards the opening in the wall. Liz inspected the footprints in the dust closer and noticed that one or both of the intruders had exited through the entry hole by back tracking over their earlier footprints. Liz tugged Robert's arm and pointed to her find. It was Uncle Bob's turn to nod his silent acknowledgement.

Uncle Bob got down on his hands and knees, quickly darted his head through the hole and into the rain filled night. After doing this two more times, he then stood back up, and holstered his gun.

"Looks like there were two of them alright. I saw two sets of motorcycle tire tracks in the mud. It looks like they both high tailed it after not finding the ledger."

Uncle Bob ran his hand over the near perfect circular opening in the way.

"Shaped charge, low directed detonation, most likely dent cord. We better get back upstairs and lock that book away."

"First we need to block up that hole. No sense in letting them or anyone else back in." said Liz.

In the shipping area were some large wooden pallets that had untrimmed stacks of unprinted paper on them. After a quick search, Uncle Bob found an 1860's style pallet jack. He maneuvered the jack into place and with some effort pushed the one thousand pound pile of paper up against the hole in the wall. He then removed the pallet jack and returned it to where he had found it.

"There, if anyone can move that, I don't want to meet them."

"I need to let Liam and Kyle know what has happened. They need to watch their backs."

Liz, with Uncle Bob close behind, started to pick her way through the pressroom machinery back to the elevator. Liz walked past some pallets of antique stock certificates, waiting to be cut and trimmed.

"What was Joe Bousquet going to do with this place? Open a ...

Uncle Bob didn't finish his sentence because from out between two of the pallets a figure came up behind Uncle Bob and hit him with a large cast iron wrench once used on the presses.

Liz turned when she heard Uncle Bob crumple to the floor, then she saw the tall, pock marked face intruder with the wrench in his hand taking a step towards her. She didn't scream because she had been trained to conserve her energy in times of crisis, and hysterics can zap energy from a person just as quickly as exercise does. Instead Liz took off at a full run, weaving through the machines with the interloper fast at her heels screaming at the top of his lungs.

"Stop, I want that book, get back here, I won't hurt you!"

"Yeah right." Liz murmured to herself. "You have just killed Uncle Bob and you won't hurt me? Bull shit, I won't give you a chance."

Liz kept on running, moving from machine to machine, all the while being highly aware of the ancient, non-safety guarded equipment and their vast array of moving parts.

She had tried to make it directly for the elevator cage, but her assailant was good, very good. He kept just a pace off to Liz's left, never running directly behind her in case she threw something into his path in order to trip him up. This technique caused Liz to very slightly keep veering to her right.

After her third lap around the warehouse floor, she realized what her pursuer was up too. He was slowly closing the gap by forcing Liz into a smaller and smaller circle every time she completed a lap. Hoping to catch her in the middle. She quickly calculated that she had just three more circuits to run before he would make his attempt to grab her and to get the ledger.

All through this exercise the thug continued shouting obscenities at Liz. Screaming for the ledger and the greenback. Describing in sickening detail what he was going to do once he caught her. Trying to fluster her into making a mistake.

Liz had to get out of here, but she knew it would not be possible with this person between her and the exit. Towards the end of what would have been her sixth circuit, she stopped to catch her breath. As she stood against a printing press, she watched as her hound moved one more ring closer to her. She gauged that she had about three minutes before she was cornered so to speak. She quickly scanned the room searching for anything that would help her. She overlooked what she was looking for. She looked around the room once again and then she saw her object and destination.

Liz had to time this out just right if it was going to work. She had to cover about sixty feet but she had to let her unwelcome guest get closer to her. One thing that made it easier was that he had kept yelling at her the whole time. Liz was always able to tell where he was in the room and about how far away he was from her position.

Liz calculated that the sixty feet was about fifteen strides. She took a deep breath; counted to ten, just as she had with the thunder and when she reached ten she took off like a shot. Liz counted her steps to herself as she crossed the pressroom floor. One, two, three, four...

"I see you, you bitch! Now we're going to have some real fun!" screamed the pocked face man. He then threw the cast iron wrench at Liz. Liz felt the air move as the ten-pound tool passed to her side, hit a stack of paper, then clanged harmlessly to the floor. This was just the type of diversion that she needed. Liz screamed as if in pain and fell to the floor in front of the aged guillotine, out of view from her would be executioner.

The thug, believing that he had struck Liz with the wrench, stopped his circle advance and ran straight to where he had seen Liz go down. Liz quickly crawled the last ten feet she needed then stood up with her back to the man, a calculated risk. She now stood as if shaken and placed one hand on the machine as if to steady her. The assailant walked quickly to where she was and began to slow ten feet from her, being wary of a possible trap.

Liz turned and now faced her aggressor still appearing to be stunned, pretending that she was unsteady on her feet. He took three steps closer and screamed his demand.

"Give me that book you little shit!" he pointed his outstretched finger at the book she was holding, when Liz did nothing he screamed louder.

"Do you hear me? Give me the fucking book, NOW!"

Liz teased him a bit by wagging the book in front of her. This pissed him off even more.

"Why you slut, wait until I'm done with you!"

The pock marked face was now beet red. His anger and irritation was like a raw nerve. He screamed once more with a volume that hurt Liz's ears.

"GIVE IT TO ME, NOW!" as small drops of spittle flew in the air.

Just then Liz tossed the ledger into the jaws of the guillotine and screamed.

"Get it your fucking self!" She twisted to her right and threw herself three feet towards the large lever on the side of the machine. Her timing had been perfect. Just as she reached the lever, her assailant reached into the jaws of the guillotine to retrieve the book. His right hand was just touching the spine of the book when the guillotine's drive engaged. First the clamping weight came crashing down on the book and his hand. Within a split second the 400-pound, razor sharp, knife blade sliced cleanly through the book and his hand.

Liz wasn't sure what surprised or disgusted her more in the next five or so seconds. The sound of the man's bones being sliced off, or the look of absolute shock and horror when he pulled his appendage away from the knife blade to reveal a hand devoid of four fingers and half his thumb.

The man stood there, blood shooting in spurts to the rhythm of his beating heart, from all five appendages.

"You, you... you cut off my god damn fingers!"

Liz knew that she should run but she just stood transfixed at the sight of a man over six feet tall with his hand held up spurting blood every which way.

"I'll kill you for this you bitch! You're dead!"

Then, fumbling with his left hand, he reached to the small of his back to retrieve a semi-automatic pistol. With trembling arm the thug tried aiming the gun at Liz's head.

"Say good bye you slut!"

Frozen in fear, with her eyes closed, Liz just stood there.

Just as the man's index finger squeezed the trigger, two loud concussive slaps filled the room. With her eye's still tightly closed, Liz waited for the excruciating pain to course through her body. After a few seconds and no such sensation, she slowly opened her eyes to see her assassin standing before her with one red dot in the middle of his forehead and another dead center of his chest. His eyes were staring straight ahead until they slowly turned up in their sockets. The big man fell to the ground in a heap.

Liz's brain was still not processing what had just happened in front of her. It was almost a full minute before she heard Uncle Bob's voice drift into her ears.

"Liz? Liz? Lizzy! Can you hear me? Are you hit?" screamed Uncle Bob.

Liz's brain slowly started to come back into focus. By then Uncle Bob was standing right in front of her shaking her, begging her to respond.

"Uncle Bob? Where did you come from? I though he killed you?"

"It's takes more than a love tap to take this old boy out. Are you okay? Have you been hit?"

"No, no I'm fine." Her head cleared. "Just a bit of shock I think."

Uncle Bob released Liz's arms and turned to the mess before them.

"What the hell happened?'"

"He tried to flush and trap me like a rabbit. He was good Bob. You were right, he knew about the ledger and the greenback. That's what he wanted. So I lured him to the guillotine and threw the journal in. He just naturally reached in for the journal, that's when I hit the release."

Uncle Bob looked to the guillotine and the bloody mess. After retrieving a handkerchief from his pocket he reached to the platen of the large knife and slowly extracted one of the dead man's fingers. He then removed the other four cleaved appendages before he extracted the two halves of the blood soaked journal.

"I'm afraid that it's ruined."

Liz still staring down at the body answered nonchalantly.

"That's not the real ledger."

"What?" answered Bob.

"That's not the real ledger."

"I heard you the first time, but I don't know what you mean. You never set that book down from the minute you let me into the building."

"I just had this uneasy feeling when we first saw the mess in clerk's office, so I switched the journal with one of the journals from the pile on the floor. I thought it would be safer there. After all, they all ready looked there."

Uncle Bob gently took her by both arms and hugged her. He then kissed her blood-specked forehead.

"Miss Elizabeth Gallagher, you are a genius!"

31

Uptick

138 Basking Avenue
Levittown, New York
May 7, 2013
4:00 AM

The Foreign Exchange (FOREX) market is the largest financial market in the world, trading around $1.5 trillion each day. However unlike conventional market trading the trading in the FOREX is not done at one central location, but is conducted between participants through electronic communication networks (ECNs) and phone networks, in various markets around the world. The market is closed from Friday 5:00 PM EST until its open on Sunday 5:00 PM EST.

Currencies are always in high demand, thus the need for a twenty-four hour cycle. The international scope of currency trading means that there are always traders, somewhere, who are making and meeting demands for a particular currency. Currencies are also constantly needed around the world for international trade, as well as by central banks and global businesses.

Central banks have relied on foreign-exchange markets since 1971 - when fixed-currency markets ceased to exist because the gold standard was dropped. Since that time, most international currencies have been "floated", rather than pegged to the value of gold. The pegged value of gold had been fixed at $35 dollars per ounce in 1944 and did not fluctuate until 1968.

From World War Two until the early sixties, the United States had been considered the world's central banker. Trust in this system began to erode and by the late sixties the once balanced world monetary system began to tip in favor of newly emerging economies.

By the early 1970s, as the Vietnam War accelerated inflation, the United States as a whole began running a trade deficit. From the 1800's until this point in time the United States Government had a gold reserve equal to approximately one half of all issued United States paper currency. Thus guaranteeing an even standard of paper for gold, better know as the Promise To Pay method.

The crucial turning point was in 1970, which saw the United States gold coverage deteriorate from 55% to 22%. This, in the view of neoclassical economists, represented the point where holders of the dollar had lost faith in the ability of the United States to cut budget and trade deficits.

In 1971 more and more dollars were being printed in Washington, then being pumped overseas, to pay for government expenditures on various military and social programs. In the first six months of 1971, assets of $22 billion fled the United States. In response, on August 15, 1971, President Richard Nixon unilaterally imposed 90-day wage and price controls, a 10% import surcharge, and most importantly "closed the gold window", making the dollar inconvertible to gold directly, except on the open market. Nixon made this decision without consulting members of the international monetary system or even his own State Department, and was soon dubbed the *Nixon Shock*. By March 1976, all the major currencies were *floating*—in other words, exchange rates were no longer the principal method used by governments to administer monetary policy.

As so often happens, history has a tendency to repeat itself and we are the fools to not heed the past. In late 2008 the United States and much of the world, started down a path to a new economic crisis.

Over three hundred banking institutions failed in the United States alone during this new panic. Rampant unemployment, loss of hundreds of billions of dollars in savings and retirement funds wiped out virtually overnight. Real estate, the once venerable safety net, became cinder blocks, tied to investor's necks, as they sank deeper into financial morass. The rich got richer and everyone else just became poor.

Gold was once again in favor by central banks and even more importantly governments. A major push was in play to once again tie all of the world's currencies to gold. Soon governments were stock piling as much of the precious metal as possible. Soon prices soared to almost two thousand dollars an ounce.

Dwayne Peters sat at the keyboard in the dimly lit basement of his parent's house in Levittown, New York. As his fingers flew across the keyboard inputting line after line of code his lips parted in a small smile as he remembered that day two years ago at the DEF CON Hackers convention in Las Vegas.

He was trying to convince some fellow hackers that he had found a way past any firewall, through any security system, in order to reset the internal clock of any computer remotely. Making it behave to accumulated historical data, even data from before the computer age, without being detected by the user of the computer. In essence he could re-write history. His friends would have none of it. Calling him a crackpot and a loser. Loser? If only those losers knew about his Cayman Island numbered account.

He remembered the woman that approached him as he spilled nacho cheese sauce down the front of his shirt. Cara the knockout! How she cooed and batted her eyes, calling him a pure genius, a stud! Her nipples pushing against the fabric of her skintight, low cut shirt. That day couldn't have gotten any better! (Well, maybe if she was dressed in Princess Leia's metal bikini from *Star Wars Episode Five: The Empire Strikes Back)* What he didn't realize was that his life was just about to become a dream.

Later that evening she introduced him to her boss who hired him on the spot for a super secret government job. He had two years to complete the Shadow Trap. For his work he would receive $250,000 up front and another $250,000 when he was done. Two years of telling his parents that he was designing websites. What they hell did they know or care as long as he paid them their paltry $100 a month rent! This time next week he would, hit the convention again, pick up a new client or two with his proven hack, then head to Grand Cayman with his money.

All of his preliminary tests had gone flawless and he was feeling damn proud of his code. Cara would visit every four months to check on his progress. Each time she came to Dwayne's home, she would wear something sluty and tell him how smart he was. When she leaned over to view the monitor, checking his work, her boobs would be so close to his face, sometimes he moved just an inch closer so he would brush up against them. He remembered the time his dick got so hard he couldn't stand up to walk her back out to her car. Maybe, he would ask Cara to go to the Caribbean with him, after all he had bucks now. He also decided that he had to come up with a new handle, a new nickname. He would be up there with Condor, Captain Crunch, even Tesla! Except what Dwayne failed to register at that moment was that as hackers they all had been caught.

Three more address lines and it would be complete, ready to launch into cyberspace. He was told this was the next step in cyber defense and that his work would help the government and financial institutions for years to come. The list of targets numbered over ten thousand, but each one would have the Shadow Trap downloaded and installed with seconds, once he pressed the send button.

First, according to the instructions that Cara had left on her last visit, he had to log into a chat room and get his final briefing. Final briefing. That was so cool! He thought of himself as a cyber 007 and Bond always got the girl, right?

He logged into the dedicated IP address and waited for the connection. He had already pinged this IP just to see who it was. The Who Is Registration came back with a Washington, D.C. street address but no name, maybe the CIA? That was so cool!

Within 15 seconds of connecting a prompt appeared on the screen asking Dwayne for his log in information. He entered the alpha-numerical sequence that Cara had made him memorize. (Once he had memorized the code he looked at her and asked if he needed to eat the paper. She just looked at him and said "What the fuck? Sure.") Once the code was accepted he received his instruction to send his Shadow Trap out at precisely 4:25 AM.

What Dwayne did not know was this was the exact time that the Federal Reserve sent their daily percentage and set pricing of monetary reserves to all worldwide financial institutions.

Dwayne watched the countdown on his monitor and when the clock reached 04:25:00, Dwayne hit the send button. With that simple command, millions of bits of information found their respected destinations allover the Internet. Now he just had to wait until his Shadow Trap reported back to his client that all was operational. He had been given another IP address to receive this information and was told that it was the only address that was to be programmed. But Dwayne was smarter he thought. He wrote a carrier pigeon program that would piggyback the information to his server.

Dwayne had programmed his incoming mail signal with a chord from a cyber-rock band called *Up Your A-D-D Ass*. Wayne was counting down time, to himself, and reached zero just before the computer chimed with a "finger nails on a chalk board" chord. Less than a minute later a chat room prompt popped on the screen confirming receipt. Then a few seconds later, a confirmation code appeared for a money transfer to his Cayman account, then just the word – END – appeared.

Dwayne clapped his hand together looking at the figure displayed on his monitor and shouted "I'm Fucking Rich!" so loudly that his mother called down to ask if he was alright.

"I'm more than alright! I'm fucking terrific! Now for Vegas and some pussy!" he shouted back to her.

Once his mother heard this language, she shouted down to him

"Do you want that filthy mouth washed out with soap?"

She then slammed the door. Dwayne heard her footsteps as she tramped across the hardwood floor above his head, calling to his father.

"Herb, did you hear what your son just said?" Then another muffled door slam.

For two years, Dwayne had been told that he was helping the world stave off a future cyber attack on the world's banks. That with his Shadow Trap they could test all computer systems and find any holes where Al-Qaeda, the Tailiban or any home grown terrorist might infiltrate and launch an attack. He felt good knowing that he was doing something so patriotic and important. Of course he didn't know the truth.

Dwayne had just launched a terrorist cyber attack, not preventing one. His trap was now telling most of the worlds financial computers to reset their internal clocks and revise historical data reflecting gold at $18.90 per try ounce, a price that hadn't been traded since the Great San Francisco Earthquake of 1906.

Once the computers had been set back in time, buy orders were sent by the thousands, first for small quantities, then slightly larger amounts. All going to over a hundred thousand dummy accounts with over a hundred thousand fictitious owners.

The end result was really quite simple, genius in fact. Buy gold at 1906 prices, make all necessary transfers, deplete holdings by the corresponding amount, then reset the computers, showing that a transaction never took place. By the time anyone noticed the anomaly, most of the world's free market gold would be under new management. Effectively cornering the market on gold. This had not been attempted since American financiers Jay Gould and James Fisk tried in September 1869, thus causing Black Friday.

This time the Centum would not fail. Every precaution had been put in place. The end result was too great to have any unknowns. That is why, five days later, when police tried to locate Dwayne Peters in Las Vegas at the DEF CON convention to tell him about the horrible fire and tragic deaths of his parents, they were unable to locate him. They left numerous messages at his hotel and would keep trying over the course of the event week. After all people got lost in the crowds of Las Vegas conventions all the time.

What the LVPD did not piece together until almost a month later, was the body they had found four weeks earlier in a vacant lot in Henderson. A John Doe in his late twenties stripped naked, showing telltale signs of a hooker's john that had recently been rolled. Cause of death was having had an ice pick thrust into the base of his skull. The John Doe was in fact Dwayne Peters.

32

Silver State

Nevada State Railroad Museum
Carson City, Nevada
May 7, 2013

Liam felt as if he had been asleep only minutes when the wheels of the jet touched the tarmac. He groggily stretched and yawned as the plane taxied to the hanger. He looked over at his friend and realized that Kyle was still dead asleep. Liam picked up a magazine and threw it the prone figure.

"Rise and shine sleeping beauty. Time to punch in."

The two quickly picked up their supplies and bags and waited for the purser to open the door and lower the stairs.

" Gentleman, it was a pleasure having you aboard." The purser said.

"Thank you very much. Wonderful flight." Liam replied as he exited the plane.

Just as Kyle was about to deplane he jokingly called to the purser.

"Just to let you know, I never got my peanuts!" he shouted.

Kyle jogged to catch up to Liam.

"Peanuts? You didn't stop snoring for the last four hours let alone even sit up in a seat! Give the man a break" Liam chastised his friend.

Liam and Kyle spent the next hour unloading all of their gear and double-checking it to make sure all was accounted for and in good working order. They loaded the cases into the back of a midnight blue Range Rover that Uncle Bob had arranged.

"Where to first Boss?" Kyle asked as he started to program the onboard GPS system.

"First stop, the Nevada State Railroad Museum. If anybody knows anything about old abandoned rail lines, someone there should."

Kyle punched in the name of the museum and the directions to the museum appeared on the touch screen

"Co-ordinates locked Captain." Kyle said in a mock Russian accent as he pushed the Begin Route button with some flourish.

"If that's your Chekov, you had better seek help my friend. It sounded more like Miss Piggy than Pavel." Kyle laughed at the reference to the Star Trek character.

After thirty minutes driving they arrived at the Nevada State railroad Museum. They parked the Range Rover and walked to the main entrance. They entered the mostly empty Museum where a short, silver haired woman, perhaps in her late sixties was seated at the Ticket/Reception counter. Liam and Kyle crossed over to where she was seated. She greeted them both warmly.

"Good morning gentleman. It's a lovely day. How might I help you?"

"We are from a film company in Los Angeles." Liam took a card from his wallet and handed it to the receptionist "We are here to do some research for a film that we are working on. A Civil War documentary, about how the railroads were so important to both the Northern and Southern armies. Would there be any one here that might be able to tell us about any railroads in this area during and after the war?"

The silvered haired woman took Liam's card and verified that he as indeed from a film company. He had given her one of the actual business cards that Liam had used over the years. If anyone called to verify their story, the phone call would be automatically rerouted to Liz, where she would answer any questions that a suspicious person might ask.

The woman didn't even have to check a directory, make a phone call or even think about the question.

"You want to talk with Steve Bertrand. He's one of our most knowledgeable docents. I'm sure that he can help you out. He's helped on many, many movie projects. Mostly, real Hollywood type ones though."

"Is Mr. Bertrand here today?" asked Liam.

"Steve is always here." She leaned closer to Liam and Kyle and whispered her nugget of gossip.

"I think he sleeps here, I really do."

"Where might we find him, Miss?" asked Kyle.

"Miss?" she blushed "That's so sweet of you young man."

As she blushed she reached at patted Liam's arm.

"Both of you, please call me Ruth."

"That would be nice, thank you Ruth. Where did you say we could find him?" countered Liam.

Ruth stood up and pointed over to a set of double doors on the opposite side of the museum near a display of a railway Post Office car.

"Just go through those doors, over three sets of tracks and you will find him in the roundhouse working on Bessy." She said.

"Bessy?" quizzed Kyle.

"She's one of our steam locomotives. We use it to give

excursion rides during summer." She replied.

Liam took out his wallet and extracted a few bills.

"How much do we owe you Ruth?" Liam asked.

"Oh, there's no charge for research. But if you want to make a donation on your way out you can. There is a collection box right next to the exit."

"We will do that. Thank you again Ruth." Liam answered as he and Kyle went to find the docent.

When Liam and Kyle passed through the doors into the roundhouse they felt as if they had stepped back in time. There was not a single item in view that was made after 1900. Box cars, passenger cars even a very strange looking bicycle that rode on the railroad tracks.

Three tracks into the roundhouse stood a large black hulk from a bygone era. Liam walked up to the massive steam locomotive. He knew from his education and love of trains that this was a 2-6-0 Mogul. On the boiler above his head was the builder's plate. Proudly displayed was that this locomotive was manufactured by the Brooks Locomotive Works in Dunkirk, New York in 1890.

The 2-6-0 designation was based upon the Whyte Wheel Classification system. Devised by Frederick Methvan Whyte in 1900, encouraged by an editorial in the *American Engineer & Railroad Journal* for a standardized classification and identification system. The system counted the number of wheels, from the front of the locomotive to the rear, not counting any tender car. This Mogal bore a two wheel leading truck, six drive wheels and no trailing truck (generally found right below the cab of the locomotive). About 8000 of this style of locomotive were manufactured from the early 1860's until the early 1900's. The top speed for this particular locomotive class averaged around fifty miles per hour, making these engines more practical for freight service instead of passenger service.

Liam walked toward the rear of the locomotive around the rear of the tender and stopped. Laying on the ground just yards ahead were a pair of legs jutting out from between the large fifty-six inch drive wheels. Appearing as if the train had run over a person and cleaved their legs from the rest of the body.

Liam waved Kyle over to join him. Liam softly called out in order so he not startle the person under the dangerous piece of equipment.

"Mr. Bertrand?" spoke Liam.

No response. He tried just a bit louder this time.

"Mr. Bertrand?"

Still the legs just lay there.

Liam shot Kyle a puzzled looked and motioned that they should move closer. They were now standing over the outstretched legs that appeared to be clothed in traditional engineers coveralls.

"Mr. Bertrand?" Liam spoke in a normal volume, still no response.

Kyle was showing little patience for this game so he stepped in, kicked one of the work boots that were on the legs and shouted.

"MISTER BERTRAND!"

The legs jerked in under the locomotive and after a count of three, a man that appeared to be in his early fifties, appeared on his hands and knees poking his head out from between the drive wheels. In his ears were a pair of ear-buds, explaining his nonresponse.

Removing his right ear-bud, he looked up at Liam and Kyle.

"Can I help you?"

Music blaring from the ear buds. Liam recognized Long Train Running by the Doobie Brothers.

"Sorry to have startled you Mr. Bertrand. When you didn't hear us we wanted to make sure that you were okay." spoke Liam.

Righting himself to a standing position, the man covered in grease from head to toe, was as tall as Liam and looked as if he spent time daily in a gym. His forearms and biceps were sculpted in muscles. His hands looked to have the fingers of a surgeon, long, thin and nimble. His dark hair was just showing signs of what most women refer to as salt and pepper coloring. He removed a rag from his rear pocket and wiped his face.

"You seem to know my name, how about the return favor?" he asked.

"My name is Liam Ross and this is my colleague Kyle Gale."

Liam proffered his hand to the man standing in front of him and when Steve Bertrand shook it, Liam's assumption of the man had been correct. He had a grip that could rip the tops off of cans.

"Pleasure to meet you both. Sorry I didn't hear you but when I work on the locos I tune everything out."

"Like Bessy here?' asked Kyle.

Steve Bertrand's response took them both a little by surprise.

"What damn fool jackass called her Bessy? That just steams

me!"

"Um, Ruth directed us too you. We're sorry if we have offended you in any way." apologized Liam.

"You didn't offend me. It's just that some of the locals around here run from the doddering to a sandwich or two short of a picnic. No respect for great items from our past. That's the main reason why I wear the ear buds and listen to music, so I don't have to hear them." He waved a hooked thumb over his right shoulder, back towards the main building.

Steve Bertrand crossed over to a large drafting table not too far from the locomotive, wiping his grease stained hands as he walked. On the table were what appeared to be the original builders plans of the 2-6-0 loco.

"So, how can I be of help to you gentleman?" he asked.

"Well Mr. Bertrand, may we call you Steve?" Liam asked.

"Please do." he responded.

Liam extolled the story of the documentary and their interest.

"In our research we've come across some information regarding a rail line built specifically for the war here in Nevada. A line that ran from here in Carson City south to what is today Las Vegas."

"It's looks as though someone is having a laugh at your expense gentlemen. The only line that was anywhere near Carson City during the war was the Virginia and Truckee. The Crookedest Short Line in America and there wasn't even a foot of track laid."

"We don't follow you sir." Kyle said a looking a bit confused.

"Two different companies tried to start a railway here in

Carson in order to connect to the line north of here that would become *The Overland Route*, the original transcontinental railroad. The main purpose was to use the line to transport freight to the mining communities in the hills. Both companies failed to raise enough money to build anything. It wasn't until 1870 that the first train ran on rails laid from here to Virginia City." Steve Bertrand explained.

"Why was it called the Crookedest Short Line in America? Were the owners, corrupt?" asked Liam.

"Well it was 1870, soon after the war, and no body trusted no body around here. So I'm sure that some people were shady, no the meaning of the nickname is that the turns on the line from here to Virginia City were so tight that the gandydancers laid twenty-one miles of track to cover sixteen miles."

Steve chuckled as he walked over to the locomotive and retrieved a part that was on the floor where he had been working. He returned to the drafting table, set down the part and retrieved a set of calipers from the desktop so he could take some measurements. Liam and Kyle still listened attentively.

"There were enough curves in that line for a train to go around in circle seventeen times. But all of that was north of Carson City. There just weren't any lines leading to the south. Sorry, hope you didn't come all the way out here for that one item, besides, at that time, there wasn't anything down near the Vegas area, except an old Yankee Army post. No reason to have a railroad." he concluded.

"Would you mind taking a look at something Steve?"

Before he could answer Liam pulled the stack of images that Kyle had downloaded plus a hyper detailed elevation scan of the western and southern portions of the state.

"These are some maps and images using some of the latest mapping technology. This is what we have found."

Liam pointed to a section south of Carson City paralleling the mountain range then cutting south and east. The scan showed a graded elevation, ten feet wide and with no more than two percent rises in any area. Liam then showed Steve the images with the old abandoned culvert trestle and what could have been evidence of a larger bridge further south, all evidence of an abandoned railroad.

"This grade looks to have gone directly from Carson City to what would have been that old Yankee Army post."

Steve Bertrand put down the calipers and repositioned his glasses on his nose. The look on his face was pure surprise as well as intrigue.

"Well I'll be damned. Sure looks like old roadbed."

He opened a drawer beneath the table and pulled out a magnifying glass. He then bent over the image and scanned the outlined path. He then pointed to various clumps of earth, overgrown with weeds and years of wind blown earth, evenly spaced along the route.

"These here, if you dug one up, it would be piles of ties. These clumps every, thousand feet or so, is standard practice on a railroad. Iron was expensive during that period of time most steel rail was imported from England. After abandoning a line they would save the rail to resell but leave the ties behind. These would be indisputable proof of a railroad."

Liam looked at Kyle and Kyle immediately knew what they were going to do next.

"Mr. Bertrand, thank you for your time. You have

provided the next piece of the puzzle."

Liam took the man's hand. The handshake was anything but normal but the look in Steve Bertrand's eyes spoke volumes.

"You're not just going to pop in here, show me this and then just runoff now, are you? This could be the biggest news in the railfan community in over fifty years!"

"We only have a couple of days sir and we have to travel quickly." said Kyle.

Steve looked at Kyle with a bit of skepticism. He closed one eye and tilted his head at a Kyle. He then poked a finger at Kyle's chest.

"You think I'm too old don't you?" Now raising his voice a bit. "Well I'm here to tell you that I am seventy-one years young, strong as an ox and have the stamina of a middle line backer. Most people half your age can't keep up with me."

Both Kyle and Liam were amazed when they heard his age. They could have sworn that he was twenty years younger. He was about to lash out with act two at Kyle so Liam stepped in.

"Steve, it's not that we don't want to invite you along, it's just we do have a very tight schedule and I'm afraid that our employer might have issues with insurance. But I do have an idea." Liam offered.

"What's that?" he returned.

"We have absolutely no interest in the discovery of this line if it is a rail line. I will draw up a paper right now; that credits you with the discovery of the first solid evidence. Does that sound fair?" Liam asked.

"And just how are you going to tell what kind of line it was? I could just follow you two." he countered.

Liam knew that taking him along on this trek or having him follow could prove to be too dangerous. Liam had an idea but he had to sell it.

"Steve, could you give me a minute while I call our employer and ask a few questions?"

"Be my guest."

Liam pulled out his iPhone and realized that he had not turned it on since landing in Carson City. He pushed the on button of the smart phone and waited for it to go through its paces. Once it connected to the network the device vibrated and chimed a number of times. Seeing that all the texts were either from Liz or Uncle Bob concerned him. He navigated to his *favorites* page in the phone application; then tapped Liz's name.

She answered on the first ring and it was a one sided conversation for almost ten minutes as Liz and Uncle Bob filled Liam in on the events at the loft back in New York. Once they were done Liam filled them in on the progress in Carson City and the potential problem with Steven Bertrand following them. Liz's accounting of the incident ratified Liam's mind that taking Mr. Bertrand was a bad idea, But he did have an even better idea.

Liam quickly outlined his idea to Liz and Bob, got Bob's approval, then closed the connection after promising not to turn the phone off again. Kyle walked over to where Liam was standing, noticed the look of concern on his face.

"Bad news Boss?" he asked.

"I'll tell you later. Let's talk to Mr. Bertrand first."

Liam began to outline a plan that called for Mr. Bertrand to join the search, but not in person. Liam convinced him that he would be more valuable asset back here at the roundhouse to verify any evidence that they might find.

"Makes sense. Got a plan to get me the information?" asked Steve.

"Do you have access to a computer with web camera?" Kyle asked.

"Follow me." Liam and Kyle followed him over to a small office near the machine shop area of the roundhouse. Steve opened the door and flipped on the lights. There, in the very modern office, was the latest Apple tower computer with a forty-inch LCD monitor, drafting tablet and large-scale plotter. "Mission control men."

"Well, that answers my next question regarding opening jpg images that we send to you." Kyle said sheepishly.

"I can also tie into the UNLV servers if you want to create any wire frame images of any structures or pieces that you may find. I was the Dean of Engineering down there until I retired last year."

"Now I feel like a complete idiot." Kyle said as he turned and walked out of the office.

"That's pretty rough terrain where you are going. How you going to get there?" Steve asked Liam.

"We've got a range rover outside that should suffice." was his response.

"Preppy toy, won't get ten miles in that kind of country." Steve responded.

"Do you have a better idea?" Liam inquired.

"I just may." was all that Steve said.

Liam and Kyle were back in the main parking lot of the museum where Liam brought Kyle up to speed on the events in

New York. Kyle started to blame himself by saying he should have stayed in New York. Liam explained that Uncle Bob was there and that he was needed right there when all of a sudden a blast of an air horn sounded and one of the strangest vehicles that Liam had ever seen pulled up beside them. Steve Bertrand jumped out of the soft-top, sand colored, six-wheeled transport and walked over to Liam and Kyle.

"What is this vision?" asked Kyle with excitement in his voice.

"It's a Pinzgauer. It's an amphibious vehicle that was named after a breed of Austrian horse. The horse can go over any kind of terrain and so can this puppy. Let me give you a quick how to then you can get on the road so to speak."

Steve spent the next forty-five minutes going over the all terrain vehicle with Kyle. Kyle was impressed with the trucks design and ease of handling and Steve was impressed with Kyle's knowledge of engineering and machines.

They loaded all their gear in the back of the truck, climbed into the cab, Kyle behind the wheel, Liam at shotgun, hooked up a laptop into the onboard GPS and then Kyle started up the behemoth.

Steve walked up to the passenger side of the Pinzgauer, Liam rolled down the window.

"I don't sleep much, so don't worry about the time. Send me a test video once you leave the roads and hit the dirt. That way I'll start a trace track with the GPS for any future trips."

"Steve, I can't thank you enough. This is over the top generous. We'll pamper her."

Liam called out as they started to drive away. Steve waved

as the 6x6 pulled onto the highway form the parking lot.

Liam and Kyle made there way south. Liam was impressed with how smooth the ride of the Pinzgauer was. He asked Kyle how it handled.

"She drives like a dream. Better than my pickup back home."

They had traveled about thirty minutes south on Nevada state route 395 to Dresslerville, Nevada. It was here that Kyle pulled the 6x6 off the main road .

"Time to go overland."

"Let me link up to Steve so he can start the trace."

Liam opened the video chat program and entered Steve's email address into the computer, he answered on the first ring.

"Steve, I've must tell you, traveling in this so far has been pure heaven."

"Just wait till you start off road with it, it's the only way to fly."

"How's our signal?" Kyle asked of the engineer.

"I have you at full strength. What's your plan of attack?" Steve asked.

Liam laid out their route first with starting at a dry creek bed that looked like it dissected the old roadbed about six miles in. Then follow the roadbed south until they reached the first telltale sign from the aerial shoots, the culvert trestle.

They found the dry creek about one hundred yards from the road and went down the gentle slope of the creek bed. The Pinzgauer handled as if it just went over a speed bump. Kyle maneuvered the vehicle into the center of the wash and started down the cobble-strewn path. It was slow going at first, not wanting to miss anything should they be going to fast. After a half an hour and only two miles Kyle picked up the pace and soon they had gone another three miles.

"We should be coming up on the culvert in about two miles." Liam relayed the information to Kyle over the din of the six-cylinder diesel engine. Liam picked up a pair of field glasses and focused them on the horizon, hoping to pick up the culvert. After scanning the horizon line once, Liam reversed his direction and started to rescan when he saw the depression up ahead.

"Culvert coming up in about two hundred yards."

"Got it. I'll head a bit west and come up from that direction." Kyle said.

They reached the old abandoned wooden trestle, pulled the 6x6 up as close as they could, shut off the engine and got out. It was still early spring but the temperature was fast approaching the mid nineties. The engine ticked softly as they walked over to the wood beam structure. Liam pulled his iPhone and connected with Steve once again. Steve's face filled the entire screen of the smart phone.

"Steve, we're found the culvert. Let me activate the rear camera so you can see what we see."

Liam touched the activate button and Steve's image was replaced with the arid Nevada landscape. Liam walked closer to the dark wooden beams and focus the camera on the top of the trestle. Steve was the first to comment.

"Well, it's a small one, but the square Bent style is typical for the period."

"What's a bent?" Liam asked.

"A Bent is a support system for wooden bridges. The are similar to columns in modern construction." Kyle interspersed.

"Right on the money young man." Steve complimented Kyle. "How about some measurements?"

Kyle produced a three hundred foot tape measure from the 6x6. Liam took the free end and started to walk across the ditch to the beginning of the trestle. Kyle walked to the opposite end. When they both stopped they pulled the tape taunt and Kyle shouted out the reading.

"One Hundred and ten feet in length. Meet you in the middle to get a width." He shouted.

The trestle top was only about six feet from the base of the ditch, but walking on the unevenly spaced, antique ties made the walk cumbersome. They met in the middle and took the measurement of the trestle's width.

"These ties are six feet wide. Doesn't that seem small?" Liam asked Steve .

"For mainline track, about three feet too short, but not for narrow gauge. With that tie measurement I would say that the line was a 36" narrow gauge line. Do you see any sign of rail attachment to the ties?" he asked.

"The ties are fairly well rotted and the top faces are fairly chewed up. Some though are in okay shape." Liam said.

"I've got some spike holes over here!" Kyle shouted as he crouched down to take a measurement.

Liam carefully made his way over the rotten wood and focused the camera on the holes that Kyle had found. Steve studied the live image and replied.

"It doesn't make any sense, none at all." He said puzzling.

"What doesn't make sense Steve?" counted Liam.

"Well the spacing of the holes is standard to heavy weight rail, not narrow gauge. I don't know of any one single narrow gauge line that everused heavy weight, flat-bottomed rail. Most used bullhead rail, that's where the top of the rail is almost the exact small profile as the base. It just doesn't make sense."

"What is the main purpose for using a heavy weight rail on railroads Steve?" Liam asked.

"Generally for weight and speed. A heavy, fast train on a light-weight rail would push the rail out as it moves, causing derailments. Main line railroads are all heavy weight due to train size, weight, and volume of traffic served. There is just no reason for the heavier weight rail to have been used on a narrow gauge line. This may not be a railroad after all guys. I need some more proof."

"Then proof we shall get. Let's continue down the line to the piles we saw on the sat images." Liam said.

Liam closed the connection with Steve, promising to call no matter what they found, then he and Kyle returned to the 6x6. Traversing the ditch bank was effortless for the Pinzgauer. Once out of the wash, Kyle steered a course due south. The surface of the abandoned right of way was generally smooth and allowed the two friends to move along at a fairly good pace.

After three miles of this straight line the course started to veer to the east ever so slightly. Liam noticed that they were now fairly close to state route 395. It was Kyle that made the next observation.

"Looks like the line meets up with 395 Boss. What do you make of that?"

Liam looked ahead at the rising hills.

"I would think that, like the state road, if this was a railroad, they would have chosen the easiest route through the hills. It just so happens that over time the roadbed became the road."

The Pinzgauer approached the paved surface but Kyle had to head back north, paralleling the road so he did not break through a cattle fence. He found a gap in the fence and steered onto the blacktop. Able to travel at full speed they drove into the hills toward Topaz Lake, Nevada.

The shadows began to lengthen as the sun started its descent in the western sky. Liam and Kyle were about twenty miles from Topaz Lake and would have missed their mark completely if it had been a different time of day. Just as the 6x6 was approaching the turn off to state route 208, the last rays of the setting sun hit an object to the side of the road that created a flash of light. Out of curiosity Kyle slowed the truck to see if he could see what caused the flash of light.

Off the side of the road, nailed to an old fence post was a fairly new sign with shiny metallic letters advertising a bed and breakfast named Gold Hill Inn. On the other side of the fence was the telltale path of the former railway.

"I think we turn here Liam. That sure looks like the roadbed."

Liam consulted the hyper-accurate topographical map of the area and checked the elevations that the computer marked for them. Sure enough the route took them east of here then a broad curve south at Holbrook Junction. The path then went further south until it crossed the West Walker River and headed east towards Hawthorne. From there it appeared that the path was the same route as state route 95 all the way into Las Vegas.

"The first batch of the mounds that Steve identified, are just south of Holbrook Junction. Let's go off road there and follow the roadbed and check out a couple of them."

"Your wish is my command, Mon Capitain." Kyle shot Liam a comical right-handed salute and put the vehicle into gear and headed to Holbrook Junction.

Liam checked in with Steve again and updated him on their plan. They would check out a couple of the mounds then head back to Carson City in order to return the Pinzgauer, pick up the Range Rover then head to Vegas.

They made it to the first mound about an hour later. The sun had fully set and the moon had yet to rise, making for a very dark work area. Liam asked if they had any lanterns in their gear.

"I've got something even better." Kyle quipped as he inserted a key into what looked like a second ignition.

He turned the key and a generator powered to life. Kyle then flipped a series of switches on the control panel that separated the driver from the passenger. The darkness gave way to brilliant light coming from work lights spaced around the vehicle.

"Instant daytime! I've got to get me one of these when I get home." The technical guru said to himself out loud while caressing the steering wheel.

Liam went over to the mound as Kyle retrieved some shovels from the back of the Pinzgauer. With the night air just a few degrees cooler than the day, the pair didn't even break a sweat as they dug into the brush covered mound. They were about thirty shovels into their excavation when Liam's shovel struck something in the dirt, producing a hollow thump.

"I think I hit wood." He said.

"Sounded like it to me as well." Kyle answered in return.

Kyle then returned his shovel into the sandy loam when the blade hit something as well. The sound, as well as the shock wave that went through Kyle's arms down to his spine, indicated that he had struck something metallic and very dense. As Liam dug out the railroad tie, confirming Steve Bertrand's mound observation, Kyle went to work on his quarry.

After a quarter of an hours dig Liam had produced a bucket full of rusted, bent rail spikes as well as the tie. Kyle's find was much more exciting. After another ten minutes of digging Kyle unearthed a misshapen, twisted steel bow tie like object.

"Rail, and old rail at that." He said. "Well, I think this pretty much confirms the existence of a railroad, don't you think?"

"That my friend is what they call irrefutable proof. Too bad it's so big or we could take it back to the museum." Liam said.

Kyle just stood there in silence, held up his index finger, signaling that he had an idea. He turned around and walked back to the Pinzgauer. He returned in less than a minute this time carrying what looked like a large chop saw.

"A K-12 rescue saw. Cuts through steel like the preverbal hot knife through butter."

He set the saw on the ground and pulled the starter cord once, bringing the saw to life. He then proceeded to cut a four-foot section off of the twisted rail. Sparks flew in every direct and the sound was deafening, but true to his statement the saw made short work of the steel.

With the section of rail cut, Liam and Kyle loaded the steel rail, whole tie and bucket of spikes into the bed of the Pinzgauer. They covered the remaining twisted rail up with dirt and tried to leave as little evidence as possible in their wake.

They headed north, this time staying to the state roads and returned to the rail museum in a little less than two hours. If Steve Bertrand had been speechless when Liam called him to relay the news, he was like a child on a sugar overload when he saw the tie, rail and spikes in person.

Liam and Kyle spent the next hour going through details with Steve about the find and assuring him that they had no intention of announcing it. The world of railroad historians would find out about this lost railroad from S. Bertrand. Steve told Liam that he would research the origin of the rail, spikes and mystery of the heavy weight rail on a narrow gauge line and get the information to him as soon as possible. The tie that they brought back confirmed that it was indeed a three-foot narrow gauge. The wood, having been buried for years, retained transferred oil marks from the underside of the rail to the topside of the tie, showing the exact distance between rails.

It was getting late and the pair needed to get on he road to Las Vegas. They repacked the Range Rover and said their goodbyes to Steve, thanking him for all of his assistance and the marvelous use of the Pinzgauer. Promises were made to keep in touch, and then Steve produced a bag full of roast beef sandwiches and some bottles of water out of thin air. He waved as the SUV made its way onto the highway.

Moments later a silver Audi A8, with a driver and one passenger, pulled out onto the highway after the Range Rover's taillights disappeared around a curve.

33

Puzzle Pieces

Bellagio Hotel & Spa
Las Vegas, Nevada
May 8, 2013

The phone on the bedside table rang at precisely 12:00 noon. Liam shot his hand from under he covers in order to grab the handset before the vile device rang again. He had just crawled into the soft king size bed just three hours earlier. The drive from Carson City took longer than they had anticipated.

Liam sat up after replacing the telephone receiver back in its cradle. He stretched and yawned then he focused on the mess in the middle of the floor at the foot of his bed. He had forgot that it took three trips for Kyle and he to bring up all the gear from the Range Rover. They had decided to self-park the car, which meant that they didn't dare leave anything in the vehicle. No matter how good the security system.

Liam took a quick shower, dressed and then called Liz and Uncle Bob. Things were getting back to normal at the loft. Uncle Bob had been able to keep the shooting out of local law enforcements hands. The body had been quickly removed from the pressroom and flown to Washington for an atopsy, just standard operating procedure. Uncle Bob had a cleaning crew from the agency take care of the rest of the mess.

Liz had the whole in the wall repaired and had returned to

her research into Octavious Gass. She also told Liam that John was being released from the hospital and would be back in New York in the morning, itching to get back to work.

"You just tell him to sit still and recooperate." said Liam.

"Right, tell John Andrews to sit still? That's like telling a shark not to swim!" Liz replied.

Liam gave Uncle Bob and Liz the rundown on the last 36 hours and told the two in New York how helpful Steve Bertrand had been.

"I honest don't think we would have pulled it off without his help."

Liam then outlined his and Kyle's next steps. Uncle Bob weighed in that and said that it was a sound plan. Bob then asked Liam if he needed any additional help.

"I'll let you know if we do Uncle Bob. As of right now, I still don't know what we are really looking for."

Liam disconnected with Liz and Bob then called down to room service for a late breakfast. That was one thing that he loved about Vegas, he could order breakfast 24 hours a day. He placed his order and pulled out the information on Gass that Liz had compiled to date. He needed to find a starting point and he guessed it might be at the historical society.

A knock on the door announced the arrival of both his breakfast and Kyle Gale. Kyle waited until the room service attendant had set up his cart and left before telling Liam 'Good Morning'. Liam had taught him years ago to never discuss company affairs with a stranger in the room. Kyle lifted the silver dome that covered the plate of Liam's Eggs Benedict.

"Looks much better than what I had for breakfast." he

said.

"And what was that?" Liam asked as he sat down to eat.

"Two bean and cheese burritos over at the Gas N' Go on Paradise. We needed fuel and water before we headed out today." Kyle let out a burp and patted his stomach "a breakfast that keeps on giving!"

Liam finished his breakfast while Kyle unrolled the topographic maps on the dining area table.

"So, what's the plan Boss?" asked Kyle.

"I just finished reading the background information that Liz sent on Octavious Gass. The details were pretty lean so I thought that we would go and try to fatten them up at the Las Vegas Historical Society."

Liam and Kyle left the Bellegio by the main entrance, which automatically took one through the casino. This had been the same design in every Vegas hotel since Benjamin Segal built the Flamingo in 1946. They were no more than five feet out the front door when it hit them, a blast furnace like heat that would melt an ice cube in three seconds. A digital sign near the valet stand announced that it was 104 degrees Fahrenheit, and that was in the shade!

"Holy shit, this heat is brutal." Kyle remarked as they walked over to the self- park garage.

"Yes, but it's a dry heat." was Liam's reply.

He had heard this saying years' ago from some acquaintance and never really knew what they meant until the first time he was in Las Vegas in the summer. By the time that the two made their way to the SUV, both their shirts clung to them like they had been dipped in wallpaper paste.

The left the casino's parking lot and headed to Fremont Street, the actual downtown of Las Vegas. They found the historical society and pulled into a mostly empty parking lot. When they walked into the building the air-conditioned air brought them back to the real world.

"Thank you Mr. Carrier." with prayer folded hands Kyle quipped.

At the front desk they inquired as to where they might find information on the Las Vegas area, pre 1900. The clerk retrieved a pre-printed building directory and marked the spot on the floor plan and handed it to Liam.

"Not much to find there. Just some old newspapers that have been scanned into the computer and a couple of old maps." The clerk called after them.

After a short search, they found the area devoted to Las Vegas pre-1900. The clerk had been right the information was minimal. They quickly searched the computer for the scanned old newspapers and didn't find any different than the information that Liz had sent. However there was one thing that was not in Liz's info.

Along with some assorted newer books on the subject was a small ledger. Inside the book was a list of original maps and documents that had to be retrieved from the archival holding vault. Liam scanned the list of fifteen items. Ten of the items were the original newspapers that the scans were made from and they would provide nothing new. The other five items however piqued Liam's interest. One map was dated June of 1863 and was actually an old territory map, the second was dated October 1864 and marked

Statehood Map, the third was marked 1867 and the last marked 1876 *Centennial Map*. The last item in the collection was labeled Diary of *Sandra Yorke, 1801-1899*. Liam filled out a request form and handed to the docent in the collections vault. The clerk told him that it would be a few minutes but before they brought the items up he needed to see some identification.

Liam handed the woman his New York drivers license and she copied the information in a register. She asked Kyle if he was going to be in the room as well and if he was, she needed his identification as well. She copied Kyle's information then handed him back his license. She then went over to what looked to be an old card catalog, removed five cards and brought them back over to Liam.

"I only need one of you to sign the removal slips. Who will it be?" she asked.

"I will m'am. " and Liam took the cards.

Liam was about to just automatically sign his name on each card when he noticed something. Each item that he had requested with the exception of the diary, all had the same requests. There were a handful of requests that dated back to the 1960's, these Liam dismissed as they had a woman's name and LVHS Librarian next to her signature. Then there were no requests until a Kelly Kanard in 2003, the notation next to her name was LV Centennial Committee. Then just six months ago an, R. Black, with no notations, had requested the maps.

"That's odd." He murmured to himself, signed the cards then handed them back to the clerk. She took the cards, handed each of them a paper with the Society's rules and regulations told them to sign it and she would collect it when she returned with the artifacts.

Kyle and Liam waited in a viewing room that was assigned to them by the clerk. Ten minutes had passed when the clerk returned, handed each of the men white cotton gloves, collected their signed papers and left the five articles that they had requested.

They started first with the maps. Surprisingly cartography had made major advances by the 1800's. Where as some modern maps claimed to be accurate to 50 yards most hand drawn maps of the 19th century could be accurate to 50 feet. The first map was the dated June of 1863. This was a territorial map that primary showed natural boundaries and Native American encampments. There was, however, a notation in a different hand than that of the cartographer, an area labeled as United States Army – Ft. Baker.

"Doesn't Liz's research show that Octavious Gass purchased a former Army outpost?" Liam asked of Kyle.

Kyle scanned the computer, page after page of the notes that had Liz sent. Kyle found the information on page sixteen.

"Affirmative, he bought the land that was Fort Baker from the War Department after it burned to the ground in October 1863. He purchased over 20,000 acres!"

Liam reached for the map that was labeled 1864 Statehood Map. This map showed primarily the same information as the first but instead of Fort Baker being marked, there in wonderful calligraphy was the name *Rancho Gass*. The third map depicted the area around *Rancho Gass* as starting to develop. It shows a small settlement to the east called *Las Vegas Springs*. As Liam finished with each map, Kyle took multiple photos of them.

The last map was unique in many ways. Instead of being hand drawn this appeared to be a mass produced printed map. The map was labeled 1876 Centennial Map of the United States. Where Octavious Gass's rancho had been in the two previous map, there was nothing in the area on this document.

"So by 1876, Gass is completely forgotten. Does any of the research show what happened to Gass's rancho after he disappeared in 1868?" Liam asked.

Kyle paged through Liz's research, he double checked all of the information and came up empty.

"Nothing, it just says that he disappeared in the spring of 1868."

"Okay on to the diary."

Liam picked the small leather bound book up off the table and carefully opened the book to the beginning. For the next ninety minutes he read in silence. Looking up from his reading to once and again to recheck one of the maps. After he had turned the last page, Liam stood up and began to pace around the room.

"What's bothering you boss?" Kyle recognized the pondering behavior of his friend. Liam outlined the tome for him.

"Well, the book is not a daily dairy but almost a biography. It turns out that Sandra Yorke was Octavious Gass's sister. She writes of her brother's birth in 1809 when she was eight. This was after her mother lost four other children to miscarriages. She was very fond and protective of her little brother because he was thought as a miracle baby. They had a normal childhood growing up in Marceline, Mo. Time passes and she falls out of touch with her brother. She gets married to an Arthur Yorke of St. Louis and settles down. Then she finally receives a letter from him at the beginning of the war. That he had been in California since the gold strike in 1848. Made himself a nice little nest egg. She hears nothing until after the war. Then in 1867 around Christmas, she receives a letter inviting her to come live on his Rancho. That he has finally made it big. She writes him back apologizing that she can't as her husband is taken with consumption."

"Consumption?" asked Kyle.

"Tuberculosis." Liam continued.

"She writes him in January 1868 that her husband has passed and if the offer was still available, could she still come? But she hears nothing for five years when in 1873 an official from the State of Nevada visits her in St. Louis and tells her that she and her brother Samuel, were listed as next of kin on the claims to there brother's land. They had spent the last two years trying to locate Samuel Gass, only to find that he died unexpectedly in Washington D.C. in the Spring of 1868, thus making Sandra the only heir.

The state has officially declared Octavious Gass as dead, and with that event all his property reverts to her. After a moment of sadness and a silent prayer for each bother, she signed the transfer documents. Before the state agent left she asked about the wonderful ranch that her brother told her about. She is told that there is nothing on the land but some ashes from what could have once been, a house. She inherits the property and never even thinks about it until she herself is near death, where she wills the property to her church with instructions to do with it as they see fit. That's all she wrote, she died in October of 1899."

"So we're at a dead end?"

"I wouldn't say that. Let's overlay the cartography from the early maps and see if we can pin point where the property is today. Then we can see if we are at a dead end."

Kyle uploaded all the photos to Liz and they spent the next

twenty minutes creating the overlay. After a couple tiny adjustments they felt confident that they had an accurate GPS coordinates. Kyle inputted them into the Goggle Earth search page. After he pressed enter, the image on the screen went from a satellite's view of the earth and zoomed right down to a 1000 foot elevated view of the coordinates.

"Of all the dumb luck." Kyle chortled.

"Smack dab on a vacant lot " added Liz via the link.

Liam just had a huge grin on his face. On the computer screen, the blinking green dot was located right in the middle of a vacant lot off Las Vegas Boulevard south of Russell Avenue. More commonly known as the Las Vegas Strip.

"Liz, cross reference this location with the Post Office data base." Liam asked.

"Already on it Boss!" She replied as her fingers hit the keys at an accelerated pace. The response was almost instantaneous.

"The address is 4863 Las Vegas Boulevard."

"Okay let's cross reference the address to the tax roles. Let's see who owns the land." Liam requested.

Liz did her magic once again and almost as fast as before retrieve the needed information.

"Tax roles are indicating that is a no tax property."

"No tax, what does that mean?" asked Kyle.

"It means that it is most likely owned by a non-profit entity." Liam answered.

"It's going to take me a while to run through the non-profit data bases Boss" Liz added.

"I've got a better idea, we can be down there in twenty minutes. Let's go and check out the site in person." Liam said.

"Be careful." added Uncle Bob. "Remember, just look, no breaking and entering."

Liam and Kyle cleaned up the table, returned the documents to the clerk and headed back into the oppressive heat of midday Vegas.

They miscalculated the time that it would take to get to the site as they had decided to go straight down Las Vegas Boulevard from the Historical Society. The traffic was horrible and Kyle complained about it.

"This is nothing." Liam added. "I was here for a convention once and it took my cab almost an hour to go just two miles up the strip."

They finally arrived at the location and pulled across the road onto a barren strip in front of the address and remained in the SUV. A chain link fence surrounded the property, which appeared to be almost twenty acres in size, with a dilapidated wood structure that sat back a hundred yards from the road.

"The only signs I see are Keep Out." Kyle observed.

"This is one expensive piece of empty real estate to be just be sitting here." Liam said to himself.

Kyle tapped him on the shoulder.

"Liam, look over there." Kyle was pointing across the street.

Directly across from the property was the Las Vegas Police Department.

"Someone there will know who owns this dirt." Kyle suggested.

They crossed the street and entered the Visitors Lot. Kyle decided to remain in the car because it was cooler than the hell that was outside, so Liam went in alone. He was only gone a few minutes when Kyle saw him exit the building and return to the cool vehicle. Liam opened the passenger door and quickly got in the SUV.

"Well, that was pretty damn easy. The receptionist remarked that they get close to thirty individuals a month coming in and asking the same question."

"The answer is always...?" Kyle asked.

"Gods Children Unitarian Ministry, a church society. Dates back to the early days of Las Vegas the receptionist said. That's why it's not on the tax roles."

Liam called Liz and gave her the information and asked her to run a search on Gods Children Unitarian Ministry. He also told her that he and Kyle were going to head back to the hotel.

The same silver Audi A8, that followed Liam and Kyle from Carson City, pulled out from the parking lot of the Little Chapel of the West and pulled into traffic behind the Range Rover, just as it had done since the SUV left the parking garage earlier. The car always stayed at least one hundred feet behind but it need not. For a GPS tracking transmitter had been placed under the car, on top of the fuel tank so that they would know where it was at all times.

Liam took the elevator up to his room and before he had even unlocked the door he received a text message from Liz to call her. He let himself into the room went to the dining area table and powered up his PowerBook. Liz appeared on the screen within a minute.

"So what did you find out about Gods Children Unitarian

Ministry?" he asked her.

"A plethora of information. I found multiple hits on the organization on web sites devoted to early United States religions. The Las Vegas Historical Society had some info on them as well. But the interesting find is that Gods Children Unitarian Ministry was organized in St. Louis, MO in 1890. It was a women's temperance organization and the principal organizer was Sandra Yorke. The organization moved to Sin City in 1910 to try and clean it up after the first big building boom of 1905, the one that really placed Vegas on the map. The organization remained in effect until 1920 and the beginning of Prohibition."

"So this is the church that Sandra left Octavious's land to. So I wonder who controls the land now?" Liam asked.

"Once I had the organization's name I was able to run that through the Non-profit data bases. It turns out that the good old gals of Gods Children Unitarian Ministry set up a trust in perpetuity to take care of their assets, in case they ever needed to reestablish themselves. The trust manager is listed as Yorke, Martin and Howard, Attorneys at Law, St. Louis, MO. Even today they submit the necessary filings and tax reports for the trust. "

Liz guessed Liam's next question.

"Yup, Yorke, Martin and Howard was started by Arthur Yorke, husband of one Suzanna Yorke. Arthur Yorke, Conrad Martin and Justin Howard were the partners in the largest law firm in St. Louis until 1941. There is still a Yorke on the letterhead today, as a matter of fact; the only attorney at the firm is an S. Yorke. I called the office and was informed that they are a private client firm and Ms. Sandra Yorke is not accepting any new clients at this time."

"The picture is beginning to form. I am beginning to think that I don't need that hammer anymore for the puzzle pieces. This Sandra must be a grand niece to the first Sandra. Liz you need to talk to Sandra Yorke."

"We're on it Boss. John is here and he can help with the light lifting," she said.

"Liam, you both need to be extra cautious now. If this is connected to Rex and Joe's murders, there's no telling what could happen. Are you carrying?"

"We haven't been, but we will from here on out." Liam assured his uncle.

"We need to get a look at that property. During the day might prove, let's say difficult, as it is right across from LVPD. Looks like Kyle and I are going out for an early morning hike."

Liam and Kyle mapped out their plan. Liam always liked to work to the SCUBA divers adage, Plan your dive, and dive your plan, that way you limit any potential for danger. This what he and Kyle now did, then went over their plan a dozen times, each time finding something that could use a little adjustment.

It was nine o'clock when they finished and they weren't going to head out until 3:00 AM. Kyle was going to assemble all of the gear that they needed and then head to his room for a nap. Liam was to wired thinking about the connection to Rex and Joe. So he decided to go down to the casino and waste of couple of hours.

34
Baccarat

There is one card game whose odds could be perhaps the best in any casino. This is the card game of the rich and famous, or so the casinos would like the general public to think, Baccarat.

There are three popular variants of the game: *punto banco* (or "North American baccarat"), *baccarat chemin de fer*, and *baccarat banque* (or "*à deux tableaux*"). *Punto banco* is strictly a game of chance, with no skill or strategy involved. With each player's moves forced by the cards each player is dealt.

By contrast, in *baccarat chemin de fer* and *baccarat banque*, both players can make choices, which allow certain skills to play a part. (These two forms of the game are very rarely found in American casinos. Owing themselves more to Asian and European play).

Like Blackjack, Baccarat is a comparing card game played between two hands, the "Player" and the "Banker". Each baccarat coup has three possible outcomes: Player (Player has the higher score), "Banker, and "Tie". The goal is simple, much like that of Blackjack. But instead of the target number being twenty-one, the target goal is nine.

In Punto banco the casino banks the game at all times, and commits to playing out both hands according to a predetermined system of drawing rules, unlike the other more historic Baccarat games where each hand is played by a separate person who can choose freely whether or not to draw an additional card. Customers may bet on either the "Player" or the "Banker", which are merely designations for the two hands dealt in each game. In punto banco, the Player hand is not associated with the customer, nor is the Banker with the house; Player and Banker are simply two competing hands, which any bettor can back.

A traditional Baccarat table is oval with seven players spaced around each end with the croupiers and banker situated in the middles. The cards are dealt from a shoe containing 4, 6 or 8 decks of cards shuffled together.

For each coup, two cards are dealt face up to each hand, starting with the player and alternating between the hands. At this point the drawing rules are used to determine firstly whether the player should receive a third card, and then, based on the value of any card drawn to the player, whether the banker should receive a third card. The outcome is then determined by comparing the totals. If either the player or the banker (or both) achieves a total of 8 or 9 on the initial deal, a "natural", no further cards are drawn and the outcome is immediately determined by comparing the two totals.

Face cards and tens are considered zero with all others cards their respective numerical assignment. (Aces are always counted as one.) So if the first coup cards dealt are a Queen and five for the player, that hand is considered "five", with the Banker cards being a four and five, that is "nine" and considered the winning hand. The house, generally with one to one odds, then pays winners. If the banker wins, a five percent commission is paid to the house.

In American casinos Baccarat is usually played in special

rooms separated from the main gaming floor, ostensibly to provide an extra measure of privacy and security because of the high stakes often involved. The game is frequented by very high rollers, who may wager tens or hundreds of thousands of dollars on a single hand. Because Baccarat attracts wealthy players, a casino may win or lose millions of dollars a night on the game, and the house's fortunes may significantly affect the owning corporation's quarterly profit and loss statement.

Liam had neither millions nor thousands of dollars to wager, this was just a way to relax and have predetermined circumstances guide his time. Plus he had fun sitting at a table betting one hundred dollars at a time when others seated could be betting a quarter of a million on just one hand.

Liam found the Baccarat room just off of the VIP elevators on the main casino floor. He entered the room and saw that only two tables were open for play. One table was reserved for a group of very serious and boisterous Asian businessman. All of them yelling and agonizing with each turn of a card, the other table was open play and had a few open spots.

Liam saw that his "lucky" number was open so he took a seat at number five. He watched the first three hands without participating. He spent this time watching the shoe to try and determine which coup was having a run, the Player or the Banker. The three hands that he observed all favored the Bank, so he decided to play the Banker position.

He had already converted a thousand dollars to special $100 Baccarat chips. He placed a single black $100 chip on the Banker circle in front of him and waited for the deal from the shoe. Most casinos were doing away with the customer acting as the dealer, allowing them to deal the cards, switching over to the casino employees dealing all the cards. The Bellagio had not followed this trend, and retained the practice of allowing the individual players deal. After all this was part of the intrigue and fun of the game.

Liam lost his first hand when the Player was dealt a Natural Nine and the Banker was dealt a seven. Well he thought it was a game of chance and not an exact science. He now bet two hundred dollars on the Banker for his next hand. The total of the coups dealt were a five for the Player and a seven for the Banker. By the rules the Player had to take a third card and the Banker had to stand. The card was dealt and slid on the green felt over to the Player with the largest bet, a middle aged Hispanic man dressed in an impeccably cut three piece suit.

With a bit of showmanship he placed the palm of his left hand on the card and slowly raised each corner one at a time. By doing this he was able to determine if the card might be a face card or a numerical one. The look on his face when he finished this process revealed the answer to all seated at the table. He quickly picked up the card and slapped the over turned card down on the table's surface, revealing a king of spades, a zero. The Player still had five, the Banker won.

Liam collected his winnings he was now up three hundred dollars. He cut his bet back $100 on the next hand which the Banker closely won seven to six. He continued to bet Banker and by the end of the tenth hand Liam had expanded his winnings to $25,000.

Liam continued betting on the Banker and lost the next three hands, two to the Player and one to a Tie, which he never bet on. He won the next and the shoe was passed to him. He proceeded to win three more in a row. There was one hand left in the shoe. He was still up $25,000 and decided to go for broke. He placed all his chips on banker.

Eight people at the table were betting on the Player. Their wager's combined total was over half a million dollars. He was the lone Banker bet and felt all eyes at the table boring into him.

He slid the first card out of the shoe and over to the highest betting player. A very beautiful, petite Japanese woman with a stack of twenty white $10,000 chips. He then drew a card for the Banker, which he placed under the lip of the shoe. He repeated the deal once more to the Player and then to himself.

The Player repeated the process almost movement for movement as the Hispanic gentleman had done. When she finished with the second card she squealed and set the cards down one by one. The first card was a two and the second was a six, a natural eight. A chorus of cheers went up from the gamblers betting on the Player.

People from the sequestered room heard the commotion came over to the table and started to line the sides of the table so they could watch the deal. Liam felt a pit in his stomach and he knew he should have not been so greedy and stayed with a conservative bet. He slowly retracted the first of the two cards under the shoe's edge. He slowly turned the card over so only he saw the results, a jack of clubs, a zero. He placed this on the felt while more cheers of "We've got it! We've got it!" echoed in his ears.

Well might as well get this over with he thought. He slid the second card from under the shoe. Now the chants had turned to "Baccarat! Baccarat! Baccarat!" meaning zero in Italian.

Somehow willing Liam to produce another ten card. Liam decided to play this for fun at let the others have their moment. Instead of turning the card up so only he saw the face he decided to turn it in the direction of the high player so she could begin celebrating her tremendous win.

The chants from the gallery continued until Liam revealed the card. Liam closed his eyes and in one fluid motion, slowly revealed the card to the other players. When he had fully revealed the card he kept his eyes closed and waited for the cheering to commence. There was dead silence.

Liam opened his eyes and saw at least thirty people, both seated and standing, with their mouths agape. Completely perplexed, Liam turned the card so that he could see it. There in his hand was a nine of hearts, a natural nine, Banker wins. Finally comments and curses started to emit from the other players. The Japanese woman looked crest-fallen; as she had just lost the majority of her chips.

The croupier raked in all of the losing bets with his hook and then slid Liam a stack of chips that equaled his bet. Liam returned five percent of his winnings back to the house in order to pay his commission. While the dealers readied the next shoe, all of the players took a break. Liam was standing next to a small snack buffet when the Pit Boss walked up to him.

"Mr. Ross, I'm Tony Sardo, the high stakes room manager. This may seem a bit unethical, but I wanted to thank you on that last hand. The group at your table has taken us for a small fortune this week. This is the first that they have lost big. You saved us almost three-quarters of a million with that natural nine."

"Well thank you Mr. Sardo, but as you know, it was just

the luck of the draw."

"Anyway Mr. Ross, I have made arrangements to have your room comped for the remainder of your stay. Please enjoy the hotel." He walked back to the table to watch the loading of the shoe.

Liam looked at his watch and realized that three hours had slipped away. He decided to stay for one more shoe then call it a night. He returned to his number five spot at the table and took his seat. Some of the original players returned but most went off to lick their wounds for the night. Over near the high stakes Blackjack table a heated conversation ensued between the Japanese woman who lost $200,000 and an irate Japanese gentleman that was most likely her husband. All the while the woman was pointing over at Liam as if to claim it was his fault that she lost. Liam made a mental note to steer clear of the Blackjack table.

The shoe was completed and a burn card was removed. The card was a queen of spades so ten more cards were removed from the deck and discarded without the players seeing their values. Just as the shoe was being passed to Liam to start off play, a hard looking, serious man around Liam's age approached the table and set twenty bundles of $100 bills, another two hundred thousand dollars on the player spot. He then announced to the croupiers.

"Money plays." The croupier relayed the directive to the pit boss, which took notation and made an entry on a casino form.

"Money plays!" the pit boss called in return.

The gentleman remained standing at the number one spot diagonally across from Liam. Then he spoke up and looked directly at Liam.

"Let's see if lightening strikes twice, shall we."

There was something familiar about this man, but Liam could just not fathom what it was. He placed two $500 chips from his winnings on the Banker spot. Then the croupier called out to the table.

"All bets, place you bets." And when no one else placed a bet he announced "All bets in, no more bets please."

The croupier motioned for Liam to start the deal. Liam dealt the four cards out and waited for what was customary, for the Player to reveal his hand first. The well-manicured hand retrieved the cards and turned them over revealing a three of clubs and a four of diamonds, the Player had to stand.

Liam turned each card over separately. The first card revealed an ace of hearts, the second was a five of diamonds, the Banker had a six. This is one of the worst hands in Baccarat. The Banker has to hit on six and with a fresh shoe there were plenty of no value high cards that would decrease his chance of beating the seven. The odds were greatest that he would draw a ten and his total would remain at six. Liam withdrew the required card from the shoe and prayed to himself that circumstances would not repeat. This time he turned the card so just he saw it. When he saw the result he cursed first, then laid a two of hearts on the table. Liam looked across at the man.

"I'm terribly sorry sir."

Liam was sorry, he didn't need more people upset at him for making what is considered a paltry bet when others are betting small fortunes. The man just smiled and took the seat at the number one position. Once seated, he held up his hand and signaled for the pit boss.

"Tony, please have $750,000 dollars transferred to my

account."

"Yes sir." Was all the pit boss said and walked over to his podium and placed a call to the cage.

Liam looked at the man and wondered, $750,000, who was this? He was soon to know the answer. The man removed a cigar case from his dinner jacket, removed a dark, almost black cigar from the case. He then proceeded to clip one end of the tube of tobacco, then produced a lighter and spent a minute setting his cigar alight, producing a perfect glowing tip.

"Mr. Ross, allow me to introduce myself. My name is Edward Pitchman, and I have been a fan of yours for some time. You are quite the talented auteur."

"Thank you for the kind words Mr. Pitchman." Liam returned. "Again I am truly sorry that you lost that last hand. I feel that my luck is ruining this evening."

"Ah yes, luck" Pitchman responded. "Instead of luck how about a game of skill instead?"

"What do you have in mind sir?" Liam asked.

The man took a long pull from his cigar, savored the smoke for a moment then released the bluish haze into the air.

"How about some real Baccarat, Baccarat Banque?"

Referring to the European version that pitted player against player instead of the house.

"Mr. Pitchman, my skill as a Baccarat player is just luck. I am here for amusement. I do not know how to respond to your offer."

"I too am here for amusement. Let's just play a friendly game. The hotel has arranged a $250,000 line of credit for you."

Liam thought about this and knew that it was crazy.

$250,000 dollars was a small fortune, but he knew that with recent events he could afford it.

"Alright Mr. Pitchman, I accept your offer if it is allowed by the casino."

"I assure you Mr. Ross it is more than acceptable."

Liam looked to Tony the pit boss and received his nod of approval.

"Then let's play. Do you mind if I go to the restroom first?"

"Be my guest. It will take the casino a few minutes to get things set up."

Liam excused himself and went to the private VIP restroom that was in the baccarat room. The second he closed and locked the door he had his phone out and was calling Liz in New York. The phone rang five times before she answered sleepily.

"Liam, what's wrong? It's two o'clock in the morning. I thought you and Kyle weren't heading out until four. I was getting a little rest so I could be on station when you two started out."

"Liz, I think I'm about to do one of the craziest things I have ever done and I need your help."

Liam explained what was about to happen and Liz just laughed.

"Only you can get yourself into that kind of situation."

"Okay enough of the comedy relief. I need you to tell me who this guy is. He is definitely connected."

"Give me a second to get over to the computer." Liz had been using the small bedroom that Joe Bousquet had set up in the control room.

"Okay, all set, shoot."

Liam gave her all the information that he knew, leaving out the feeling that he had. It didn't take long before Liz had a response.

"That's odd." Liz said.

"What do you mean odd?" Liam asked.

"What's odd is that there is nothing anywhere on an Edward Pitchman unless he is a one hundred and twenty year old former marine that is buried in Arlington National Cemetery."

"When you mean nothing, as in not one scrap of information?"

"That's right, he's a ghost as far as the Internet is concerned. Which is not all that unusual with people of substantial wealth." Liz added.

"Well, now my interest is piqued. I guess I'll have to play him. Do me a favor and call Ken Whitelaw and have him transfer $250,000 to my account. Wake him up and have him do it the minute the bank opens."

"Will do Boss, and good luck." Liz disconnected.

Liam retuned to the table with his curiosity really piqued. Who was this person that just challenged him and why did he seem so damn familiar to him. Well worry at it, not about it he told himself.

"Are you ready Mr. Ross?" asked Mr. Pitchman.

"As ready as I will ever be, shall we start."

"How do you feel about a $10,000 minimum bid?" he asked Liam.

"It's only money." was all that Liam could muster.

"A very healthily attitude Mr. Ross. You will indeed live a long life if you adapt that adage as the bedrock of your personal policy."

"Gentleman are you ready?" asked the croupier.

A crowd larger than before had gathered around the table. There were no other players, just Liam and the unknown millionaire.

"Just a refresher of the rules." continued the croupier. "The banker retains the shoe until he loses a hand, only then the shoe is passed. Unless a player was to call "Banco". When "Banco" is called the stakes are just like "going all in" in Texas Hold 'Em. The shoe is passed to the caller and the hand is played. If the person refuses to play, then they forfeit the game and loose half of their holdings. Any questions before the first coup is played?"

Both men shook their heads in the negative.

"Then as the larger holder, Mr. Pitchman has first honors with the shoe, Sir do you care to bank?" asked the croupier.

"No, I think I will pass the shoe to Mr. Ross."

The croupier removed one card from the shoe and revealed a four of clubs. He then removed four more cards and discarded all five cards. The shoe was passed to Liam. Both men started with the minimum bet of $10,000.

Liam distributed the first two hands of two cards each. Mr. Pitchman had honors to start and turned over a seven of hearts and a six of diamonds, producing a three. Unlike in punto banco Baccarat, there are no set rules as to when you receive a card or not. To improve your hand you may ask for one more card, if you wish, Mr. Pitchman requested another.

"Card."

Liam extracted a card and the croupier's paddle delivered it to the man. He lifted the card and placed a five with his current three. He had improved his hand to eight. Liam could only win with a nine or tie the eight. He turned over both cards and revealed a king of clubs and a jack of diamonds, baccarat, a zero. Liam automatically took another card from the show and displayed a four of spades. Liam lost this hand eight to four. The croupier collected Liam's wager and passed it to Mr. Pitchman. Liam then passed the shoe across the table.

The next three hands produced similar results with Liam first losing another $10,000 dollars, six to five, $20,000 dollars with a two to Pitchman's natural eight, and yet another $20,000 with a seven to a nine. Liam was down $60,000, so he decided to take a chance and bet a larger amount. He bet $50,000 and beat the man with a four to his three. Liam was almost back even and he would control the shoe. Before he even had a chance to place his wager Mr. Pitchman spoke the word that increased Liam's pulse.

"Banco."

"Do you accept or forfeit Mr. Ross?" asked the croupier.

Liam just closed his eyes and replied.

"I accept."

Liam returned the shoe to the millionaire and placed all of his chips on the wager line. Liam's hands returned to the table in front of him with some trepidation.

There comes a time when common sense gives way to stupidity. Liam felt that this was his time. He had just placed $290,000 worth of chips on a bet that was at best 50 − 50 but depending upon the first card could change to 90-10 in a heartbeat, not in his favor. Mr. Pitchman dealt the cards and the croupier placed them on the felt in front of Liam. His throat was dry and his palms were beginning to feel damp as he reached for the two small cardstock objects. Liam brought the cards up slowly, one covering other completely. He looked over at Mr. Pitchman and watched as the man blew a smoke ring towards the ceiling. He was perfectly calm, as if he did this a hundred times a day.

Liam's heart fell when he finally looked at the first card. It was a knave, the Jack of Spades. He prayed that the next card was a natural nine and he could then continue to breathe. He slowly revealed the second card. If he could have he would have started this day all over again. There paired with his Jack of Spades was the Queen of Spades. He had been dealt Baccarat. He laid both cards down and a slight gasp went up from the assemblage. He had no choice but to draw another card. With his parched throat he asked for another card.

"Card please if you would Mr. Pitchman."

"Of course Mr. Ross. It would be a pleasure." He spoke as he smiled.

Mr. Pitchman removed a card and left it on the table in front of the shoe. With a continued deft motion, the croupier swept the card from where Mr. Pitchman had placed the card and slid it off the paddle in front of Liam face down.

Liam stared at the card for what seemed like an hour. He reached for the card and with breath held, turned the card over displaying a single mark, he had overturned the Ace of Diamonds. Liam felt his stomach give way as a collective moan rang up from the crowd. It seemed that he did not have a snowball's chance in hell to pull this off.

"I am sorry for you this time, Mr. Ross." Pitchman said with a condescending tone.

He turned his first card quickly and displayed a ten of clubs. He dismissed this as an inconvenience; his calculation in his head told him that there were still over 200 numerals left in this shoe, so he need not worry about a zero card. He turned the second over and the same gasp that Liam had heard on his hand had accompanied another zero point card, in front of Pitchman, a King of clubs.

Pitchman stared at the cards incredulously. Almost as if these were not supposed to be his cards and he just wanted them to disappear back into the shoe. Once he regained his internal composure Edward Pitchman drew his last card.

The chances of drawing a card higher than an ace felt like they were a million to one in his favor. The card appeared and was turned over as if one was removing a band-aid from a sore. You really didn't need to see the card to know that Pitchman had been beat. The gasp, then the stony silence told the entire story. Pitchman had drawn one of only a handful of tens left. His hand was worse than one.

"Mr. Ross wins, one to zero!" called the croupier.

Liam just stared at the pile of chips that had been raked in front of him, a half a million dollars! He stood up and ran his fingers through his hair. He couldn't believe that he had won. The adrenaline was coursing through his body making him tremble. He finally caught his breath then returned to his seat. Ready to call it a night.

"Gentleman, are we ready to continue?" asked the croupier.

"I don't know how Mr. Pitchman feels, but maybe we should…" but Liam was cut off before he could finish.

"Banco" came from mouth of the flushed face man. His cigar had been crumbled into a pile in front of him. Liam could see the anger building behind the eyes.

"But…"

"Banco!"

"Mr. Ross, do you accept?" asked the house agent.

Liam ran through some mental math. He had his first $50,000 that he had won earlier, the $250,000 line from the casino, $50,000 from the fourth hand with Pitchman and now another $290,000. He adjusted the total after losses to Pitchman and he had $580,000 sitting in front of him. Pitchman had $400,000 dollars left. Liam watched as the man moved all of his chips to the wager line.

"Mr. Ross?" repeated the croupier.

"I accept."

With those two little words Liam was moving $400,000 to the wager line in front of him. Pitchman still had the shoe so he began the coup. Liam had realized that this man was out for more than sport. If he could he would have Liam's head mounted on a pike.

With the cards dealt Pitchman asked Liam a question.

"Would you mind if we had the croupier overturn the cards for us both?"

Liam didn't have a reason to accommodate the request. So he just nodded his head in the affirmative.

The croupier collected Liam's cards and placed them in the center of the table he then collected Pitchman's and did the same. His hand hovered over Liam's cards. He then picked up the first card and turned it over to uncover a ten of hearts. He then went directly to the second card and revealed the nine of clubs. Liam stared at the natural nine and looked on in disbelief. It was the perfect hand. The best Pitchman could wish for was a tie. The subdued gallery erupted with applause and whistles.

After the crowd calmed down it was time to divulge the final coup. The next two cards would determine who collected the $800,000 and the game. The croupier turned over the first card and another gasp went up, a nine of spades was placed on the soft felt. If the next card were a ten, the entire process would begin again. Liam's throat went dry thinking of that prospect.

Liam looked over at Pitchman who had become so transfixed at the play unfolding before them. The final card was picked up and disclosed to all there. Pitchman's nine was reduced to zero with the addition of an ace of spades! The crowd let loose a cheer that drowned the sound coming from the slot machines in the main casino. Liam still could not believe that he had just won $800,000. Liam felt as if he would just collapse.

Edward Pitchman had a much different response. He stood up from the table with a start, threw a glass of water than had been placed in front of him then stormed out of the Baccarat room without a word.

Tony the pit boss came over and shook Liam's hand.

"Well done Mr. Ross, well done. But I'm afraid you have not made a friend tonight. "

"I do believe that you are right Tony." was all that Liam had said.

35

Spelunking

Las Vegas Boulevard
Las Vegas, Nevada
May 9, 2013

Liam called Kyle in his room so that they could head out to the Gods Children Unitarian Ministry property. When he came down to the casino Liam was waiting for him in the coffee bar by the main entrance. Kyle placed his order for a very strong, black cup of coffee with the barista. He then joined Liam at a small stand up table once he retrieved his java.

"Get any sleep Boss or are you on autopilot again?" he asked.

"Didn't really feel like sleeping so I came down to the casino earlier to loose some money."

"So how much did you loose this time?"

Liam removed an envelope from his coat pocket and handed it to Kyle. Kyle had just taken a large mouthful of coffee when he opened the envelope. Liam ducked as coffee spewed from Kyle's mouth and nose when he read the amount on the check.

"How the hell did you pull this off? The casino must be pissed as hell about loosing so much."

"As a matter of fact Mister Doom and Gloom, the hotel has actually comped our rooms while we are here. You see it's not the casino's money."

Liam told him the story of the last few hours.

"So he knew that you and Liz couldn't find a thing on him. Sounds a little fishy if you ask me. What are you going to do with the money?"

"Haven't really thought about it yet. If this was last week I would have said invest it into some stamps. But look what a week has wrought."

Liam downed the last of the coffee in his mug.

"We had better get a move on." Liam said.

Kyle quickly finished his coffee and they walked out to their SUV. Liam was always amazed at how many people were always on the streets of Las Vegas, even at three o'clock in the morning. Instead of heading directly down Las Vegas Boulevard, Kyle maneuvered the Range Rover down a parallel street. When they did their planning they both concluded that it would be prudent to enter the property from the northern side. That side abutted up against some undeveloped land owned by McCarran International Airport.

They turned off the main road onto what looked to be a service road for the airport. Kyle turned off the headlights and only ran with his parking lights. It was still extremely dark as the moon was in its new moon phase. They continued down the access road, until ahead of them in the distance, a pair of headlights was coming directly towards them.

"Must be security on rounds. See anyplace we can hide?" Liam asked Kyle.

"It's so damn dark, I can't even see five feet in front of us!" Kyle snapped.

Liam rolled down his window and scanned the area to his right to see if anything presented it self. They went about fifty more feet when he saw it. A small section of the chain link fence surrounding the Gods Children Unitarian Ministry property was missing.

"Pull in there. Looks tight but it may be our only chance."

Kyle killed the running lights and left the rutted track. He pulled through the rusted wire fence with inches to spare. Once through the fence Liam noticed an abundant number of tumbleweeds that had accumulated against the fence.

"Kill the engine. It's time to hide in plan sight." Liam said excitedly.

They jumped out of the SUV and started piling the brittle tumbleweeds around the Rover. Within a minute the front and drivers side of the SUV were covered. The on coming headlights were now less than fifty yards away.

"Okay, let's hope they're tired and don't notice anything." Kyle hoped.

As the lights neared, Kyle and Liam realized that the security truck was on the other side of the airport fence. One thing that had gone their way. Still, it would have been very suspicious to be out next to the airport in the dead of night.

They could now hear the drone of the engine and the tires on the broken gravel.

"Ten seconds more and they'll be here."

They both held their breath as the truck was now along side of their camouflaged SUV. They both exhaled as the truck continued its steady pace and rolled past them.

"That was easy. Looks like your luck is holding tonight." Kyle said.

"Let's give them some room." Liam counted.

They both watched the taillights of the passing truck. All of a sudden the brake lights came on and illuminated the dark.

"Oh, Oh, spoke to soon." Kyle whispered.

The driver's door opened and the driver stepped out into the warm evening. He hurried over to the fence and proceeded to relieve himself. His partner from the truck yelled at him.

"You've got a bladder the size of a gnat! Hurry it up will you, I want to get back to the break-room and get a little sleep before I head home!"

The driver finished relieving himself and rushed back to the truck. After a minute the truck resumed its course. Liam and Kyle watched until they could no longer see the red glow from the taillights.

"That was too close." Kyle said as he started removing the tumbleweeds from the Range Rover.

They uncovered the truck in less than a minute and were back on their way. During their planning they consulted Google Earth images to find the perimeter of the property. They mapped out some basic service roads on the property and they were now looking for one.

They had continued to travel along without any lights and came upon the road they were searching for by accident. The road had at one time been paved in parts. The pavement was raised a good six inches from its surroundings. The front wheels of the SUV hit the asphalt with a bone-jarring thud.

"Found it" quipped Kyle.

Liam trained the blue light from the pencil thin LED flashlight onto Kyle's face.

"Really?" He said sarcastically.

He then focused the light on the map in his lap and located their approximate location.

"Okay, lets head to the south about 300 yards. There should be a right turn that will take us right to the building."

The truck moved slowly down the uneven road, hitting several deep potholes on its journey. The turn was right where Liam said it was. After the turn they had a straight shot to the building.

The building came up faster than either of them predicted. So quickly that Kyle had to stand on the brakes so he didn't run into a smaller outbuilding that loomed directly out of the darkness in front of the truck. They continued to drive around the main building and several smaller out buildings to find a place to hide the SUV from prying eyes. Liam spied the perfect location off the north side of the main building. Ten yards from the building was a pile of lumber. Wood that must have been bought to expand the building for this lumber was old and decayed.

Kyle maneuvered between the main building and the pile. This proved to be an ideal hiding place from anyone viewing on the property from the Strip. They got out of the truck and started to retrieve only gear that would be needed for a fast reconnaissance. If they found anything, which was doubtful, they would come back to the Rover.

The plan was to split up inside the house in order to complete a sweep faster. Each man would carry a small flashlight, earwig communication device, their weapons, their iPhones and their high tech Swiss army knives.

It was a two-story building that Liam estimated to have five thousand feet of living space. Entry into the building was not an issue as the rear door leading into a kitchen area, hand been lifted from it's hinges ands lay splintered and broken on the sandy ground. Kyle offered to survey the upstairs so he went off to find the stairway. Liam went to his left out of the kitchen into what at had been a communal dining room.

Here, strewn about the room was decade's accumulation of trash and dirt. Liam extracted a collapsible security baton from a holster on his belt. He flicked his wrist and the compact hardened steel rod extended to total length of twenty-four inches. Liam proceeded to use this to poke through the piles on the floor. After spending maybe five minutes Liam learned that kids must have been using the building for many generations for parties. He uncovered soda cans from today as well as pop bottles from the 1940's and 1950's. There were newspapers from every decade since 1920 and what Liam assumed to be rodent droppings from at least that many generations of rats. This building was a time capsule of twentieth century filth.

Liam heard footsteps on the floorboards above his head. Kyle had finished sweeping through a labyrinth of sleeping quarters upstairs. As most were barren, Kyle finished the task quickly, so he rejoined Liam downstairs.

The first floor plan was one of simplicity. A large kitchen in the rear, off that was a dining area that led into a general workroom/storeroom. That room led to a larger room with remnants of old wooden pews anchored to the floor and large double doors set into the outside wall This must have been the main meeting room of Gods Children Unitarian Ministry. The room measured out to be fifty feet long by twenty feet wide. Liam and Kyle were able to deduce which direction that the pews had faced. On the facing wall, at what would have been directly behind a dais of some sort, was a large stone fireplace, discolored from years of neglect.

"There just isn't anything here but a truckload or two of garbage." Kyle said.

Liam trained his flashlights beam on the aged pews and warped floorboards. There was dust and dirt everywhere. At least a quarter of an inch of the Nevada desert covered everything.

"Kyle, do you notice anything odd?"

Kyle watched as Liam trained the light back and forth over the dust and dirt. He then moved the flashlight over to the fireplace hearth.

"I don't follow you boss. What do you mean?"

"Well, there is a full patina of dirt over everything in this room. The only footprints in here are ours. You would think that there would be dozens of prints all over the room. Plus, the same dust that is everywhere is not in front of the fireplace, why?"

Liam shifted his light to reveal the dust line in an almost perfect arc about four feet from the hearth, delineating the scuffed, barren pine boards from the dirt.

"Maybe the wind is coming down the flue and dispersing the dust?"

Liam crossed to the front door and removed a wooden brace that was keeping entry into the building blocked. Once he removed the brace he pulled on the right half of the ornate double door until he freed the stuck portal. He walked out onto the small porch with Kyle following close behind. Liam walked about ten yards away from the building, stopped, turned around and pointed his flashlight at the roof, illuminating the decaying cedar shingles.

"No chimney." He related to Kyle.

"Now, how in hell did you know that?" Kyle asked. "What's the trick?"

"No trick, just observation, I remembered the satellite images. I didn't recall there being a chimney, that's all."

Kyle just shrugged his shoulders giving into his Boss's uncanny ability to remember even the slightest, insignificant detail.

"So I ask again, Why no dirt in front of the fireplace?"

"Let's go find out." Kyle retorted.

The two men went back into the dilapidated building. They both stopped at the apex of the delineation between dirt and clean wood. Liam bent down and picked a handful of dirt from the floor then he tossed it close to the fireplace hearth. Within seconds the dirt started to blow away from the hearth. Within a minute all of the dirt had been swept clean by the invisible breeze.

Liam moved closer to the hearth and put hand close to the floorboard right next to the stone.

"Do you think it's coming up from a crawl space?" Kyle asked.

"If it was from a crawl space wouldn't the entire floor show signs of air movement? No, I think it's coming from underneath the fireplace."

Kyle crouched down and put his hand near the large slab of rock. He felt a steady breeze against his palm.

"It's definitely positive air pressure, but from where?" he queried.

Liam took out a knife and tried to fit it between the floor and slab. He drew the blade edge along the rear of the fireplace hearth and noted that a seam separating wood from stone was the same constant opening across the entire front of the hearth. He then focused his flashlight where the slab met the left pillar of the fireplace and traced it up until it ended. Atop the pillar was a hand hewed wood mantle made from a wood that Liam did not recognize. He retraced the light back down the pillar and held it steady at the junction of the hearth slab and the pillar. Here too Liam found a crack that when followed went across the hearth to the base of the right hand pillar. He placed his hand against the crack and detected similar air pressure as at the floorboards.

"It appears that the lower slab is a single stone that is not connected to the rest of the fireplace. Check the rest of the fireplace for any similar seams."

Liam and Kyle methodically went over the entire fireplace, inch by inch, from top to bottom. As Liam was working his way across the mantel, he stopped in the exact center and noticed a slight breeze coming from around the keystone, directly beneath the mantel.

Liam bent closer to the breeze so he felt it on his check. He then traced the seam surrounding the stone and verified that the breeze surrounded the stone. He shown his light and closely inspected the igneous rock. He handed his flashlight to Kyle.

"Here, train this on the keystone."

Kyle trained the beam center on the stone. Liam touched the rock and moved his fingertips all over its surface. He then placed both hands, one on top of the other, on the keystone and pushed with his entire body. On the first thrust the stone didn't budge so Liam tried again. This time he detected a small movement in the rock. He let up pressure and tried once more, third time was the charm. The stone depressed, from the rest of the stones, a good two inches until the stone bottomed against a hard stop. When the stone stopped a loud click was heard near the slab at the floor.

Liam sat on the floor in the front of the fireplace slab. He placed both feet up against the stone and pushed with his legs. Slowly the stone gave way. As Kyle was holding the light he noticed an iron roller recessed in the floor under the slab.

"Hang on, I think a good shot of penetrating oil might help."

He removed a can from his pack and sprayed the both iron rollers. Liam let the lubricant set in for about a minute then he pushed on the slab again. This time the ashler moved a good six inches. The two men repeated the process of alternating lubricant with pushing. After the fourth sequence the stone revealed a dark opening.

The air that poured from the opening had coolness unlike the air in the house; it also carried with it the telltale odor of water.

"Well, that's a surprise." Kyle said.

"Looks like stairs. We had better get all the gear from the truck."

"We're going down there? We have no idea what's down there!" Kyle said brusquely.

"The only way we find out is by going down." He slapped his friend on the back. "Let's get the gear."

They went back to the truck, called Liz and extolled her of the discovery. Liam asked her to track each of them via the GPS chips in their smart phones. He also told her that they would check in two hours. They then distributed the gear between themselves and headed back into the house.

When they returned to the fireplace the rock had returned

to it's original place covering the hole. The pair did a quick scan of the room and did not notice anything different since when they left. Theirs were the only footprints in the dust.

"Must have some type of a return mechanism." Kyle observed. "The keystone is back in place as well.

Liam repeated the process, this time both the keystone and the slab moved with ease. Kyle inspected both the slab's rollers and the keystone looking for some type of catch, he found it in the keystone. Two groves had been chiseled in the walls off the keystone's socket. Kyle searched for anything that would fit into this receptacle; he finally found that one of his carabineers fit snugly into the grooves.

"Let's wait and see if anything happens before go down." Kyle suggested.

""Good idea. No telling if there is a release down there."

As they waited patiently to see if the rock moved, they projected their flashlights into the gaping darkness. Kyle unpacked five Cyalume sticks, bent them in the middle and shook them, activating the chemical reaction. He then tossed the glowing green sticks into the hole. They both heard them land on solid earth when they hit bottom. After fifteen minutes and no movement in the stones, it was decided that they begin their descent.

Liam stepped into the hole first. The stairs were hewn from solid rock carrying evidence that they had been carved by a stonemason. Each tread was exactly ten inches wide with each rise being eight inches in height. Liam was down six of the steps when Kyle followed him.

There were solid rock walls on both sides of the companionway. To the right, what had once been a handhold, attached to rings inset into the stone, were remnants of a rotted hemp rope. They continued down the steps, Liam counting and doing the math in his head as to how far down they were going. Kyle was using an app on his iPhone that marked elevation to make the calculation. So far they had descended almost fifty feet below the fireplace.

"I think we are almost there. I can see the glow on the ground surrounding the Cyalume, maybe twenty more feet." Liam announced.

When they reached the bottom, they activated their battery powered LED headlamps. They had landed in a room with rough-hewn walls, small droplets of moisture leaking at varying intervals, a yawning black tunnel opened on the opposite side of the cave.

Near the tunnel entrance in a seated position leaning against the wall, as if just resting, sat the skeletal remains of an individual that had not seen the light of day in over a hundred years.

36

Eureka!

Liam and Kyle did a cursory exam of the skeletal remains. From the style of the tattered clothes, they guessed that this person most likely died in the 19th century. They searched the ground immediately around the skeleton and didn't see multiple foot tracks. There was only a drag mark in the dirt from the base of the stairs to where the skeleton now sat.

Further examination revealed a massive crack and depression on the back of the skull. Kyle began a search of the stairs and the surrounding area. He was on the eighth step from the bottom when he called to Liam.

"I can't be certain, but I have a stain on one of the stairs that could be blood."

Liam gently pulled the skeleton from the wall, cradling it in his arms. Behind the remains was a dark streak that ran from where the head had rested against the wall to the base of its spine and coccyx.

"I think it might be from a pretty massive head injury. Could have been an accident." He offered as he returned the skeleton to its resting position against the wall.

Liam then searched a pocket that was definable in the remaining blue canvas pants removing a pocket watch and fob. As he withdrew the watch, the cloth disintegrated into a clump of threads and powder. Liam turned the golden color watch over in his hand. The front of the watch displayed the ornate inscribed initials – O.G. When he opened the case it reveled a Waltham watch in near mint condition.

"O.G. - didn't Otavious Gass disappear in 1868?" asked Kyle.

"I was thinking the exact same thing."

Liam started thinking and pacing, holding the watch tightly in his hand as he walked back and forth. He tugged at his lower lip as he mulled this new piece of the puzzle.

"How does this scenario sound?" Liam poised. "We know from newspaper accounts and from Sandra Yorke's diary that there had been some type of fire at Octavious Gass's home in March of 1868, also Gass disappeared around that time as well. How about the house caught fire, Gass had this hiding place but he fell in the commotion. Hit his head and then died as a result."

"Or got hit…"

" Then his sister inherits the land, her church builds a compound on the exact spot where Gass's house was, because fireplaces don't burn in a fire. So they incorporated the old fireplace that still stood from the fire fifty years earlier, into their design?"

"However, this is all an assumption based upon the fact that that is Octavious Gass." Kyle said pointing to the remains.

"We can have Uncle Bob contact the local authorities and retrieve the skeleton when we leave. I don't really want to explain what we are doing here, do you?"

Kyle just shook his head no. Liam looked around the room and continued.

"Well, we are obviously in a man made cavern, so let's see where the tunnel takes us, shall we?"

Liam started down the darkened tunnel, his headlamp illuminating the way. Kyle kept in step about ten feet behind his boss.

"Watch the floors for openings. You never know when you might come up on one. When you do, nine out of ten times it's too late." Kyle offered.

They had gone about fifty feet when they happened upon another small room larger than the first, but not by much. On the ground in the center of the room were mine rails connected to a turntable. On the table, pointed towards the wall, was a device, similar to one that they had seen in Carson City. A bicycle mounted to an outrigger that one could pedal on the rails. Connected to the rear of the bicycle was a small flat car for transporting various items. A set of tracks continued down another tunnel. The rails were set eighteen inches apart, each one covered in a patina of rust.

Kyle tried to rotate the turntable. He pulled up on a lock pin that kept the table from moving. He then grabbed a handrail and when he put all his weight into a push, the platform rotated with such ease that Kyle lost his balance and fell to his knees.

"Whoever built this really knew what they were doing. It's counter weighted so you could move it with one finger when it has been greased."

Liam stepped onto the turntable and started to sit on the seat of the bicycle. When his butt touched the old tanned leather seat, it fell apart into a hundred unusable pieces. Kyle pulled out a small blanket and a roll of duct tape and fastened a make shift seat on the metal stem. He then lubricated the chain and gears of the bike with the can of WD-40.

Liam tested the pedals and they moved without any

binding.

"Now boarding on track nine…"

Kyle jumped on the service car as Liam started pedaling off the turntable. The minute his weight settled on the rail car Liam had to triple his pedaling effort.

"Two hours of this and you would have Quadriceps and Gluts of granite. This is a work out. You might want to consider the veggie plate on the ride home."

Liam kidded his friend.

The tracks went straight ahead with very few curves. Kyle was using this opportunity to try one of the hyper-secret apps on his iPhone, a Ground Penetrating Global Positioning System or GPGPS for short. Liam had been pedaling as if the devil were on his coattails. Kyle estimated that they were moving at approximately nine miles per hour. Kyle pressed the mark location on the app and the calculation popped on the screen.

"You've gone a mile and three quarters. Can you keep it up or do you want me to take a turn?"

"I can keep it up for a bit more. I'm more thirsty than anything."

Kyle produced a bottle and handed it to Liam. He downed the bottle in one gulp and continued peddling on. The walls of the tunnel inched past as the rusty conveyance carried the two men. They made a gentle curve to the left and then to the right before the line straightened out. After twenty minutes Liam was nearing exhaustion and his legs were screaming in pain. He was about to have Kyle take over the pedaling duties when ahead an identical turntable appeared. Liam was approaching the turntable too fast.

"We're coming in hot! We've got to slow down, drag your

feet!" he yelled.

On the trailing car Kyle noticed a pedal positioned over the far most rail. He pressed on the pedal with all his weight. Kyle felt the pedal make contact with the rusty rail moving beneath the wagon.

"I've got a brake! Save your shoes!"

Kyle kept his weight on the brake until the bicycle and the trailing cart began slowing down. By the time they entered the turntable they were still moving to fast.

"Get ready for an abrupt stop!" yelled Liam.

Rail stops had been mounted on the turntable. Kyle saw them at the last second in the gloomy dark and heaved his body off the side cart and onto the hard stone floor. He rolled until he hit the cavern wall. The next thing he heard was the side cart smashing through the bumpers and hitting the end wall. Their packs and equipment launched airborne, scattering around the cavern. Liam had ridden the cycle to its stop.

"Ronkonkama, next station Ronkonkama!" mocked Liam as a train conductor.

"Next time I'll take the bus." Responded Kyle.

Liam and Kyle surveyed the damage to the pedal cycle and determined that it was minimal. They righted the vehicle and placed it back on the turntable's track.

The pair then maneuvered the turntable so the pedal cycle was pointing in the return direction. Liam found his pack and hefted it onto his back.

"So, where are we?" Liam asked

"According to the GPGPS we are about three miles directly west of the entrance." Kyle answered as he pulled out a survey map that they had packed. Using his finger as a make shift ruler he scaled out three miles.

"So that puts us right at the base of Desert Hills."

The air in this cavern seemed to be more humid than the entrance cavern. A low rumble was felt in their feet more than hearing it.

"So what do you think that is?" Kyle asked.

"Haven't the slightest idea. How about we find out. There are two exits from the cavern. Shall we split up and see where they take us?"

"Had a feeling that you were going to say that." Kyle added.

" Why don't you take the tunnel on the left and I'll head right."

"Let's only head out five minutes in each tunnel and report back."

"Good idea."

They each stepped into their respected entrances. After only a minute Kyle called out to Liam.

"Not going to take five minutes! My path dead-ends into a door. How about you?"

"About sixty paces in and more tunnel to go!" Liam called back into the dark. "I'll head back your way so we can check out the door."

Liam double-timed it back down the tunnel to find Kyle working on a large lock inset into the old oak door.

"I almost have it" reporting to Liam as he entered. Kyle continued to fumble with a make shift lock pick every forth word an expletive.

To the left of the door, carved into the rock, was a small alcove. Set into this nook, were a pair of wooden shelves. Hanging from a cob nail on the upper shelf was a skeleton key. Liam took the key and tapped Kyle on the shoulder and held the key out to him.

"Hey Houdini, try this."

Kyle looked up and grabbed the key from Liam.

"Sure, go for the easy way in!"

Kyle stood up and inserted the key into the lock and turned it to no avail. He removed the key and sprayed some of the lubricant that he used on the pedal cycle into the mortise. He reinserted the key and jiggled it back and forth until a large audible snap was heard. He pushed on the door and shoved it with all his might. The door only moved a fraction of an inch. Liam helped on the second opening attempt and enlarged the crack by another whole two inches.

Kyle grabbed the can of lubricant once again and soaked the three door hinges.

"Can't live without it!" Kyle struck a pose holding the can as if in a commercial. Liam let out a quick laugh.

They let the penetrating oil do its job for a couple of minutes and then made their third attempt. This time pushing the door open until it came to rest against a wall.

Their headlamp beams pierced the darkness revealing a well-kept, well-appointed room, resembling that of a working business office. Mounted on the walls in six foot intervals were oil lamps. Kyle removed one of the wicks and rubbed some of the contained liquid between his fingers and smelled the result.

"Smells like kerosene. I think it will still light."

He replaced the wick assembly and tried lighting the oil soaked wick. The flame licked up towards the ceiling until Kyle adjusted the wick so it produced a steady burning flame, illuminating the corner of the cavern. They lit the remaining lamps around the stone room.

"This office could be in New York in the 1800's." Kyle said

Liam picked up a sheaf of papers from the desk.

"Well, this confirms it, this was Octavious Gass's office. These are receipts for building supplies all made out to O. Gass. Most are dated from mid 1865 through the fall of 1867."

Kyle continued to probe the corners of the office, locating mining relics from the 19th century. He opened a series of filing cabinets containing more and more files.

"This guy was meticulous. I don't think he ever threw anything away"

Kyle removed a stack of papers tied with yellow ribbon from a cabinet drawer.

"He even saved copies of articles from some San Francisco rag called the *California Daily Record*." This stack is from 1850."

He picked up another stack and tossed it to Liam.

"Those are from Chicago's *Daily Tribune* in 1848."

Liam carefully leafed through the brittle yellowed papers. He spotted a common theme with the articles.

"These are all assay reports from the California gold rush. What are yours?'

Kyle quickly scanned a few of the articles.

"Same here, different paper, but all about California gold strikes and their assayed ores."

"So it looks like Gass had an interest in gold mining."

"I don't recall there being a gold strike in this part of Nevada?"

" There was a fairly large strike in Nye, Nevada, but that was in the early 1900's."

Kyle returned his focus to a series of wooden crates neatly stacked in one corner. The top crate's lid was loose. Kyle removed it and shown his flashlight into the crate. Inside, were a bunch of small cylinders about two inches long with a papery string attached. He removed one and held it up to Liam.

"Any idea as to what these are?"

Liam looked up from his search of the desk and nonchalantly answered.

"Looks like a very old eighth stick of dynamite and a timing cord. They used to be used as fuses to set off bundles of TNT. Not very safe in the day as they weren't considered very stable, kept prematurely igniting and blowing off various body parts."

Kyle stood rock still when he heard this news. He took a deep breath and then slowly returned the relic to its rightful place. Once safely in the crate, Kyle replace the wooden lid and slowly backed away from the stack of boxes, praying that a misstep wouldn't send them all to their maker.

They continued searching through the office, looking for any information from the past that could explain why Rex and Joe were murdered and why Liz and John were almost killed.

Frustrated, cold and hungry after an hour of searching, they were ready to call it a night. They put everything back where they had found it and took a series of photos of the office.

"Okay Kyle that should do it." Liam said putting the camera back into his pack.

"Let's kill the lamps and get out of here."

Kyle started at the rear of the office and extinguished the burning wicks by turning the wick adjuster counter clockwise. When he reached the lamp directly behind Gass's desk, he turned the adjustor and started to move to the next lamp when he realized that the flame had not been extinguished. He tried the wick raiser once again, achieving the same result.

"Damn pain in the posterior!"

He reached for a metal can that sat on the desk so he might smother the flame by placing it on the chimney. As he started to place the can over the glass chimney he grabbed hold of the base of the lamp. As he did this the lamp started to rotate to the left, causing some of kerosene to leak from the oil font onto the stone floor of the office. Liam saw this and warned his friend.

"Careful there bud, don't want to burn the place down."

With the can placed over the chimney the burning wick quickly snuffed itself out from lack of oxygen. Kyle then turned the lamp back clockwise to realign it. Once the lamp was back into the original position both he and Liam heard a click come from the cabinet next to the doorway.

"What was that?" Kyle asked.

Liam knelt down next to the cabinet and placed his ear against the wood. Hearing nothing he methodically started to press on various sides and panels of the cabinet but to no avail.

"Kyle, try turning the lamp again."

Kyle obliged and turned the lamp counter clockwise again, but it did not yield any results.

"How about I try the other direction?"

"Worth a try. Just turn it slowly."

Kyle slowly returned the lamp to its perpendicular position. Nothing happened until he went past the twelve o'clock position and continued turning until the lamp was in the two o'clock aspect. Liam called out.

"Just heard another click. Very slowly, turn it to the left again."

Kyle guided the lamp until a third click was heard and a panel in the rear of the bookshelf popped open.

"Oh you have to be kidding me! What a cliché! A wall lamp opening a secret panel, how B movie-ish!" quipped Kyle.

"B-movie or not, when this was built it was cutting edge technology with most work being done by hand not machine."

Liam turned his attention back to the secret door.

"Let's see what this cliché has to offer."

Liam opened the panel door to reveal a niche in the stonewall. From the cubbyhole he removed two folded sheaves of documents. One set turned out to be the plans for a ranch house and the other set was a detailed map of Gass's rancho with well locations marked for his water pumping stations. He passed these to Kyle who packed them in a small waterproof tote bag that they had brought with their equipment.

Liam then removed a small ledger from the safe with entries dated from early 1865 until March of 1868. Each entry noted number of cars and estimated weights and volumes of ore mined. A quick calculation revealed that whatever ore it was had been mined from Gass's property, with an unheard of weekly weight of 5,000 tons!

Liam passed the ledger to Kyle then continued to remove items from the hiding place. Out came some small pieces of jewelry that in today's antique jewelry market would net a small fortune in their own right. He found another book that turned out to be a daily diary. He passed this one to Kyle as well. Next he removed a chunk of ore the size of a baseball with an assayers tag attached. He read the tag out loud.

"According to this tag, it states the ore is 99.9% pure. Making it the finest ore that had ever been submitted to this assayer."

"99.9% pure what?" Kyle asked without looking up from the diary.

Liam turned the tag over in order to reveal the answer. Then simultaneously with Kyle whom had come to a certain entry in the diary, they answered.

"GOLD!"

"According to the ledger and diary, over 400,000 tons of the stuff!" Kyle exclaimed.

Liam just sat there slack jawed and mouthed the words - 400,000 tons? Kyle turned the page and then reported.

"That's not even the half of it, Liam. According to this entry all of that ore came from a, and I quote, "the smaller of the two veins", end quote.

"What the hell did Gass's find out there?" Liam asked out loud.

Kyle could not return a response to Liam, as he was still stunned at the thought of 400,000 tons of gold ore being a smaller vein, his mind finally returned to reality.

"Anything else in there like a map to an equally as big

diamond mine?"

Liam reached into the back recesses of the hiding spot. At first he thought he had hit the rear of the niche, but he quickly realized that what he felt was not stone. He slowly reached into the alcove with both hands and removed a large oilcloth wrapped bundle. The package was about the size of a large boot box and Liam estimated its weight at close to twenty pounds.

Liam delicately started to remove the oilcloth wrapping. First he untied a series of twine closures. He then peeled back a corner of the fabric and gently placed it upon the stone floor. He then lifted the second fold of the linseed oil impregnated canvas. Liam just stared as to what sat before him, as he removed the final folds of covering. Kyle's face was frozen in awe as well.

Stacked neatly in two bundles about four inches in height were one thousand greenbacks identical to the half printed one that had been stolen from Liam.

"Is that them?" asked Kyle.

Liam thumbed through first one stack then the other. He then measured out about an inch of the notes and counted that pile. He then measured both stacks and calculated the total.

"Mr. Gale, what you see before you, are approximately one thousand, one million dollar notes, or easier stated as one billion dollars!"

Kyle took a note off a stack and held it in his hands. Slowly turning it over and over in his hands if it were not real.

"This is a million dollars?" he muttered.

"To be more precise, each certificate in 1868 was worth one million dollars in gold."

"Wow!" Kyle responded staring at the piece of paper.

Liam finished reading the rear of the greenback as his copy did not have the reverse printing. What he found printed on the back of the note made his throat go dry. He removed his iPhone from its case and launched a commodities conversation app. He input a few numbers and when the final calculation was complete, Liam looked up from the screen that he held in his hands. His hands began to tremble.

"Listen to this, *Promise To Pay The Bearer, Cash Amount or True Returned Weight In Gold, As Of Date Specified Or At Later Date, No Sooner, Which Ever Is Greater For Payment of Interest. Note Matures in The Year Of Our Lord Eighteen Hundred and Eighty*".

"Holy shit, returned for weight in gold?"

"What's even more amazing is that the one million dollar figure was based on 1868 gold prices. Which was roughly $19.00 an ounce. Making a certificate equal to approximately 52,000 ounces, or after doing the math, roughly 3000 pounds of gold!"

Kyle let loose a long whistle.

"I'm not an expert." Liam added. "But I think that these certificates are redeemable at the going market rate of gold based on the original issued weight."

"What's today's going rate?"

Liam referred back to the iPhone's conversion app.

"According to this, gold is set to open this morning at almost $2,000 an ounce!"

"So you're saying that each one of these pieces of paper are worth, what?"

Liam entered some figures into a calculator app, the resulting calculation made his dry throat even drier, if that were at all possible.

"About $104,000,000."

"You mean just one of these is worth $104,000,00!" Kyle shouted.

Liam just nodded his head and took a deep breath to remain calm. The certificates in a pile in front of them, which had once been hidden by Octavious Gass in 1868, were worth close to $105 Billion dollars today.

"$100 Billion dollars, $100 Billion dollars." Kyle kept repeating the figure over and over again to himself. His eyes narrowed and his pupils constricted into tiny pinpoints. The specter of greed was beginning to seep into him.

"Actually $105..." Liam stopped short of continuing. "In order for these certificates to be issued for actual gold in 1868, over four million pounds of it, that meant that Gass had to have mined over one billion tons of rock!"

"More like one billion, five hundred million tons."

Liam and Kyle looked up to see Edward Pitchman standing in the doorway pointing a pistol at them.

37
R.I.P.

"Thank you gentlemen for doing all the hard work, it is greatly appreciated. So, if you would please return the certificates to the package and pass it over to me."

All the while the 9mm semiautomatic in Pitchman's hand did not waver a fraction of an inch. Liam and Kyle returned the certificates to the oilcloth bundle. Liam then retied the bundle and started to stand up. His movement caused Pittman to draw a direct bead with his pistol on Liam's head. Liam stopped in mid-crouch.

"Now, now, now, better be careful there." Pitchman said as he scolded Liam with his left index finger.

"Now, with your left hand, thumb and index finger only, remove your gun and set it on the desk. Liam complied with the man's request and removed the gun from his vest and reached over and placed it on the desk with the grip towards Pitchman. Pitchman retrieved the gun from the table and secured it in the waistband of his pants.

Liam stood up slowly and threw the bundle at Pitchman's feet.

"Your cell phone please?"

Liam slowly removed his iPhone from his pant pocket and held it out to Pitchman.

"Just toss it on the ground."

Liam complied and Pitchman crushed the device under his boot heel. Rendering the device useless.

"Now hands above your head Mr. Ross, lacing your fingers."

Kyle was still kneeling on the ground near the bookcase's hiding spot, his back towards the intruder. Like Liam, his pistol was in a chest holster; incorporated into his tactical vest. He inched his right hand towards the Glock 19 Gen 4 - 9mm. Pitchman registered this slight movement with his peripheral vision and quickly aimed the gun's guttersnipe sight on the middle of Kyle's back. Pitchman cocked the pistol.

"It will not have even left the holster before the first bullet severs your spin." He delivered in a cold, mono-toned voice.

"Same as your Boss, left hand, thumb and index finger, slowly remove the gun and put it in the safe."

Kyle looked to Liam as if to read some sort of signal as to what to do. All Liam did was mouth the words "Do it". Kyle removed his semi-automatic and placed it in the hiding area that he and Liam had removed the greenbacks from.

"Now, close it up please." Pitman asked politely.

Kyle complied by closing the panel, then he slowly stood up with his hands behind his head; lacing his fingers as he stood next to Liam.

"Now, your phone if you would please Mr. Gale.?"

Kyle repeated Liam's motions and Pitchman followed with the crushing of the phone.

"Very nice. Now, that didn't hurt one little bit, did it gentleman?"

Pitchman gathered up the bundle of certificates while still aiming his gun at Liam and Kyle. Liam was running various scenarios through his mind as to what their next move should be.

470

"What are you going to with us, Pitchman?" Liam asked.

"Do with you?" the gambler chuckled.

"You seem to be a bit misguided Mr. Ross. I do not plan on doing anything with you. But I do know of someone that has a very spectacular future all laid out for you."

Liam looked at Kyle, who had a quizzed look on his face; who then shrugged his shoulders. A voice, coming from the cavern behind Pitchman continued where Pitchman's words had left off.

"We could have continued where we last left off. But sadly, I'm afraid too much has transpired since then."

At that second Liam would have sworn that his heart had stopped cold, if it had been medically possible. Those few words tore through Liam as if a blade had been plunged between his ribs.

Stepping around Pitchman, and into the light of Gass's secret office, was the Centum's Recipient, Rebecca Hodge.

"Rebecca?" was all Liam could muster.

"Are they cleared Pitchman?" she asked coldly of her accomplice.

"All weapons are secured, Ma'am." His response was how one would answer a superior officer.

Rebecca walked up to Liam so that she was six inches away from him. She put both of her palms seductively on his chest, leaned in and whispered into his left ear.

"Surprised? So was I when I heard you were still alive. I really thought that I had hit you that night I killed the old man in Little Italy."

Upon hearing her words, a flash of anger over powered Liam's rational. He started to bring his hands down in order to grab this monster's throat. He wanted to squeeze the life from her for killing Rex. His action was too slow. Rebecca grabbed his shoulders then brought her left knee up and connected with his crotch. The blow did not hit him squarely in his groin, but glanced to the left hitting more of his inside thigh that anything. The pain was still immense and Liam buckled and slumped to the carpet covered stone floor.

Kyle tried to jump on Rebecca as Liam fell to the ground but he was pistol whipped in the back of the head by Pitchman. All went black as he fell to the cold floor.

"Kyle? Kyle? Can you hear me?" Liam whispered as he tried to nudge his friend with his foot. He was sitting up, his back to Gass's large oak desk.

After a brief time a low moan emitted from the prone figure. A few more nudges, Kyle was able to open his eyes.

"What the hell?" he asked as the swelling knot on the back of his head started to throb. "Why can't I move my arms?"

"Pitchman clocked you with his gun. Then bound your hands with some plastic cuffs. He cuffed my arms around the desk leg."

"Man, my head hurts. My kingdom for an aspirin."

"No doubt it does. I think you dented his pistol grip when he hit you."

Kyle let out a stifled laugh, wincing with pain.

"Please, don't make me laugh! So what's our next move? Also who the hell is the redhead?"

"It's a long story."

"Well, let's hope you have time to tell it someday. Where

did they go, anyway?"

"They've been gone for about fifteen minutes. I keep hearing drilling and hammering every so often."

Just then they heard someone hammering on rock not far from the door, which had been left open.

"Any ideas Boss?" Kyle asked.

Before Liam could answer Pitchman appeared in the office doorway. His clothes were coated with rock dust. He carried with him the familiar yellow Dewalt battery operated hammer drill that Kyle had packed.

"Wonderful, you're both up!" Pitchman quipped as he set the drill on the floor near the door. "Also, thank you so much for bringing this beauty with you. Saved me a boat load of time."

"So glad we could help." Kyle answered sarcastically.

"Pitchman, where is Rebecca?" asked Liam.

"That's right! You only know her as Rebecca Hodge."

"Then what's her real name?"

"Such a pity, I don't think even she remembers her real name anymore."

Liam struggled against his bonds and cursed at Pitchman.

"Easy now Mr. Ross. You wouldn't want to hurt yourself before the party begins."

"Party? What the hell are you talking about you asshole?"

Rebecca entered the office just as Liam was about to continue on his tirade.

"Liam my dear. Why so angry my love?"

She walked over and stroked his check. Liam turned his head in disgust.

"Who the hell are you, you bitch?"

"Bitch? Now that hurts, it was just five days ago that we were in bed, me on top of you, with you saying much nicer things."

Rebecca stroked his face once more but before she finished she slapped Liam hard.

"Oh how soon they forget."

She turned around and crossed the room to Pitchman.

"Have you finished?" she asked.

"Yes Ma'am." Pitchman stood tall and erect as he answered.

"If anything goes wrong this time Pitchman, it will be your ass that I come looking for."

"I understand Ma'am. Nothing will go wrong, I assure you."

He returned to the outer cavern.

"Famous last words." she answered to herself.

She turned back to Liam and Kyle.

"So lover, I guess you want to know what is going on, don't you?"

Liam did not respond.

"You see, this is unlike the movies when the hero is trapped and he outsmarts the bad guy into revealing his plan so that the hero can escape and save the day. Well, not this movie. Tonight Sweetie, you and your friend shall be tragic accidents number seven hundred twenty five and seven hundred twenty six in our little historic saga."

"Okay Red, now you've peaked my interest." Kyle spoke out as he lay on the floor next to Liam.

"Well Mr. Gale…"

Kyle looked surprised that she knew his name and his

query registered on his face.

"Oh, I know all about you Mr. Gale. Who you are, where you came from and every single movement you've made for these past eight days. In my profession if I don't do my homework bad things can happen… to me."

"Just what is your profession, if I may ask?"

"She's a professional assassin Kyle." Liam's answer was cold and flat.

"Bravo, my love, bravo" she started to clap at Liam's recognition.

"All of this for a worthless stack of paper?" Liam asked.

"You call one hundred billion dollars worthless? Good god, what is real money to you? Besides it's only seed money. You've heard the expression; from an acorn the mighty oak must grow."

"So you are also an opportunist as well as a thief." Kyle added. "There is no way you will see a dime from those certificates."

"Mr. Gale, you know little, where as I know much."

Rebecca walked over to Kyle and leveled a kick to his ribs. Kyle expelled all the air from his lungs in a groan. Liam spoke up garnering her attention before she could administer a second blow.

"So Rebecca, there was one thing that has been nagging me since our dinner at the loft. I didn't give it much thought until just this minute."

"That you had been set up from the very first minute?"

"No, that when you arrived that night at the loft, how you knew what door buzzer to ring. I never told you what number I was in."

"And I thought you were too stunned by my beauty to notice. Well too bad you didn't figure it out sooner. You might be seeing tomorrow if you had."

She turned back towards the doorway.

"Well enough chit chat. It's time to close things out for the night."

Pitchman returned and handed her a small control box.

"Everything is packed and ready to go. Plus, all of the circuits are completed. Once you press the ignition we have fifteen minutes, as requested."

"Well done Pitchman, well done."

Pitchman turned to return to the outer cavern. Before he exited the office Rebecca called to him.

"Pitchman?"

He turned smartly in response, a smile on his face. When he stopped he saw the silenced pistol in her hand, his mouth hung open in puzzlement. She quickly squeezed the trigger sending two hollow point bullets into his lower abdomen. He unconsciously grabbed his stomach with both his hands where the projectiles entered his body. He removed his hands and saw the sticky crimson fluid covering his fingers. He looked up at her.

"Why?"

"Because, it's what I do."

She then leveled the gun and squeezed the trigger once more. The lead bullet left the barrel and found it's way to the middle of Pitchman's forehead. He remained standing for about three seconds, as if nothing happened. Then a small trickle of blood emerged from the perfect circle running down to his nose. His body collapsed as if some unseen specter had removed his skeleton.

Rebecca turned to Liam and Kyle.

"So, I guess we get a bullet to the head as well?" asked Kyle.

"No, Mr. Gale. Because of my deep affection for your boss, I am going to let you see him die, or is it maybe he sees you die. Oh never mind, six of one half dozen of another."

She held up the small transmitter that Pitchman had given her.

"What we have here boys is your alarm clock. Push once for fifteen minutes, your last fifteen minutes. Sadly there is no snooze button on this particular model. One and done, so they say."

She bent down to Liam and whispered into his ear once again.

"So sorry lover. You were the best fuck I ever had."

She then kissed him hard on the lips. When she pulled away Liam spit in her face. She wiped the spittle from her check.

"What? Hard feelings?"

She walked over to where Kyle continued to lay and kicked him in the side once again. This time connecting with three of his ribs, clearly breaking them. Once again he let out a groan.

She then crossed to the prone body of Pitchman, which was blocking the door from closing. She bent down and with one arm deftly and with great ease, suggesting great strength, dragged his body from impeding the closing door. Before she left she turned towards Liam once again, held up the transmitter and pushed the single button once, then dropped the device.

Once it hit the floor she brought her booted foot down on the electronic trigger and rendered it to an unusable form. Without another word, she blew Liam a kiss, turned around and left Gass's office, pulling the door closed behind her. They both heard the key turn in the mortise as she locked the door. Kyle broke the silence.

"Well doesn't that just cut it?"

"What?"

"You get the girl and I get a kick in the gut!"

Kyle then blacked out again from the searing pain in his ribs.

Rebecca had jogged hard and non-stop back down the underground railway tracks, carrying the bundle of certificates in a pack on her back. She was almost out of breath when the dim light from the stairwell appeared before her. She had just set her foot on the first stone step to head up and out into the Nevada desert when the series of explosions started.

"Goodbye Liam Ross." She expelled as she took the stairs two at a time.

38

Withdrawal

Airport Designation - DCA
Washington D.C.
May 9, 2013

8:00 PM EST

The tires of the Gulfstream V gently touched down on runway 1/19 of Ronald Reagan Washington International Airport. The plane was one of the very few private aircrafts still allowed to land at DCA since the restrictions tightened after September 11, 2001.

The jet used half of the runway to diminish speed before it turned onto taxiway N then quickly onto taxiway K. It continued down the tarmac past the general aviation terminal to a little known disembarkation area normally reserved for high government officials.

The plane rolled to a stop next to a Lincoln Town Car limousine. Once the jet's stairway had been lowered Rebecca Hodge exited the aircraft. She walked the short distance to the car with the darken windows and opened the rear passenger door. She stepped into the climate-controlled interior and took a seat next to the limousine's sole occupant.

"Let's dispense with the customary pleasantries, shall we. Your last phone message was rather cryptic. What is the project's current status?" asked the Chairman.

Rebecca handed the Chairman the worn knapsack that contained, the oilcloth wrapped bundle of gold certificates.

"They have all been recovered and Pitchman has moved onto the next phase of his life."

"And Ross?"

"I am happy to report that Liam Ross is no longer a stone in our shoe."

"Very good, one less distraction we have to worry about."

"How is the acquisition part of the operation proceeding?" asked Rebecca.

"As of market close today, we will have obtained over sixty billion ounces."

Rebecca did the math conversion in her head almost faster than a human could key the decimals into a calculator.

"That is over one million, eight hundred seventy-five thousand tons."

"Which will be in our possession in our various worldwide accounts by market opening tomorrow. That's the beauty of the world's precious metal market. It never sleeps, not even on Christmas."

"Then the Shadow Trap program has worked?" asked Rebecca.

"Flawlessly, each ounce was purchased at the trading price on this date in 1896. Not a single individual, anywhere, noticed the anomaly. The prospects for this program are endless.," replied the Chairman.

"So, tomorrow morning we run the price of gold up, present the notes for redemption. Redemption in gold, which the United States will have only a fraction of available. It will be unable to purchase or borrow anymore, because what's left on the any market would barely fill a tooth. We are sure that the Chinese will not fund another loan and bail out the U.S. again?"

"Mr. Fa is not only the Chinese financial controller, he is also been a full member of The Centum since his father died fifty years ago. He has acquired more wealth with us in one year than he would in a thousand lifetimes in China. No loan will be granted, not with over three trillion dollars in loans already outstanding."

The Chairman pressed a button on the small consol inset into the rest arm of the cars seat.

"Wilson, back to the office."

The black car exited the airport through the "Official Business Only" gate and drove onto the George Washington Parkway northbound. Wilson then crossed the Potomac over the Theodore Roosevelt Bridge and headed back to the office in Foggy Bottom.

39

Smoke and Mirrors

Las Vegas Desert
Las Vegas, Nevada
May 9, 2013

Rebecca had just closed the heavy oak door when Liam's mind jumped into high gear. If what was going to happen that Liam thought was going to happen they had fifteen minutes to get there asses in gear and stop it.

"Kyle, are you awake? Are your legs bound?"

Returning from the darkness.

"No, they're free. What do you have in mind Boss?"

"Can you wiggle on your back and place yourself under the desk?"

"Shouldn't be a problem."

Kyle wiggled on his side like a snake until he was directly under Octavious Gass's desk. The pain in his ribs screamed.

"Okay, now what?"

"How's your leg press strength lately?"

"Gotcha!"

Kyle centered himself under the desk. Rolled from his side to his back, wincing from the pain caused by his broken ribs. He lifted his feet up and connected with the underside of the desk.

"Okay Boss, on three. One, two, three!"

Kyle pushed upwards with the strength of an unharnessed bull. He lifted the end of the desk a good four inches from the floor. This provided more than enough room for Liam to slide his bound hands down the leg, freeing himself.

"Okay, all cleared." Liam called to Kyle. Kyle lowered the desk back to the floor.

"Well, I hope Pitchman was a better card player than a henchman. What kind of bad guy was he? He didn't even think that binding through very well. Now what?" Kyle asked.

"Snake back over here and position your hands near my boots."

Kyle moved with renewed energy. Positioning his back and bound hands near the top of Liam's boots.

"Left boot, inside leg. My old riggers knife is in a fitted holster."

"Do you still have that old glorious, wonderful, thing?" Kyle said as he fumbled with Liam's pant leg in order to retrieve the knife.

"Had it since my first junior high show and every project since."

Kyle fished his fingers under the top of Liam's boot and connected with the wooden handle of the ancient stage relic. He grasped the knurled wood with his two fingers and slowly pulled the knife from its sheath.

"Damn it!" Kyle spat.

"What's wrong?"

"Nothing, just dropped it on the floor. I've got it again."

The two men positioned themselves so that they were sitting on the carpeted floor, back to back of each other. Kyle held the knife in his hands as Liam rubbed his plastic cuffs on the blade. After five tries the knife finally cut through the nylon.

"They're off!"

Liam rubbed his wrists to regain some of the circulation. He then cut Kyle out of his cuffs.

"Okay, now the door."

"You don't think she's out there?" Kyle asked.

"I think she's long gone. She probably didn't want to hang around for the explosion."

"I thought she might change her mind and just leave us down here to rot."

"Don't think so buddy. While you were out she started the timer. I think all of Pitchman's drilling; was him setting multiple charges. I think we've got about ten more minutes until we're buried down here for eternity. I don't know about you, but my plans today didn't include dying."

"I left the key in the lock so that's out." Kyle said.

"No problem, it's a pull door. Hinges are on the inside."

Liam inspected the hinges and turned to Kyle.

"In any of Gass's old tools, did you see a chisel and hammer? The hinges are just hand formed iron. With the amount of rust on them I think they'll crack like an egg."

Thy both started rummaging thought the multiple piles of antique tools. Liam spotted what he needed first.

"Found a cold chisel! Now we just need that hammer."

"Got it! " Kyle yelled as he was tossing tools left and right. He tossed the carpenters hammer over to Liam. Liam went right to work on the rusted metal.

He was on his third stroke when the corroded metal shattered into tiny pieces.

"One down…"

The second hinge was a bit more stubborn. After a full minute of wailing on the chisel with the ancient hammer the metal finally gave way. Liam then inserted the chisel's point into the crack between the door and it's jamb, moving the wooden egress just enough so that they could grab hold of the door and pull it open. Once clear of the jamb the door crashed to the ground.

"Old joke. What did one shepherd say to another Sheppard?" Kyle asked.

"Let's get the flock outta here!"

Liam and Kyle took off down the tunnel in the opposite direction from the underground railway. The pair got about twenty yards down the tunnel when Liam stopped suddenly in his tracks level with some of the wired charges set into the ceiling and walls

"I've got an idea."

"I'm all for anything that prolongs my life." Kyle returned.

Liam studied the explosive set into the rock. He then leaned in and smelled the plastic substance.

"Sweet odor, its Semtex, with a DC charge blasting cap. Let's disconnect as many as we can in the next two minutes."

"How about just disconnecting the power source?"

"Let's work down equal paths. You look for the power source and I'll start disconnecting as many as I can. Pitchman only drilled for thirty minutes. He couldn't have set that many units."

Liam set his watch timer to two minutes and then started pulling the ignition charges from the pockets of Semtex plastic set in the tunnels walls and ceiling. He found three charges drilled into some of the timber support braces. The two minute imposed time limit was fast coming to an end.

"Any luck with the source?" Liam called out.

"Not yet. Give me a few more seconds." Kyle yelled out.

Liam's watch timer started to emit a steady beep.

"You don't have a few seconds! Times Up!"

"Found it! He buried it in one of the holes packed with the explosive."

"Make sure that it doesn't have a redundancy before you disconnect!"

"No redundancy, just a battery wired in parallel! Disconnecting!"

Liam didn't even know why he closed his eyes. Just out of reflex or waiting for the first boom? Nothing happened until Kyle yelled out again.

"All clear! Now what?"

Liam jogged back down the tunnel to where Kyle was standing, holding a battery in his hand.

"First things first. Rebecca may still be waiting for the explosion. Let's give her one. Lets pack together enough Semtex and send it down the tunnel on the Railrider's sidecar. That should give off enough of a signal to not send her back down the tunnel to snoop."

Liam put together the ball of plastic explosive while Kyle disconnected the cart attached to the bicycle conveyance. He had just finished removing the last bolt with help from Octavious Gass's antique tool cache when Liam appeared with the deadly package.

486

"We've got to work quickly, we only have five minutes left."

"All set Boss. Place the plastic in the cargo box and I'll reconnect the battery."

"The battery!" Liam shouted. "I'm such an idiot! We no longer have a timing circuit. We just can't chance reconnecting the current source. It will most likely just blow!"

"Any ideas then Boss?"

Liam started to rack his brain for any idea that would work. He was reconstructing everything in his mind as if he was rigging an effect on a movie set, he just couldn't come up with an alternative ignition source.

"What we need is a way to time the ignition."

"How about using one of our cells?"

"Pitchman destroyed both of them. Tell me how else can we time a charge?"

"Electronic, as with the cell, physical, as closing a contact, like a switch or twisting wires together, or exothermically..."

Liam cut him off.

"How?!"

"Exothermically, a reaction of some type..."

Liam turned on his heel and took off on a full run back to Gass's office. He was gone for less than a minute returning with an object that Kyle recognized immediately, one of the dynamite fuses.

"What the hell are you going to do with that!?"

"Exothermic reaction. We can cut the fuse to the desired length and be safely away when the charge blows, thus igniting the Semtex."

"How do we know that thing won't just blow when you

hook it up?"

"I don't. You have to take some chances in life."

Kyle just stood there with his mouth agape, unable to respond.

Liam packed the plastic explosive, much like packing a snowball, around he stubby stick of dynamite. He cut off six inches of the aged black powder fuse.

"We need to get an idea as to how long the fuse is going to burn. I'll light this piece and you time how long it burns."

Liam produced an old *Strike Anywhere* match from a pile on Octavious Gass's desk. He drew the phosphorus sulfur tipped splinter of wood across the rust covered wheel of the Railrider. The tip of the match erupted into a miniature pyre of white flame. Liam then set the tip to the end of the half foot long piece of fuse. Meanwhile Kyle started his watch timer.

The fuse sparked and sputtered and emitted an enormous amount of smoke. When the cherry red dot had reached the end of the cord, Kyle stopped the timer.

"Thirty seconds give or take a second." he reported.

"So, to give us two minutes of time, we need to leave two feet of fuse."

"And run like that the hounds of hell our on our heels!" Kyle added.

Liam roughly measured out what he needed, twenty-four inches of the aged fuse and cut the single length.

"Okay, after I light it, we have to push the cart for fifteen seconds and let it loose. Then run like all get out back down the tunnel. Check?"

"Check Boss. On your count?"

Liam produced another match and lit the fuse. Kyle was already pushing the cart as Liam set the flame to the fuse. After the spark of ignition, Liam fell in beside Kyle and the two ran down the narrow gauge tracks, pushing with all strength, meanwhile Liam was calling out a *Mississippi* count.

They reached Fifteen Mississippi about thirty yards down the track. They gave the cart one last massive shove, the inertia causing Kyle to trip and fall. Liam reached down and pulled his friend up. They both then ran in the opposite direction of the rolling cart.

The explosion erupted with such force that the shockwave, concentrated by the confines of the mine walls, sent Liam and Kyle tumbling twenty yards down the jagged dense rock tunnel floor. When the dust and smoke finally settled enough that the two were no longer gagging for air, Kyle calmly sat in the middle of the tunnel floor, brushing debris from his clothes.

"I really, really hope that your night with that bitch was worth it. Because the next time I see her..." Liam cut his friend off.

Liam, covered head to toe with dust and rock sat on the hard rock floor. A constipated smile was locked hard on his face.

"Oh no you don't! Back off brother, I saw her first! She's all mine. I owe her!"

The friends collectively checked themselves for any severe injuries from the blast. The worst that had were bruised shins and egos.

"Well buddy, time to find a way out of here."

They started back towards where they set off the explosion. Gass's office was upended. The subway railroad track was bent and misshapen at grotesque obtuse angles. A large wall of rock and boulders now blocked the tunnel that led back to the fireplace exit.

"Well, if you can't zig, zag." Kyle quipped.

Liam was lost is his thoughts pawing through a small pile of debris near the damaged door of Octavious Gass's underground office. The Dewalt hammer drill that Liam and Kyle brought with them was a melted heap of plastic slag; small fires had started in the collected papers within Gass's file cabinets.

"Kyle, help me put some of these small fires out. We may need this information as evidence latter on."

The men found two old, hand formed iron miners spades and went to work spreading dirt and sand on the small pyres, paying particular attention to the aged dynamite fuse boxes. When they had all the fires smothered, they collected some tools that they figured might come in handy for their extraction out of the mine.

"Okay, lets start back down the opposite tunnel, checking any anomaly or side entrance. How are we set for light?" Liam asked.

These LED lamps should burn for days, no possible downside there. Plus I've got extra lamps and batteries. Could last us a month."

"That's great, at least our bodies will be illuminated for the search and rescue teams after we've died from dehydration and starvation."

Liam turned to his friend.

490

"Hey it was my turn for a smart ass remark. Kill me!"

"I promise you that if you do go first, I'll prop you up against a wall and put a drink in your hand with one of those tiny little umbrellas, sound okay?" Kyle countered.

"Just wait, someday, I'll be looking down from the heavens and see you writhing in torment." Liam smirked

"How do you know you won't need a periscope for all the stuff you've done in your life?"

"You mean me? You think that I'm going to hell?"

"Don't worry Boss, I'll save you a seat!"

After years of working so closely together, the two friends found that humor would get them through just about any trying circumstance.

They gathered up want equipment that could find or scavenge. Their guns and iPhones had been taken care of by Rebecca and Pitchman. so that had no protection and no way of communicating with Liz and Uncle Bob. They started off down the mine tunnel. Kyle pulled out an old fashion Boy Scout compass.

"Be prepared!" he said

"Do you think any massive ore deposits down here will give us a false direction?"

"Maybe one or two degrees, but nothing catastrophic. Right now I've got us going almost due west. With the distance we covered on the rail tracks to the office, we should be real close if not directly under the low foothills."

"Okay, here's what we have to do Kyle. Gass was a crafty old geezer. We have to check every false lead, every crack, anything suspicious."

"Got it Boss. Do the same as before and split up. Five minutes out then back?"

"That would be the plan."

They split up and found nothing in their first half an hour of searching. Then Liam stumbled upon it completely by accident, a large boulder, standing over ten feet tall and eight feet across, perhaps weighing sixty tons. Liam called for Kyle to join him.

Kyle jogged about sixty yards down the tunnel that Liam had walked. He stopped when he came to Liam's pack lying on the floor in the center of the tunnel. His headlamp was on top of his pack, turned on and illuminating the large rock to the left.

"Boss! Boss! Liam! Where are you?" Kyle shouted. The resounding echo and action almost caused Kyle to have a stroke right there on the spot.

The enormous boulder started to shimmy and tip towards the unsuspecting Kyle. The noise of rock scraping rock was deafening.

"Holy Shit! Cave in! Liam, Where are you?" Kyle screamed at the top of his lungs.

Just as he was going to scream again the enormous monolith stopped and all went silent. Liam stepped out from behind the boulder.

"Ta Da! It's magic" he mimicked the patter of long past magician Doug Henning.

Kyle jumped a foot in the air when Liam revealed himself. He bent over trying to catch his breath and to stop himself from keeling over.

"What the hell?" asked Kyle "How the hell did you do that?"

"You mean this?" Liam stepped back behind the rock and proceeded to duplicate its motions from earlier only in reverse. Kyle just stood there perplexed.

"I see it, but I don't get it?"

"Well, it happened this way. I was walking down the tunnel kicking at some of the small rocks. I kick this apple sized one and it went flying into the large boulder."

"So?"

"I mean it went flying through the large boulder!" Liam bent down and showed his friend the hole in the large boulder. Kyle reached out and touched the rim of the hole.

"It's really old papier-mâché, expertly treated to look like a boulder. The whole thing is a concealed entrance."

"Entrance to where?"

"That my friend is the surprise! Come follow me down the yellow brick road!"

Kyle followed Liam behind the false rock. Liam told him to turn off his headlamp. Kyle complied and when his eyes adjusted to the dimly lit cavern his pupils dilated to the size of silver dollars! Behind the false boulder was the proof to the cryptic message in an old diary. The walls of the tunnel were streaked with veins of pure gold, silver and a multitude of gems.

The veins ranged from the size of a pencil leads, to others the thickness of a strongman's thigh. The veins ran floor to ceiling down a tunnel that disappeared into the darkness. Liam pulled out a small single lamp LED light and shown it on the walls. The walls sparkled gold and white with specks of green and red at intervals.

"Are those jewels as well?"

"Best I can tell they are rubies and emeralds!" Liam excitedly explained.

He then focused his lamp on some not so small veins of a silver material.

"Silver as well?" asked Kyle.

Liam took the old cold chisel and hammer to the rocks vein. With a deft swing he connected hammer to chisel breaking a piece of the metallic mass from the larger vein. It fell to the caverns rocky floor with a small metallic tinkle. He picked it up and examined it closely under the light.

"A hundred years or so ago, this would have been identified as silver/silver ore. However, what I think you are looking at is a .99999% pure piece of Platinum."

"Platinum? That can be as much as twenty times more valuable than gold!"

"It would have to be tested, but I think we're looking at perhaps the richest strike ever found in the world." Liam said.

"And Octavious Gass was sitting on it all those years ago."

"He was also sitting on another surprise, all that time ago. Follow me."

Liam disappeared into a small alcove in the vein-lined wall. Kyle squeezed though as well. Once through they stood in a small alcove that had two small shelves or seats hewn out of the rock.

"I found this as well." Liam removed a piece of rock from a seemingly seamless rock wall. Once he removed the rock by him he duplicated his movement with another chunk nearer to Kyle.

"How did you find these holes?"

"Simple really. I came in here and dropped my penlight. I

used a match to find it, but not before a small breeze coming from this wall blew out the match."

Darkness emanated from the two viewing ports.

"So what's on the other side?" Kyle asked.

Liam removed a slightly larger flashlight from his pack and trained its beam into the dark abyss.

"This is the real surprise."

Kyle moved closer to the port and almost retched at what he saw.

40

Mass Grave

At first the shapes in the darkness were hard to make out. But as a one's eyes adjusted to the dark, the shapes revealed themselves to be things that nightmares are made from.

Scattered about a cavernous room the size of two in-door football fields were mummified lumps of human bodies, dozens maybe evens hundreds. A larger unidentifiable mound was just out of the illumination of the flashlight. After a moment the distinct sound of moving water could be heard coming from the dimly lit room.

Liam and Kyle set to work widening the holes to gain access to the cavern. After thirty minutes they had been able to widen one hole large enough for a person to enter the cave. Once inside the two started the task of setting some make shift work lights with the spare batteries and LED lamps that they had. Within the half hour the perimeter surrounding the mummified remains was lighted.

The bodies did number into the hundreds, large ones, small ones, old and young. Some were skeletal remains but most had been mummified from the constant cool airflow in the cavern. Some bodies were curled into the fetal position, upon a dried dark crimson pool, while others held one another. Upon further inspection, it appeared that most of the bodies had multiple entry wounds, the size of large caliber bullets. Many bodies had appendages rent from their torsos. It became very apparent that these people had been murdered.

Kyle had started an inspection of the larger piles that they couldn't identify in the darkness. The first central shape turned out to be a mound with a large canvas oilcloth over it. Kyle removed the covering and found another cache of old tools similar to the one in Gass's office. Also with the tools were kegs of grease and kegs of pitch once used for the now dismantled mine railway.

He moved to the second pile and removed the oilcloth. He then stood ramrod straight and stared at the horror he had revealed.

"Hey Boss! over here!"

Liam stood up from examining one of the bodies more closely and started to walk over to Kyle.

"Looks like they were Chinese from the looks of their facial features and clothing. I would guess to say, mid 1800's. What did you find out?"

Liam was just steps away when he stopped dead in his tracks.

"They way they were murdered." Kyle replied with just a whisper.

Mounted on an old wagon, the two stood in front of one of man's most horrible inventions, the tool that hastened the turning point of the United States Civil War, the Gatling gun.

"They just executed them." Kyle choked out. "Who were they?"

"I bet you anything they were the miners and rail workers that cleared the mine and laid the track to Carson City. I would even bet that if we searched the old roadbed, we would find evidence of even more mass graves, just like this one."

"All of this for just gold? It just doesn't change does it?" Kyle asked.

"What doesn't change?"

"The rich, getting richer, by the extermination of the poor and uneducated. So what do you think, the former President covering his tracks? If the world only knew!"

"It may yet, if we can get out of here. We had better explore the cave and see what our options are. I'll go this way and you go the opposite and we'll meet on the other side."

"10-4 Boss." Kyle still seemed a bit shaken. They both walked off in silence in opposite directions.

Liam found the source of the running water. On the far side of the cave, a small stream cascaded down a two-meter fall into a crevasse in the floor. Liam climbed the rock face to see where the water emanated from. When he reached the top, a low-slung shelf of rock prevented him from doing anything but to lay flat on his stomach.

He shown his flashlight into the dark hole that the water streamed from. The rock ceiling only went back about three meters before it opened up once again into what appeared to be another large cavern. The depth and width of the sluice cut by millions of gallons of water traveling over the rock was perhaps a meter and a half deep by two meters wide, with perhaps a third of a meter from the top of the water to the base of the rock ceiling.

Liam dipped his had into the water to discover a cool but not ice cold water. He tasted a small handful and noticed a slight effervescence tingle on his tongue. Indicating to him that the water was traveling over a course of limestone and calcium carbonate. What this truly meant to Liam was the possibilities of more caves and a possible way out!

Liam climbed back down from the top of the small waterfall. He had just stepped off the first rock ledge when Kyle appeared from his reconnaissance.

"Well, good news & bad news Boss. Good news is we have plenty of air and it looks to be you found plenty of water."

"And the bad?"

"I found what used to be the entrance to the mine. It's been sealed up with perhaps one or two thousand metric tons of rock. No way we are getting out that way. Also from my recon, it looks to be this cavern is man made, as in every ounce of material that was once here has been mined and removed."

"Didn't Pitchman say something like one billion, five hundred million tons of ore had been removed? Also with what we just saw I would guess that there is again, that much more down here."

"Too bad, we won't be able to tell the world about this place. I can't see any possible way out." Kyle lamented.

"Oh yea have little faith."

"Oh really? Just how do you propose we get out of here? Dig straight up?"

"Oh nothing so strenuous. I thought we might take a little cruise."

41

Panic

Centum Offices
Washington, D.C.
May 10, 2013

Octavious Gass's stack of certificates was now piled on the edge of an 18th century, English desk. The expanse of the highly polished wood dwarfed any object that was placed upon it, making the pile of greenbacks look more like a packet of Post-It-Notes than the single most valuable objects in the world. The Chairman was seated at the desk; Rebecca sat across, waiting in silence, as others lined the perimeter of the room. An ornate grandfather clock was marking the passing time with its soft whirls and ticks as all eyes watched the hands as they displayed 8:00 and the soft chimes of the antique filled the silence. All heads turned to where the Chairman was seated.

A lone man that appeared to be in his forties entered the room and walked directly to where the chairman was seated. He stooped and quickly whispered into the chairman's ear. He then left the room as quickly as he had appeared.

"Ladies and gentlemen, I have just learned that the market has reacted to the sudden shortage of gold bullion. Gold opened just three minuets ago, and the priced has adjusted to over $5500.00 an ounce. Within a few minutes there will be uncountable cries of anguish and desperation from around the world. Within the hour many of those voices will turn their impulses too much darker avenues. Some will act on those impulses and will leave this world, by their own means, believing to be complete and utter failures."

The room was silent. The Chairman continued.

" A short while later the realization will begin to set in and the phone calls and emails will be sent telling even more individuals that they too are destitute, many not even possessing enough cash to buy a loaf of bread. Because you see, with in just a few days, that loaf of bread will cost as much as a weeks salary. An archaic means of compensation that even millions more world wide will no longer have."

All eyes were locked on the Chairman, waiting for the next shoe to drop.

"Within the hour simultaneous messages will be delivered to the President of the United States, the Vice-President, all sixteen cabinet members, the heads of the FBI, the CIA and NSA. The messages will all read the same. That the United States will have forty eight hours to come up with compensation for approximately $320 trillion dollars worth of *Promise To Pay The Bearer* notes."

The room remained silent.

"As we have all discussed, and as mentioned on the certificates themselves, the payment can be made either in cash or comparable recompense in gold. A commodity, that as of last night, no longer exists any where in any worthwhile quantity."

It was a brave soul that asked the question of the Chairman. A question that Eileen Leonard wished he had never asked the second it left her lips.

"What if they won't pay?"

Dr. Leonard waited for a shot to ring out or a pain to appear but neither ever came. Instead the Chairman answered the question in a very calm voice.

"The U.S. government will have no other option available than to pay. For there is a piece of the puzzle that has not been shared. The same message is also being delivered the President of China, where he will have no other option available to him but to call in the U.S.'s debt. Adding another $50 trillion dollars to the mix. Making this a rather expensive day for our President."

Dr. Leonard pushed her luck with even one more question.

"If they still refuses to pay? What are our options?"

"Doctor" the chairman started but stopped, changed a mental course, and continued. " I would then wonder how the U.S. would like to default on the world's largest military. I assure you Doctor, the Chinese will get what's owed to them, either by a wire transfer or by force."

The Chairman almost sensed what the next question from Eileen Leonard would be and offered a response before the question was asked.

"And no Dr. Leonard, the United States armed forces will not be able to stop the People's Republic of China's armed forces."

The Chairman walked over to where she was standing. Dr. Leonard's attention was solely focused on the Chairman. The Chairman stood nose to nose with her. She had not seen Rebecca Hodge slide in behind her, nor did she feel the needle slide into het left leg.

"Because Dr., patriotism is trumped nine out of ten times by greed. Simply put, how can you afford to pay an army if you have no money?"

It was the last thing that Eileen Leonard heard.

42

Demands

Bousquet Loft
Bronx, New York
May 11, 2013

Liz had just poured herself a fresh cup of coffee. She had just turned into the hall from the kitchen and walked straight into Uncle Bob, who had slept in the guest room.

"Mmm... that smells good. Any left?" he asked.

"Just brewed a fresh pot. It's on the counter by the sink." Liz explained in between bites of a donut. She then continued down the hall to the stamp room.

Uncle Bob rubbed the sleep from his eyes as he went to pour himself a cup of the magic elixir. He contemplated a day old donut from the nearly empty box sitting on the counter next to the coffee maker. He looked down at his stomach and patted it.

"A half of grapefruit and a run is what I really need."

Speaking to no one there. Ignoring the box of deep fried dough.

"Congratulations Robert. You do have will power after all."

As he turned around triumphantly and started back towards the door, he made it exactly two steps, wiped back around to the counter and quickly picked the last glazed donut from the box. He then walked out of the kitchen towards the stamp room muttering, to himself.

"Oh well, baby steps, just got to do it in baby steps."

Uncle Bob entered what the small group was now referring to as "mission control". John was seated at one terminal and Liz had just settled into the second station, ready to check on any information that had come in over night. Uncle Bob stuffed the last of the sugar delivery system into his mouth.

"That had better not be the last glazed!"

John pointed an accusatory finger as he focused on Uncle Bob like a dog staring at a steak. Uncle Bob took a gulp from his coffee cup, nearly scalding himself.

"Any word from Liam and Kyle?" He asked, quickly changing the subject at hand.

"No it's been only been thirty-six hours." I say we give them twelve more before we worry."

John answered, his eyes never leaving Uncle Bob. Liz then spoke up.

"I'm just a little concerned. I can't pull up either of their phones GPS tracking."

What Liz did not know of course were that both Liam's and Kyle's phones had been smashed to pieces by Rebecca Hodge's lapdog, Pitchman. They were now a pile of useless transistors and printed circuit boards.

John continued with culling information from various agencies and wire services when the alert came across. A loud steady alarm started to sound and three lights installed on the control counter started to blink in time with the noise. Throwing his hands in the air, afraid that he might be electrocuted at any moment.

"What the hell is that?"

John asked while looking around the room.

"I don't know what in God's name it is!" Liz reacted by angrily typing commands on the keyboard. "But I do know it's locked us out of the system! I can't control a thing! John…?"

"Me either!" Shouted John "I'm dead in the water here as well!" Uncle Robert just stood rock still.

The alarm continued for another agonizing sixty seconds. Then as quickly as it started, the noise abated and all the computer screens went black.

"Wait for it!" Uncle Bob announced to his two associates.

Slowly, a crawling graphic went from one screen to another on the bank of monitors before, Liz, John and Uncle Robert.

"What the hell?" Liz asked.

"Wait for it!" Uncle Bob repeated.

Just then a higher pitched tone emitted from somewhere in the control console. The crawling graphic, from right to left of the monitors, was now flashing the word "ALERT…ALERT…ALERT.

"I'll be a son of a bitch! The old fart Bousquet was NSA. This is a NSA – AES!"

"A what?" Shouted John over the ear splitting pitch.

"An NSA - Alert Encryption System. It's the most classified paging system in the world! There are only supposed to be three systems built."

"And where might those be?" asked Liz.

"Well I'd only be guessing, but if I had to venture to say one would be in the Pentagon, number two would be the Director of NSA office …"

"Number three?" Liz asked prodding Uncle Robert.

" Um, the Situation Room at the White House."

There was silence among the three even though the alarm was now louder than a minute before. The alert message stopped flashing and a series, of what appeared to be, coded text now appeared on the screens.

"This must be coded, its just gibberish!" added John.

"If this truly is an AES it will start to decipher itself in about five…"

Uncle Robert didn't even have time to finish his statement. The text on the screen went from "gibberish" as John had put it to a highly classified message. At the end of the message a single line of type stated that they had just ten seconds to securely capture. John started banging on the keyboard attempting anything to give him access to the system, Liz was failing as well. A voice that had started counting from ten had now reached four and was not stopping for anything that Liz and John attempted.

In a quick desperate attempt, Uncle Bob grabbed Liz's iPhone from the desk and quickly snapped a picture of the screen. Just as all three heard the device emit a shutter sound, the alert alarm stopped and the computer screens went black.

The silence in the room was pure tension. It was at least thirty seconds before Liz's question punctuated the still.

"Did it work?"

Uncle Robert was still just holding the iPhone in his hands seeming frozen in time.

"I don't know? I just grabbed the first thing that came to my mind."

Liz retrieved the iPhone from Robert and opened the phone's photo album program. There, as the last picture taken, was a crystal clear image of the text that was on the computer screen just a minute before.

John started connecting a cable to the projection display system. Liz plugged in the phone and the screen came to life. On the 7 x 10 screen was the following:

NSA – AES ALERT / NSA –AES ALERT / NSA – AES ALERT

The DDO of the NSA has confirmed a credible threat to the safety of the United States. At 0805 EST the following actions occurred thus resulting in this AES Alert.

At 0801 EST the world's gold commodity market collapsed, sending gold to an all time high of over $5,000 USD a troy ounce. Once this information was revealed there was an automatic hold circuit breaker placed on all international markets. The NTSE, the NASDAQ and the S&P 500 markets are on open hold until further notice. This has been the directive of POTUS and Sec/Tres. There have been reports of multiple cases of high-level suicides around the world in connection with this information.

Additionally, the following correspondence was received at 0803 EST. It was hand delivered by a paid courier service that is known not to be a party to this action. Courier was located and is being held for questioning. Text of correspondence is displayed next:

Mr. President,

By the time you receive this, the world's economic markets will find themselves a bit strapped for liquid funds. We will have done what Gould could not do during a feckless administration. We are now the physical owners of over 83% of the world's gold bullion.

That however is not your major concern this morning, we are in possession of a debt that is long past due and this is a collection call. (We have attached a copy of one of the actual notes for authentication. We are feeling magnanimous today. You can deduct this note's amount from monies owed!)

All three gasped as a photo of a "Promise To Pay the Bearer" note, like theirs, was displayed. The message continued –

As you can see we are in possession of 1000 of these demand notes that that are payable in either one of two ways. 1) Payable by original weight in gold (don't think you have enough) or 2) Payable by monetary equivalent, or so you do have to strain at the math - $320 Trillion Dollars. I assure you that these are legitimate, legal tender, a bit past prime, but legitimate just the same.

Not to appear to be pushy but you have exactly 48 hours to make arrangements and complete transfers or we will have no other recourse than to offer these notes to a primary competitor of yours, at a reduced rate. From what we understand they will take over ownership of collateral immediately upon transfer. (Think noodle stands at the Grand Canyon for their workers as

508

they strip mine the length and breadth!) Tick Tock. The clock has started!

Sincerely,

Chairman of the Board
The Centum

The text continued for another paragraph –

We have also detected communications from the Chinese State Council that in 2 hours, the president of China will be recalling loans totaling, $50 Trillion USD, made to the United States over the past twenty years.

We have also intercepted communications from the Chinese State Council that they will be deploying their enforcement arm to protect their investments. Deployment Starts by days end.

The words on the screen ended.

"This is a blackmail, pure and simple, and with one of Octavious Gass's notes!" Liz shouted.

"What do they mean "deploying the enforcement arm to protect investments?" John asked.

All of the color had drained from Uncle Bob's face:

It means that by days end the People Republic of China's Army will be on it's way to the mainland United States, all one million of them."

After taking a minute to realize what had just happened, Liz broke the silence.

"Uncle Bob, now I'm really concerned about Liam and Kyle. They are obviously mixed up in the mess."

Uncle Bob remained silent and started to pace back and forth in front of the control console. After about ten trips back and forth he finally responded to Liz.

"Quickly, we have to put everything that has happened in the last 72 hours into a timeline. We need to be able to show my superiors a direct link to what has happened to what's going on here in New York, D.C. and Las Vegas."

Liz and John dove for the keyboards, both accessing an online project management timeline creator.

"Liz, this isn't a secure website." John relayed as he feverishly clicks various icons on the screen.

"I know it's not, but we don't have an option. Let's keep the info vague. That way anyone snooping around will just think it's just a project. Bob, how far back do you want to start?"

"Start with Joe Bousquet's death and take it up all the way through the receiving of the AES. That should tell the whole story."

They spent the better part of the next hour adding items to the timeline. From Joe Bousquet's death, then Rex's death, to the break-ins to the attack on Liz in the pressroom, ending with the AES alert earlier.

"Well that seems to be all and it's starting to make sense as well. From the strong-arm tactics to get Joe's stamp collection to the attacks on Liam, John and Liz, to the discoveries about President Johnson. It all boils down to those damn bearer bonds that Liam and Kyle have tracked back west. Now somehow, someone, somewhere has these bonds and is blackmailing the U.S. Do we have enough to pass this on up the food chain?"

Uncle Bob recited to no-one listening and did not receive any responses. John and Liz were focused on the monitors in front of them, deep in concentration. Bob picked up a near by book that happened to be the National Banknote ledger and slammed it down loudly on the table in order to get their attention.

"Hey! I ask you. Do we have enough to take this to the next level?"

The sudden noise made the pair snap to attention.

"Sorry Uncle Bob" Liz spoke up "We seem to have a few major holes in this scenario that we need to plug."

"Like?"

"Well, for openers, why did Joe Bousquet have an NSA – AES system in his home? Second, the gold run makes sense. Someone has bought up or stolen as much available gold so that the bearer bonds become more valuable. Whoever has made the price of gold skyrocket so the Blackmail amount is astronomical. So, how did they pull off such a fantastic worldwide scam? Whoever bought the gold either had to pay for it or commit to paying for it. "

"I'm following you so far."

"So there has to be a money trail, there always is. The close of gold the night before was $1,938.00 per ounce. I have, make that had, a small amount of gold in my portfolio. My broker had a standing sell order for $2,500 per ounce. He sold it and I should have seen a deposit for roughly $250,000 in my account."

"$250 K! What the hell are you being paid!" quipped John

as he was now paying closer attention to Liz since her revelation.

"Good investments and diversity. That's all I'll say on that subject."

She directed at John, she then continued on.

"So I should have roughly $250,000 in my gold account, an even 100 ounces. But for some reason I'm only showing proceeds from the sale at $1,890. That works out to $18.90 per ounce."

"Since Liz found this out, I've been scanning for any other info on the web pertaining to the gold sale. The one thing that keeps popping up doesn't even relate to this instance. Hell, it doesn't even relate to this century!"

"What are you talking about John?" Uncle Bob asked.

"The reference that keeps popping up is an historical gold assay price being quoted as the longest fixed price of gold, $18.90 per ounce – in 1868!"

"The reference to Gould in the note! I thought it was a typo of gold, it wasn't! It was referring to when Jay Gould tried to corner the gold market during Grant's administration in 1868!" Uncle Bob expressed.

"So, I received an 1868 price per ounce for my gold? How in hell did that happen?"

Liz was asking herself as she dove back into the computer keyboard.

"Someone had to manipulate historical data for current." Se said

"This must be a sick joke. John, can you find anything on The Centum?" asked Bob.

John started reading off his computer screen.

"Well this is from the free dictionary". He read on

"designating those Indo-European languages, including the Italic, Hellenic, Celtic and Germanic subfamilies, that merged the palatal velar stops with the plain velars k, g, gh and maintained a distinction between them and the labiovelars k^w, g^w, g^wh.."

"What the hell does that mean?!" quizzed Uncle Robert.

"It's the definition of centum. Right from the dictionary." John said.

"Centum is also Latin for one hundred you dolt!" chimed in Liz who was still hunched over her terminal.

"Is there any historical data on the Centum on the internet?" ask Uncle Bob

"I can't seem to find any." Said John. "Anytime I think I have a lead, it ends up at a dead end."

"Uncle Bob how about any contacts at the agency?" asked Liz.

"I would be more likely to get an audience with the Pope than trying to reach someone over there right now. But what the hell, I'll try."

Uncle Bob retrieved his iPhone from the projector hook up and scrolled through his contact list. He finally landed on one name.

"Here's someone that's so far out of the loop he just might be able to help."

Uncle Bob pushed the call button and listened to the hollow ring on the other end of the line. After five rings, the line connected. Bob pressed the speakerphone function.

"Jason Cantrell" came a response.

"Jason, Bob Ross."

"Uncle Bob! How the hell are you?"

Uncle Bob put his hand over the phone and whispered to Liz and John.

"Big family!" he returned to the phone. "Jason, I need a favor. I have two colleagues here, Liz Gallagher and John Andrews."

"How you doing? Is this on book or off?" he replied.

"Whatever you want, there's nothing covert with this one."

"No problem. What do you need?"

"I need your special expertise on some historical data on a group called *The Centum*."

"No problem. How quick and how deep?"

"Quicker than humanly possible and just scratch the surface. We can do a deeper search later."

"Got it! Hold the line let me fire up the ole' laptop. Just take a sec."

Jason Cantrell was an analyst for the CSS; specializing in off beat, rather obscure information. Some might say his theories often bordered on conspiracy theory.

"Coming online now. Now what's the information you need?"

"Historical data and background on a group called The Centum."

The only noise that they heard over the phone was the sound of a keyboard being manipulated. After three minutes of the seemingly non-stop data entry Jason exhaled loudly.

"Jason, what is it?" asked Uncle Bob.

" Nothing really."

"Jason, even something that may seem insignificant could mean something."

"It's not that. I mean it's really nothing, not one byte of anything on an organization called The Centum. That's near to impossible!"

"What do you mean?"

Liz answered.

"Because there is nothing new in this world, just reworks of older ideas. It's highly unlikely that there is absolutely no information on anything referred to as The Centum."

"Give the lady a prize Uncle Bob. Someone is scrubbing the net daily and removing any information what so ever on anything related to the word centum. Not an easy feat, would take an army of searchers everyday to do that."

"Who has those abilities Jason?" Bob asked.

"Well, we do for one. We do it all the time."

"When you mean we, do you mean the CSS or we as in U.S.A.?"

"Both, we all have the resources."

Uncle Bob didn't even wanted to start that conversation, which this whole affair had been cooked up by a U.S. government agency.

"Who else, besides us?"

"Any major government, some well financed, shall we say, less than honest, organizations."

"I can't see this being this being an affront from another country. They don't go to this much trouble to get something they want. It has to be one of those, well financed, organizations."

"Um, Uncle Bob?" broke in John. He was pointing at the computer monitor in front of him.

"Yeah John, what is it?"

"Well for shits and grins I did a search on Joe's system, seeing it's more than just a home PC, for the Centum, and look what happened!"

The screen in front of John was opening files at a speed that only a super-computer could generate. File after file would flash on the screen as it opened and remained opened on the computer's desktop before the next file would open. The file counter on the toolbar as of that minute was showing that 2,300 files of 112,000 were open. Liz, John and Uncle Bob caught small glimpses of names as each file opened. Napoleon in Louisiana, Kennedy Assassination, Lincoln Assassination, Moon Landing, and Benedict Arnold... the names flashed as fast as the files opened. Watergate, Clinton Administration, Bush/Gore Election, what the hell had John found?

Uncle Bob just stood there transfixed on the screen and it's images flashing by. He didn't realize that he was speaking the file names out loud until he heard Jason's voice over the speakerphone.

"Where the hell are you finding those files? They sound like Level AA – Most Secret files, they aren't even supposed to exist! Man, I give my right arm to get copies of those. Say anyway you can shoot me you server IP?"

You could almost sense Jason foaming at the mouth. Uncle Bob snapped back to reality.

"Jason, so sorry! Got to go!" He quickly closed the phone connection.

"Holy shit John, what have you done?"

"Well, I just did a search for *The Centum* and a password prompt came up. So I entered the password that we have been using on Joe's stamp collection, just as a hunch, and viola. Instant electronic paper storm."

"More like instant shit storm. As Jason said, these look like Most Secret Files. How the hell did Joe Bousquet get them?" asked Liz.

After a half an hour the computer stopped opening files. Whenever the word Centum appeared in a document, it was highlighted yellow. At first look the name appeared numerous times in each document.

After more research into the open documents it was concluded that most of the information had come from the same source. For each document was stamped with the seal of the United States and the notation – AA then numbers ranging from 1 to 45. Some of the files were new only a few years old, most were decades old. But every file had the mark and notation.

"Okay, each of us take a few of the files and read over them for any pertinent information on The Centum, any questions?" Uncle Bob asked.

The three were silent as they each scanned a computer screen, looking at document after document. Every so often one of they would break the silence with an "Oh my God" or "Holy Shit" or even a "What, you got to be kidding!" Each person would read for a bit then scribble something on a yellow legal pad before returning his or her attention back to the document on the screen.

"I think I've figured out the coding of the stamp!" cried Liz.

"What have you got?" asked Uncle Bob.

"The numbers so far only range from 1 to 45. When you read a document, place that document in time. For instance, here's one written in 1932 about the Lindbergh Kidnapping. The date is

March 1932 and the stamp is AA-31. This next one is about the lunar landing, its date is July 1969, and the stamp is AA-37."

"So?" questioned John.

"Don't you see, the date, the number? 1932, number 31, 1969 number 37? Who was president in 1932?"

"FDR." John shot back.

"Not in March of 1932. He wasn't elected until November of '32. It would have been Herbert Hoover." Added Uncle Bob.

"What number president was he?" she asked.

"I don't know. I don't keep inane trivia in my head like Liam and you!" quipped John.

"Call up a list on the computer." Uncle Bob told John.

John typed in the Google Search request and up popped a dozen web sites, including the public White House site.

"Might as well go to the horses' mouth." Said John.

The historical list of presidents was displayed, Herbert Hoover was number 31. Without asking John confirmed that number 37 was Richard Nixon.

"So the presidents are aware of these files. It still doesn't answer why a stamp collector from New York had them." Said Uncle Bob.

"What's even more mysterious is that all of these documents refute public knowledge of these events." Liz added. "Take this one dated January 1815 and stamped AA – 4."

"Number 4 would be James Madison" contributed John.

"This document is saying that Napoleon Bonaparte was at the Battle of New Orleans and the a group called *The Centum*, financed his armies involvement as well as financing the British armies as well." Liz paused "Wouldn't that make The Centum almost 200 years old and a bunch of traitors?"

"Who ever heard of Napoleon fighting in the U.S.?" ask John.

"Well it was considered but history tells us he never acted upon it because he was short funds for his own revolt against the British. But what you are saying is that Napoleon indeed led a troop of mercenaries hired by this organization and actually fought along side the British at the Battle of New Orleans?"

"What else is in there at The Centum?" asked Uncle Bob.

"Would you believe that Benedict Arnold was paid by this group to spy on Washington's troop movements?" read John. "Here's a dozy and it might be relevant to our case, would you believe that The Centum financed the group that assonated Lincoln? It also says that where we were led to believe that Andrew Johnson was a target he was in reality a co-conspirator! This document is even stamped AA – 17! He admits that he had Lincoln killed! That's cold! That's hubris folks, go ahead and confess in a document that only you can read." Liz paraphrased her screen this time.

"So quickly in recap, we have a centuries old organization that has been directly linked to some of the blackest days in United States history? That President Johnson dealt with them? That the Promise To Pay The Bearer notes were authorized by Johnson? We have the evidence! I have to report this." Shouted Robert.

"Just to be the devil's advocate here, report to who? We don't know how high up this goes! You could be reporting to someone that will have you assonated next!"

John's points brought them back to the real world. Uncle

Bob started pacing again and started thinking out loud.

"I wish Liam was here, he would see the obvious."

"The obvious!" Liz shouted startling both John and Uncle Robert.

"There is one "obvious individual" that we can talk to and trust!"

"Who?" Uncle Bob and John asked simultaneously.

"The man that the letter was sent to. Someone that should have no self-interest in blackmailing the country only protecting it, the President of the United States!"

43

Report To The Boss

Uncle Bob and Liz now sat in the Roosevelt Room of the White House, just steps from the oval office. Their journey since New York could be described as whiplash at best.

Uncle Bob had called his superiors in D.C.; he had to follow the chain of command. At first his Deputy Director thought Robert had come unhinged. He didn't believe anything of what Bob said until he was told to transport Robert to the White House ASAP.

From then it was a big blur. Within ten minutes of hanging up with his DD, he, Liz and John had compiled all the facts that they had. It was decided that Liz should accompany Uncle Bob to D.C. to present what they found. A knock at the door to the loft started things rolling at breakneck speed.

From the loft it was red lights and sirens all the way to LaGuardia Airport where a CSS G-5 was fueled and waiting with priority take off the minute Bob and Liz were on board. They landed at Reagan National within 30 minutes of taking off. A dark windowed, standard agency issue, black Suburban SUV meet them on the tarmac, hurtled them through D.C. traffic, then deposited them at the West Wing Entrance to the White House.

There they were met by the presidents Chief of Staff and taken to the Roosevelt Room. They had been offered coffee but both of their stomachs were still in knots from the furious trip. They were told to wait, that the President would be with them shortly.

They had been seated only a scant few minutes when a plethora of Secret Service agents swept into the room and surrounded Uncle Bob and Liz. Ten seconds later POTUS walked in and without even a greeting directed the two to follow him.

"You two" pointing and Robert and Liz, "Follow me this way. We're expected in the Situation Room." POTUS said.

Robert and Liz followed closely on the heels of the President and all the while being surrounded by a dozen Secret Service agents, some who had special automatic machine pistols. A variant of the MP7A1, the US-SS-MP7A-2 was a 4.6 mm x 30 (4.6 caliber by 30mm long shell, 50 shot magazine capacity) lightweight machine pistol designed specifically for the Secret Service by Heckler & Koch of Germany. One burst from this gun could literally cut a man in two. It had a firing rate of close too a thousand shells a minute.

The small parade made it to the Situation Room and Uncle Bob and Liz were asked to wait in the outer room. They both took seats and were immediately surrounded by the agents with the machine pistols. Uncle Bob thought he recognized one of the agents and called him over.

"Agent Walter, can I speak to you for a moment?" ask Uncle Bob.

The agent broke away from another agent that he was talking with.

"What can I do for you?" he countered.

"I thought that was you" Robert held out right hand "Robert Ross, CSS, we met on the Childress case a few years ago."

Agent Walter looked at Uncle Bob for a long while as if

searching his memory for a clue, it then came to him. He returned his right hand towards Robert and shook the pro-offered hand.

"Agent Ross, I thought you looked familiar."

"So, Tony, isn't it?" Uncle Bob asked politely, " Why all the hardware?"

"This whole thing came down in the matter of minutes and nobody, sorry Robert, had ever heard of you. My director was just a bit leery of letting in two people that no one, outside of your agency, could vouch for or confirm who either of you were. We've been hopping since 8:00 this morning."

"So much for inter-agency trust." Said Robert

"You said it, not me." replied Tony Walter. " But you guys have a tendency to be so deep, even the brass forgets who's out there."

The door to the Situation Room opened and the President's Chief of Staff came out.

"Agent Ross, Miss Gallagher, could you join us inside please?"

The Secret Service agents all lowered their weapons simultaneously as Uncle Bob and Liz entered the Situation Room, where the President greeted them officially.

"Agent Ross, Miss Gallagher, I'm so sorry for the rather cold reception. As you can imagine, we are playing things fairly close to the vest today." said POTUS.

"We understand sir, we did rather sneak up on everybody." replied Uncle Bob.

"Well Agent Ross, could you please tell us what you have uncovered." asked a rather portly five star general seated at the large, dramatically lit table in the center of the room.

"Or perhaps it's another CSS theatrical trick that you've concocted. I know what goes on over there." spoke the inflated five star.

"Agent Ross, Miss Gallagher, please be seated." POTUS gestured to two open seats.

"Please excuse General Washburn's assessment. He does not speak for everyone in this room. What have you uncovered? POTUS continued.

" Well sir, it's like this." started Uncle Bob.

The debrief continued on for the better part of an hour. Uncle Bob, supplying information with back up and additional facts from Liz. They led the assembled dignitaries through the rat's nest that was the past seven days. Upon hearing it told in an unbroken linear fashion, even Liz felt that it seemed a bit outlandish! She was a central figure in all of this, and even she was having a hard time believing! What they hell would the President and Joint Chiefs say?

They didn't say much; they just sat there and listened. Every once and a while you would hear a comment muttered under a hushed breath. Uncle Bob continued until he re-counted every detail from just three hours ago, in the loft in the Bronx.

It was the pompous five-star that spoke up first.

"You see gentlemen, right here is a classic example of a CSS trick and lie, in order to garner favor and funding. There is no way that a NSA – EAS site is hidden in an old mans stamp collection!"

POTUS just mentally dismissed the windbag general and after a moment's contemplation, asked all to leave, except Robert,

Liz and POTUS's Chief of Staff.

When the room finally cleared POTUS cleared his voice and spoke.

"Agent Ross, I'm would like to apologize for the General's comments. He can be a complete horse's ass sometimes. Trust me, he does not speak for me." he continued, "I've asked you to stay because you and Miss Gallagher, have in a very short time, stumbled upon a secret that very few people know of."

"Joe Bousquet?" Uncle Bob asked.

"Joe Bousquet" replied the Chief of Staff.

"What are we talking about here, sir? If you don't mind me asking.," asked Liz.

"Joe Bousquet was not a retired stamp dealer. He was hand picked by me, as a White House staffer, who alerted my office to the existence of the Centum five years ago. What they were suspected of doing in the past and what they were capable of doing today."

"We've seen their handiwork up close and personal." Uncle Bob replied, remembering the chaos back at the loft.

"How can we help?" asked Liz.

"Well, for starters, keep digging. This threat is for real. From what you have told us, your nephew and you are further along with this in a week than Joe was able to obtain in five years. We had our suspicions on this Centum, however we were never able to get anything concrete." replied the COS.

"The U.S. is between a rock and a hard place Agent Ross. We do not give in to terrorist threats or demands. It may be a home-gown threat, but it still is terrorism, financial terrorism, plain and simple." POTUS added.

The assembled four were lost in silence for no more than a few seconds when the COS continued.

"Sir, we may not have an option. We have a good suspicion as to what they are capable of, we may just have to pay the ransom."

"But, Raymond, we can't. We would be declaring open season on the United States from every crackpot organization that crawls out from beneath the slime!"

"Uh, Sir?" Liz quietly spoke up, while unconsciously raising her hand.

"Yes Miss Gallagher, we don't raise our hands here.," replied the COS.

Liz withdrew her arm so fast, that it hit the table in front of her with a loud crack.

"That's going to hurt, would you like some ice?" asked POTUS.

"Thank you, but no sir, I'm fine." Liz continued all the while holding her hand.

"What if we were to pull the same trick on the Centum. We make it look like we pay them, but not really pay them."

"Just how do you suppose we do that?" asked the COS.

"Well, they gave you an option, payment either in cash or in gold. Gold is no longer part of that option, there is not enough." Liz stood up and walked over to a sideboard that hand pitchers of ice water and glasses. She picked up a glass and with a motion that seemed to ask POTUS if it was all right.

"Please, help yourself." POTUS offered back.

" Well we also know that they are highly computer savvy or at least they have a highly intelligent co-conspirator, we just turn the table on them with their own software."

"How do you propose that?" asked the COS.

"I can reverse engineer the pathways and send them the same type of historical data that they traded on. We fabricate an account that lived in the past with a high level balance." Liz responded.

POTUS was quiet while he turned Liz's idea over in his mind.

"If we do this, we have to keep it quiet. No one outside of this room can know."

POTUS looked around the room at the assembled three. In unison they shook their heads in affirmation.

"Liz, do we have everything we need back in New York at the loft?" asked Uncle Robert.

"From what I've seen so far, Joe Bousquet's system is more that just your run of the mill agency terminal. I can handle it there just as well as there than here in D.C. In actuality I rather do it there with no one breathing down my neck. But first, we need to find Liam and Kyle." She said.

"You get right to work on the accounts. Let me worry about finding your friends." POTUS said.

" When were they last heard from?" he asked.

"Thirty-six hours ago sir." answered Uncle Bob

"And, where were they?" POTUS asked.

"Oh, Las Vegas." Liz answered sheepishly.

44

Going Up

Las Vegas Desert
Las Vegas, Nevada
May 10, 2013

Liam and Kyle were about to set off to find their way out of the old Gass Mine. It had been thirty-six hours since Rebecca had left them there to die.

"Cruise? Did you hit your head or are you just going batty?" asked Kyle.

"When I was reading Sandra Yorke's diary, she wrote how her brother Octavious Gass had plans to turn the desert into Eden." Liam said.

"Just how the hell was he going to do that?" asked Kyle.

Liam just bent down and scooped up a handful of the cool liquid.

"Water!" exclaimed Kyle.

"Gass's main interest from when he mustered out of the army was farming. He had heard tales of the local natives growing all kinds of fruits and vegetables in the hidden valley. He must have figured out that there was an underground river system. So he bought the land and started on the transformation of the desert. In her diary Sandra Yorke told of letters from her brother writing of the fresh citrus and vegetables that he grew on his ranch. That he had invented a system for "mining" the water up from below." Liam continued.

"In other words, he must have sunk a series of wells on his property in order to get at the streams. Also according to one of his letters to his sister, the vegetable fields were on the northern part of the property."

Liam pointed his flashlight beam upstream.

"So, I suggest we head that way."

"But you mentioned a cruise?" queried Kyle.

"Back in Gass's secret office, there is plenty of wood and oil cloth as well as tools. I propose we make a small raft out of the wood, cover it with the oil cloth and follow the stream until we find a well head."

"Take a boat in the desert, this has to be a first! Let's get going."

Kyle resigned himself to Liam's idea.

They headed back to Gass's office and picked through the damage to find certain items that they would need to accomplish their task. In the rummaging Kyle found a door that led to a storeroom.

"Hey Boss, look what I found here. It looks like a root cellar."

Liam poked his head into the storeroom. All along the walls, from floor to ceiling, were boxes, crates and barrels. Upon closer inspection they were indeed in an old root cellar that Gass had used for food storage.

Hundreds upon hundreds of sealed Mason jars were carefully labeled and categorized, containing everything from peas to peaches.

"Think they are any good?" asked Kyle "After all it's been a while since we ate."

"I wouldn't take a chance with those."

Liam grabbed his pack off the floor and rummaged through an outer pocket. He retrieved a protein bar and tossed it to his friend.

"Here, this is considerably safer."

Kyle opened the bar and greedily ate the peanut butter protein bar.

"Sorry Boss, I didn't save any for you."

Liam did not looking up from his scavenge.

"That's okay, I have more. You can thank Liz later. Years ago, after a shoot that ran 16 hours overtime, she always made me carry them. I guess I was a little cranky after take sixty-three!"

Liam uncovered some same casks that were on the bottom of a pile of cases of empty Mason jars.

"Just what the doctor ordered."

" If that is beer or whiskey, I rather eat the canned peaches!"

"They are actually kegs of hardtack, an old style cracker made from wheat flour, water and a little salt. It was thought that they would last forever."

Liam picked a cracker out of a keg and nibbled at the corner.

"Still edible, that is if they ever were!"

He spit the cracker out on the floor.

"Help me empty six of these casks. They will make excellent pontoons."

After dumping the cracker barrel contents, Liam and Kyle

took all of their needed supplies back into the cavern. Within an hour they had fashioned a serviceable raft from the cracker casks, some oilcloth and the planks from the storeroom door. Liam had also brought along a few other "surprises" from Octavious Gass's old office, just in case.

Liam and Kyle transferred their packs and supplies onto the raft and pushed it to the edge of the river.

"How fast do you think the current is running?" Kyle asked Liam.

Liam walked about fifty feet down stream and placed a medium sized rock at the waters edge. He then paced ten strides going upstream. He knew his stride was roughly 36 inches, heel to toe, so at 10 paces or roughly 10 meters he placed another rock near the streams edge. He then took the small drinking cup out of his pack and placed it into the water. Before he did this he asked Kyle to time the cup from rock to rock.

Kyle started the count the instant that Liam let the cup loose. The cup traveled in a fairly straight line and did not encounter any interference. Kyle noted the time.

"Sixteen seconds!" shouted Kyle.

"Okay, so that's 1.6 meters a second or roughly 3.5 mph.," answered Liam.

"A little over 3 knots. Almost the speed of the East River! That's cruising!"

" We just go slow and low and we'll find what we are looking for."

To avoid any clearance issues the two friends laid face down on the raft. They had crafted some short paddles out of small shovels they had found with the other tools. Slowly they developed a rhythm as the raft strained against the current. The going was slow, but when clearances allowed they sat upright on the raft for more leverage in paddling. Giving their strained back muscles a rest, every hundred yards or so, one of them would scan the walls and ceilings for any sign of Gass's water wells.

Their search proved somewhat profitable about an hour later. During a brief break, to let the soreness leave their cramped muscles, Liam almost missed the first sign of a wellhead.

"Well, good news and bad news."

He remarked as his flashlight beam focused on a spot about forty feet off the ground. There were the ruins of a wooden ladder with a pipe strapped to it heading straight up and disappearing into the blackness.

"No way we are ever going to reach that. So what's the good news?" Kyle asked.

"We're on the right path. Where's there is one there must be another!"

Liam clicked off the flashlight and took up his modified shovel once more and began paddling. Kyle did the same.

They came to a low out cropping of rock that would not allow their progress while on the raft. The two slipped into the cool water and held onto the raft as they ventured beneath the rock overhang. The submersed section took longer they both wanted. By the time they reached the next cavern they were both shivering and their teeth had started to chatter. They had to get out of the water or risk hypothermia.

They decided to take a break and to start a small campfire, dry their clothes, have something to eat and to just let their aching limbs rest. They dined like kings on some MRE (Meals Ready to

Eat), military provisions, that Liam had the good sense to pack in his sack.

These were not just ordinary rations, they were FRH rations, *Flameless Ration Heater* MRE's. These meals were contained in a package that housed a water activated exothermic reaction, much like a sports hot pack. This packaging allowed Liam and Kyle to have a nice hot meal after being chilled to the bone. Kyle dined on Southwest Chicken and Beans while Liam enjoyed Spicy Penne Pasta.

Staying hydrated was not a problem. In fact both men had noticed how the water had a refreshing, revitalizing effect, when drunk.

"Someone should think about bottling this." Kyle said.

"It could be you. Kyle Gale, water magnate! You'll be swimming in cash before you know it!" laughed Liam.

Their clothes dried rather quickly due to the fire and after a short rest they decided to head back out. They had only gone about 400 meters (about ¼ of a mile) when they spotted the next well bore site, this one looked more promising.

Instead of being forty or so feet from the cavern floor, this one was about twenty feet up and positioned right next to the cavern wall. Where someone, most likely Gass, had chiseled steps out of the bare stone.

They flipped a coin to see who would go first; or rather they would have if Kyle hadn't taken off for the rock wall at a sprint. Liam caught up just as Kyle reached the top of the stone steps. He was about five feet short of the bottom rung of the ladder and the pipe that was attached.

" It's a short jump, I can make it." Kyle told Liam.

"I don't doubt it. I'm more worried about what happens if you miss the ladder rung."

"Worry wart!"

With those words Kyle leapt from the stone steps into the air towards the lowest rung of the wooden ladder. Liam held his breath until his friend caught the wooden slat in his right hand.

"Don't try that again, okay?"

Kyle slowly tested the lowest rung with both hands and it held his weight.

"Well, this has possibilities!" he said as he pulled himself up to the next rung.

It was slow going at first, testing each slat of wood before moving upwards. Kyle made progress, moving up about a dozen feet, testing as he inched along, all the while receiving encouragement from Liam below.

"It looks to be about fifteen more feet to the top. You're doing great!" Liam cheered on.

"Yeah, but what do I do when I get up there?"

"I thought that was pretty obvious."

"But you have all the tools."

"Hey, I'm not the one who wanted to play flying squirrel! When you get up there, you can assess and then we can make a plan."

"Sounds like a pre-plan." Kyle responded.

Kyle made it all the way to the top only to find the way permanently blocked.

"Bad news Boss, looks like maybe fifty or sixty yards of concrete in the way. We're not getting out through here."

"Shit! Might as well head back on down then. We can

check the next one further up stream."

"Next stop, First Floor, ladies perfume and unmentionables." Kyle joked.

An accident is called an accident because it is unexpected. Kyle had scaled the century old wooden ladder without so much as a splitter. When he moved his left foot to go down a rung he knew he was in trouble.

"Oh Crap!" was all he said.

"What?" Liam barely got the word out before all hell broke loose.

A board first tested, sometimes, cannot be used a second time. That is just what happened to Kyle. Kyle's weight on the termite-ridden slat gave way, throwing Kyle off balance. He tried to grab another rung, but each rung he tried to secure, shattered into a worthless pile of toothpicks.

Liam tried to at least cushion the landing of his friend by jumping into Kyle's fall path. The only things that it managed to do was knock the wind out of him, produce a number of well-placed bruises and cause him to loose consciousness.

Kyle heard the sickening crack before he felt the pain. When Kyle hit the cavern floor his left thigh landed on a rock the size of a football. The crack he heard was his left femur breaking. Kyle screamed out, the pain that followed was excruciating. Kyle quickly grabbed his leg and felt a sticky, warm, substance on his leg. He looked at his hands and saw that they were a dark shade of crimson. He started to feel light headed from the pain and also from the severe blood loss. When Kyle's femur had broke it caused a compound fracture. If the bleeding didn't stop he would bleed to death.

"Liam, can you hear me? I can't move! Liam can you hear me?" Kyle shouted.

He finally picked up a small rock that was lying by his hand and he tossed it at Liam in order to get a response. Nothing. He tried again. Nothing, The third rock was the charm before all went black.

Liam regained consciousness, and tried to make sense out of what happened. The cavern was near total darkness, Kyle's flashlight was damaged during his fall, his friends falling body knocked Liam's from his hand. It now lay about twenty feet away, near the edge of the rushing stream.

"Kyle! Kyle! Where are you?" shouted Liam.

He didn't receive an answer. He stood up, his head ringing as if he had used it as a battering ram. He located his flashlight and swung the beam around the cavern. Seeing his friend's body, in a rumpled fashion, at the base of what was left of the ladder. He rushed over.

Liam performed a quick triage and found the compound fracture. His first concern was to stop the bleeding. But in order to do that he had to reset the bone so it was not protruding through the skin.

Liam flashed back to his teenage days working with the local fire departments. They carried a device on the rescue trucks that was designed for the immobilization of broken femurs.

Designed by a British orthopedic surgeon, Hugh Owen Thomas, his splint was called the Thomas Half Ring Splint. The splint was attributed with the reduction in military femur fracture mortalities from 80% to 7%. Mainly helping to assist in the stoppage of bleeding from open fractures, like Kyle's.

It was easy enough to fashion a Thomas splint. All Liam needed was two dissimilar length poles or boards, some rope or cravats, and some patience. Liam had what needed on the raft. He striped two of the planks off the raft, ripped some of the oilcloth into bandage strips.

He placed the longer of the two boards on the anterior of Kyle's left leg, snug up into his armpit. The second board he placed, interior of his leg, snug into his crotch. He fastened the boards around Kyle's leg at various points, staying both above and below the wound. He then brought the end points of the two boards together to form a "V". This junction was about 12 inches below his foot.

Next he took a bandage of the oilcloth and formed an ankle hitch around his friends boot. He left a loop on the end of the bandage large enough to accept another bandage. Liam took another bandage and thread it though the loop bringing the ends down to the ends of the boards. He slid the bandage between the meeting points of the two boards; he then attached a small block of wood to the bandage, making a windless. He started to twist the windless in a clockwise motion. The screw action pulled on the bandage, which pulled on the ankle hitch, which in turn put pressure on Kyle's leg pulling the broken bones in alignment. It wasn't a precise alignment, but Liam was worried about the amount of blood his friend had lost. The doctors could always re-align later if need.

As the bones pulled into alignment, Kyle screamed, bringing him back from unconsciousness.

"What the hell are you trying to do, rip my leg off?" he

shouted.

"Hang on pal, one more turn and the pain should subside."

With one more turn, the bones slipped into alignment and the majority of the bleeding ceased.

"You were right, that feels much better."

"You're not out of the woods yet. I still have to stop the rest of the bleeding and get this splint cinched down for transport."

"Transport? My, aren't you being the optimist. I was rearranging this dump in my head as our final resting place."

"Sorry to disappoint you, But my plans include getting the hell out of here."

"First we get you on the raft, then we head out to find the next well site. It should be about the same distance as the last."

"Then what?"

"My turn to play flying squirrel."

" You do realize that if you miss, we really are dead, right?"

"I won't miss, simple as that."

"Famous last words, Rocket J."

Liam got Kyle loaded onto the raft. There was still enough room for him to be onboard as well. While Liam paddled, Kyle was able to use his shovel as a rudder, to keep them going as straight as possible. Liam had to get back into the water at the next rock outcropping. There was barely enough room to wedge Kyle between the rock and the raft. This time Liam was in the water for a much longer than previous. After an eternity, they stopped and Liam pulled the raft onto the bank of the stream. Liam was freezing. He wanted to start a fire and dry off, but they didn't have the time. He took the last flashlight and started a recon for another wellhead. He found it about thirty yards from were he left Kyle.

This ladder looked to be in one piece. The ladder went straight up into the darkness above. Liam guesstimated the climb at seventy-five feet. Liam went back to Kyle and reported the find.

"This one looks promising." Liam said.

"Stay to the outer edges, the wood should be strongest there."

"I've got a better idea." Liam remarked as if a light bulb just went off inside his head.

Liam again rummaged through his pack and came up with a one hundred foot long piece of climber's utility rope. He quickly fastened a ten-foot piece into a climber's assist, a knotted rope that gives a climber a foothold. He would use this on the adjacent pipe, so this way he was not putting his full body weight onto the rotted wooden slats. He would slide this knot up the pipe as he inched forward. Also to this rope he attached the large flashlight. This way he would always have light on his feet. He then retrieved a LED headlamp from their supplies. He placed this over his wet hair.

"Okay, here goes." Liam spoke softly to Kyle.

"You're dripping wet from the swim. You should dry off first."

"We don't have time buddy. I've got to get you to some help."

Liam started his assent. The going was very slow at first because of his wet shoes and clothes. Liam was still shivering from the immersion. He found his rhythm at twenty-five feet up. Everything was working well. He would put one foot on a slat, slide the foothold knot up the pipe until placed just right, put his weight into it and reach up for the next slate. He calculated he was climbing at about five feet every ten minutes.

"How's it going up there?" called Kyle.

"Just like using the Grand Staircase at the Ritz!" Liam called back.

"Just be care…" Kyle didn't finish his warning.

At that moment, Liam's weight on the next wood slat collapsed the pine board,   thus causing him to fall back ten feet before the foothold knot and his aching arms caught the rough-hewn lumber ladder. The bad sign was loosing the flashlight in the stumble. The sound of the cracking wood and subsequent noise of the flashlight crashing down alarmed Kyle.

"Boss, you okay?" called the prone Kyle.

" I would have been better if you hadn't have jinxed me, now keep quiet!" Liam yelled back in jest as he hung by his legs.

It took all of what was left of his strength for Liam to re-right himself. After hoisting himself upright, he rested a few minutes, before starting to make up the lost distance that he fell. After his heart rate returned too normal, Liam re-attacked the climb. He made good time of his fallen ten feet, as well as the next fifteen. It was trickier going without the flashlight, not being able to see his foothold, but he would have to make due with whatever ambient light was in the cavern and from the headlamp.

Liam didn't put one and one together for another ten feet. There was ambient light in the cave! All of the other caverns had been pitch black. Liam didn't notice at the beginning of his climb because his pupils had adjusted to the light levels from the flashlight. But without the extra light, Liam could make out faint details of the rocks surrounding him. Liam kept moving upward. He maybe went another fifteen feet when he looked up and saw he was maybe twenty feet from the ceiling of the cavern.

Liam turned off his headlamp and let his eyes adjust to the darkness. Perhaps darkness was the incorrect term to use. The light around him was more like an early morning light. Faint yellow specks of light shown directly above his head, casting little light dots on the wood ladder and on his clothes. Then he heard a noise, it started growing in intensity. The ladder and pipe began a gentle undulation that as the noise got closer and louder, the vibrations became more intense.

Liam knew this noise, he knew it well. It was the sound of a jet, a large jet starting to take off.

He waited until the aircraft has passed overhead and shouted down to Kyle.

"Hey, what time is it?" he shouted.

"Was that what I think it was?" replied Kyle.

"Yes sir, and I bet you are going to tell me around 6:30 am. Because, that is when flights are allowed to leave Las Vegas International Airport in the morning."

Kyle consulted his watch and called back to Liam.

"6:30 on the dot. Hey, what's wrong with your watch?"

"Well both of my hands are kind of busy right now."

Liam was holding onto the ladder and pipe for dear life as the plane's vibrations slowly subsided.

"We really didn't want me to die looking at my watch, did we?"

"I don't know. It's a really nice watch." answered Kyle.

"Smart ass!" was all Liam responded.

Another ten minutes of climbing and Liam reached the end of the ladder and pipe. Both seemed to end at a rusted steel grate that covered a rotted series of wooden planks. Liam removed a Black Diamond piton hammer that he had strung on his belt. He used the chisel end to hack at the rotten wood.

The wood chips gave way and fell to the ground revealing clods of earth wedged in between the bars of the grate. Liam kept hacking at wood and earth, slowly revealing a circular grate approximately one meter in diameter. The warm, morning Vegas desert air started to reach his face. With each lump of dirt and grass, more and more light streamed through. Kyle shouted that he saw it from below.

Liam identified which was the hinge side and which was the release side. The grill was rusted in place and was not going to budge.

"Time for one of my surprises!" Liam shouted to Kyle.

"Are you going to do what I think you're going to do?" called Kyle.

"Now, It wouldn't be a surprise if I told you, would it?"

Liam carefully removed a small TNT charge that he had liberated from Octavious Gass's office. He wedged the small cylinder into a clod of earth right next to the latch of the grate. He then measured out four arm lengths of powder cord. From their timing experiment, Liam remembered that one foot of fuse gave him one minute of burn time, so two, six -foot arms length would be approximately twelve minutes of fuse. He figured plenty of time to get out of the way of the blast.

Liam's plan was to use the rest of the climbers rope and repel part way down to the ground and wait for the TNT to do it's magic. He figured that in ten minutes he should be way out of harms way. He attached the rope to a bar that had been secured to

542

the water pipe. He tested the connection and declared as well as can be expected.

Liam then lit the century old fuse and waited until he was sure that it had caught hold. He then released his grip on the rope and slid down to his calculated position, unfortunately the rope had plans of it's own. When Liam was just fifteen feet below the grate, Liam jerked to a sudden stop.

He was unable to release the rope and continue his descent. The end of the rope had wrapped itself around the water pipe and had tied itself tightly at Liam's waist.

"Houston, we have a problem." Liam called to Kyle.

Liam quickly explained the predicament to Kyle.

"Can you cut yourself out?" Kyle asked.

"Sure I can. Then I end up down there next to you, broken leg and all. I don't think that helps our situation much."

"I see what you mean. What do you propose?" he asked.

"Well I guess I just hang around and wait."

"Oh great answer. Is there anyway you can stop the fuse by pulling it out?"

"Nope, too far away."

As Liam was looking up he noticed that the fuse was traveling much faster than before.

"You know what we forgot to take into consideration?" asked Liam.

"No, what?" replied Kyle.

"That fuse burns faster on an unobstructed vertical surface. This thing is going to blow in about two minutes!"

"Now you find that out, oh well." Kyle delivered in a flat monotone.

It was less than two minutes. The charge exploded in less than a minute. The force of the concussion sent dirt and steel raining down. Large portions of the aged wooden ladder collapsed on itself, cascading down on Kyle, who had the good sense to cover his head in a duck and cover motion, as best he could. The rope fell free of the pipe, when the section that held it fast broke way and crashed to the stone floor. Liam was swaying back and forth on the thin rope.

The real excitement happened outside of the cavern. Liam and Kyle had traversed underground back towards Las Vega International. What Liam didn't know was that the old abandoned grate was buried about ten yards from an active runway. The wellhead went undiscovered through the decades with all of the airport expansions. Unlike the wellhead that they located that has been sealed by concrete, most likely from the runway construction.

A United Boeing 757, bound for Seattle, had just started its power up to head down the runway, when the blast to the starboard side of the plane erupted, sending a large metal object into the air. Only to land on the runway directly in front of the accelerating aircraft.

The pilot and co-pilot took evasive action, shut down the engines and veered the large plane off of the tarmac onto a grassy strip. The pilot then instituted emergency procedures and started the evacuation of his aircraft.

Meanwhile the explosion and it's aftermath had been witnessed by the tower and a line of aircraft awaiting takeoff on the nearby taxi way. The tower crashed the airport into emergency shut down and dispatched emergency services to the accident. Because of the report from the pilot of an explosion, ATF and Homeland Security were dispatched.

Once the aircraft had been evacuated and the taxiing jets diverted to another runway, officials started to search the area for the cause of the mystery grate now in the middle of a runway. After a short search a Homeland Security agent, in turnout gear and holding an AR-15 rifle, found the hole in the ground. He called for backup over to his location. Within one minute there were twenty agents, from a multitude of departments, pointing various firearms, into the blast hole. It was at that moment that Liam Ross had made his way backup the rope, and popped his head out.

"Too late to catch my flight?" he quipped.

45

Summoned

Liam had been hauled out of the hole and quickly thrown to the ground and cuffed. It took the better part of an hour to get Kyle up from the cavern. When he reached topside and the morning desert heat, he too was quickly cuffed and escorted to an ambulance.

Homeland Security took lead on the investigation. They took Liam to their offices inside the Las Vegas terminal where he was put in a windowless, ten-foot by ten-foot room, which smelled of bad coffee and stale air. In the center of the room was a table, bolted to the floor, with four lightweight aluminum, ladder-back chairs, and a two-way mirror mounted on one wall. Liam took a seat facing the mirror, as he knew that they would want him there so Homeland Security could observe him.

After a short wait, two Homeland Security officials entered the interrogation room and sat in the chairs across from Liam.

"Mr. Ross, I'm agent Hines."

Liam shook his extended hand.

"This is agent Cornell. So tell us about the bombs you and Mr. Gale were placing under the runways. If you cooperate with us, this will go a lot easier for you." said agent Hines.

"Agent Hines, Mr. Gale and I were not doing anything even remotely related to what you suggest. As I told the other agent, we are with the CSS from Washington. We were doing some reconnaissance of an old tunnel from the late 1800's, nothing more." Liam replied.

"CSS, never heard of it. It's not even listed in an official U.S. Agency Directory. You, my friend, are in deep shit here. Now tell the truth." Agent Cornell snidely spoke.

Liam flashed back to New York and Lieutenant O'Brian and Detective Conner. Did all cops read the same, good cop, bad cop, instruction manual? Liam chuckled to himself.

"What's so funny RCSS?" Cornell sneered.

"Oh, you just remind me of someone, that's all." he said.

"Oh, someone funny maybe, huh?"

Cornell spouted angrily and pushed his chair back as he shot up.

"I'll show you funny!" he yelled.

"Now Agent Cornell, yelling will get you no where." Liam responded calmly.

"What were you doing below the runways? You know, we have agents down there now, they will find out!" now Hines got into the yelling.

Liam sat calmly and replied.

"I'd pull your men out of there right now agents. It's not safe."

"Are you threatening us? Are you? Right now we have you on multiple counts of domestic terrorism. Also multiple counts of attempted murder you mother fu…"

Cornell couldn't finish his thought as a loud knock on the door through off his cadence. Cornell crossed to the door and wiped it open.

"This had better be a fucking emergency!" he was yelling even before he saw who knocked.

Once the door was open, three well-dressed men in suits,

and black Way Farer sunglasses, stood in the doorway.

"Who the fuck are you!" shouted Cornell.

The lead gentlemen displayed his credentials.

"Agent Greenbauer, Secret Service. I have orders to take Mr. RCSS and Mr. Gale into custody. Orders of the ..."

Once again, Cornell shot off his mouth.

"I don't care who the fuck issued you orders. These two terrorists are in my custody! They are going no where!"

It was now clear that Agent Cornell was in charge and not Agent Hines. Agent Greenbauer started to take a step inside the room and Agent Cornell moved to block his way. In one swift move, Agent Greenbauer countered his move and was behind Agent Cornell, holding him in a chokehold. Agent Hines began to rush to his aid.

"Stop where you are please, you are both attempting career suicide. We are here on official business. Mr. Ross and Mr. Gale are not a threat to this airport or to this country. The are both employed by the CSS." regaled agent Greenbauer as he held Cornell.

"What the fuck is the CSS?" croaked Agent Cornell.

Commotion at the door drew everyone's attention. The Homeland Security Agent in Charge of Las Vegas International was trying to squeeze through the Secret Service agents, while yelling to let him in.

"Agent Greenbauer! Release my agent right now!" he demanded.

Greenbauer released Cornell; Agent Cornell slumped into one of the chairs, rubbing his neck.

"Mr. Ross, you are free to leave. I am sorry that we

detained you."

"What?" screamed Cornell and Hines simultaneously?

"I demand to know on whose authority?" barked Cornell.

Agent Greenbauer stepped up to Agent Cornell and stood nose to nose with him.

" If you had allowed me to finish before, I could have finished. On the authority of The President of the United States." Greenbauer spoke.

Cornell swallowed hard and took a step back; he continued to back up towards the door. When he reached the door he pointed at Liam.

"I'm not through with you Ross!" he yelled. He then turned around, was joined by Hines, and they both left the interrogation room.

"The President? What in hell did I do?" Liam asked.

"We've been told to escort you back to D.C. as soon as possible. We had better get going. I was told to give this to you."

Agent Greenbauer handed Liam a folder with "Eyes only" stamped on the sealed cover.

Liam broke the seal and scanned the top sheet.

"Gentleman, First I have to retrieve my gear from my hotel room."

"I hope you don't mind Mr. Ross, but we already have. It's waiting for you on the plane."

"I need to see Kyle before I go."

"All due respect. My orders are very clear, get you to D.C. ASAP. You can check in with him from the plane. We must be going now sir."

Agent Greenbauer stepped aside and motioned for Liam to come with him. After a short walk through the bowels of LVI Agent Greenbauer, Liam and two other Secret Service agents were crossing the tarmac too two waiting Airbus ACJ330 corporate jets. Both of the planes carried the tail markings of the U.S. Air force.

They approached the stairway to the first jet and Liam started to climb the stairway. He was half way up the stairs when he noticed that none of the Secret Service agents were following.

"Aren't you coming agent Greenbauer?" he asked.

"Our instructions, direct from the president, were quite clear. You were to fly alone or with Mr. Gale. We are to follow in the second jet. We have also loaded some equipment and supplies, that a very persistent Liz Gallagher, told us you would need."

Liam turned and entered the aircraft. There set up in the center of the luxury airplane was a mini effects shop, complete with most of his portable location filming tools. As usual Liz thought of everything he might need. The plane must have gone to New York before coming to Vegas.

Liam asked the pilots how long to Washington, they told him they would be landing at Reagan International in about five hours. They also told him that they would be taking off in five minutes. Liam found a seat that didn't have one of his effects cases strapped to it. He chose a small couch, sat down and buckled up for the take off. He finished reading the "Eyes Only" file, and knew exactly what he was up against.

Liam had five hours to pull off an effect that would normally take twelve. He had to pull this off. His president and country were depending on him.

46

Reversal of Fortune

Three agents escorted Uncle Robert and Liz back to New York from the Secret Service and five from the CSS, all on the president's authority. Liam and Kyle had been located in Las Vegas and plans were in the works by the time they left the White House.

When they arrived at the loft, Uncle Bob gave the agents a grand tour of Joe Bousquet's building. Even showing them the museum floor. Uncle Bob deployed the agents in the most tactical spots around the building, given what he had experienced from The Centum. The Secret Service agents insisted they stay upstairs near he and Liz.

During their flight to New York, Liz called John and talked him through the process of setting up a clean machine. A computer that had absolutely no information on it, wasn't connected to a internal network and had to go through multiple firewalls to get to the outside world, a machine that could not be pinged or back-traced to its source. This terminal was at the ready when Liz walked into the stamp room.

Her next step was to install a copy of the program that the CSS Cyber Crimes division was able to clone from an infected terminal at a local gold traders office in New York. After installation, Liz set the parameters for the program.

She programmed the date change to a day before The Centum had cornered the market on Gold. She felt strange knowing that with this program she could affect every single person on the planet that had banking access.

"This is just way too much power for anyone to have." she spoke to herself.

After an hour she had the program ready to go and informed Uncle Bob that she was ready to brief the president. Uncle Bob contacted the Situation Room at the White House as he was instructed; POTUS was waiting for their call. The Air Force lieutenant that was in charge of the Situation Rooms technical crew switched the video call to the large projection screen. Uncle Bob and Liz did as well in New York.

With the video feed completed, Uncle Bob and Liz could now see the entire Situation Room. The main conference table was empty but for POTUS and his Chief of Staff.

"Sir, I am calling to report that the shadow program is ready to be implemented."

"Good job Agent Ross, Miss Gallagher. How quickly will we see results?"

"We wont see any tangible results for at least twenty-four hours sir" reported Liz. "It takes that long to infect the host and get the computers clock to reset. If we reset the clock to fast we run the risk of alerting someone. How we manipulate the clock, is we roll the time back six seconds every second, or six minutes every minute. This way in twenty-four hours, the computer will think it is five days ago."

" How fast did The Centum accomplish this?"

"All evidence points to just over a week. That way no one

was going to catch any discrepancy."

"What is the next step?" asked POTUS.

" When the computers clocks are reset, we start to erase all traces of the gold purchases. After that is accomplished, the program then accelerates the clocks back to the current time and date. With the outcome appearing as if the transactions never occurred."

"What about the physical gold that was transferred?" asked the chief of staff.

"A bit trickier, that's where Liam comes into play. Once he locates the identities of the vaults, I'm afraid sir, you are going to have to send force in to recover the gold."

"Agent Ross, Ms. Gallagher, how confidant are you both that this will work and The Centum will not find out?" asked the President.

"We've taken every possible precaution.," offered Uncle Robert.

"One hundred percent confident?" he asked.

"You can never be one hundred percent about anything. One thing that this job has taught me sir, is there are too many variables." Responded Robert.

The President mulled Uncle Bob's response over for a minute before closing the conversation.

"Very well. Good luck to you all. Report back to me at 1500. White House off."

With the President's response, the screen went black.

47

Mirror Image

Reagan International Airport
Washington, D.C.
May 13, 2013

The Air Force executive jet taxied to the congressional terminal at Reagan International. Rebecca Hodge and a squad of Centum security forces were waiting in the dusky shadows of the late spring evening. The jet stopped about thirty yards from the secure terminal. A rolling staircase was moved into position then the hatchway was opened and a flight crewmember hurried down the stairs.

"Everyone hold until the target is fully present. I've got the first shot, is that understood?" radioed Rebecca.

All team members singled an affirmative by pressing their radio switch. No words were spoken.   Rebecca subconsciously counted ten clicks. All had reported in. They had continued to wait and no one appeared. The jet meanwhile had begun its shutdown procedure. The flight crewmember, that had left the plane when it first landed, reappeared at the base of the stairway, this time with a wheelchair. Rebecca thought this odd.

At last a figure appeared at the top of the stairway. The person started down the staircase with a cautious walk of an elderly individual. Rebecca pulled a pair of Ziess field glasses out of her

554

coat in order to better observe.

It was a man, but it was not Liam Ross. This man was at least ninety years old and had a strong resemblance to Senator Robert Worthington, a ten-term senator from Utah whom was the oldest serving member of congress. Rebecca watched as Worthington slowly lowered himself into the awaiting wheelchair with assistance from the crewmember. Once the senator was seated, the crewmember released the chair's wheel locks and pushed the elder statesman over to a waiting black Suburban SUV.

"All hold! It's not Ross! Again all hold! It's not the target. We were given bad intel. Stand down and report back to base. Do you copy?"

Once again she counted the ten clicks. Rebecca then unscrewed the silencer from her antique WWII German produced Volkspistole. Dejectedly, she returned to her awaiting car and left the tarmac in a cloud of smoke from the singed rubber of her tires.

"It's all clear. We're not being followed." Reported Agent Greenbauer.

The hunched over, aged senator in the rear seat suddenly sat up straight as if he were a twenty year old. The man then placed the tips of his fingers, from his right hand, under a fold of skin at the base of his neck. He slowly pulled upward on the skin revealing the face of Liam Ross.

The plan had been for Agent Greenbauer's plane to land at least thirty minutes earlier than Liam's flight and to land on the other side of the airport. Information that Liam received in fight indicated that there might be an attempt on his life when he came to D.C., his movements having possibly been leaked by a high-ranking government official with ties to The Centum.

The plan was to return to D.C., infiltrate the inner workings of The Centum and to try and identify where they were physically storing the gold that had been scammed.

Joe Bousquet's files contained a list of possible high-ranking officials that may be connected to The Centum. A surprising name on the list was that of Senator Robert Worthington of Utah.

Worthington had been detained by the Secret Service and taken to an out of the way safe house in Provo, Utah. The success of the mission was hinged on the fact that Liam could assume Worthington's identity, and get into the building in Foggy Bottom that had been identified as The Centum's headquarters.

The minute Liam's jet had reached altitude out of Las Vegas; he set to work on his Worthington identity. During Liam's Hollywood period as a special effects make up artist, and CSS operative, Liam designed a special 3-D replicating machine. Not unlike a 3-D printer that one would use to make a prototype piece of an airplane or car design, Liam's invention could create amazingly lifelike masks of any being, either human or creature.

Additive manufacturing also known as 3D printing is defined as the "process of joining materials to make objects from 3D model data, usually layer upon layer, as opposed to subtractive manufacturing methods, such as traditional machining". With Liam's machine, you programmed data in the form of photos or artwork of the wanted mask. The information then controls a series of nozzles on a x,y,z axis.

These nozzles move back and forth over a highly accurate cast of Liam's head and shoulders. Short bursts of a specially formulated liquid silicon, are built up, layer by layer, until the subject mask is complete. Through this process, a series of nozzles follows the silicon nozzles, laying down microscopic layers of pigment, painting the mask. Producing a translucent, skin-like appearance. Additionally lasers had been curing the silicon and pigment, leaving a remarkable lifelike prosthetic.   Liam had produced thousands of these masks during his career. He had always had time to finish his flawless characters, but time was not on his side tonight. He had been unable to separate the masks lips and adequately secure the mask to his head before the plane had landed. So here he was, bouncing around the back seat of a Suburban, trying to secure a mask to his face.   From this point on every move was extremely dangerous, they were walking on eggshells. The Secret Service had been successful with Senator Worthington back in Utah, securing certain coded phrases that Liam would need to get into The Centum's headquarters. Agent Greenbauer would pose as the fake Senators Worthington's aide. Explaining, when need be, that the senator was down with one of his most frequent bouts with an upper respiratory infection. Where Liam could never impersonate the senator's voice, he was sure that he could hack up a lung and gesticulate wildly if the need arise.

With Agent Greenbauer driving, they arrived at the nondescript office building in Foggy Bottom. The suburban was stopped at the main entrance, where Liam produced the senator's, house floor credentials; they were then allowed to pass. Once through the gates Liam and Agent Greenbauer realized that what was displayed to the outside world was but an illusion. The black Suburban and it's occupants were now in, if what best to describe as a compound. The outer building, while functional, ringed the true campus of The Centum. There had to be over twenty acres of buildings and parking facilities. In the center of this compound, Slightly elevated on a hill, stood a building design very much in line with the District's many 19ᵗʰ century edifices. In fact, if Liam had time to research the building further, he would learn that no other than Thomas Jefferson had penned the original drawings of the compound's centerpiece.

An awaiting attendant directed Agent Greenbauer to pull up to the center building. Here a valet helped Liam, disguised as the senator, out of the rear of the Suburban. Agent Greenbauer left the keys with the attendant and took up station behind the wheel chair.

Agent Greenbauer whispered as they approached the door to the Greek revival columned building.

"I've seen hundreds of satellite photos of D.C. and I have never seen this place, not once."

"I wouldn't be surprised if The Centum has enough pull to get even Keyhole images retouched." Liam whispered back.

As the wheelchair approached the front steps, Agent Greenbauer noticed a wheelchair ramp off to the left. He wheeled Liam over to the ramp and up to the front door. They stopped at the solid mahogany door and they were about to wonder what to do next when the door opened and Rebecca Hodge greeted them. A flush of anger washed over Liam. It was gone as fast as it had appeared.

She was dressed for business. A severely cut lightweight, grey, wool suit and a black button up, men's style oxford shirt. She wore a single strand of pearls around her throat and her ears were unadorned with any jewelry. Her footwear was the biggest puzzle. She was wearing the same crepe soled boots that she was wearing the last time Liam saw her in the mine.

"Senator Worthington, how nice to see you again." She said as she stepped forward with her hand extended.

Liam did not want her to feel the coolness of the silicon appliances on his hands. So as he started to return the handshake, Liam launched into a coughing tirade. He shot his hands so quickly to his mouth to try and cover the coughing fit. Rebecca automatically recoiled her hand to ward off any germs.

When Liam finished coughing, he mumbled his thanks, and continued coughing into a proffered handkerchief from Agent Greenbauer.

"I'm sorry m'am, but the Senator has one of his nasty colds. No disrespect."

"None taken." Rebecca responded. "Please follow me. The others are assembling for lunch and the remainder of the countdown. This way please."

Rebecca led them through a metal detector where a guard had to hand wand the seated senator. After she turned and started to lead them off into the building.

"I'm sorry, but I didn't catch your name, Mr...." she directed at Greenbauer.

"Baldwin, Thomas Baldwin." He responded. Greenbauer had the flight to D.C. to study up on the role that he would be playing. They continued to walk down the marble lined hallway.

"What happened to Kenneth?" Rebecca asked.

Greenbauer knew that the senator's aide was being held

with him. Greenbauer took a chance and went off script.

" Apparently Mr. Cole's sister took ill. He's off to spend some time with her." Greenbauer lied.

What Agent Greenbauer did not know was that Rebecca and Ken Cole were screwing every time they met in D.C. He also did not know that Ken Cole was an orphan as well as an only child, this had not been in the brief. They continued down the lushly carpeted hallway when all of a sudden Rebecca Hodge abruptly stopped, spun around, all while un-holstering a Glock 17. She aimed the pistol directly at Agent Greenbauer's chest.

"Who are you?"

"Like I said, I'm Thomas Baldwin." He started to reach to the small of his back.

"Stop right there."

"I'm getting my identification."

Rebecca relaxed just a fraction, as she knew that both men had been through one of the most sensitive metal detectors ever made, actually it was the only one. She knew that there was just one gun that either man could have but most likely not. She would have been told.

Liam and Agent Greenbauer had thought about this in the ride from the airport. What Rebecca did not know was that the Secret Service had just started supplying all vehicles with a specially designed polycarbonate and ceramic handgun. The Service had some air-soft handguns modified that could shot traditional ballistic rounds. This was what Agent Greenbauer was reaching for. Liam as well was reaching for his pistol secreted in a book that he was carrying.

"Don't move! Either of you!"

Rebecca was now motioning the pistol back and forth between the men.

"You" pointing at Agent Greenbauer 'Turn around slowly and put your hands up."

Greenbauer complied. His death would accomplish nothing.

"You" she now directed to Liam "Slowly drop that book on the floor."

Liam did as he was directed. Greenbauer now had his back to Rebecca. She found the small gun in the small of his back. She retrieved and pocketed it. She bent down to retrieve the book, never loosing eye contact with of either the senator or his aide. She found the second pistol.

"So, you're both Secret Service. A feeble, feeble attempt by your president to go around our negotiations, no doubt."

Greenbauer spoke.

"I beg you pardon m'am, but I am licensed to carry a gun when I am with the senator, I am his body guard as well as aide."

" Cut the shit, I know a Secret Service weapon when I see one."

This was surprising news for both Liam and Agent Greenbauer to hear. There was there a leak high up at the service or in the White House. They would both shudder at the thought.

Rebecca turned her attention back to the man in the wheelchair.

"I must say Liam, you're looking simply alive since I saw you last."

"I'm like a bad penny Rebecca." Liam stood up from the chair "You can't get rid of me."

Liam reached up and removed the mask of Senator Worthington and dropped it at Rebecca's feet.

This deviation of Liam's actions and the disturbing feeling of seeing a face dropped at one's feet, caused Rebecca to relax her guard for fraction of a second. Greenbauer sensed her muscles relax ever so minutely. As they did he then lashed out with all his strength, his left foot targeting her gun hand.

When his foot connected to her hand, he felt bones shatter. She cried out with a small yelp of pain, having to drop her Glock to the carpet. Liam dove for the discarded side arm and received her right foot in the back of his neck as a reward. Rebecca had stumbled back; Liam had rolled with her kick, sending her off balance. As she fell back she retrieved Agent Greenbauer's pocketed handgun. Liam watched her as she took aim at the Secret Service agent. Liam was lying on his side on the carpet. He felt Rebecca's Glock beneath his rib cage. He pulled the gun out and pointed the gun directly at Rebecca, flicking his thumb down to make sure that the safety was off. In a fluid motion he fired a double tap directly to Rebecca's heart, slamming her body against the Vermont marble wainscoting. He felt nothing for the woman he had made love with just a short while ago. He did feel hatred for the person who left him for dead beneath the Las Vegas desert.

Unfortunately Rebecca was able to get one shot off as Liam was ending her life. The shot hit Agent Greenbauer in the right thigh sending him crashing to the ground. He was lying in an expanding pool of blood holding his leg.

"Agent Greenbauer, are you hurt badly?" Liam asked.

"I'm not going to be pulling any limo duty anytime soon, that's for sure."

He thought about running aside the president's car at 17 miles per hour.

"That may not be a bad thing though!" he laughed.

"Well, I figure we have about ten seconds to get out of this hallway and into hiding somewhere before all hell breaks loose."

Liam grabbed the handkerchief that Greenbauer had given him and pressed it into the agents wound, he then retrieved the mask of Senator Worthington. They decided to leave Rebecca's body where it was, to not risk leaving a blood trail while they searched for a place to hide in order to call in help. Agent Greenbauer was able to stand up and hobble on his own. As they started down the hallway, they tried every door they passed. They were all locked. After the tenth door Agent Greenbauer spoke up.

" You know we have a mole in the White House. It seems like it's someone really high up to."

"Agent, I'm going to asked you a pointed question that may seem like it's out there, Could it be the President?"

"I suppose it could really be anyone, but I doubt it's him. He really is as much as a boy scout as he appears to be. If I could tell you just a fraction of what I know."

"You would be fired on the spot."

The next door that Liam came to was unlocked. It revealed a stairway going down.

"Feel like exploring Agent Greenbauer?"

They heard the sound of people running down the hall.

"Just get us out of this damn hallway, okay?"

It was a short flight of stairs. At the bottom was another hallway with offices lining each side. They found an open door and went inside. It looked to be a clerk's office. A cup of hot coffee on the desk told them that someone had just stepped out for a moment.

"We don't have a bunch of time before the occupant gets back." Greenbauer said.

They each pulled out their cell phones. Liam looked at his screen.

"No service."

"Same here. What now?"

Liam looked at the desk and nodded towards the phone.

"Are you out of your mind! How do you know they won't be listening?"

"I don't." Liam responded.

Liam picked up the phone receiver, pressed nine, and was greeted with a dial tone. He then pressed the eleven digits he knew so well.

Uncle Bob had returned to Washington D.C. in case he was needed. Liz had stayed in New York monitoring the computer transfer for the president. Uncle Bob was just getting out of his SUV when his cell phone rang. He did not recognize the incoming number.

"Robert Ross."

"Uncle Bob, It's Liam. I'm afraid I'll be late to dinner. I've gotten bogged down here at the office."

"No problem kid, see you when we see you."

Uncle Bob closed the connection.

Liam returned the receiver to it's home.

"That was rather cryptic." mentioned Agent Greenbauer.

"Old habits die hard.

" How do you know they didn't trace that?"

"The odds of someone listening to that phone line at that specific moment are incalculable, Agent Greenbauer." Liam said. "But let's move just in case."

They went further down the hallway and entered a door marked service. Here they entered a labyrinth of subterranean hallways and tunnels. They continued to try each door with the initial objective, find evidence as to where the ill-gotten gold was stored. They kept striking out. Agent Greenbauer located a computer terminal.

"This terminal is for service personal only, it's not password protected. It's basically a computerized directory." he said.

"Do a search for gold."

Agent Greenbauer just looked at him.

"It's worth a try!"

The agent typed GOLD into the search box. It inquiry returned no results.

"Do a search for Chairman." Liam spoke up again.

Liam moved over to where the agent was typing the information on the keyboard.

"Way ahead of you."

He finished inputting his search request. A list of twenty different locations compiled on the screen. Liam scanned the list over Agent Greenbauer's shoulder.

"There, number five, Chairman's Office, third level northwest corner."

Liam noticed the security designation as L-5 on the list.

"What's L-5 mean? As if I don't need to ask?" asked Liam.

"Can't be good." Responded Greenbauer.

Agent Greenbauer went back to the original search screen and typed in Security Levels. The responding list confirmed their suspicions.

"It says here, that L-5 is a "must be accompanied" level. Any ideas on how we're going to get by that?" asked Greenbauer.

"I haven't got a clue." Liam answered.

Liam wanted to proceed alone up to the third floor, but Agent Greenbauer refused to hear any of his idea, calling it shear suicide. Liam argued with the agent that someone had to get back outside and lead the cavalry to the rescue and seeing where as Greenbauer was injured, that made him the perfect choice. After a few more moments of discussion the two men parted ways.

"Keep your head down Greenbauer. Just tell everyone to

be careful whom they shoot. I'd like to get back home. I left something on the stove."

Liam laughed as he started down the basement corridor. They both had to pick their ways through a series of corridors to the opposite ends of the building before it was safe for either of them to start ascending. Liam was perhaps halfway to his destination of the kitchen when the shrieking alarms started, alerting the staff that there were interlopers about. He had hoped that Agent Greenbauer had made it to his destination safely and undetected.

Liam made it to the kitchen, but clean access was blocked with a slew of waiters and service personnel going about their duties, getting ready for what looked like a rather large luncheon. Liam had an idea. He found a break room off of the service hallway and went to search for what he needed.

He struck pay dirt the minute he entered the break room. On a rolling rack against the far wall, were service uniforms in an array of sizes. He located one in his size and stepped into the men's room in order to change. When he emerged he checked himself out in a full-length mirror.

He stuffed his own clothes and mask of the senator into a black laundry bag that he also found on the rolling rack. He hid the bag in a soiled linen hamper that was in the hallway just outside of the break room. He went back over to the throngs of service personnel.

He watched for a few minutes in order to read the pattern of the room. A waiter would collect a service tray, laden with the meals for what appeared to be five individuals. There were at least twenty waiters along with busboys, chefs and a maître de, all franticly going about setting a meal.

Liam made his way over to the door that all the waiters were whisking their trays through. Without upsetting the unending flow he was able to peek into a rather large function room that he estimated, currently held one hundred, well dressed individuals both male and female. Liam wanted to get a closer look. He made his way back into the kitchen prep area and slipped his way into line to receive a tray.

The servers were now on the main course, Liam's stomach rumbled as the aroma of the luncheon filled his nostrils. He received a tray of five service domes and as others were doing, he lifted the domes, one at a time, in order to check the contents before being served. Under each dome appeared to be an 18th century hard porcelain china plate, possibly from Limoges, France. On each plate was on half of a crispy duck, petite baby red carrots and a white truffle risotto with about $500.00 of shaved white truffles on top. Liam sighed wishing he had a fork.

He replaced the dome and moved along towards the entrance to the function room. Once in the room he saw that there were twenty tables of five individuals each. He found the closest table without food and walked up to the table. Waiting at the table were five more servers, however these men were dressed in formal attire, each one displaying a telltale bump of a shoulder holster under their three-quarter length coats. One man alone, off to the side of the table appeared to be in charge. He ordered Liam and the five table staff to take station around the banquet table.

As if this procedure had been done hundreds of times, the dome plates were all set in front of the diners at the exact same time, then the silver domes were removed with a choreographed flourish. The domes were then returned to Liam's tray and he was excused by one of the armed waiters but not before Liam overheard one of the diners thank the man in charge.

"Bradshaw, the meal once again is superb! Bravo to the chef!"

Liam surveyed the room on the way back to the kitchen. There were five of these men stationed at each table. That meant at least one hundred guns in the room, most likely many more.

Liam walked close to a table set near the kitchen entrance, where he over heard.

"So after luncheon the Chairman, personally, is to reveal the split from the latest endeavor and deliver the preliminary's for the next project."

Liam could not linger any longer. He had to move back to the kitchen lest he be detected.

So the Chairman was in residence. Perhaps there was an easier way to find where the gold stores were, just ask!

Liam reentered the kitchen and took a calculated risk. He headed over to the head chef and lied through his teeth.

"Bradshaw wants the Chairman's luncheon delivered immediately."

Without even a question or rebuttal of Liam' authority, a tray with gold chargers and domes were prepared. These were then presented to Liam on a service trolley and he was told to take them to the third floor dining room. There he was to set service for the chairman. Liam was about to roll the cart away when an oversized, iron vise of a hand clasped his forearm.

Liam looked to the end of the arm to see the owner was none other than Bradshaw from the main room. Liam had pushed his luck.

Bradshaw took a long deep breath, concentrating on Liam's terror. He finally spoke. Liam was positive that he had been found out.

"You forgot the wine you imbecile." Barked Bradshaw.

Bradshaw proceeded to call out for the sommelier, his voice lifting over the din of the kitchen.

"Marcel! Marcel! The Chairman's wine!"

A funny little man, who walked like a bird, crossed over to Liam and Bradshaw. In his hands were two bottles of 2002 Domaine LeFlaive Montrachet Grand Cru.

"Put these on the sideboard and I will be right up." Marcel told Liam.

"Yes sir." Liam responded as he rolled the cart over to a dumb waiter. The Chairman was about to have his lunch with $12,000 worth of the rarest white Burgundy that the Cote de Beaune has ever produced.

Liam pushed the call button and waited for the dumb waiter door to open. Once the dumb waiter arrived, Liam pushed the trolley inside, selected the third floor from the control panel, stepped back and closed the doors. He watched through the window as his cart started to rise upward. Liam walked down the hall to where the staff stairway was. Before he headed up the first flight, he retrieved his hidden pack from the soiled linen hamper.

When Liam reached the third floor he immediately stepped into the Chairman's private dining area, the room was from a bygone era. The opulence of the furnishings all around seemed to belong more in the gilded age than that of the 21st century.

In the center of the room was a very old, cherry two-person dining table, elegantly set for one. Liam located the dumb-waiter in a service area off to the rear of the room. His service trolley sat waiting for him ready to retrieve it. He extricated the trolley, stashed his bag under the white linen cloth and moved the two bottles of the liquid gold wine to the sideboard that was next to the dumb-waiter door. A noise from behind him startled him and he turned to see Marcel the sommelier huffing and puffing into the tiny service area.

"You idiot! You have not put the wine in the ice bucket yet! What a numb-skull!" he shouted.

"I'm sorry sir, but I have just arrived as well. You specifically told me to place them on the side board." Liam responded.

"Sideboard, ice bucket! Do as I want, not as I say!" Marcel spouted sounding quite flustered.

"Why the nerves?" Liam asked.

"I have never served the chairman privately before and I'm a bit off my game."

"I'm sure everything will be just fine. All you have to do is take a deep breath."

The two men went about their duties, with Liam bluffing most of his. Before long the Chairman's private table was prepared and all they had to do was wait. They waited in the service area until they were called for.

Not long after, the two men heard a door open into the private dining room and they heard voices. There were two people, what sounded like a male, deep bass voice and a female with a mid range alto voice. Marcel, took this as his cue and retrieved a bottle of the Grand Cru and delivered ii to the Chairman.

Marcel returned and told Liam that the Chairman was ready for luncheon.

"I heard to two voices, I only have food for one." he answered.

"Only the Chairman is dining, go ahead and serve." Marcel countered.

Liam picked up the chargers for the luncheon service and entered the dining room through the swinging door.

The door was positioned behind the seated Chairman. Liam wasn't shocked, but surprised to see that the seated individual was the female that he had heard. The owner of the second voice, belonging to the male, was standing at the other end of the room near a door. This was obviously a bodyguard.

Liam approached the table from behind ready to serve this very powerful person lunch, but to also catch her off guard and if need be force the gold information out of her. How he was going to accomplish this, he had no idea. It was at this point that Liam realized that his plan had some gaping holes in it.

He stopped just behind the seated Chairman, and served to the right while standing just behind. He then stepped forward and while looking across the room at the bodyguard, removed the golden dome from the Chairman's meal with the same flourish that he had witnessed downstairs.

When he was done with this act, he stepped one step to the side, all the while his eyes were still on the bodyguard. The Chairman responded to the offered food.

" This smells wonderful. Please send my compliments to

Chef Shelton."

Liam turned his head to respond. When his eyes locked onto the Chairman's eyes, Liam dropped the golden dome service piece. His blood ran cold.

48

It's A Go

Liz sat staring at the computer screen, willing it to work faster. One hour more and The Centum's shadow program, turning on itself, would be complete. The second it was finished, she was to call Uncle Bob and they could start an assault on the Centum's headquarters and in turn get Liam out of the hornet's nest.

John walked into control central of the stamp room.

"I just got off the phone with Kyle. He's been given a clean bill of health but he'll be bedridden in Vegas for the foreseeable future. I filled him in on what the boss and Uncle Bob are up too. He called them both reckless children. He filled me in on what happened in the mine. It was not pretty. He said to give him a call anytime. He wouldn't be going out."

"I'll call him when this nightmare is over." Liz replied to John. She then yelled at the computer once again.

"Faster you son of a bitch. We don't have all day!"

At the conclusion of her tirade the computer signaled with a soft chime. The upload was complete.

She reached for her iPhone and pushed the screen button, prompting her phone's personal assistant to ask her what she required.

"About bloodily time." She responded to the computer finishing.

"Call Uncle Bob, private number." She spoke into the

phone.

"Calling Uncle Bob, private number." Came the disembodied recorded voice.

Uncle Bob picked up on the third ring. A signal that he had long trained Liam and his team to mean he was not under any duress.

"Elizabeth, tell me you have good news." he answered.

"Uncle Bob, it's all done. The program was successfully planted on The Centum's core server. All of the trades have been reversed. There are no longer any records of gold trades being made."

"Good work Lizzy!" was all Uncle Bob replied before he closed the connection.

Uncle Bob made on call to a number he had memorized just the night before. It was answered on the first ring.

"Mr. President, It's a go!"

49

Shock and Awe

The hair was now blonde, but the face was classic beauty, a live classic beauty. Liam was starring at a women he thought he had just shot and killed thirty minutes ago.

"Not who you expected Mr. Ross or may I call you Liam? I feel that I have known all about you for some time now." the Chairman asked.

The bodyguard stationed at the door was moving fast towards Liam and the Chairman, his right hand reaching underneath his coat. The Chairman raised her hand and he returned to his post at the door.

" At least what my sister has told me about you." She continued

Liam stood frozen in his stance, unable to move. He started to feel unsteady and reached for the table's corner to steady himself.

"Please, Liam, have a seat before you fall and hurt yourself." She waved to an empty seat at the table. Liam reached for a chair and landed clumsily in the seat.

"There, now isn't that better?" she asked.

"I am truly sorry, I am being very rude. Here I know all about you, and you, it appears, know nothing of me."

She reached her left hand to Liam.

"My name is Sandra Hodge. I am Rebecca's monozygotic twin sister."

Liam looked at her hand as if he were looking at a specter, afraid to even touch it. He had still to utter a single syllable to this woman.

Sandra Hodge withdrew her hand and returned her focus to her glass of wine. Liam's eyes followed her every move.

"Again, where are my manners, do you care for a glass of wine?" she asked Liam then called out "Marcel! A glass of the Burgundy for our guest!"

Marcel shot out of the service room door in his bird like manner with a fresh wine glass and the cloth wrapped, chilled Grand Cru. He slowed to a dead stop when he saw whom he once thought was just a server, seated with the chairman. He continued forward, set the glass on the table and poured Liam some of the coveted wine. Liam just sat at the table and stared at the wine glass.

"Please, do try a sip Liam, I assure you it is not poisoned."

The Chairman took a long swallow of her wine, she then picked up a fork and started at her luncheon, she also continued on talking.

"So by your look, Rebecca never mentioned that she had an identical twin. It was fun growing up. Fooling our parents and family. Boyfriends were the best! Some never could figure it out. It was only when Rebecca would seduce them that they knew something was up. You see Mr. Ross, being identical twins does not mean we did everything alike. I was, how would you put it – chaste. Now Rebecca was, lets just say – friendly, no doubt as you know."

Sandra Hodge continued to eat.

"How, why? What is this organization?" Liam asked.

The chairman set her fork on the plate, and then wiped her lips with the linen napkin.

"The Centum, Mr. Ross, is a very, very old organization. We have authenticated our roots back to one of the first English explorations to land on North America." Sandra Hodge sat straight in her chair, almost pedagogic.

"I'll keep this short so that I won't bore you. It was in 1587, a small group of ill prepared English settlers were left to fend for themselves amid the woods of a small isle in what is now modern day Virginia." she started

"You're telling me that you can trace this organization back to the Missing Colony of Roanoke?" Liam asked incredulously.

"No Liam, I am stating fact that I can trace my family back to the Missing Colony of Roanoke."

Liam swallowed hard at hearing this news. The Missing Colony of Roanoke was the oldest mystery on the North American continent.

"Please, continue." Liam responded.

" It was from this betrayal, being abandoned, that our hatred for government started. My ancestors swore that they would never let anyone get the better of them, ever again. So with the help of a local Hatteras native tribe, showing my ancestors how to survive the never ending hardships of the new world, we were able to prosper quite nicely in Colonial America."

Sandra Hodge continued. Liam was fascinated.

"When we had an opportunity to help the Colonists against King George we were there with money and other services to offer. We have had our services utilized by every president from the very beginning."

"Thus becoming very rich and powerful along the way. Tell me then, just what service did you do for president Andrew

Johnson?" asked Liam.

"We were able to help him out of a nasty little debt collection issue."

"By murdering people in 1868 and today, not to mention blackmail and theft!"

Sandra Hodge rose from her seat at the table and walked over to an antique sideboard. Here she picked up a small silver bell and rang it.

"Collateral damage. I don't allow anything to get in our way"

Within seconds Marcel, the sommelier returned.

"Could you please have coffee and Armagnac sent to my office?" she asked of the wine steward as she walked towards Liam.

"Yes m'am. They are on their way." Marcel replied.

"Barry" she called to the bodyguard "Please show Mr. Ross to my office. I'll join you shortly Liam, maybe you can show me, what my sister saw in you."

She stroked Liam's left cheek with the back of her hand. Liam pulled his head away in disgust. Barry came over to the table and grabbed Liam by the shoulder. Sandra left the room via a doorway that was expertly camouflaged by the room décor. Liam and Barry however left through the door that Barry had been stationed at.

Barry escorted Liam to an office with similar décor as the private dining room, very opulent, extremely plush. Soft lighting, accentuated by period oil lamps, set among the furnishings and on the desk. Barry shoved Liam into a chair in front of a large partners desk. Marcel came into the room, directly behind the two men;

wheeling the service cart that Liam had hidden his pack on. On top of the trolley were a china coffee service and two snifters, partly filled with a deep amber liquid, the Armagnac. A decanter of the same liquid was off to the side.

It was at that moment that another concealed door behind the desk opened and Sandra Hodge entered, holding Liam's pack containing the mask of Senator Worthington, his clothes and more importantly his gun. When she left the dining room she had been dressed in a conservative business suit, very similar to the one that Rebecca last wore. She had changed into a very casual affair of designer jeans and a cashmere crew sweater. On her feet she wore some very expensive New Balance custom trainers. She looked like she was ready for a weekend in the country, not a blackmail demand.

"Gentlemen, can you give us the room please?" she asked of Barry and Marcel. Marcel left with a bow, leaving Barry.

"But m'am, I must not leave your side." protested Barry.

"Please wait just outside the door Barry. Mr. Ross is of no threat to me."

She hefted the bag she held into the air.

Barry left the office but not without starring at Liam seated at the desk. Sandra Hodge did not say a word until Barry left the room and closed the door. She walked over to the coffee service and poured a cup of black coffee.

"May I pour you some?' she asked Liam. Liam's silence was his answer.

"So where were we? Oh yes, you had asked about President Johnson."

She returned to the desk and took her seat opposite of

Liam. Not before she set one of the snifters of the aromatic Armagnac on the desk in front of Liam.

"Johnson was a stooge, a puppet of the confederacy. We helped him with his Lincoln and subsequent money problems and how did he repay the favor. He had my great, great, great grandfather Homer Black along with his identical twin, hanged in the Lincoln conspiracy."

She took a sip of her coffee.

"Jamaican Blue Mountain. Are you sure you would not like a cup?" she asked.

Liam starred in disgust at this woman. He was trying to figure out how much more time the cavalry needed. He still had not found out where the gold was being stored. He started to poke.

"So, blackmail the world over gold? Isn't that just a bit cliché-ish?" Liam asked as he reached for the snifter of the brandy.

"It's what is owed to us for the years of promises made but not fulfilled."

"So you would crash an economy of good hard working citizens for what, payback?" Liam countered.

"The economy will recover, it always does." She said flippantly.

"And the killing of my good friend? Just collateral damage?" he asked.

"He had what we needed, beside's that was my sister's expertise." She responded.

Liam was mid sip of his Armagnac, he almost inhaled the liquid. He had to stop himself from choking.

"Then, my killing of your sister is just part of the collateral damage as well?"

Liam drained his snifter, letting the words linger in the air.

Finally comprehending what Liam had just said, Sandra Hodge hissed a question behind clenched teeth.

"My sister is dead? How can this be? I just was with her an hour ago!"

"It was only thirty minutes ago that I shot her, in self defense if I may add."

Liam had expected this to elicit a major reaction from her, but oddly it didn't. She took a deep breath and wiped one tear from her right eye. Liam stood up and crossed to the coffee trolley. He took the poured snifter of brandy and this time he set it in front of the Chairman. He then returned to the cart intending to pour another snifter full from the decanter. This would become a part of his action plan.

He turned around to return to his seat when the first explosion hit, the shock wave gently swinging a chandelier in the middle of the ceiling.

"That would be my associates, they want their gold back. You see, for the past twenty-four hours we have been erasing all evidence of any gold trades that your little computer program made. As a matter of fact, we also took whatever other money you had laying about. So to put it gently, your sister is dead and you are broke."

That got the rise out of her that Liam had hoped for. She started screaming for his blood. The bodyguard outside of the office, reacting on the explosion, now compounded with his bosses screaming, came charging into the office with his gun drawn. Liam threw his snifter of Armagnac onto the highly polished surface of the desk, splashing some of the liquid onto the hysterical woman's sweater. Liam then knocked over one of the lit oil lamps that were positioned on the desk, igniting the alcohol. The flames spread fast but the brandies vapors were faster. The blue flame leapt from the desk onto the wet spots of Sandra's sweater, igniting small patches of the wool. Sandra grabbed Liam's formally hidden pack and started to use it to pound out the spreading flames.

The sound of small arms fire started to resonate from the hall. Barry took a shot at Liam but Liam dove behind the desk for cover. Having put the flames on her sweater out, Sandra ran to the concealed doorway that she entered from. She paused at the wall and reached to a spot at the wainscot molding. The door slid open and the Chairman exited through with the door closing silently behind her. Barry fired more rounds from his nine millimeter automatic. Splinters of wood from the desk rained down on Liam. He had to move before Barry made it to the desk.

His only option was to try for the secret exit. All Liam had to defend himself with was the empty brandy snifter. If he threw it at Barry it might be enough of a distraction for him to get to the exit. Liam weighed the heft of the crystal glass in his hand. He then moved into a crouch, building up the nerve to race to the wall.

Barry moved closer, he was now in the center of the room and moving cautiously towards the desk. Liam started to count to three. On three he would pop up, throw the snifter and dash to the secreted exit way.

Liam reached three and popped up and threw the leaded glass crystal at Barry's head. It achieved the desired effect. Barry ducked as the glass flew over his head. Liam leapt for the spot in the wall where the exit was located. At that very moment the room erupted into chaos. An explosion in the outer office caused the five hundred pound iron and crystal chandelier to loose from its mount and crash onto the unsuspecting Barry below.

Liam located the hidden switch, he depressed the wood block that was covering it and waited for the door to open. The door reacted slowly, most likely caused form the earlier explosion. Just as the door was wide enough for Liam to squeeze through another explosion rocked the old house to its foundation. The rescuing interlopers did not cause these blasts as Liam had first thought. What Liam was to find out was that this sequence of explosions was set into motion by the fleeing Sandra Hodge.

50

Rabbit Hole

Liam found himself in a narrow brick lined passage that he was sure dated back to the original house. Many Colonial era homes had these hidden passages and keeps, not unlike Octavious Gass's tunnels beneath the Las Vegas desert.

Liam followed the hallway until it ended at a larger version of the dumbwaiter he had used earlier. The car had been sent down, Liam pressed the button in order to bring the elevator car back up. Once the car arrived Liam noticed that the floor call buttons were older push buttons. The last button pushed was for the basement level of the house. Liam pressed the button once again, only to have the button pop out. He quickly pressed the button once more, this time the button stayed in.

The car was bigger than the service version he used earlier. It was also much older. Liam climbed about and started his descent to the basement. He was halfway down when he realized that he could be stepping into a major trap and he with no weapon.

The car finally came to a stop with a jolting thump. He listened intently but all he could hear was an occasion round of handgun fire and more explosions. He could not tell if anyone was on the other side of the dumbwaiter door. He slowly pushed the door open an inch and was met with the resistance of something made of glass being thrown at the opening door. Liam tried once again with the same result. Liam then began to smell the tell tale aroma of red wine.

Liam called out to whoever was throwing what he assumed were bottles of wine.

"I mean no one any harm. I'm just trying to get away from the explosions!" Liam yelled.

"I don't know that! You could be lying!" came the reply.

"Marcel?" queried Liam.

Marcel answered back sheepishly.

"Yes?"

"Marcel, don't throw a bottle that you will regret, I'm coming out."

With that Liam pushed the door fully open. No bottle came crashing through. The dumbwaiter opened into a wine cellar. Marcel was crouched next to a rack of bottles marked Boudreaux, a bottle grasped firmly in his righty hand.

"I certainly hope that that is not a Chateau of any consequence?" asked Liam.

"I would never! This is from a lot that my predecessor bought ten years ago. Some sort of awful plonk if you ask me." Marcel responded with a smile when he saw that it was Liam.

"Marcel, this is very important. Which way did the Chairman go?"

"I don't know if I should tell you. What if I get into trouble?"

"You won't get into any trouble Marcel." Liam reasoned with the man. "You should tell me where she went then you should get out of here before all hell breaks loose."

"What about my wine?"

Liam gently took a hold of the man's shoulders and looked

him straight into the eyes.

"You can look to it when this is all over. Right now I really need to know which way the Chairman went. It really is a matter of life and death."

Marcel saw in Liam's eyes that he meant him no harm. He pointed down an aisle to the left of the wine racks.

"She went that way!"

"That's great Marcel, now get yourself to safety, now." Liam said firmly.

Liam started down the aisle. He was halfway down when another explosion, this one located quite near by, rocked the racks of wine. Liam heard bottles crashing and Marcel crying off in the distance.

"Marcel! Are you alright?" Liam shouted back.

"My babies! They killings my babies!" he started to weep.

Liam's thoughts quickly reminded him of his newly acquired wine cellar. He should find Marcel when this was over. The man was certainly passionate about wine.

Liam kept tracking the Chairman through the house's old cellar. He came to a hallway and the only way she could have run. Liam proceeded with caution, unsure what was awaiting him at the next turn. The next turn, lead out into a small, connecting hallway. Liam had no idea, which way she was headed. He stopped at each of the three entrances hoping to hear the fleeing woman.

No luck with the first two hallways. When he came to the third hall he did not hear the echo of running feet, he heard someone struggling with a heavy door. He headed down the darkened hall. He remembered that his iPhone had a built in flashlight application. He retrieved his phone from his pocket and paged through the applications until he reached the one he needed. He now could proceed not being blind to what lay ahead.

He cautiously continued down the hallway until he came to a tee branching left and right. The noise off to the left seemed to be close, very close. Liam turned off the flashlight so its beam would not reveal him. He quietly crept up to an open door set back from the hallway. Liam approached the open door with trepidation. He knelt down low and peered into the open door.

He was peering into a vault, an old one, filled with filing cabinets and many works of art, all cataloged and stored in this subterranean shelter. Sandra Hodge was there too, franticly rummaging through drawers in a file cabinet, the one furthest from the door. After a minute of searching it appeared that she found what she was searching for. She took a sheaf of folders and stuffed them into the black bag containing Liam's items. Liam crept slowly and quietly into the vault, hoping that he could ambush her.

Liam was not that fortunate. He stepped onto a small crate that was on the floor right in the middle of his path. With the resulting sound, Sandra retrieved a pistol and opened fire in Liam's direction.

"Stop, no further or I will shoot you!" she barked.

Liam had no option other than to stop, which he did. Sandra pickup another small bundle and with the gun trained on Liam told him to move to the back of the vault as she exited. He fully complied; he was not about to die today.

When she cleared the doorway to the vault she took off running again. Liam took off right on her heels after her. He had started to gain on her when he noticed that there was a dark, wet trail on the floor leading away from the vault. The odor of gasoline was heavy in the air. Liam proceeded closer with caution.

He stopped when he saw her, about twenty-five feet down the hallway. She just stood there with an object in her hand.

"That's far enough Ross, it ends here."

"It's the end Sandra, you can't run. You have nothing."

"Oh, there is always something!" she shouted.

She threw the object in her hand down the hallway towards Liam. When the metal orb was about ten feet from him, Liam recognized what the object was. It was an old WWII incendiary grenade. Liam could easily tell that this was no dud as smoke curled from the center seam of the device.

Liam reversed course and took off back towards the vault running at a full sprint. He had just reached the door of the vault when he heard a sharp crack and a wall of flame started traveling down the brick lined hallway. He skidded into the vault and started to pull the heavy iron door closed.

He felt the heat start to build and smelled the acrid smoke that was emitting from the burning gasoline. Liam pulled the door closed just as the fire raced past the doorway opening. He was safe inside the vault, or was he. The temperature in the vault soon started to climb. Paper near to the old iron door started to smolder from the intense heat. Liam was trapped inside an oven.

Liam heard the inferno, outside the vault, raging. He started to toss the boxes and stacks of paper to the back of the vault in order to stop the smoldering. He was about finished when a very loud explosion occurred. Dust and rock fell from the ceiling, shelves that were up against the walls collapsed into piles in the center of the room.

After the dust settled, Liam listened at the door. He no longer heard the conflagration outside. The explosion had most likely extinguished the fire. He quickly touched the door it was molten steel hot. He had to try and open the door. Liam found some old ledger books amongst the mess, whose thickness might protect his hands from the searing heat. Another explosion erupted, sounding the closest yet. More rock fell from the walls and ceiling. The electricity finally gave out; Liam was plunged into inky blackness. He tried to push the door open but it would not yield. The hallway and for all he knew the whole house had collapsed around him. Was this to be his grave?

51

Search and Rescue

The team that Uncle Bob had assembled was the best of the best. He had been given Carte Blanche by the president personally. He had over one hundred of the most elite special force troops from all branches, S.E.A.L.S., Delta Force, Marine Recon, and Air Force Pararescue.

Uncle Bob had the teams deployed around the circumference of the Centum's compound. Uncle Bob and the Marine Recon unit would be the first through the gates. They would be followed by local law enforcement by the hundreds, whose primary purpose was to collect and detain anyone trying to leave the compound in the chaos. The president had to draft and sign an emergency order authorizing the use of military troops on U.S. soil.

The minutes slowly ticked by, all they were waiting for was the signal from Liz Gallagher that the computer program had run its course. Uncle Bob was on his fourth cup of coffee, the acidic brew turning his stomach sour. His iPhone finally chimed that he had a call. He picked up on the third ring.

"Elizabeth, tell me you have good new." He answered.

"Uncle Bob, it's all done. The program was successfully planted on The Centum's core server. All of the trades have been reversed. There are no longer any records of gold trades being made."

"Good work Lizzy!" was all Uncle Bob replied before he closed the connection.

Uncle Bob made on call to a number he had memorized just the night before. It was answered on the first ring.

"Mr. President, It's a go!"

Uncle Bob picked up the microphone of the UHF radio that all units were tuned into.

"All unit leaders, it's a go! We move on my mark.," he announced.

He took a deep breath, checked his service weapon and started the count down.

"We go in three, two, one, mark, go, go, go…"

The units swarmed out, they were soon met with small arms fire. It seemed like nothing larger than 9mm rounds. Then the first explosion went off.

"Who release a grenade?" Uncle Bob called on the radio.

The units all responded with a negative. No one had used a grenade.

"Point Unit 1, explosion came from inside the main house, repeat explosion from the inside the main house."

"This is Point Unit 1, affirmative, all units proceed with caution. Be on the lookout for Liam Ross. Over." Uncle Bob relayed out.

The second explosion blew out the windows on the second story. Hundreds of people came running out of the central compound building. Local police agencies started corralling the individuals to safety and for interviews.

It wasn't until the third blast that the flames appeared. The fire seemed to start on the first floor but soon spread to all the floors. Because of the age of the building and the method of 17th century construction, the entire structure was soon totally engulfed in flames.

Uncle Bob radioed for fire support. The fist units arrived within three minutes. The firefighters had water on the blaze within two more minutes. The noise of the inferno and continuing blasts elevated the chaos of the scene to a frantic level. You could barely hear a person standing two feet from you. It was pure chance that Uncle Bob heard or rather sensed that his iPhone was ringing.

He answered it on the third ring, it was Liz.

"Have you got him yet?" she was referring to Liam.

"Lizzy girl, we have a situation here. The building is totally in flames and explosions are going off all over. It must have been rigged. I wouldn't know where to start looking."

"You can't just stand there!" she shouted " I have him on GPS. He is about two hundred yards from you at 292 degrees WNW."

Uncle Bob radioed for a battalion commander to join him ASAP. He returned to his phone.

"Sit tight Liz, I've got help coming." He told her.

A white helmeted firefighter soon appeared at Robert's side. He told the chief about the situation and gave him the coordinates to where Liam was.

"Are you out of your mind!? he shouted, "Look at where you say he is."

The firefighter pointed to the middle of the inferno.

"No one, and I mean no one can live through that. I'm not endangering any of my men by even thinking about going in there for a search and rescue. I'm sorry, but your man is most likely gone."

After that, the largest of the explosions went off leveling

the western side of the building. The captain left Uncle Bob to go back to his command. In shock he slowly lifted the smart phone to his ear to relay the bad news to Liz. He heard her sobbing; she had heard the conversation between the two men.

"I'm sorry Liz, our hands are tied."

She just closed the connection and Uncle Bob stood amid the chaos, feeling numb.

It took almost five hours when the last of the hot spots were attended to by the fire department. District of Columbia police had detained members and employees of The Centum and held them in an office building that faced the road. Once all the names and I.D's had been confirmed Uncle Bob and his team started the long tedious task of sorting out the suspected players from the many office workers employed by The Centum.

A Captain with the D.C. police took a bit of initiative and categorized the lists of individuals first by sorting the VIPs' from the remainder. He then had the individual groups situated into different rooms.

Uncle Bob scanned the list twice but it wasn't until he slowly read the list for a third time that the name jumped out at him. Senator Robert Worthington from the great state of Utah. Uncle Bob ran from room to room searching the faces. He saw the police captain that organized the list and the detainees.

"Captain! Captain!" Uncle Bob yelled at the top of his lungs. He finally got the D.C. cop's attention.

Uncle Bob was franticly pointing and stabbing the list with his right index finger.

"Captain! Where is this man? He's not with any of the

groups! Where is Senator Worthington?"

"We sent him to the hospital. He was having hard time breathing and he didn't look so good. The president's chief of staff was with him."

"You idiot!" Uncle Bob screamed as he threw the papers into the air and stormed off to find out which hospital the Senator had been taken to. Uncle Bob started calling every assistant that was left at CSS to have them start tracking down where the Senator had been taken and by whom.

After about twenty minutes of more phone calls and dead ends, Uncle Bob's calls were interrupted with a priority call.

"Excuse me sir, I should really take this.," he said.

"Robert Ross."

"Agent Ross, this is Gregory Simon with the Maryland State Police. I am responding to a BOLO for Senator Robert Worthington. I have the ambulance that transported the Senator from your site, to John Hopkins Hospital."

"John Hopkins? Why in God's name would anybody go to Baltimore if they had difficulty breathing?" Uncle Bob asked.

"I don't think they would agent Ross. I fear that something has happened to the Senator. You see his ambulance has been found abandoned and the two attendants and one patient have had their throats slit. That's after one had the deliberator paddles turned on himself, on full charge no less."

"Is there any evidence at the scene?" he asked.

"The ambulance is down a 150 footy embankment. It's going to take a while to bring it and the bodies up." The trooper responded.

"Alright, I'm sending some lab techs out. They should be

there within the hour. Thank you, very much" he disconnected with the trooper.

Liz thought that she was all cried out over the loss of Liam. Time after time, Liam had shown the world what he was made of, she remarked to herself.

"I guess his time just ran out."

John came into the stamp room after retrieving a bottle of Tequila and a couple of glasses. He poured them both a glass equal to three fingers. They both downed the liquor in one gulp. John poured two more.

"How did Kyle take the news?" she asked John.

"No better than either one of us. He said he was going to try and make ac break from the hospital in the morning. He was going to head back here."

Liz downed the second glass and was about to pour a third when her text notification on her iPhone chimed. She retrieved the phone from the desk so she could shut it off. She didn't want to be bothered for a while. When she picked up the phone the message on the screen made her jump.

"Does anyone know a good restaurant here in D.C. that will deliver? I'm getting hungry."

"It's Liam! He's alive!" she screamed with glee.

"What?! What are you talking about?" Jon cried.

Liz started to call Uncle Bob. The phone started ringing in her ear.

"It's Liam! The text is from Liam!" she cried in return.

Uncle Bob answered somberly.

"Yes, Liz. What is it?"

Before he could even get the whole question out, Liz was screaming into the phone.

"Uncle Bob he's alive! He's alive"

"Who's alive dear?"

"Liam is!"

"Liz, there is no way that Liam can be alive, just no way." He calmly replied.

"He texted me! He texted me Uncle Bob! He's alive!"

Liz's text notification went off again.

"Hold on Bob. He's texting again.

"Could also use some ice water. Also make sure restaurant is not BBQ. Repeat NO BBQ!"

Liz forwarded the text to Uncle Bob. He received it and let out a shout. He ran to where the battalion commander was.

"Chief, Chief! My guy is alive! My nephew is still alive! We've got to start digging!

An all hands alarm went out across the compounds debris. Within minutes over one hundred fire fighters and rescue personnel where digging through piles in the area Liam was last thought to be. When the rescue teams hit large foundation stones they had no choice than to call for heavy equipment.

A large backhoe arrived within minutes. The rescue team set right back to work. After ten more minutes of clearing one of the rescuers let out a call.

"We've got an intact room over here, some kind of vault if you ask me.

The firefighters, with the assistance of the backhoe removed three very large foundation stones that had fallen in front of the door to the vault. Once they were gone a female firefighter/rescuer surveyed the iron door.

"It's badly banged up. We may have to use a Frac-Pack on it in order to open." she said.

"A Frac-Pack is a low yield explosive charge that fire departments use to gain entry into an otherwise inaccessible structure. The pack was attached to the door and was about to be blown when someone asked if there was any communication with the individual inside, he might want to get back from the door.

Uncle Bob had been on the phone with Liz since she received the texts. He now asked her to send Liam a text telling him what they were about to do. Her fingers flew on the keyboard of the smart phone. After typing she pressed send and waited for a reply. Three seconds later, she received it.

"Aye Aye boss."

She relayed the message to Uncle Bob. He acknowledged to Liz that he received it.

"Blow It!" he shouted.

The charge went off and the damaged door buckled to the ground. Three firefighters entered into the vault followed by Uncle Bob. Liam was seated at the back of the vault with his head protected by a heavy hardwood, packing crate. He removed the crate and its packing material. He looked up and saw the firefighters and his Uncle.

"We may have a small problem. I only ordered enough food for one."

52

Laying Down Roots

Bousquet Loft
Bronx, New York
May 27, 2013

It had been two weeks since the *Gold Rush Incident*, as it was now called, had come to a rather explosive conclusion in Washington, D.C. and all were back in New York.

John was still hobbling about with the aid of a cane from the attack on him in Washington. Kyle would be incapacitated for a little while longer. Luckily, the only bone that had broken was his leg. Because of this, he was tearing up the sidewalks of New York, not to mention the carpets in the loft, with a motorized wheelchair, that he had removed all speed governors from shortly after receiving it.

Liz had been working directly with the CSS and NSA tracking down the physical deposits of the gold that The Centum had stolen. They had been able to compile a short list so far. The depository's ranged from being in the United States to Great Britain, India and Japan. Liz was sure that they would find it all. It would just take time.

Uncle Bob had a big surprise for everyone. He had been promoted to Deputy Director of Operations for the CSS on direct recommendation of the President of the United States. He would have free reign over the re-organization of CSS operations.

Liam had spent the past two weeks going from one debrief to another, from one lawyer to another. Every iota of information that Liam and his team had uncovered over the past three weeks would need to be confirmed, dissected, and then confirmed again.

Locations of Gass's reserved gold in the desert were mapped. The bodies of over five hundred Chinese rail workers, killed by Sandra and Rebecca Hodge's great-great-grandfather had been unearthed and given proper recognition.

No one had found Sandra Hodge yet. She was now on various United States agencies, most wanted lists, for black mail, murder and primarily for terrorism. The United States congress had declared the acts of The Centum as terrorist acts against the U.S. and the world.

Liam had to admire her; she had a superior intelligence, charisma and a survivor's ability. She had used Liam's own Senator Worthington mask, to get out of the compound and away from incarceration.

But, tonight they would not talk about her; tonight was about friends and family. Liam had been cooking up a storm since early that morning. He had prepared Colorado racks of lamb, roasted new potatoes and slow-roasted tri-color peppers with olive oil and Kamalatta olives. He had shucked six-dozen oysters, brought in fresh from Montauk only two hours ago. For desert he had prepared a Pavlova with fresh berries, whipped cream and rare fig balsamic vinegar.

He had selected some wonderful wines from his cellar and was looking forward to the evening. To begin the night, two bottles of Laurent Perrier rose champagne, for the main course a 1990 Chateau Mon Bousquet and 1985 Chateau Lynch-Bage. For the desert, a bottle of 1941 Chateau Yquem sauterne.

He was removing a sheet of sour dough rolls that he had been proofing for two days, from the convection oven when his cell phone rang. It was from the 315 area code, and from a number he did not recognize.

"Liam Ross."

"Liam, it's Susan Bousquet. I hope I'm not disturbing you?"

"No Susan, not at all, I was going to call you in the morning. I should be wrapped up here in a couple of weeks. I then plan to bring in a packing crew to start packing up all of your father's collection. It's taken a bit longer than I had expected. I've also made some calls about your father's museum collection on the second floor. The Smithsonian would love to get their hands on it. They would love to get the entire contents on permanent loan."

"Liam, as far as I'm concerned, if it has anything to do with stamps, it's yours to do with what you want. Also, I've been doing so thinking."

"Susan, are you sure? I couldn't…"

"Liam, I'm 100% sure. Now as I said I've been doing some thinking. How would you not have to move anything?"

"I don't quite follow you Susan."

"My boyfriend up here in Syracuse proposed to me. We are going to settle up here and I have no need for the property there in New York. How would you like to buy it?"

"If's its in my price range, I would seriously consider it."

"Well, that is where you are in luck. I have spoken to my father's private banker. He and his bank are very well educated with my fathers' collection. So they are willing to hold a mortgage for you, based upon the collections as collateral. My attorney tells me that I could get almost 10 million for it on the open market."

"Well, to tell you the truth Susan, ten million is a bit out of my neighborhood. So I don't…"

She cut him off.

"Now I didn't finish. I care about the building about as much as I care about the collections. How about I make you an offer that you just can't refuse?"

"Oh, and what would that be?"

"Can you scrape together $250,000 dollars? If you can, its all your."

"Susan, I couldn't consciously take that offer. You would be losing a fortune."

"I would rather have someone in the building I trust. You see there would be a caveat with thus deals. You would have to grant each remaining tenant up to five years free rent. You see, my dad never charged any of the tenants any rent. He believed in helping those that needed helping. Do we have a deal?

Liam did not even have to think.

"I'll have a cashiers check sent to your lawyer in the morning. Could you ask him to extend or write up the tenant agreements for me?'

"Liam, thank you so very much for carrying out my fathers wishes."

"No Susan, thank you. It's my pleasure."

Liam returned to the kitchen and his friends. They were all eating oysters and drinking Champaign. Liam took a glass of the wine out to the balcony and stared off at the Manhattan skyline. Everyone joined him for the setting sun. Liam was lost deep in thought. The air smelled fresh with rain.

"Penny for your thoughts boss?" asked Liz.

Her voice brought him back.

"I think I'm moving to New York."

He lifted his wine glass and toasted his friends.

Liam Ross will return in

Toy Train

www.ingramcontent.com/pod-product-compliance
Lightning Source LLC
Chambersburg PA
CBHW052343020726
47503CB00001B/86